ALYSSA BELFIGLIO

You Don't Know Nana

Chapter 1

A very inhaled, or at least tried to, but every breath became trapped in the shallow cavity of her chest. Which was odd, because it was a quintessential, early June day in a suburb right outside of Philadelphia, when the weather in the northeast still had a chance for being hot but not humid, sunny without suffocating. At least, that's how the weather performed in Avery's memories. Everything seemed more unpredictable these days.

The sun was blessing the world today, casting golden hues on the nourished leaves of the sidewalk trees. Birdcalls could be heard, even if one wasn't paying attention, because the neighborhood street was silent. No cars coming. Nobody leaving. Avery stood on the sidewalk of her nana's suburban neighborhood, squinting at the simple, two-story house before her. It had white siding and black shutters; all the houses in this neighborhood were two stories, with white walls and black shutters. When Avery was little, she'd loved the organization and uniformity of it all.

It was a large neighborhood, in relation to the small cul-de-sac Avery had grown up in, but Avery had grown enamored with the sidewalks where her nana and her would go for strolls. The pebbled concrete would bend with the quiet roads, and most of the time they would be greeted by a friendly neighbor or pass children laughing, riding bikes, or playing hockey in the street. Her nana's neighborhood – and her nana's home, for that matter – had always felt safe. Now, as Avery squinted at the black, paint-chipped front door, all she could do was look around and wonder about the different lives hidden behind each one. It felt as though she were walking back in time, into an era that had never existed. At least, not really.

So lost in thought, she hadn't even noticed the luxury SUV pull into Nana's driveway.

"Aunt Avery!"

Avery snapped her head in the direction of the familiar, squeaky voice. Before she could respond, her niece, Lily, was pummeling towards her as if she were a tiny NFL player ready to make her tackle. Her niece's wild sun-streaked curls, though secured in a bow as big as her head, bounced with every step. Avery braced herself just before her niece made impact, but she was still knocked off balance. Lily was not the two-year-old she'd once been. She was nearly five, now, and tall.

"Lily," Avery said, wincing at her throbbing hipbone and then smiling at her niece as she knelt on the dry grass to reach Lily's eye level, "I'm so happy to see you!"

"Auntie A, what'd you get Nana?"

"Huh?"

"What'd you get Nana?"

Just as the words left Lily's mouth, Avery's eyes landed on the biggest bouquet – or perhaps it was more like a small chunk of a garden – coming her way. Carried by none other than Avery's oldest sister, Brinkley. Vivid shades of pink and orange flowers obstructed her sister's face, so it looked as if the bouquet had grown legs, her sister's legs, and it was getting closer by the second.

"Well shit ..." Avery mumbled under her breath.

"You said a bad word!" said Lily, her little mouth forming into a circle.

"What makes a word bad, Lily?"

While Lily scrunched her sunburned nose in thought, Avery watched the bouquet making its way towards her.

"Did you buy the whole garden, Brinkley?" Avery called.

Brinkley poked her head around the rich green leaves, her striking hazel eyes coordinating perfectly with the wild flora. "Do you think it's too much?" Brinkley asked. "I hope it's not too much. I have just been so nervous about this whole thing, you know? Like why did Nana only want us to come? Why can't my husband or John come? We're all family! Is she about to unleash some crazy family secret? Are we all about to inherit a lot of money?"

Avery felt her head spinning. The birds were still busy singing their morning song.

"I don't ... think so?" said Avery, scratching the small tattoo of a pen on her forearm. It was her first tattoo and sometimes she found herself itching at it, as if that would make it go away. Not because she didn't like tattoos – she had over ten of them inked over her arms – but because she had tattooed the pen on herself when she was sixteen, using the stick-and-poke method. Now she was left with a symbol on her arm that reminded her of herself as a teenager in defiance of her mother's refusal to let her get a tattoo; the pen was an object she no longer felt connected to.

"What are you thinking about?" Brinkley asked, her eyes studying Avery.

"Nothing."

When Brinkley continued to eye her sister, Avery filled the silence. "Yesterday, Mom said Nana's not doing well, so she wants to keep her last visits to as few people as possible," Avery said with a shrug, crossing her arms. "Chase and John got their chance to say goodbye over the weekend, anyway. Do they really need another? Nana's always more reserved around the in-laws. I want her to just be herself and say whatever she wants during our last moments with her."

Before Brinkley could respond, and before Avery could muster enough courage to ask if they could claim the bouquet was from both of them, a white Mustang blaring music zipped around the corner. But it wasn't fun, upbeat music. It was opera, and it sounded like the singer himself was experiencing a breakdown.

"Mama Donna's here!" Lily screamed with the kind of joy only a child can have when seeing a relative.

Avery and Brinkley exchanged looks.

With the white Mustang now parked behind Brinkley's SUV, and the melancholic music turned off, Lily ran to the car to greet her grandmother.

"Don't run in the street!" Brinkley yelled after her daughter.

"Oh my gosh, Auntie Liz is here, too!" Lily shrieked once she reached the Mustang.

"Of course they showed up together," Brinkley mumbled.

"The two best friends," Avery agreed.

The excitement was too much for Lily, who began to jump up and down as her grandmother, also known as Mama Donna, and her other aunt, Elizabeth, greeted her with a hug.

Traitor, Avery thought as Lily squealed with joy when Elizabeth bent down for a kiss.

Brinkley carefully set the bouquet down with a huff. "That thing is so heavy."

"Hi girls!" Avery and Brinkley's middle sister, Elizabeth, called across the yard as she got out of the car.

Elizabeth was dressed in an expensive-looking, all-black ensemble comprised of thick-rimmed, square-shaped sunglasses, a slim-fitting jumpsuit, and a simple oversized blazer. Small gold hoops dangled from her ears, offering the only pop of color. Her long, dark brown hair that always seemed to reflect light and stay smooth, even on humid days, was parted in the middle and pulled back into a low ponytail that almost touched her perky butt. Even for a visit to someone on their death bed, Elizabeth looked both appropriate and fabulous.

Their mother, on the other hand, looked as if she'd been kidnapped. A black scarf covered her hair and framed her face. The same thick-rimmed, square-shaped black sunglasses that Elizabeth was wearing adorned her face, but looked even bigger on Mama Donna. She was also dressed in black, but nothing about her outfit was fabulous. Despite the distance between them, Avery could hear bursts of sobs. The sobbing was so loud, in fact, Avery swore she could hear the snot bubbling from her mother's nose.

Avery searched Elizabeth and her mother's hands for any sign of a gift, but they were empty. She breathed. Then Elizabeth waltzed to the trunk of the Mustang and out popped a cube-shaped box wrapped in all-black paper complete with a gold bow.

"What the hell do you gift a dying person?" Brinkley whispered.

"I mean, that's exactly what I was thinking ..." Avery glared at the bouquet.

Elizabeth and their mother were getting closer, with Lily leading the way.

"That's beautiful, Brinkley," Elizabeth noted, nodding towards the bouquet.

In all the years Avery had grown up with Elizabeth, she had heard her sister change her tone of voice only once – when their parents had announced they were getting a divorce. Elizabeth had been in high school and had squealed with joy at the news, congratulating their mother.

"It's not too much?" said Brinkley, nodding at the bouquet.

"No, no one loves flowers more than Nana," Elizabeth assured her, pushing her black-rimmed sunglasses to the top of her head.

Mama Donna blew her nose, and perhaps her entire naval cavity, into an already-crumpled tissue.

All eyes looked at her.

"Are you okay, Mom?" Brinkley was the first to ask.

"No, I'm not okay," said Mama Donna, dabbing at her nostrils with the dirty tissue. "My mother is dying."

They all offered a moment of silence, not sure what else would be appropriate to say.

"What'd you get her?" Brinkley was eyeing the box in Elizabeth's hands.

"Socks," said Elizabeth, looking at the present in her arms as if it were her baby. "When John and I were in Paris last week, I gave Nana a call and asked, 'If you could have anything in the world, Nana, what would that be?'"

Avery wanted to snatch the gift and run.

Elizabeth's eyes appeared to water as she continued looking at the box. "And she said ... 'socks'." Her voice cracked. The tears that had been forming in her eyes began to pour down her cheeks. "She said she's never bothered to invest in a really good pair of socks, and now ..." Elizabeth's shoulders heaved as she tried to speak between sobs ... "her feet get cold."

The sounds of Elizabeth's cries seemed to trigger something in their mother, whose own briefly repressed tears now released themselves into a steady stream past her sunglasses, onto her black blouse.

"That is a bit sad," Brinkley said, her voice cracking with emotion.

"Auntie A, why is everybody crying?" Lily tugged on Avery's hand.

"Well, Lily, they don't teach you how to deal with death," said Avery, feeling proud of the honest conversation she was about to have with her curious niece, but of course her mother had to interrupt.

"You know what, you always blame your mother," said Mama

Donna, still using the same crumpled tissue to blow her nose.

"Mom, I'm not blaming you," Avery said, "I'm blaming our education system."

"Can we go see Nana now," Lily whined. "I'm hot."

"Yes," said Brinkley.

Brinkley wasn't crying – not exactly – but her face looked disfigured from her Botox and holding back tears. It was something Avery had never understood – the purpose of not allowing her tears to fall.

"Come on, guys," Brinkley sniffled. "Let's go see Nana."

Avery inhaled deeply, this time forcing the air past her chest and into her stomach as everyone followed Lily to the black, paint-chipped front door.

Nana is dying, Avery confirmed to herself as everyone around her wiped their fallen tears and suppressed any future ones.

The truth was, their nana had been dying for the past few years, as the elderly often do. But during their nana's dying years, time had kept ticking and life had kept moving just as fast as ever before, so it had seemed fine that their nana was the only thing slowing down. That is, until their nana had broken her hip and was no longer moving, not even slowly. Now they were forced to face the fact that they were almost next in line to this slowed way of life, of aging. Avery imagined her nana's death getting announced to the heavens, causing the grand circle of life to turn less than a centimeter forwards with one simple click.

The thought made her dizzy.

"At least Nana's going out in style with this in-home hospice care," said Elizabeth with a shudder, flipping her ponytail over her shoulder.

"Yes, I do not want to pass away in a hospital," Mama Donna announced, trailing closely behind. "And when I am gone, do not put me underground. Cremate me and sprinkle me in a meadow."

"Oh my gosh, Mom, can we get through one death at a time?" said

Brinkley as everyone huddled around the front door.

"Do we ... ring the doorbell?" Elizabeth asked.

"Oh, don't be silly, just go in," said Mama Donna, ripping off her sunglasses to reveal bloodshot eyes framed by puffy, dark eyelids.

"Mom, you look like shit," Brinkley gasped.

"You said a bad word!" Lily said, pointing her little finger at Brinkley.

Mama Donna's bloodshot eyes were focused on the bouquet Brinkley was shifting between her arms.

"Oh, wow, Brinkley. This is gorgeous," Donna cooed, running her finger along one of the fuzzy green leaves. "Absolutely gorgeous! You've never gotten me a bouquet like this."

"Mom, are you serious right now? You're not dying!" Brinkley snapped.

"Dying?" Lily shrieked and looked at Avery. "Is that a bad word?"

Mama Donna didn't offer a chance for anyone to answer.

"Oh what, Brinkley, so I have to be dying to get a pretty bouquet from you? Give me a break."

Brinkley rolled her eyes. "You know what? I'm not doing this with you, Mom. Not today. Come on, Lily." With her bouquet and child in tow, Brinkley stormed through the front door of Nana's house.

Mama Donna looked at Elizabeth and Avery. "Is that not the craziest thing you girls have heard? You have to be dying to get a bouquet from her?"

"I'm going to go see Nana," said Elizabeth, and walked straight past them, into the house.

And then there were two, Avery thought as she stared at her mother, who still had her black scarf wrapped around her head.

"Oh, Avery, you couldn't wear long sleeves to cover up your tattoos?" Mama Donna grabbed Avery's arm. "You know Nana's not a fan of tattoos."

8

Avery snatched her arm back. "It's going up to ninety degrees today," she said. "Besides, Nana's about to leave this world. I don't think tattoos are going to be on her mind."

"Are you ever going to fill the spaces between them?" Mama Donna wondered aloud, squinting her puffy eyelids at Avery's arms. "It looks like Lily and Daisy got into a pack of stickers and stuck them all over your arms. Blindfolded."

Closing her eyes, Avery released a long exhale through her nostrils.

"Anyway, did you get anything for Nana?" her mother continued. "I mean, what do you get someone who probably only has a day left? The morphine keeps putting her in and out of it – the other day she told me she's going to a dinner party with John F. Kennedy. Said she's going to find out what happened. I don't think she'll remember getting socks." Mama Donna was shaking her head, looking at the opened, paint-chipped front door.

Avery noticed the beads of sweat pooling on her forehead. Tucking a damp strand of her wavy hair behind her ear, she offered a shrug and said, "I don't know, Mom, I guess you're supposed to get them something to help with the transition. Flowers and socks are nice. Something beautiful to look at and comfortable to wear ..." Her heart grew heavy as she felt the emptiness in her hands. She glanced at her mother, who was busy blowing her nose into the ever-dwindling tissue. "This must be hard for you."

"It is."

There was a silence that sank between them. They both seemed to search for words that would comfort the experience of death. But this was the human condition: it would happen to everyone, and had been happening to everyone, long before words were even created.

Perhaps that was why they couldn't find any.

Chapter 2

Everyone surrounded Nana in a semi-circle, as if to form half a halo around her lower body. When they first entered the room, Nana's gray hair was covered by her favorite Italian headscarf – blue, with simple white polka dots scattered throughout – and all the wrinkles surrounding her eyes were hidden by black, cat-eye sunglasses. Even though Nana was not Italian, Avery couldn't remember a time their nana had left the house without an Italian headscarf and sunglasses, claiming the objects "made her feel put together". Then Nana would usually go on to detail a trip she had taken to Italy in her early twenties, praising the fashion, food, art, architecture, language. As a little girl, Avery would listen to this tale of her nana's travels with a dream-like haze, but as she got older, a sadness crept into the repetition of memories, because Avery realized there were no new memories being made. At least, not ones her nana wanted to share.

Now they were inside, and their nana wasn't going to leave the house probably ever again. There was something comforting and haunting about a woman wanting to feel "put together" for one last time.

At first, Lily had been concerned, asking why Nana was hooked up to a machine as she slept. Brinkley had whispered that Nana wasn't feeling well, so the machine was going to help her for now. It seemed a sufficient answer for Lily, who had then asked for her tablet so she could play games. The family had waited close to an hour before Nana awoke, and when she did, she was conscious. With the help of Mama Donna, the sunglasses were removed to reveal her clouded eyes, and stories were shared, questions asked, tears dabbed with tissues. They laughed and cried as they admired their dying icon of strength and love from fold-out chairs. The sisters' other grandparents had died years earlier, so Nana was their last living link to a past they would always be part of, but would never get to experience.

Nana was smoothing the ice "lollipop", as she called it, around her probably dry cotton mouth. Her breath was labored, every movement of her body, even if it was just a finger, appearing to be done with maximum effort.

"These are more delicious," said Nana, her words slower than normal as her shaking hand raised the ice lollipop, "than any lollipops they're feeding the kids these days." Then Nana looked at Lily. "She's always been such a light in my life."

After waiting so long for her great-grandmother to wake up, Lily's boredom seemed to transform into pride, especially after hearing this public declaration. The four-going-on-five-year-old sat straighter in her chair – which was seated right next to Nana, the VIP of the afternoon – and her little hand squeezed her great-nana's arm.

Nana shifted her gaze around the room. "I don't know when life is going to leave me," she said. Her strained voice snapped everyone's attention back to her. "I have last words for all my grandchildren. But only if you want to hear them."

"Nana," said Avery, "of course we want to hear."

Nana nodded, but her gaze looked to the others.

"Yes, tell us!" Elizabeth and Brinkley encouraged.

A crooked smile spread across Nana's papery face when her eyes rested on Brinkley.

"Brinkley, my first grandbaby ..." she began, her voice becoming even more strained.

Oh wow, Nana's wasting no time, Avery thought as she stared at Brinkley, who was beaming just as brightly as her daughter Lily.

"Just like your daughters," Nana continued, "you have always been a light. I've watched you grow ... You used to be such a tiny ..." Even though Nana's eyes were resting on Brinkley, she seemed to slip into a time and place that no one else could see. Nana breathed, regaining focus. "You are a wonderful ... mother ... and wife."

Avery watched as Brinkley responded with a smile that stretched towards her ears, revealing her dimples. The Botox kept the rest of her face smooth as a baby's bottom.

"You have so much love in your life, Brinkley. You live such a ... lucky life." With trembling fingers, Nana began to wiggle a pink-and-gold ring off her ring finger.

"Mom, let me help you." Mama Donna sprung off her chair.

"Just wait, just wait," said Nana. "Let me try first."

Avery smiled when her nana's determination worked, and the ring slipped off. A thin gold band bounding a circle-shaped rose quartz now lay in her palm.

"I want you to have this," Nana said, her deep-set eyes trained on Brinkley. "It was one of the first gifts your grandfather ever gave me ... I've been wearing it ever since. It's a symbol of love, Brinkley."

Brinkley accepted the ring through a tear-streaked face. "I love you, Nana."

"Mommy, that's a beautiful ring," Lily cooed, leaning towards Brinkley to admire it closer.

As Brinkley clutched her gift and her daughter, Nana turned her head slightly towards the window to face Elizabeth.

"Elizabeth," she breathed, the name rolling off her tongue as if it were a celebration. "Oh, how I love hearing stories of your and John's travels. You two make me ... made me ... feel alive again."

All the tears Elizabeth had released earlier had smudged her mascara across her lids. She resembled a smiling raccoon.

Nana took a long breath, her chest dramatically rising and falling. "When I go to heaven, Elizabeth ... I'll still come to you to brighten my heart."

I don't think you'll need any brightening up there, Nana. That's kind of the whole point of heaven, Avery thought, fidgeting in her seat as she continued to wait her turn.

Their nana reached for an item on her wooden nightstand before holding out a small, red leather pouch with fleur-de-lis symbols embroidered with shimmering gold thread throughout. "For you."

"Oh, Mom ..." Mama Donna almost seemed to wince. "You really want to give her that?"

"Yes, Donna, I do," Nana said with a little cough.

"Yeah, Mom, why wouldn't she?" Elizabeth said. "It's beautiful!"

Mama Donna studied Nana for a moment before pressing her mouth shut and sinking into her fold-out chair.

Avery watched as Nana eyed Mama Donna before returning her gaze to Elizabeth.

"I bought that coin pouch when I was in my twenties, visiting Rome."

Here we go again, Avery groaned in her mind, bracing herself for a half-hour retelling of the best gelato shop her nana had stumbled on while in Rome.

Nana's hands trembled as Elizabeth delicately took the crimson-colored pouch between her fingers. "It was the greatest trip of my life ... That pouch is the only souvenir I got."

"Oh, wow!" Lily gasped as she watched Elizabeth smooth over the gold fleur-de-lis embroidery. "That's beautiful!"

"It's my favorite gift," Nana breathed, "to this day."

"Nana, I don't know what to say—" Elizabeth began, but Nana held up her hand for silence.

Nana's gaze lingered on Elizabeth for a moment, the corners of her mouth curled into a slight smile, before she closed her eyes, sucking in a long breath. When she blinked her eyes open, she craned her neck even more towards the window, to Avery. Her eyes, which were highlighted by the golden light of the summer sun, locked onto Avery's. "My last grandchild," she said.

Avery felt herself sit straighter.

"Do you remember when you were younger?"

Avery paused for a moment, waiting for Nana to take her usual heavy breaths before continuing. Yet Nana's lips remained closed.

"Um ... Yes?" Avery responded.

Nana kept her lips pursed shut.

"I mean, I remember parts of it ..." Avery felt a tightening sickness in her stomach. "Most of it," she corrected.

"Ah," Nana nodded. "I never could get a read on you, Avery. You ... confuse me."

Nana let out a deep, raspy cough. Her breathing was becoming even more shallow, but she continued to lock her eyes onto Avery. "You confuse me," she repeated with a rasp.

"What?"

Avery scanned the room to try to make eye contact with someone – anyone – to confirm Nana was just high, no longer making sense. Yet everyone seemed to be avoiding her "this is weird" gaze, too busy pretending to study their new gifts or the plain brown carpet beneath them.

Even Lily kept her eyes trained on Brinkley's ring.

"I don't know where you've been ... So, I have no idea where you're going," Nana said as Avery felt her mind flood with thoughts and memories. There were too many to see individually, so all her recollections existed as one blurry loud mess.

"I don't even know if *you* know where you're going, Avery," Nana continued. "But I want you to have something."

The strain in Nana's voice pulled Avery's focus back into the room. Nana's chest rose and fell with every breath as she searched her nightstand with trembling fingers. Everyone seemed to hold their breath to see what this last gift would be, especially after an introduction like that.

From the table, Nana produced a small, nondescript tan leather journal.

"Oh," Lily blurted, her face scrunched in clear disappointment.

Avery dropped her gaze to study the object. Its cover was smooth, with minimal cracks and creasing. The gift almost looked brand new.

"I bought this journal when I was fifty-three years old ..."

Okay, here comes the explanation, Avery thought.

"I wrote in one page and decided ... Eh." Nana gave her bony shoulder a slow-motion shrug.

Elizabeth snickered.

Avery blinked. "What?"

"Realized it wasn't for me. But," Nana said, and patted her chest as she released another raspy cough, "I held onto it. And now I ... I want you to have it."

What the fuck, Nana.

"You write, don't you?" she said, eyeing Avery's forearm as if searching for the tattooed evidence.

Suddenly ninety degrees didn't seem too hot for long sleeves. Avery uncrossed and re-crossed her arms.

"I mean, I ... I used to," Avery said. "I stopped like, years ago ... after graduating high school."

Avery tried searching Nana's eyes for answers, but they were cloudy.

It was as if Nana's pupils were no longer a black circle. They were a murky puddle that spilled into her pale gray irises and faded into the window's sunlight.

Her sisters clutched their precious presents, their own closures, as they looked at Avery and Nana for the next move.

"Ah," said Nana. "Well, here you are."

Avery took the journal from her nana's outstretched, trembling hand.

"You know, Nana," Avery began as she clutched the soft leather, "this is a beautiful gift, but I'm confused about what you said—"

Nana lifted her hand for silence.

Avery pressed on. "I mean, if you want to know where I've been, or where I'm going, I'd be happy to answer any—"

"No need for that now, my dear," Nana interrupted with another cough, keeping her hand in the air.

Avery wished the lights had gone out then, with her nana slipping into a morphine haze and everyone agreeing that Nana had been a little out of it for Avery's turn. *What a shame,* everyone would say, and Avery would nod along and pretend to accept her fate with grace.

But that didn't happen.

Instead, Nana remained conscious for another half-hour. Everyone continued making conversation as if it were any other visit, even though it wasn't. They were conversing with a woman who was saying goodbye to this world and her people in it.

Avery inched towards the edge of her fold-out chair, her mouth opening and closing, but for the last half-hour, no more words could leave her lips. The family members around her were laughing and sharing stories, and it took all of Avery's energy to try to laugh along, to conceal her own emotions so she could fit in with everyone else's.

When their nana closed her eyes and drifted into a sleep between this world and the next, everyone stood in line to give their final goodbye.

Avery stepped to her nana's side and leaned forwards, planting a kiss on Nana's tissue soft, wrinkled skin.

"Goodbye, Nana," she whispered. "I hope you know I've always loved you."

Final kiss and words complete, Avery stepped aside and fled towards the door.

With every tick of the clock, the blob of emotion in Avery's mind began to take shape into thoughts, and she was forced to face what she had felt all along.

She was never going to get an explanation for Nana's last words.

Chapter 3

"What is Nana's problem!" Avery said once their mother closed the black, paint-chipped front door.

"Shh!" Elizabeth scolded. "Are you kidding right now, Avery? We're in Nana's front yard. You can't wait until we make it to the sidewalk?"

"Elizabeth, she could barely hear us when we were *in the room* with her! She can't hear us out here!" Avery was no longer yelling, but still speaking in a raised volume to prove a point. She looked at Brinkley, who was clutching Lily's hand, walking towards their SUV, though they were walking so slowly, it appeared they were merely looking at the car. As if Brinkley legitimately believed that having her back turned was enough to prove she wasn't eavesdropping on every word. Rolling her eyes, Avery stormed a few steps towards her mother, who now had her oversized black sunglasses shielding her face. "What is her problem?" Avery said again, waving the journal in her mother's face.

Mama Donna pulled her black cardigan closer to her chest. "Avery, please calm down. You are making a scene."

"Did you set her up to that?"

"What? Avery, what are you talking about?" said Mama Donna.

"Nana doesn't know where I've been, Mom? She doesn't know

where I'm going, and couldn't even be nice enough to lie, like she did for everyone else?" Avery felt her body shaking as she spoke.

With her mouth agape, Elizabeth smoothed her hands through her ponytail. "Just because you're jealous that I brighten Nana's heart better than heaven doesn't mean she was lying, Avery."

Mama Donna nodded. "This is true. My mother keeps it real."

Clutching her stomach, Avery lowered the tan leather journal to her side and forced herself to take a slow inhale through her nose. "It just seems odd, Mother," Avery spat, "that I'm the only child she didn't have anything nice to say about. Does it not? Am I that terrible of a human being to you all?" Avery crossed her arms and squinted towards the quiet road. "When Chase and John were here on Saturday, she had nothing but love to share. Now all of a sudden, she wants to bring up an issue with me? Those are her last words to me?" Feeling her voice rising again, Avery took one more breath and snapped her gaze back towards her mother. "I mean, what the hell, Mom. Why would she—"

"Avery, enough," her mother hissed. "I don't have these answers for you. If that's how Nana feels, that's how she's allowed to feel. What she said was not even that bad, so don't be dramatic." Mama Donna waved her hand as if to shoo Avery away. "Nana just wanted to get to know you better over the years. You need to calm down."

Nostrils flared, Avery drilled her gaze into her mom's dark shades. "Then why wouldn't she tell me she feels this way when we *had time*?"

"Avery, Nana did try!" Elizabeth snapped. "You were the one who kept your distance. Screaming about Nana at all, let alone in her own neighborhood, is rude."

"I'm not even yelling!" Avery yelled.

"Okay, okay," Lily called in her squeaky voice as she ran towards them with Brinkley close behind. "It sounds like everyone needs to take a time-in."

"You mean a time-out?" said Elizabeth.

"No," Brinkley sighed. "Time-outs feel punitive. Time-ins are for reflection." Even Brinkley rolled her eyes at her own explanation. "It's this new thing Lily's summer camp is doing ..."

"Okay, anyway—" said Elizabeth, just as Brinkley said,

"Look ..." For the first time, Avery noticed faded dark circles under her oldest sister's eyes. "We're all feeling sensitive right now, and my daughter is here, so we need to *process* our emotions *before* we take them out on one another." Brinkley looked at everyone with a tight smile. "Okay?"

"That's like ... really smart, Mommy," said Lily.

Brinkley's gaze landed on Avery. "You know how much Nana loves you. I'm sure whatever she was trying to say just came out weird. She's not completely with it right now."

Brinkley's rose quartz ring glinted in the sunlight as she spoke.

Avery raised her eyes to meet Brinkley's. "Must be nice to be a wonderful mother and wife," she retorted, turning on her heels to storm across the front yard, back to her car that was as old and beat up as she felt.

No one called after her. All she heard was her mother's voice say, "Do you think she's safe to drive?"

To which Elizabeth responded, "She'll be fine."

Tears welling in her eyes, Avery ripped open her car door and locked herself inside. Once again, her breath felt caught in her chest as if the stale air that had once felt trapped was now making her body its permanent home. Still, she couldn't stop staring at the smooth cover of the journal.

It only took a few seconds before she ripped the cover open, ready for the moment of truth. Nana claimed she had written in one page of the journal. There had to be a message on that page. All the holidays Avery had spent with Nana, all the *I love yous* exchanged over the years

– there had to be something else her nana wanted her to know.

But when Avery opened the cover, an empty, yellowed page stared back at her. Empty, except for two sprawling words scribbled in cursive at the top:

Dear Self.

Avery stared at the two words. She flipped through the other pages, but they were all blank.

Dear Self.

"What the fuck."

The world felt as though it were collapsing into her chest. She jammed her key into her car's ignition and followed the empty neighborhood road until she was out of view from her mother, sisters, and niece. Once alone, she parked her car by the curb of an empty, familiar street. White houses with black shutters lined the road on either side.

Chapter 4

B rinkley padded down the creamy travertine hallway that led to her master bedroom. Even though the stone was cool beneath her bare feet, she couldn't help but linger outside her own bedroom door. After purchasing this house on the Main Line three years ago, the interior of her and Chase's master suite was finally complete. Yet ever since Brinkley and her interior designer had added the final touches, adjusting the lamps on their nightstands just so, fluffing the already fluffy pillows, lighting the candles, Brinkley found herself lingering on the other side of the door more often, imagining the room she had spent years helping design.

The once carpeted "sitting room" the previous owners had left behind was now replaced with walnut wooden floors and handwoven, neutral-toned rugs; the shelves that once held books had been torn down, along with the walls that had supported them to create an addition for the Calcutta marble bathroom that overlooked their backyard's sycamore trees. Brinkley had spent a full year working with a renowned interior designer based in Philadelphia to transform the room into her and Chase's personal paradise. She had spent months waiting for custom-made furniture, testing swatches of the softest fabrics and most durable woods while also trying to determine which neutral tones worked best to soothe her and Chase's senses.

The chandelier alone, with air trapped inside its glass, falling from their ceiling to appear more like a work of art than a fixture to light their room, had taken over half a year to complete. And now it dangled from their ceiling, the wire that was holding it so thin it was almost invisible, ready to light their room in whatever shade they wanted.

It was all waiting for her on the other side of the door.

She tightened the silk robe around her waist, hoping it would give her curves less of that pear and more of that hourglass shape that had become so popular these days. Looking down, she wasn't sure it had worked.

With a sigh, she tucked her short, warm blonde waves behind her ears, pushed her rose quartz ring and wedding band further up her fingers, then nudged open the door.

Chase sat upright in their custom-made, sandalwood bedframe, the blue glow from his laptop illuminating his clean-shaven face.

"Another late night, huh?"

Chase's thick-but-groomed eyebrows creased behind his rectangular reading glasses, but he remained focused on his screen. Brinkley rolled her eyes with a sigh.

"Sorry," he mumbled, his eyes still focused on the screen as he began to type something.

She released another sigh, this time louder.

"Jeez, Brinkley, what?" he asked, but removed his reading glasses to look at her. "Did the girls fall asleep?"

"Daisy needed a few bedtime books. Lily fell fast asleep." Brinkley pulled down their gray silk sheets to let herself into her side of the bed. Once she was tucked in, she looked at her husband, but he had already replaced his glasses on his face and resumed typing. "My nana is doing well," she continued. "Miraculous recovery. Ran a marathon and everything. Today wasn't difficult at all."

The sound of his typing stopped.

Chase closed his laptop and eyed Brinkley. "I wanted to finish sending a few emails." He set the laptop onto his nightstand before Brinkley had a chance to snap it in half. "I'm sorry ... How did today go?"

Brinkley's arm collapsed across her forehead as she stared at their ceiling. "I hope letting Lily see her great-nana like that wasn't traumatizing for her. She's only four. I worry."

"I mean, she's about to be five ..."

Is he trying to be funny? Brinkley wondered, but kept her mouth pressed shut.

Chase took the hint. "Look ..." he said with a sigh.

But when Brinkley did look at her husband, she saw him eyeing the laptop on the nightstand.

As if he could feel her glare, Chase focused his gaze back to her. "Lily and your nana had a special bond," he said. "You can't withhold a goodbye from them. Now Daisy, she feels too young. I'm glad you didn't take her. But Lily ..." He shook his head. "She needs closure, too."

"Yeah," said Brinkley, "I just ... I'm not good with death, you know? It freaks me out. So, if I can't handle it, why did I think it'd be okay for Lily?"

"Okay, well what normal human is 'good' with death?"

"I don't know – some people seem to deal with it better. I'm not one of those people. I won't even be able to sleep tonight."

"That's part of the grieving process," Chase said with a shrug. "You told Lily Nana was sick. You gave her a choice if she wanted to go, and she wanted to go." As if that were a sufficient answer, he pulled the computer onto his lap.

"She's four, Chase. Do you really think she knew what she was agreeing to?"

"Seeing someone go in and out of naps isn't scary. Kids are too sheltered from their own lives these days."

"And the adults are becoming too detached," Brinkley muttered, glaring at the glowing blue screen.

Chase shut his computer again and looked at his wife. "I'm sorry ... One of my houses has been on the market too long. The sellers aren't happy."

"No need to apologize," Brinkley said softly, opening the computer for him. "Sell away. It was just ... a weird day."

"Wait," Chase paused. "Speaking of weird, can you explain your text ..." He began to scroll through his phone. "And I quote, *Only my family would create drama at a deathbed. We're all fine, but o-m-g.*" Chase pushed the phone to her face. "What happened?"

Brinkley swiped it away. "I don't even know if I want to relive it," she groaned.

When Chase didn't fight for more information, and instead began typing, Brinkley used her pillows to prop herself up. "Okay, okay," she said. "Basically, my nana had last words to say to everybody—"

"No last words for the in-laws, huh?"

"Guess not. Anyway," said Brinkley and turned her body to face her husband, snuggling herself into this new position, "Nana said she had last words for all her grandchildren and went around the room saying really sweet things—"

"That sounds nice."

"It was, until she got to Avery ..." Brinkley paused for a moment to draw the suspense. "She told Avery, like, she doesn't know who she is, and doesn't know where she's going—"

"What?"

"I know. And then she gifted Avery this old journal that she basically said she never liked. How crazy?"

"Well ... what did your nana tell you?"

"Me? She told me I've been a light in her life, and that I have a lot of love, and live a lucky life ... Oh, and that I'm a wonderful mother and wife," Brinkley said, emphasizing the word "wife". She could feel her eyes dazzle as she recalled the moment. "Look what she gave me." And she stretched out her manicured hand in front of Chase's face to show off the rose quartz ring.

"Oh, wow," Chase marveled as he examined the crystal. "That's beautiful, Brinkley."

Brinkley beamed. "She said it was the first present my grandpa ever gave her. She's been wearing it ever since. Isn't that crazy?"

"A one-of-a-kind ring for my one-of-a-kind wife," said Chase, tucking a strand of Brinkley's hair behind her ear, which made Brinkley remember she needed to get her roots retouched soon. Maybe during the week when the girls were at summer camp.

"So, wait," Chase said, withdrawing his hand, "you are the light in her life, and ... she has no idea where Avery's life is going?"

"Yeah." Brinkley looked down at the ring. "Avery was so upset by the whole thing."

"I bet," Chase said, staring into the distance for a moment before looking at Brinkley. "Was Nana ... you know, 'with it' ... when this all happened?"

"I mean ..." Brinkley scrunched her face the same way her daughters did. "She seemed pretty conscious. Even for a while after ..."

"What did Avery do?"

"What do you mean?"

"Did Avery ask her why she was talking crazy?"

"Okay, I don't think Nana was talking crazy. I think she was being very honest," Brinkley said, admiring her ring for a moment longer before meeting her husband's gaze. "I mean, Avery tried asking, but Nana just put her hand up like this." Brinkley held her hand in a "stop" position to demonstrate.

"Your nana did that?"

26

"She was feeling sassy today," Brinkley said with a nod.

"And no one asked her why?"

"I mean, Nana needed to get things off her chest. She probably didn't have the energy for any talk-back, or persuasion, or ... whatever." Brinkley shrugged. "She's on her deathbed, Chase. I don't think anyone should disrespect her wishes during her last moments, you know?"

"Why not?" Chase argued. "If anything, your nana should respect all her grandchildren's wishes. You're the ones who will be stuck living with her words while she's drinking Mai Tais with Jesus."

"Chase ..." Brinkley looked at her husband with wrinkled eyebrows, but could feel the muscles of her mouth suppressing a smile.

They held the moment together, their eyes locked, smiles hidden.

"I'm just saying ..." Chase glanced at his computer. "Your sister has every right to ask why she'd say something like that. This," he said and held up his hand in a mock "stop", "is rude."

Brinkley's phone chimed from her nightstand. "Speak of the devil," she murmured. "It's Avery."

"How's she doing?"

Brinkley's mouth hung open for a second.

"Well?" said Chase.

"She just texted ... *Nana can rot in hell.*"

Chapter 5

E lizabeth found herself staring at the framed pictures hanging on the beige wall of her future in-laws' living room. Every wall was painted a shade of beige in this house.

The picture frames were of varying sizes, but each one was composed of thick black borders that formed clean lines and sharp edges against the wall. Black-and-white photographs filled the frames, showcasing essentially the same thing – smiles of straight white teeth, belonging to bodies dressed in black tuxedos or evening gowns, adorned with diamonds and pearls. Each photograph was set in an extravagant place – ballrooms, courtyards, rented rooms of museums – as noted by a chandelier here, a floral backdrop there, shiny hardwood floors and wall moldings everywhere.

It was, as everyone in John's family called it, the "welcome wall", as it was situated in their living room, the place they most often welcomed guests, and featured the finest photographs of generations welcoming new eras of life over the past two centuries. Business mergers, charity events, pictures with local politicians, and weddings.

As Elizabeth studied the photographs, she noticed that no matter what decade or event was showcased, the people pictured always possessed a certain gleam in their eye. A gleam that could only come from the kind of power money can bring.

"Pretty soon your wedding will be up there," a smooth voice cooed.

Elizabeth looked at Mrs. Astor, her future mother-in-law, who had snuck up behind her. Mrs. Astor's eyes remained on Elizabeth as she brought a delicate champagne glass to her carmine-red painted lips. Even her eyes twinkled like jewels, two blue sapphires amid unnaturally taut skin and charcoal colored hair.

"John told me Hotel Aurore is all booked for the ceremony and reception?" Mrs. Astor said with a smile.

"Yes, it is all booked," said Elizabeth, smoothing over her long, low ponytail that she hadn't had time to redo after visiting Nana. Once her mother had dropped her off, John was already waiting in his car to take them on the half-hour drive from their isolated cabin in Wynnewood to his parents' estate in Chestnut Hill. Elizabeth had been too drained from the emotions of the day to bother with her hair. At the time, wiping the streaked mascara from her eyelids had felt like enough of a win, but now she prayed there were no loose strands slipping from her ponytail.

"A little more than three months and we'll be ... married." Elizabeth took a sip from her own champagne glass and cleared her throat. "At Hotel Aurore."

"Oh, that makes my heart so happy, you have no idea." Mrs. Astor clutched her chest as she spoke. "I know there had been whispers of some old barn-type of wedding—"

"Um, an outdoor wedding, yes—"

"Right. Well, trust me when I say Hotel Aurore will not disappoint. The owner is a friend of a friend, so I know we are in good hands."

Elizabeth looked down at her nearly empty champagne glass. She had long dreamed of an outdoor wedding ceremony and reception, with everything from the tables to the ceiling adorned with flowers and greenery, romantic string lights – but her future in-laws had warned her about bugs, and weird smells, not to mention how dependent the whole day would be on the weather.

Weddings are for sophisticated interiors, they'd insisted.

Whatever that meant.

The Astors had offered to pay for the whole thing, so it didn't really matter, anyway.

Save your money for a beautiful honeymoon, Mrs. Astor had instructed her and John.

Elizabeth had been so touched, so relieved when the Astors had offered help. Her own father had claimed she and John were old enough to pay for their own wedding. Then he'd spent his money on a four-carat engagement ring for Sin, short for Cynthia, his girlfriend of a few months.

So, the magic of Elizabeth's wedding fantasies had been corrupted by the reality of the wedding industry, when the Astors had offered relief. It was an offer she could neither refuse nor pay back. Which, she worried, as she saw the twinkle in Mrs. Astor's eyes, was maybe the whole point when they'd made such an offer.

"There you are." John's deep voice cut through the air as he stepped into the beige living room.

Elizabeth felt her muscles relax. No matter how many years they had been dating, she still found the depth of John's voice insanely attractive and somehow comforting. His publishers took notice too, and often tried to persuade him to narrate his own audiobook. John had two books published and a strong cult following. While his first book had been published with little fanfare and decent reviews, his second book had been a critically acclaimed success. It was a love story following a tourist who falls in love with her scuba instructor's underwater world.

John had spent the last two years working on the follow-up to that book, to reveal whether the tourist could ever love the scuba diver when not underwater. Over those two years, Elizabeth had frequently found her fiancé ripping up papers and sobbing through the stress of trying to follow up his life's biggest success.

Elizabeth thought turning his masterpiece into an audiobook would be a profitable idea to help take the stress off. But John refused, always claiming he "wrote words for people to read, not for people to listen to".

"The fire pit is lit." John's voice pulled Elizabeth away from the memories of him sobbing on the ground.

"Oh, good, I told our new housekeeper to do that," Mrs. Astor said. "You two enjoy the fire – I'm going to check on Chef Monroe."

"Yes, please do," John said, looking at his mother. "It smells like Lamb Chop is getting roasted alive in there."

"Oh, John," Mrs. Astor said with a chuckle. "We're not having lamb tonight. We're having cow."

Elizabeth watched John's jaw tighten as his mother walked away.

"We can always fill up on bread and wine," Elizabeth said, though she could feel her stomach rumbling. "I think your parents are still adjusting."

"Adjusting? Elizabeth we've been vegetarian since I started *researching* my last book!" John shot back. "And how many years ago was that?"

This was true; John had spent months researching the state of the oceans' ecosystems for his book, and neither he nor Elizabeth had eaten an animal, land or sea, since. Though it seemed the Astors wanted them to.

"Let's leave," he whispered. "My sister won't stop talking about her baby's Mandarin lessons and I can't take it any more."

"What do you mean? The baby's not even born yet ..."

"Exactly. She hired someone to come to her house and talk to her stomach in Mandarin."

"Is she trying to learn the language too?" Elizabeth wondered in a whisper.

"What do you think?"

"I actually don't know."

"She doesn't give a crap about learning another language, Elizabeth," John said in a forceful whisper. "She's only doing it to try to one-up her elitist friends."

"Well, whatever, John. It's her baby and her life. We can't just leave over that."

"Why not?"

"Because ..." Elizabeth whispered, looking around the room to make sure none of the Astors were nearby. "Your parents threw this whole dinner for me, to help me mourn my nana. We can't leave after they did all this."

"Your nana's not even dead yet! This is not how normal people mourn the dead, Liz." John was whisper-yelling and gesturing wildly to emphasize his point. "People don't mourn by popping fancy bottles of Champagne and bragging about their bizarre pregnancy practices."

Elizabeth's gaze dropped to the empty Champagne glass in her hands, through which the image of the Astors' beige living room was magnified.

When Elizabeth had first been introduced to John's family, she had fallen in love with them almost as much as she had fallen in love with him. The Astors had seemed so ...refined compared to her family, with their tailored clothes and even temperaments.

Elizabeth appreciated that John's family had opened their hand-carved, double wooden doors – not to mention a whole new world – to her. A world that always included expensive Champagne served in the finest crystal, as if life itself were enough of a celebration. The immediate family members attended every gathering, and on the rare occasion someone couldn't make it, no one gossiped about them. The Astors also participated in sweet little rituals, like gathering around the fire pit after a meal, and hosting an extravagant New Year's Eve party every year.

Not to mention, the parents were still married and at least appeared not to hate each other.

When Elizabeth diverted her gaze to look at John, he seemed to have given up on his escape plan and had planted himself on the brown leather couch.

"Didn't you say the fire pit was lit? Maybe we should get some air?" she said.

John looked at her through narrowed eyes, then patted the spot next to him. "There's no air around here, Elizabeth. Not even outside," he said, appearing to study her every movement as she walked to the couch and took a seat.

"What?" Elizabeth asked, seeing his eyes still focused on her. They were a hue lighter than his mother's, as if someone had taken shades of gray and tried to paint a shallow, stormy sea into his irises.

"We didn't have time to talk about your nana," he said, raising an eyebrow. "How is she?"

"I mean, she's dying," said Elizabeth, smoothing her hands over her stomach. "So ..."

"Some people handle that better than others." John shrugged, smoothing his hand through his own dark, gelled hair.

"True," she said and sighed, switching her focus to something on the floor. "So, she's doing well, then. At least it appears that way. She gave me something, actually."

"Really?" John paused. "What is it?"

"An old coin pouch she bought from a trip to Italy. She said it was the greatest trip of her life."

"Wow. What made her go to Italy?"

"What?"

"What made her want to take a trip to Italy? It's a beautiful destination, but one that attracts all different sorts of reasons, no?"

"Um ..." Elizabeth paused, smoothing her hands over her stomach a second time. "I don't know? She did it when she was in her twenties."

"Well, did she go with anyone?"

Elizabeth felt the blood rush to her head as all the questions she would never be able to ask or answer rushed through her mind. "I don't know. Shit. My brain was fogged from, like, the dying of it all ... I mean, she's told stories about it before, always raving about the fashion and carbs. I didn't think to ask anything more—"

"It's okay," John soothed, but then added, "Just call her tomorrow. Or call your mom. I'm sure Mama Donna would know."

She felt her muscles relax, but only for a moment before John spoke again.

"If she said it was the best trip of her life, I feel like you should know about that, no?"

Before Elizabeth could panic or process further, John continued, "Did your Nana give anyone else a gift?"

"Yeah," Elizabeth said, trying to talk through the nagging in her head. "Brinkley got a gorgeous rose quartz ring. It was one of the first gifts my grandpa ever gave Nana." Elizabeth tilted her head as she pictured the ring shining on Brinkley's finger. "I don't really know why Nana gave Brinkley the ring. I'm the one who's been in the longest relationship and getting married in a few months, but—"

"Perhaps the coin pouch is supposed to honor your financial independence," John offered with a shrug. "I mean, if it weren't for my trust fund, your CPA salary would exceed my book royalties."

Elizabeth felt her mouth curve into a smile as she eyed John.

"Anyway, a ring is so predictable," he added.

Elizabeth tried considering every question she'd ask while inter-viewing Nana tomorrow, but John's voice interrupted her thoughts. "What about Avery? Didn't your nana have a complicated relationship with her?"

"Oh." Elizabeth snapped her attention back to John. "Avery's was weird," she admitted. "Avery got a journal."

"What's weird about a journal?"

Chapter 6

"Oh, Brinkley child, Brinkley, my sun, moon, and stars. My little tiki torch, my little nightlight," Avery cooed in her dramatic reenactment of visiting Nana earlier that day. She was in a bar, sucking down her fifth vodka tonic. "The light of my life, Brinkley," Avery finished with her arm extended towards the heavens.

She paused for a moment before standing straight and speaking like herself. Well, herself when she was drunk and in a social setting. In a social setting, any tragedy could be material for a laugh. It was when she was alone that she had to be careful.

"Brinkley is the light of my nana's life, Elizabeth makes her feel alive when she's dying for Christ's sake, and I'm just ... nothing?" Avery rocked her head back to down the last of her vodka tonic.

She looked at her longest and dearest childhood friend, and room-mate for the past couple of years, Izzy, for help. Izzy and Avery had met in middle school when Avery's parents had been in the beginning of their divorce. During a group project one day, Izzy had spotted scabs on Avery's wrists. Instead of using this information as gossip, Izzy had invited her to her thirteenth birthday party. Much had changed since then, but they had made it into adulthood and survived an apartment infested with cockroaches, as well as the ensuing chaotic move after, intact. Yet, now her so-called longest and dearest friend, Izzy, seemed more interested in making a bull's eye than helping her through this crisis.

Maybe Izzy was getting tired of Avery's crises. Avery was exhausted from them herself.

Still, she continued: "Do you believe my nana told me, 'I don't even know if *you* know where you're going'?" Avery repeated her nana's last words for about the tenth time since entering the bar. "Like, what kind of bull crap is that? She's the one who's dying! I don't think any of us has a clue where she's going, but we don't tell her that!"

"Listen," Izzy said as she used her fingers to fluff through her coils of curls, "just because someone's dying doesn't mean they're worth listening to."

Izzy's voice was calm but firm. Avery imagined it was how she spoke when chiding her second-graders.

"Shots fired," Avery said and laughed, happy someone else's voice was breaking the torment occurring in her own mind.

"I'm serious," said Izzy, piercing Avery with her dark brown eyes. "I remember after my uncle died, everyone praised him as if he were a saint. Suddenly all the trauma he put his family through didn't matter." Izzy lined her body to face the dartboard again. "It was hard," she concluded, the dart hitting just outside the bull's eye. "Took years for me to reconcile different versions of my uncle into one memory of a human being. But you know what? Taught me a lot." Izzy turned towards her. "And you'll get through it too. One way or the other."

Izzy's eyes lingered on Avery for a moment, her eyebrow cocked in the air. Avery couldn't tell if her friend was questioning the validity of her statement or checking to see if Avery understood.

"Yeah," Avery heard her voice exclaim a pitch higher than she would have liked. "Yeah, you're right," she tried again, nodding.

"Just because Nana's dying doesn't mean she's not an asshole."

Izzy broke their gaze to grab her glass of wine from the high-top table. Her eyebrow was still raised, and her eyes had widened.

"What?" Avery demanded.

"I just ..." Izzy took a breath, fiddling with the gold bangle on her wrist. "That's not exactly where I was going with it."

Avery rolled her eyes in an exasperated sigh. "I need another drink. You need one?" Her cell phone vibrated in her back pocket.

"All good," said Izzy. "I can't drink much more after this. I have yoga in the morning."

"Ah, that's right," Avery said, scratching her head, her phone still vibrating.

All it took was one look at the crowded bar for Avery to decide to head outside, instead. She needed fresh air more than another tonic, anyway. She pulled her phone from her pocket.

"Hello?" she shouted.

"Hey girl!" Brinkley's voice sang just as Avery stepped into the kind of summer air that felt warm on a good night in Philadelphia and suffocating on a bad one. She glanced down the cemented sidewalks of Passyunk, each slab tilted at different angles, as if the ground beneath had had enough of everyone walking at breakneck speed. She stared at the strangled specks of greenery forcing its way through the cracks, doing whatever it needed to be seen by the sun. "How are you feeling?"

"Um ... I'm feeling ... I'm feeling rather dark, Brinkley. I'm not really a light in anyone's life, so—"

"Well, you're a light in my life!" said Brinkley. "Look, I was talking to Chase about this whole thing, and we both think you should just ask Nana why she said ... you know."

"That's really brilliant. I wish I'd tried that. Oh, wait!" Avery said loudly, then spotted the rather large bouncer scowling at her. "I did try asking her, Brinkley. Nana didn't let—"

"I know, I know," Brinkley said quickly. "But maybe push through until you get an answer. Tomorrow you should just go to her house and demand an explanation. Tell her how much that would mean to you."

Avery watched the traffic light in the distance change from green to yellow to red.

"Are you there?" Brinkley asked but continued speaking. "She probably has no idea she even hurt you this much, Avery. I don't think a misunderstanding like this should ruin your memory of her."

Pressing the phone into her ear, Avery exhaled a long sigh.

"It's late," Brinkley said. "Just get a good night's sleep and tomorrow you'll have more clarity, okay?"

"Okay," said Avery. "Thank you, Brinkley. Love you."

Once Avery was back inside the bar, she and Izzy decided to leave, going their separate ways as they often seemed to do these days. Izzy took a cab to sleep at her boyfriend's apartment, and Avery hesitated on the disfigured sidewalk, watching the light change once again from green to red.

All Avery wanted to do was walk through these narrow neighborhood streets, past the fountain with cherub angels playing their silent trumpets, and into the center of the city, where she could look up and see buildings that reached the skies until her feet grew weary and her mind grew tired.

But it was getting late. Too late to walk alone. So, she climbed into a cab and stared out the window. The lights and cars and people, some laughing, some arguing, others simply trying to get food to eat, all seemed to blur, and for a moment Avery felt as if the events from earlier today weren't real. Because her nana couldn't be at home dying while the city was blurring as if it were any weekend night.

Once Avery stepped into her apartment, however, the realization that the day was real hit her, and the weight of that truth carried her to bed. Knowing her nana was an early riser, Avery set her alarm for sixty-thirty am, and imagined hearing Nana's voice. It was the only thought that helped soothe her to sleep.

At four fifty-two am, Avery's phone buzzed with a text from her mother:

Nana passed early this morning.

Chapter 7

Before the funeral ceremony began, everyone seated around Brinkley tried to make small talk, as if Nana's dead body weren't on display in a coffin a few feet away. At first, Brinkley attempted to entertain such talk.

People would ask about her daughters.

"Oh, my daughters are doing well," she would reply. "Chase's mom is watching them today. Last I checked, Lily was making a card for Nana in heaven, and Daisy was filling her face with dinosaur stickers, so ... that'll be fun to try to take off," she would say with her nervous laugh, only to immediately regret offering any kind of laugh at a funeral.

Some would ask her and Chase how Chase's real estate business was doing, and if he would offer a "family discount". Brinkley let Chase deal with that one.

Others, of course, would attempt to talk about the weather.

"Such a shame it's sunny today," one woman with silver hair and a cane in her hand mused. "I prefer rainy days for funerals."

Brinkley didn't recognize or know this woman, but she imagined she had already reached the stage in life when all her loved ones had died. The thought that someone could develop preferences for funerals was the final tipping point for Brinkley to give in to her emotions and bawl her eyes out. The problem was, once her crying started, it was hard to stop, so she became a wet mess of snot and tears.

No one tried making small talk with her now.

Chase kept handing her tissues she had stuffed into her purse until there were no tears left to cry, at least for now.

"I hate open caskets," she whispered to her husband once she calmed down, using a fresh tissue to give her nose one final blow. Luckily, she had remembered Elizabeth's raccoon eyes from the last visit to Nana and had at least worn waterproof mascara. She eyed Elizabeth now, but John was the one eyeing her back.

"I think spending a minute with the body of a loved one who's passed can help you heal," John whispered back.

Okay, creep.

"John's right," Elizabeth whispered.

Oh, here we go, Brinkley thought, but John pressed on.

"Spending time with the body can help you realize the person you loved was always more than their physical form, Brinkley. And then you realize you're way more than your form. And since we're all headed for death," John paused from his whispered musings, looking towards the open coffin, "you might as well spend some time with it, when it arises, and try to understand it."

Brinkley blinked.

"You're gonna die, Brinkley," John said. "Don't be afraid."

"You sound like a freak right now," Brinkley snapped.

"Oh, Brinkley, grow up," Elizabeth hissed. "There's no need to be afraid of a dead body," Elizabeth continued. "You're going to become one, too, you know."

Brinkley wanted to vomit all over them.

But John and Elizabeth just looked at each other with a shrug and joined a crying Mama Donna in the line that had formed to see the open casket.

Brinkley couldn't get over the fact that there was even a line. As if a dead body were some sort of amusement park attraction.

When the ceremony progressed and various loved ones walked to the microphone to say their eulogies, Brinkley found herself spinning the rose quartz ring around and around on her finger. The speeches highlighted what a compassionate, strong-willed, and overall beautiful human her nana was. Each speaker seemed to note how Nana had volunteered at soup kitchens, and traveled to Washington D.C. to join the marches for the Women's Liberation movement. Not to mention she was the greatest mother, wife, and friend anyone could ever ask for.

It made Brinkley wonder what anyone would say about her at her own funeral.

Brinkley loved her children and her husband. And watching trashy reality TV while drinking wine, she thought with a heavy heart, and then tried again. *Brinkley was a wonderful mother and wife. Not to mention a light. Well, she was a light in her nana's life. And her husband and children's life. Sometimes she was a light for her sisters and parents, too, but sometimes they really seemed to dim that light ... Anyway, she was a fucking light. Shining bright. And she had a lot of love in her life – don't forget that. Also, she joined the student council when she was younger and tried to make great changes for her peers at school. Pizza parties every Friday.*

She wanted to groan at her own thoughts.

Let's try this again ... Brinkley Rose Taylor was a wonderful mother and wife. She was so devoted, in fact, she quit her job in marketing so she could devote all that time to raising her beautiful children. Her beautiful children sometimes threw tantrums and tried talking back, but ...

Wait a second, Brinkley wondered, thinking of Nana's last words to her. *Why am I confined to being a mother and wife? What's up with that,*

Nana?

She tried once more.

Brinkley was a devoted mother, wife, friend, sister, daughter, human, perhaps angel, not to mention a previous marketing assistant. Until she realized America does not support working mothers and to successfully keep up with both worlds would require expensive childcare and an Adderall prescription—

"Elena was a symbol of love, and strength, and compassion," the priest concluded, snapping Brinkley out of her own obituary.

Brinkley continued spinning the rose quartz ring around and around on her finger, trying her best not to faint as the next round of prayers began.

Chapter 8

Elizabeth couldn't stop staring at Brinkley, who had been spinning the rose quartz ring Nana had gifted her around and around on her finger. It looked as though her older sister were possessed and needed the priest to perform an exorcism, stat.

The priest concluded his sermon and asked everyone to rise to sing the dirge. Elizabeth followed the instructions with the rest of the crowd and looked around. Her mother was still in hysterics. *Let it out, honey.* John was fully engaged with the hymn, belting his deep voice to the heavens. *That's my man.* Chase was holding Brinkley's hand, the same one adorned with the ring, probably to prevent his wife from spinning herself right into psychosis. He was appearing to sing, but Elizabeth couldn't hear anything coming out of his mouth. *This isn't a lip-sync battle, Chase. Just live a little already. No one's going to judge you at a funeral.* Finally, her eyes landed on Avery, who wasn't even pretending to sing. The hymn book was open in her hands, but Avery's mouth remained shut, her gaze focused on the intimidating wooden crucifix hanging at the center of church. Avery's eyes were steady as she stared. Though her face looked fallen, it also appeared relaxed. A faint wrinkle creased between her eyebrows.

Avery's gaze made Elizabeth feel as if her little sister were some-where between here, at Nana's funeral, and somewhere else. Somewhere that existed in memory and thought. This would happen to Avery. She would seem to slip in and out of places, and then say, "Sorry, I was lost in thought."

But Avery would never describe where she went.

Elizabeth glanced at the wooden crucifix, but it didn't transport her anywhere. She was stuck in the church with all her emotions and unanswered questions. So, not knowing what else to do, she opened her mouth and joined the mournful song.

Chapter 9

I zzy was right: people do praise the dead.

The entire funeral service made Avery feel as though her nana had been one of earth's VIPS, here to gift everyone with her presence. Every speech raved about what a compassionate human being and loyal loved one her nana had been. Every picture framed around her coffin showcased the biggest smiles. Even her nana's biography highlighted all the good she had brought to this earth. Avery was starting to wonder who Nana's publicist was.

Avery surveyed her surroundings: the grand church ceiling, the high-rise walls adorned with magnificent stained-glass windows featuring angels and Biblical references Avery wouldn't understand. Her gaze landed on the wooden crucifix featuring Jesus Himself. *I don't know where you've been,* Nana's voice still echoed through her brain. Avery stared at Jesus, literally hanging on the cross before her eyes. A symbol of forgiveness and strength amid suffering, of staying so true to his morals, He was willing to die for them. To sacrifice Himself for the greater good.

For a moment, it made her own issues seem petty. If Jesus could love His Father even while getting nailed to a cross, couldn't Avery find enough love in herself to get over whatever petty drama her family had put her through?

Then again, wouldn't Jesus want her questioning her family? Wasn't questioning the status quo part of His whole shtick?

As everyone started to sing the dirge, with John's deep voice crowding out all the others, Avery continued studying the crucifix. Was Avery the one who needed to ask for Nana's forgiveness, for whatever grudge Nana seemed to have held against her? Or was Avery the one who needed to do the forgiving?

After an hour of getting lost in her own questions and thoughts, the service ended, and the repast was held in Nana's home. According to Mama Donna, Nana had wanted it this way. She had wanted all her loved ones to mourn her death and celebrate her life in the very home she had been married, raised her kids, and grown old in.

While everyone congregated around the food, Avery remained alone in the living room. She could hear people from the dining room *oohing* and *aahing* over Brinkley's rose quartz ring.

"My mother never took that ring off her finger!" Avery heard Aunt Carol gush.

"I know, it really is so special," Brinkley cooed.

"Now what did Nana gift your daughter, Carol?" Mama Donna asked her sister. "Nana told Brinkley that she was a light in her life."

"Oh, Mom, stop it," Avery heard Brinkley's nervous laugh. "Seriously, stop it."

After a few minutes, Avery had to tune it all out. She studied the pictures framed on Nana's living room shelf. Avery had passed this shelf many times over the years, but as she analyzed the pictures now, she wondered if she had ever bothered to look at them before.

All of Nana's grandchildren were framed, showcased in different stages of life. She could practically see Brinkley grow up before her eyes. Yet the only pictures of Avery were from her elementary school days. Avery squinted at the pictures, searching for her adult face. Only her childhood one stared back at her.

48

Heavy footsteps came closer.

"Ah, the old grandchild shelf," Uncle Terry's voice announced to the empty living room. He let out a loaded sigh, the ice cubes of his drink rattling. "Wonder who will fight over these pictures now."

Avery eyed her uncle as he hobbled to the sagging couch.

"I'm only in here as a child," she confessed.

"What do you mean?" he asked, running his free hand through his thinning hair, his other hand clutching his drink.

"Nana has pictures of all her grandchildren at different stages in life. But I'm only in ones from when I was young."

"Huh ... Well," Uncle Terry said and clicked his tongue, "your cousin Jessie didn't make it onto the shelf at all, so consider yourself lucky, kid."

Avery snapped her head back at the framed pictures, searching for Uncle Terry's son, Jessie. *Oh, shit.*

"Nana always did say Jessie reminded her of me," Avery heard Uncle Terry grumble. "I thought she used it as an excuse not to like him, instead of having to admit she didn't like having a bastard grandchild."

Ears perked, Avery raised her eyebrow and sat on the sagging couch opposite her uncle. "Jessie's not a bastard child ..." Avery tried, even though, by definition, he was.

Over the years, Avery had a feeling Uncle Terry was the black sheep of his family. Avery had grown up hearing his name mentioned whenever her mother told tales of her childhood – he was her mother's older sibling, after all – but Avery didn't remember him coming around in her earlier years. He never came to birthdays or holidays. He didn't even attend Nana's annual Easter egg hunt.

Then, one year, when Avery was in second grade, Uncle Terry had started showing up. With a newborn infant named Jessie. When Uncle Terry had shown up with his son, everyone had hugged him hello and told him they loved him as if no time had passed at all. Uncle Terry had entered Avery's memories with such ease, she often forgot he hadn't always been part of them.

But every now and then, Uncle Terry would let a comment or insight about Nana slip. Slip from somewhere, it seemed, he had agreed to keep hidden. It would make Avery wonder ... But before Avery could ask questions, usually her mother, or Nana, would chime in and the comment would be lost, dissipating into the air.

No one was here to chime in now.

"If Jessie reminded Nana of you, wouldn't that make her want to frame a picture of him even more?" Avery questioned. "You're her only son."

"Ah, kid," Uncle Terry said, his heavy footsteps leading him away from the couch and towards the bar cart. He screwed off the cap of a whiskey bottle, poured his glass full, and sat back down. "You have a bit of a ... complicated relationship with your parents. Don't you?"

Avery felt the muscles of her stomach tighten. It made her nauseous. A comment like this would usually be the moment Avery excused herself and let Uncle Terry drink alone, but this time she stayed.

"What does that have to do with you and Nana?"

He shrugged, riffling through his pocket, and pulling out a cigar. "Your nana wasn't my nana. Your nana ... was my mom. That's all I'm saying."

He lit his cigar.

Elizabeth's voice made Avery jump.

"Didn't know there was a party happening in here," she declared. Dressed in a lacy black turtleneck, oversized black velvet blazer, and black pencil trousers, Elizabeth looked grief chic.

"No party here ..." Uncle Terry puffed his cigar.

Elizabeth glared at the smoke before she took a seat next to Avery.

"I feel like I didn't know a lot about Nana's life," Elizabeth confessed, reaching for a handful of peanuts from a dish on the coffee table. "Aunt Carol told me she had a whole plan to move to Europe?"

Uncle Terry chuckled. "Your nana had a lot of plans and dreams she never got to pursue."

"Why not?" Avery asked, but Elizabeth talked over her.

"Do you know if it was Italy she wanted to move to?" Elizabeth asked, staring at Uncle Terry. "Aunt Carol had no idea. But Italy was apparently the greatest trip of her life."

"It was probably the only trip of her life, Elizabeth," Avery corrected, crossing her arms.

Uncle Terry smirked even as he slipped the cigar between his lips. He exhaled a long stream of swirling smoke, his eyes lingering on Elizabeth. "She admitted that?"

"Uh, yeah, why wouldn't she?" said Elizabeth and reached into the hidden pocket of her blazer. She pulled out the crimson-red coin pouch embroidered with gold fleur-de-lis. Cradling the gift in her flat palm, she extended her arm towards Uncle Terry. "Nana gave me this before she passed. She said she bought it in her twenties, traveling through Rome. Said it was the only souvenir she got from the greatest trip of her life." Elizabeth paused, still studying Uncle Terry. "Do you know anything about it, or like ... why Italy was the greatest trip of her life?"

"Elizabeth, you were one of Nana's favored ones," Avery said before Uncle Terry could respond, glaring at her sister. "So why don't you be happy with your beautiful, probably handmade Italian pouch and let the less-favored offspring sort through their emotions alone, please?"

But the creases in the corners of Uncle Terry's eyes deepened. "No, that's not how it happened," he said, turning his gaze from the pouch towards something far away. "Nana said she bought that souvenir?"

"What do you mean?" Elizabeth asked. "Of course, that's how it happened. That's what Nana told me."

"Francesco bought her that pouch," he corrected.

"What?" Elizabeth's face was twisted in confusion. "Who the heck is Francesco?"

"Yeah, I've never heard of him before," Avery said, tilting her head at Uncle Terry.

Uncle Terry smiled sadly. "Francesco is a man Nana met while she was in Rome."

"Like ..." Avery started, and then stopped herself to switch to a whisper as she leaned in. "Like a lover?"

"Avery, Nana never mentioned a lover." Elizabeth rolled her eyes. "Uncle Terry's just messing with us." She tucked the red leather pouch back into the hidden pocket of her blazer.

Uncle Terry shook his head and took another puff from his cigar, the smoke clouding his face. "Lover might be the word for it," he said with a shrug. "Your nana extended her trip to stay with him, until her parents scared and guilted her into coming back home." With the cigar still dangling from his fingertips, Uncle Terry looked towards the window, his eyes narrowed. "But they always continued writing to each other, even after she got married ..."

"Damn, Nana!" said Avery.

"But that makes no sense ..." Elizabeth was shaking her head. "Why would she lie about buying it for herself? And Nana never mentioned the name Francesco before." She crossed and uncrossed her legs. "Nice try, Uncle Terry, but I'm not buying it."

Avery watched as Uncle Terry put out his cigar in the peanut dish.

"Some people are trained to be ashamed of their past," he said. "Lord knows how much shame her parents instilled in her—"

"But she loved her parents!" Elizabeth shot back, her voice growing louder. "She always told us how much she loved them. Why would she lie?"

"I already answered that," said Uncle Terry, his voice low. Clutching his glass full of whiskey, he rose from his seat. "Please excuse me, kids, I'm going to go grab some food."

Once he left the room, Elizabeth groaned. "Classic Uncle Terry."

"What do you mean?"

"Any time he starts drinking, he wants to change the story. A story that's not even his to tell! Like, I think Nana knows her life better than you do, dude."

"I don't know, I mean, that's the first time I've heard him share a story about Nana's past," said Avery.

"Okay, but don't you remember all the times Nana, or Mom, or even Aunt Carol would be in the middle of a story, and Uncle Terry would interrupt with 'That's not how it happened', or 'That's not true'. Maybe you don't remember because we'd all ignore him. The man is a pathological liar."

"I don't know if I'd call him that ..."

Elizabeth glared at her sister. It was as if she couldn't fathom the differences in their childhoods. As if growing up in the same house with the same family meant that everyone had the same insights and experiences. As if Avery didn't have the right to develop her own perspective.

"Why are you getting so upset about this?" Avery finally asked. "If anything, it makes your gift cooler. A gift from a forbidden lover."

"I'm upset because it's not true, Avery. Nana wouldn't lie." Elizabeth's eyes were still narrowed on her. "Don't take anything Uncle Terry says too seriously. He caused Nana a lot of pain while she was alive. Don't let him ruin her memory, too."

"How did he cause Nana pain?"

Elizabeth rolled her eyes. "You don't think disappearing from Nana's life and then showing up years later with a baby would be a bit ... traumatic?"

"Well, there must have been a reason he disappeared from her life," said Avery. The nausea rising from her stomach and into her throat was begging her to stop, but she continued. "Anyway, he's not ruining the memory of her. He's making it more interesting. If I hear one more thing about what a saint Nana was, I'm gonna—"

"I don't want to start with you, Avery," said Elizabeth, her lips tight. "I'm sorry you so desperately want to find a flaw in Nana's life because you're still pissed about what she said to you." Elizabeth flipped her ponytail over her shoulder. "But Nana was a wonderful woman and a devoted wife. She adored our grandfather."

With that, Elizabeth rose from the couch. She only took a few steps before turning around, wagging her index finger in Avery's face. "And she adored her parents!" Her face was flushed with splotches of pink. "Nana was pure, and lovely, and I miss her. So, I'm not going to sit here and let you or anyone desecrate her reputation."

Elizabeth stormed out of the empty living room, her ponytail swaying back and forth with every step she took.

"Some people's perspectives work so well for them," Avery muttered to the antique air.

Yet, as she sat alone on the couch, left with nothing but her thoughts and the perfect pictures staring at her from the shelf, Avery knew things weren't always what they seemed.

Chapter 10

"**F**unerals are always fascinating to me."

Brinkley side-eyed Elizabeth's fiancé, John, when he said this. It's not as if they were at a play – they were near the dessert table in her deceased nana's house, for crying out loud. Her *recently* deceased nana.

"I mean ..." he said, his gaze transfixed on the people congregating in the small dining room.

Brinkley followed his gaze. Nana's dining room had always been kept bare. A dark wooden dining table for six sat near the window and a dark wooden China cabinet lined the opposite wall. Decades ago, Nana and Grandpa had covered the walls with wallpaper that featured pastel-pink roses, but Brinkley noticed it was peeling now.

They would need to add a few upgrades before Chase tried to sell this place.

"All the emotions that arise during a funeral are ... It's a raw human experience we all have to go through." John was still talking. "Even the wallpaper!" He moved to a piece of peeling wallpaper, bending his tall body, and hunching his broad shoulders to inspect the wallpaper closer. Brinkley wasn't sure if John was still talking to her as he used his index finger to smooth over the piece of exposed wall. "Even houses grow old with the people who inhabit them," he said.

Before Brinkley could excuse herself, John deserted his fascination with the wallpaper just as fast as he had discovered it. "So where are your daughters?" he said.

"With Chase's mom."

"How are they mourning?"

"Well, Lily is four, so she's making a card for Nana in heaven. Daisy just turned three, so she's putting dinosaur stickers all over her face. I wouldn't exactly call it mourning at that age."

"Ah ..." John nodded, smoothing his hand through his wavy, dark hair. "The first funeral I went to, I was five. It was for my grandfather. My parents didn't believe in sheltering us from anything."

"Yeah, that's kind of what Chase was saying, but I hope we made the right decision." Brinkley looked at the stained brown carpet beneath her. "Chase and I were debating taking Lily to the funeral, but she still seems so young. I don't know."

"Listen. Every parent tries curating a ... a certain life for their child, but the children do with it what they will, you know?"

Brinkley felt herself nodding along and then shook her head. "Wait, what?"

Chase's presence interrupted the interaction as he slipped a stem-less glass of white wine into her hand.

"Thank you, Hun," Brinkley acknowledged, accepting the glass before widening her eyes at her husband. "We were just talking about how John is fascinated by funerals.

"What do you mean?" Chase asked, but before Brinkley could respond, John spoke for himself.

"Even the way your nana left us was poetic," said John, his gaze lingering on the dessert table before turning to Brinkley and Chase. "Gifting everyone with a little something from her past. Telling everyone her final words."

"Um, isn't that kind of what all dying people do?" said Brinkley.

"Yeah, that's pretty much how my grandparents left," said Chase with a smile that showed off his dimples. "Said a few nice words to everyone, maybe told them about some object they could take, and then passed."

"You can say 'died', Chase," said John. "We're all going to die someday."

Chase opened his mouth before shutting it and looked down, into his glass of wine.

"Can we stop talking about death and how we're all going to die?" said Brinkley.

"Why? We're at a funeral," said John, nonplussed.

"I don't know," Brinkley shook her head. "Never mind. Just don't tell Avery my nana's death was poetic." She was desperate to change the conversation, even if it required gossiping about her little sister. Feeling guilty, she took a sip of her wine and added, "I mean, I don't even think I like hearing my nana's death was poetic."

"But poetry's a beautiful thing ..." John's frown deepened. This guy was really not getting it.

"Okay, but." Brinkley looked around before leaning into the triangle the three of them had formed. "The girl did not even shed a tear at the funeral. I think Nana's last words are still bothering her. I don't know if Avery's ever going to get over this."

"What do you mean? Avery is the luckiest one. She didn't get the closure she was looking for, and she was given a journal to find it!"

Brinkley felt her heart beating faster, though she didn't know why.

"The luckiest one? I don't think so, John. We all got to hear nice things about ourselves while Avery just sat there and got the short end of the stick. I don't think that's lucky."

Shifting her weight and looking around the room, Brinkley released a small breath before leaning back into the triangle. "And I don't think she considers it lucky, either. She's still struggling."

John didn't respond. The warm sunlight streaming through the dining-room window seemed to illuminate his skin, making his gray-blue eyes appear like little worlds of their own against his pale face.

"It's not like Avery's a character in a story, John," Brinkley continued. "None of these people at this funeral are. They're real people, with real feelings. You understand that, right?"

Without any hesitation, John said, "We're all characters in a story, Brinkley."

Brinkley made eye contact for a moment before she and John took a simultaneous swig of their drinks. *Classic John response,* she thought.

"Shakespeare taught us that," John muttered.

Brinkley saw Elizabeth charging towards them from the living room, her ponytail swaying with every step.

Elizabeth breathed with a smile flashing her beautifully bleached white teeth. "I think Uncle Terry is flagged on the alcohol."

"Why?" said Brinkley. It seemed Elizabeth was always trying to flag Uncle Terry at family gatherings.

"He's talking nonsense about Nana's life," she said.

"Like what?" said John.

"Nothing, it doesn't matter ..." Elizabeth shook her head.

"Well, John was just telling us about his fascination with funerals," said Brinkley.

"Yes!" said John. "Death has a way of ... of bringing out the human spirit, you know? It knocks on all of our doors, and ... is able to somehow take the most precious things, while leaving the most valuable feelings behind."

Brinkley had been observing Elizabeth's reaction to John's words, but Elizabeth's eyes remained transfixed on him the entire time he spoke.

"Aw, John," she said, "I love the way your brain works."

Elizabeth said those words as if she actually believed him. As if she weren't at her own nana's funeral.

Brinkley felt her face growing hot. How dare they talk about death so candidly, as if it were life's work of art or some other excuse. Death was horrible. It was painful.

Brinkley couldn't wait to go home to her daughters, take off her shapewear, and put on her most comfortable, colorful pajamas. She was ready to leave this day behind.

Chapter 11

Avery made her way from the living room, down the dimly lit hallway, and into the light-filled guestroom-turned-Nana's-bedroom. It had turned into Nana's bedroom the year she had broken her hip from losing her balance while walking down stairs. Had Avery bothered to call Nana then? Check in to see how she was feeling?

With a long breath, Avery stepped further into the bedroom. The room in which everyone had spent their last moments with Nana.

The room Nana had died in.

It looked different. The bed had been stripped of the sterile white sheets, and the in-home hospice care workers had left, taking their machines with them. Family members were no longer crowded inside, swapping stories with tears and laughter. Nothing and no one stood in their place. All that was left was a mattress on a plain bedframe, one nightstand, and a stack of abandoned foldout chairs leaning against the wall.

Avery searched through the shallow drawers of the nightstand. Emptiness stared back at her. Not even an old pen lingered to go with her old journal. Nana, and her presence, were no longer part of this realm.

And yet, Avery considered as she took a foldout chair for herself, *she still manages to take up so much space.*

She plopped her body into the chair.

"Oh, sorry," a familiar, deep voice said.

"Jesus, John! I'm in the room my nana just died in – you couldn't knock?"

"I know, I'm sorry. I'm looking for the whiskey?"

"The living room, down the hall."

"Right, thank you," John said, but he lingered. "By the way ..."

She turned her head to glance at John, who was dressed in a charcoal-gray tweed suit. Its tailoring looked expensive – not a hemline was misaligned nor a string out of place – but appeared as though it were made from another era, as if the suit was inherited from a dead, rich relative. Knowing John, it probably was, and he'd probably worn it to a funeral on purpose.

"A journal is a blessing," he said, leaning against the door frame with his hands in his pockets, as if he had been going for a stroll and only stopped to import this wisdom.

"Coming from a writer ..." Avery mumbled and turned to face the bare mattress again. "Okay, thanks, John."

"I'm serious," he said. "It can be a curse, of course, so ..." He paused, giving his words a chance to fill the empty room. "Choose wisely."

Instead of processing and responding to what John said, Avery cocked an eyebrow in the air. "Nice suit."

"Thank you. It was my grandfather's," he said with a quick bow of his head before disappearing down the dimly lit hallway.

Knew it ... She could feel herself squinting at the empty doorway, her chest rising and falling in one breath.

The thing was, Avery had kept a journal before. For many years. Then, eight years ago, around the time of her high-school graduation, she had decided to read her journals. Every page of every one. It had taken Avery all day to read through the document of her life, as told through her elementary-, middle-, and high-school selves.

It hadn't all been bad. Seeing herself develop from a child into a young adult was a gift. A blessing, as John would say. Still, as she read, Avery often found her heart breaking for the child who had written the words. And she had not liked the realization that her heart was breaking for herself. She despised the victim role after seeing the people in her life play it so many times. Yet no matter how hard she tried to write about something new, it always felt as if the same experiences and emotions ended up filling the blank pages.

So, she had stopped writing. As if no longer writing about her role would release her from it.

But now, as she sat across from where Nana had said those famous last words, she wondered how, after years of writing nothing, she was still here, feeling like a victim. And how it was possible to feel stuck in a role she thought she'd never wanted to play.

Chapter 12

"So, you do this every day?" Mama Donna panted. She stopped walking on the uphill trail to catch her breath.

"Every day," said Brinkley, stopping alongside her mother for a water break. "Even though Daisy is three, I feel like I have so much baby weight I can't shed."

"I don't think it's baby weight any more, Brinkley," Mama Donna muttered. "Now it's just weight."

"Okay, Mom." Brinkley rolled her eyes and continued walking uphill.

Every morning, after making coffee and breakfast, kissing Chase goodbye, and dropping the girls off for their half-day summer camp, Brinkley took a two-mile walk through a park close to her house. It was time to be by herself and listen to the explicit music she couldn't play around her kids. Or an audiobook. Sometimes a podcast.

Perhaps it was Nana's funeral that had happened a few days ago, or the gray, overcast day, but today Brinkley didn't want her "me" time all to herself. Unfortunately, Elizabeth and Avery were working – Elizabeth was an accountant who worked every weekday, while Avery was a bartender who sometimes worked brunches – and Brinkley wasn't in the mood for any of her stay-at-home mom friends. So, she had invited her mother.

Or rather, Mama Donna, as Lily and Daisy called her. Her mother had qualms about being called a "grandma" when she still had "so much life to live", so Mama Donna she was.

"Anyway, Brinkley, you look great," Mama Donna said between pants. "I am sick of women being so hard on themselves. You'll never hear a man stressing over his gut or his wrinkles, his graying beard, or the fact that he's a deadbeat dad—"

"Okay, this is starting to get too specific …"

"Anyway, do you know how much weight I gained after having Avery? Do you know what you children did to my body?"

"Yeah, actually, you've told me before. Many times."

"Well, you were ten freakin' pounds, Brinkley. You wanna complain about your body, try pushing a ten-pound baby out of your vagina. See what happens then."

"Jesus, Mom, I wasn't trying to enter a competition—"

"Don't use the Lord's name in vain. He didn't do anything to you. And the stretch marks, oh my gosh, I couldn't even recognize my own body. But you know what? I don't give a damn any more! I'm in my sixties, I pee when I sneeze, and I've never felt more fabulous."

"I can't tell if that's happy or sad …"

"When I was younger, I stressed about everything. Turns out, there's so much more to life – to me – than my post baby body—"

"Okay, can we change the subject?"

"Fine. What would you rather talk about?"

"Literally anything else."

"Well …" Mama Donna thought for a brief moment. "Have you talked to your asshole father recently?"

"Okay, besides that too."

"Oh, don't be ridiculous, Brinkley, I just want to know if you've talked to your father. Isn't he getting married soon? Have he and his newest fling picked a wedding venue yet?"

"I don't know," Brinkley muttered, redoing her ponytail. She could feel the knots she hadn't had the time or energy to brush out this morning. "They haven't updated anyone on anything. All I know is they're engaged." Brinkley finished tying her ponytail and looked at the gray sky ahead. "Anyway, it's such perfect weather for walking, no? I kind of like walking when it's overcast—"

"Oh, Brinkley. I know you're just trying to change the subject."

"Well, I don't want to talk to you about Dad—"

"Well, why not, Brinkley? I am your mother. You should be able to talk to me about anything."

"I can't!"

"Why not?"

"Because you literally can't say Dad's name without referring to him as an asshole."

"He is an asshole." Mama Donna shrugged. "The stuff he put me through. The stuff he put us all through – I mean, you know how the fighting got, Brinkley. The yelling, and the bruises—"

"Okay, you know what? This is why I can't talk to you about him. So can we please change the subject?"

"Fine," Mama Donna said, but when Brinkley looked at her, her mom refused to look back.

Brinkley felt her heart sink.

"Anyway, I visited Nana's grave this morning—"

"Oh my gosh," Brinkley groaned, stopping in her tracks and bringing her fingertips to her temples.

"What? Oh, now I can't even talk about my own mother?"

"We just went to the funeral a couple days ago."

"That's why I need to talk about her!"

Brinkley yearned for a podcast.

"Look, I don't drink, I don't do drugs – why can't I just talk about what I wanna talk about?"

"Mom, you drink wine as if every meal were the last supper," Brinkley said.

"Well, wine was sacred to Jesus, Brinkley, so maybe it's sacred to me, too," Mama Donna said with a huff.

"What did you invite me on this walk for, anyway?" her mother asked. "What are we allowed to talk about?"

"I don't know, maybe something that makes us happy?"

Mama Donna offered another huff.

They resumed their walk in silence, Brinkley a few steps ahead of her mother. She tried breathing the fresh air, listening to the birds, admiring the leaves on the trees, but her mood felt too heavy to lift now. She began to twirl the rose quartz ring around her finger.

Mama Donna broke the silence. "Are you all set for Lily's birthday party this weekend? Do you need help with anything?"

"Everything's all set, but if you want to come over early and help set up, that would be really nice."

"Okay, I'll come a few hours early," she said.

The silence between them grew again, and now it was Brinkley's turn to break it. "Hey, if you had to write something short and sweet about me, what would it say?"

"Something short and sweet? Are you running for the PTA or something?"

"What? No. I'm just curious how some people would describe me," said Brinkley, regaining the position next to her mother so they could walk side by side again.

"Oh," Mama Donna said, closing her mouth for a moment as she kept her gaze focused on the trail ahead. "I would say you are a … caring person … sometimes … who loves your children and your husband. Occasionally your mother."

Brinkley glared at her mother.

"What?" Mama Donna asked.

"That's all you would say?"

"You said short and sweet. Besides, I'm not good at coming up with stuff on the spot. Why? What's wrong with what I said?"

"Nothing ..." Brinkley shook her head and tried tuning into the birds' chirping again.

"I can't believe I'll have to see your as— ... your father ... and his fiancée at Lily's birthday party. I mean, isn't this one named Sin?"

"It's short for Cynthia—"

"Brinkley, who wants Sin as their nickname? I mean, does she worship the devil? And to get engaged, after a few months of dating! Like, has he lost his mind? With all the different women your father has brought around over the years, do we even know who's stepping in and out of our lives any more?"

Okay, at least Brinkley could agree with her mother on this one.

But of course Mama Donna had to add, "I hope Richard's being safe. He could get an STD, you know."

Brinkley groaned.

Next time she would definitely listen to a podcast.

Chapter 13

Tick. Tick. Tick.

Avery stared at the clock hanging above the front door of the bar she worked at. When her shift was slow, the tick of time seduced her attention. There was something about witnessing the thin red second hand travel the circumference. It made her question why she was spending her days, with her able but time-limited body, here. Especially when, even after all the time she spent on her feet, smiling at customers, taking orders, mixing drinks, she was still going to struggle to make rent this month.

Business hadn't always been this slow. When Avery had begun working at this bar in Old City a few years ago, the job had allowed her to afford a small two-bedroom apartment with Izzy, with a little wiggle room for some savings and fun. At first, Avery had loved the art of bartending. She'd loved finding the perfect balance of flavors to create an intriguing cocktail. She'd appreciated the fact that her salary was based on tips. Even though some customers were cheap, or obnoxious, most of them were kind and generous, and she had loved feeling like her daily earnings were not set in stone.

Most of all, Avery had loved meeting people from all over the city, not to mention from all over the country and world. Tourists would ask for directions to Independence Hall, to stand in the place the

Constitution was written and signed, as if seeing the place with their own eyes would be enough to elicit an understanding, somehow help them make sense of the world they lived in with their modern lives. Others would stop in for a drink and ask for all the good places to eat, unenthusiastic for the food Avery's bar offered, but also hoping to avoid possible tourist traps. Avery would assure them they were in Philadelphia. It was a challenge to find a place that wasn't able to whip up something delicious. Avery loved guiding these customers through their stay in the city she now considered home, but her favorite customers were the ones who came in and told her about their own homes and lives. Where they came from, what brought them to Philly, into this specific bar. What was their drink of choice and why.

Yet, Avery had been working at this bar no more than a few years, and her job had been changing. Rents in Philadelphia kept rising, newer restaurants and bars were opening, and less people were coming through the arched doorway that would lead them straight to the stained and ripped velvet barstools that sat, empty, by the bar counter Avery was standing behind now. Some older bars in Old City had already proved themselves against all odds, yet the alchemy of their survival, their ability to maintain old customers while attracting new ones, remained hidden. As fewer people came to the bar, fewer tips went home with Avery. Not to mention fewer memories.

Maybe it was time for a new bar. Or a new job. But every time she found herself checking job postings, it made her nauseous. People with more experience and college degrees were struggling to find work right now.

She drew in a long, deep breath as she observed the second hand making yet another trip around the clock.

Tick. Tick. Tick.

Avery looked out the front window of the bar. It was more like a wall made entirely of a window. Her very own window wall. She appreciated that this bar had windows big enough for the natural sun rays to brighten the place. The first bar she had worked at was a pub with few windows. She hadn't lasted long there.

With her elbow on the counter and her cheek resting in her hand, she stared through the window wall. Philadelphia, especially Old City, always seemed to come alive in the summertime. So many people coming and going across the cement sidewalks and cobblestone streets. She observed the various passers-by, dressed in suits, sundresses, workout gear, mismatched outfits. Some of the city dwellers shared smiles; others maintained serious glares; a handful seemed to show no emotion at all – they were just bodies led by heads.

Avery always wondered where these people, these passers-by she may never personally meet but felt connected to, were going.

But before she got too lost in her imagination, the little chime above the front door rang, and an old man bowed his head to fit through.

Raymond.

Raymond had a wild gray beard, with little strands that twisted and turned, intertwining with one another. His beard dipped just below his heart along with the rest of his wavy, light gray hair. When Raymond was close enough, Avery could always spot a few strands that still held onto their sand brown color, not able to let go of their youth.

Raymond had been visiting Avery every Wednesday afternoon for the past three years. He was, according to the owner, a decade-long regular. Avery had befriended him one day when she saw him wearing a Yellowstone National Park hat. It was her lifelong goal to visit every national park in America. She had a way to go.

Raymond was a former History professor who had two children who lived in a suburb outside the city. His wife, Maria, had passed away a decade ago, but every time Raymond had a story to share about her, his deep-set eyes would appear to both smile and cry. It made Avery feel that, even though she'd never meet Maria physically, she could somehow still know her through the bond of love death could never take away.

As Raymond used his cane to assist him in approaching the bar, Avery began chilling a rocks glass for his usual old-fashioned order. After Raymond and Maria had bought a house, Maria had wanted to purchase a TV for their living room. Raymond had resisted, claiming he was unable to understand how a TV would enrich the room that was meant to be lived in. Maria had agreed not to purchase a TV, and the room became their meeting place for board games, conversations about life that lasted deep into the night, and a makeshift playroom for when they had children. After those children grew up and Raymond and Maria found their lives with new pockets of time, the living room became their favorite spot to sink into a comfortable silence with a book and a mug of tea. But it was this and other instances of Raymond's reluctance to purchase new technologies that made Maria playfully tease her husband about being old-fashioned.

A few months after Maria had died, Raymond had decided to come to the bar he was still walking across a decade later. Never a big drinker in his youth, he'd asked the bartender at the time what he should order, and the bartender had replied, *How about I make you an old-fashioned?* Avery didn't know what Raymond believed about the experience, but she knew he had been coming every Wednesday since, always to order one old-fashioned.

"You should not be here," he said.

His voice always had a soft quality to it, a special restraint – or perhaps strain – that made Avery feel as though she were being hugged by sound.

"If I remember correctly ..." He began the process of lowering himself onto his barstool as Avery added water and a dash of bitters into the glass. "Your nana's funeral was just a few days ago," he said. "Why aren't you giving yourself time to grieve?"

"My landlord," she said as she began to muddle a sugar cube.

He chuckled, his deep-set eyes smiling at her. "Well, did you learn anything? Death can have a way of putting things into perspective."

"Does it, though? Because I'm feeling like Nana's death knocked everything out of perspective."

Avery hadn't had the chance to tell Raymond about Nana's dramatic farewell.

Pulling a bottle of bourbon from the top shelf of the liquor counter, Avery poured a hefty double-shot into the glass before meeting Raymond's eyes.

"Before she died, she went on a goodbye tour and said all these really nice things to my siblings, but then told me ..." Avery set the bottle of bourbon down to look Raymond in the eyes. "*I don't know where you've been. I have no idea where you're going. I don't even know if you know where you're going, Avery.*" She blinked. "The words are burned in my brain at this point."

"That's because you're repeating them," he said, his voice soft as ever.

"I don't know how to stop. The words didn't make any sense to me when she said them. I feel like my brain is trying to make sense of them now."

"I think it's simple," he said with a shrug of his bony shoulders. "She's doesn't know where you've been. She doesn't know—"

"You want to hear what she told my siblings? Brinkley's the world's greatest mother and wife. Elizabeth offers more brightness than heaven ..." She threw ice cubes into the glass with a loud *clink*. "I'm completely lost and get a journal? Thanks, Nana."

"You got a gift?" His thinning gray eyebrows raised at this information.

"Brinkley got a ring from like the 1900s and Elizabeth got a coin pouch from a forbidden lover. I got a journal she said she didn't want, Raymond. Is that really a gift?"

"Didn't you once tell me – and forgive me if my old brain is playing a trick on me – that you once kept a journal? For many years, I believe."

Avery stirred the drink, probably more aggressively than any drink needed to be stirred. Even though she felt Raymond's eyes on her, waiting, Avery took her time holding a few oranges before selecting one with a soft peel. Slicing and then adding the orange peel to the top of the glass, she set down a coaster, placed Raymond's drink on top, and crossed her arms.

"You are correct," she muttered, glancing at her forearm's pen tattoo before hiding it by leaning onto the counter. "But my nana prefaced giving me my 'gift' by saying she felt 'eh' about the thing. I kid you not. She said the journal made her feel 'eh'." Avery's lips formed a thin line as she shook her head.

He smiled, showing his crooked, yellowed teeth. "So why did you stop writing?" His face gave nothing away as he observed her.

Avery glanced at the people passing by outside. "I don't know," she finally said.

"Well, for anyone who's written for that long, I would hope you do." He leaned his head across the counter. "Now, why'd you stop?"

All the people walking outside seemed to blur together as she chose her words. "I think ..." She stopped and sighed. "Or, I realize, there's no reward in documenting memories any more. It just makes them easier to remember. And I don't know if we're supposed to remember that much." She broke her gaze from the window and looked towards Raymond but not at him. "I mean, it's not like I would only write sad things. There were a lot of happy moments I wrote about, too," she felt the need to add, both for Raymond and herself. Once upon a time, journaling had been her savior, her therapy. It felt wrong to

YOU DON'T KNOW NANA

disrespect the practice that had once helped her survive.

Shifting her weight onto her other foot, Avery let out a long sigh. "And a lot of happy memories I could be writing about now! This is the longest I've ever held a job, I have my health, I can almost afford health insurance, I'm living in my first apartment that's not infested with something gross, and ..." Avery trailed off, her gaze drifting to the ceiling as images of the cockroaches and mold that haunted her previous apartments filled her mind. "Wait. How did we start talking about this?"

"I don't know. Somehow it all relates to why you stopped writing."

Avery hadn't felt the muscles of her face tense, but her forehead felt heavy from the strain now. "I guess it does," she mumbled, looking into his warm eyes that had never left her.

Something about his eyes as they looked at her now, beneath his wild gray eyebrows, made her feel safe. As if they could see the unspoken parts of her.

"Sometimes I just feel ... sad, Raymond." Once the words were freed, Avery was surprised to feel a softness wash over her face, as if speaking the truth for the first time to another human was helping her release the tension, the power, it held. It encouraged her to continue. "And I worry that I've been sad for a long time. So, for the past few years, I stopped writing. Because even with all the changes that have happened in my life ... There's nothing new for me to write. Not really." As she felt the tears rise towards her eyes, she released a long breath, sniffed, and looked away. *Get it together, Avery. Raymond is not your therapist; he is your customer, for crying out loud.*

"Listen." Raymond set his old-fashioned down, the glass *thunking* against the aged wood. "Your nana gave you a journal and a perspective. Her perspective. Maybe it's time you rediscover yours." His voice was still soft, but there was a deeper tone to it, an edge. Raymond narrowed his eyes as he looked at her. "The one you have now doesn't seem to be serving you, does it?"

Avery held his gaze for a moment before shaking her head. "Okay, but what does that mean?"

Raymond chuckled. "You and the younger generations always want an answer right away. But I don't have the answers to your life. I have my own life, you know."

"Oh, come on, you go to bed at like six pm."

Raymond laughed a full belly laugh, clutching his stomach before the sweet melody faded.

"I want you to go home," he instructed, a twinkle in his eyes, "and write in the journal you were given. Ask it anything. See what happens."

"You know, Raymond, I've always felt like there's wisdom in wrinkles. And you have a lot of them. So, I will try."

Raymond chuckled again, the smile spreading through his eyes. Avery knew he enjoyed when people joked about his age. Probably because the world around him so often ignored it, as if his wrinkled skin and arthritic movements didn't represent years of life and experience, but were instead a reminder of death and defeat.

"I hope you know what a wonderful joy you have been in my life, Avery."

"Thank you, Ray. Just please don't die on me any time soon."

Another chuckle. "I will try."

When she got home that night, after one of the slowest shifts of her life, Avery kept her promise to Raymond and pulled out her tan leather journal. She had been hiding it, but in an easy-to-access spot among her crumpled T-shirts in her bottom dresser drawer. Once she pulled the object out and set it on her unmade bed, she took a minute to stare at the thing. Its smooth finish and rare creases.

Avery opened the cover.

Dear Self, it read in her nana's messy cursive.

No, Avery thought. She needed a blank space.

Turning the page, she pressed her pen to the unmarked piece of paper. When she had kept a journal all those years ago, she had never written *Dear Self.*

At the top of this clean page, she scribbled *Dear Journal.* The words made her feel as if she were twelve again, but they also stared back at her, as if they were old friends. Old friends who happened to know all her inner workings and deepest secrets.

She remained in this staring match and thought of her earlier conversation with Ray. *Ask it anything,* he had instructed. *See what happens.*

Lately, her mind had been consumed with thinking and complaining about Nana's last words, Nana's life, Nana's death. Avery realized she didn't have a question. Not one that could be answered. That was her whole problem.

But even with nothing to gain, Avery knew she had nothing to lose, so she wrote her unanswerable question.

Why did you choose those last words for me before you died?

There. The question was asked. But the thing about writing, or any form of self-reflection for that matter, was that she didn't always like the answers she found. So, she shut the book.

Chapter 14

Elizabeth and her mother were seated on the plush white carpet of her mother's family room, flipping through Nana's old wedding album. Heavy sobs escaped their lips with every page turned.

Nana and Grandpa had married in a simple church ceremony followed by an even simpler backyard reception. A conservative lace gown had adorned Nana's body, her brown hair styled in a wavy bob that framed her face. A black tuxedo adorned her grandfather's body, his brown hair combed and gelled to the side. The photographs were printed in black-and-white, though some were sepia toned, with slight creases and crinkles at the edges, making each one feel irreplaceable and romantic.

Tears poured down Elizabeth and her mother's face. Just as Elizabeth reached for a fresh tissue, John appeared in Mama Donna's family room with two mugs of steaming chamomile tea.

"Here you are," he said as he handed Elizabeth and Mama Donna a mug.

"It was all just so ... painless ..." Elizabeth's voice trembled as she took the mug into her hands. She was studying the photograph of Nana and Grandpa sharing a kiss in their backyard, in front of a small group of people – probably their dearest loved ones. Only a few balloons acted as decoration, adorning a couple of backyard trees.

"Painless?" said John.

"Everything just looked so simple, so beautifully romantic. Nana and Grandpa loved each other and that was enough to make a beautiful wedding day. Their love was *enough*—"

"My mother and I were best friends," Mama Donna wailed. "What am I supposed to do now that she's gone? Who am I gonna talk to?"

"Mom, don't say that." Elizabeth took heavy breaths as she wiped the tears from her puffy eyes. "You know you can always talk to me."

"Well, since we're looking my parents' beautiful, *intimate* wedding ..." Mama Donna cleared her throat, using a fresh tissue to dab her mascara-streaked eyes. "Can we talk about how your father doesn't deserve a plus-one to your wedding?"

That was all it took for Elizabeth to snap out of her nostalgia. "Okay, yeah, maybe you do need Nana back."

"Elizabeth!" Mama Donna cried, her eyes frantically searching her daughter's.

Elizabeth kept her gaze focused on the album as she turned to the very last page.

"John, do you think my ex-husband deserves a plus-one to your wedding?" Mama Donna tried. "I mean, he's not contributing anything financially, and you know he's going to bring Sin."

Without giving John a chance to respond, Elizabeth snapped her head towards her mother so fast, she worried she had given herself whiplash. "You can't really expect us to ban Cynthia from our wedding, Mom. She's his fiancée now!"

Ever since Elizabeth had gotten engaged, her mother had whined about whom Elizabeth's father would bring to the wedding.

"Elizabeth, she flaunts her engagement ring around town, even though any decent woman knows that money should have gone to your wedding! You're his daughter. He should be contributing something. We both know he can!" Mama Donna looked at John with widened eyes. "John, don't you agree?"

John studied Mama Donna, then Elizabeth, before opening his mouth. "My parents can afford it—"

"Mom, John and I know it's messed up. But you of all people should know how Dad is when he doesn't get his way. I don't have the energy to tell him not to bring his fiancée."

Elizabeth felt every muscle of her jaw tense. "It's not worth the fight."

"Why is everyone so afraid of upsetting him?"

"We're not afraid, Mom," Elizabeth corrected, though once she said the words, she wondered if they were true. "We're just tired. Sometimes you have to learn how to pick your battles."

"Ugh, so now I'll have to be in the same room as *Sin*, and his siblings, whom I can't stand, and don't even get me started on having to be in the same room as *him* ..." Mama Donna rolled up the sleeve of her cardigan to show off her arms. "I'm already breaking out in hives at the thought of having to see him at Lily's birthday party."

"Donna! Do you need me to pick up ointment?" said John.

"John, stop playing into this," said Elizabeth, grabbing her mother's arm, and raising it in the air. "This is one mosquito bite! Not hives."

Mama Donna rolled her eyes with a huff and snatched her arm back to herself. "Okay, fine. I mean, I always thought you wanted a small, *intimate* wedding, but if you don't mind Sin being in the audience when you say your vows—"

"Well, firstly, it's not an 'audience', and she'll be seated with four hundred other people, so there will be plenty of other strangers to distract me from her."

"Wait, what?" Mama Donna gasped. "I thought you were only planning for thirty guests. Forty max."

With her lips pressed into a thin line, Elizabeth glared at John.

"Don't look at me like that, Liz! You're the one who wanted thirty. I'm fine with none."

"So how did it get to four hundred?" Mama Donna said, her eyes widening by the second.

"The Astors know a lot of people," Elizabeth said quietly.

"Oh ... Well, if they're the ones paying—"

"Yes, Mother. I am aware." Elizabeth could feel her body growing hot as she forced a tight smile onto her face. "It'll be fine," she breathed. "The more people to celebrate John and my union, the merrier."

"I don't know, Elizabeth ..." Mama Donna drew out the words as she eyed her daughter. "I don't enjoy big gatherings. I mean, what do you need all those people for? Big crowds used to give you panic attacks when you were little, you know." She tilted her chin and looked up at John. "I'll never forget when Elizabeth went to an amusement park—"

"It doesn't matter, Mom!" Elizabeth snapped, feeling the heat rise from her chest and through her cheeks. "You said yourself – the Astors are the ones paying. What do you expect us to do, tell them they can't invite all their friends right before we hand them the bill?"

"Well, no, Elizabeth. That would be rude."

"So what do you want us to do?"

"What happened at the amusement park?" said John.

"Nothing," Elizabeth said through clenched teeth.

"I'll never forget it," Mama Donna said, shaking her head. "All the other kids were so excited to enter the park – I mean, it's an *amusement* park. Ice cream, rides, games where you can win a surprise! Every kid's dream, right? Anyway, when we entered, Elizabeth had a full-blown meltdown, screaming, crying – the whole thing – saying there were too many humans and she wanted to leave.

I kid you not, she said 'too many *humans*'," Mama Donna said with a chuckle.

"How old was she?" John asked.

"Around ten."

"I would've fallen in love with you then, too," John mused, looking at Elizabeth with a hidden smile.

Elizabeth responded with a roll of her eyes. "Yeah, well, I wonder what made me so scared of humans at ten years old."

"And what's that supposed to mean, Elizabeth?"

"Nothing, Mom, I'm just in the midst of planning a rather large wedding, so I would appreciate it if you didn't remind me of my panic attacks triggered by large crowds!"

"All right," Mama Donna said, raising her hands in surrender. "Well, big wedding or not ..." she added, glancing at Elizabeth and then at John, "I still think you should consider disinviting Sin. And Richard's siblings."

"You know what." Elizabeth slammed the wedding album shut. "I have to go."

"What? Where are you going?"

"Am I coming with you, or ..." John trailed off on seeing Elizabeth's eyes narrow.

"Unless you want to walk home, John, then yes, you are coming with me," she said, then glared at her mother. "We are leaving, Mother. I love you, I truly do, but I have a big wedding to finish planning for my big guest list, and you are just going to have to put a smile on your face, and deal. Just like *I* am!" She took a few steps before turning around. "Got it?"

John and Mama Donna just blinked at her.

"You know, John, if you want to stay for a cup of tea, I can always drive you home too."

"John!" Elizabeth grabbed her fiancé's hand and tugged him out of the house.

"We'll plan another time!" he called over his shoulder.

Chapter 15

"*H*appy birthday, Liiilyyyy, haappy birthdaaaay to youuuu.*"

Lily scanned her crowd of followers that erupted into cheers after singing to her. The sun beamed onto her bejeweled pink birthday crown, reflecting brilliant sparkles of color onto anyone she looked at. She sat tall on her birthday throne – as Avery had been calling it, even though it was just a foldout chair adorned with balloons – with a gleam in her amber-colored eyes.

It didn't take long for the moment to be ruined.

Lily's blood-curdling shriek shot through the backyard. "Daisy, stop!"

Daisy had taken it upon herself to start blowing out her older sister's birthday candles.

"Mom!" Lily's face was distorted in hysteria, tears streaming down her cheeks as Daisy, apparently unbothered, blew out the very last candle.

Lily began kicking her feet like a swimming duck and slunk her body to the grass in one swift motion.

Brinkley dropped to her knees to come to eye level with her daughter. "Lily, take a deep breath," she said, trying her best to keep her voice calm yet stern. "Your sister was just trying to help you."

Just as Brinkley said the words in an attempt to calm Lily down,

Daisy, the culprit, dipped her little fingers into the icing.

"Daisy!" Brinkley barked.

The crowd around the birthday cake only seemed to grow closer, as if to watch and judge Brinkley's response to this challenge.

Where the hell is my husband, Brinkley wondered, looking through all the nosy adults and sugar-hungry children.

Her eyes narrowed onto Chase, who was talking to his older brother, Dan, beer in hand.

"Honey?" she called, plastering a smile on her face. "Little help over here."

Chase took one look at Lily, who was still wailing on the ground, and Daisy, who was frozen with icing fingers.

"Lily and Daisy," he called, not hesitating to use his "stern dad" tone. It's not like anyone would gossip about him, a father, being too harsh with the children. "Come with me. Now."

Their daughters' heads hung low as they trotted to their dad.

Of course, they listened to him. It would have taken Brinkley three tries and a crazed look in her eyes to get her daughters to walk away from birthday cake, but they always listened to Chase on the first try.

Brinkley looked up and offered a wavering smile to the crowd. "Kids, right?"

She tried to laugh, but she was exhausted. Chase had been busy all morning conducting an open house, so Brinkley had woken up at six am to set up tables, balloons, and decorations by herself. Then she had to get the girls dressed, do their hair, get herself dressed, do her own hair, all the while directing the caterers, face painters, and bounce house people where to go. Mama Donna had kept her promise and had arrived a couple hours early to "help" set up, but Brinkley soon realized her mother was only there to taste-test the catered food and complain about having to see Brinkley's father and his new fiancée today.

With a suppressed yawn, Brinkley rose from the grass, regretting her choice to wear a flowy, flower-print dress. Running a kids' birthday party of this magnitude required workout gear.

Mary, one of the moms from Lily's preschool class, approached Brinkley just as she began cutting the Funfetti cake.

"Ugh, you are just so lucky to have a hands-on husband like that," said Mary, hovering around the cake.

The bags under Brinkley eyes grew heavy and her smile stretched tight. "Yeah well, they're his children too, you know." Brinkley let out a laugh, but it sounded more like a cackle.

"Well, of course, but not every father will get involved like that, you know?" Mary said, eyeing Brinkley's white knuckles as she gripped the knife and attempted to cut perfect cake squares.

"Well then, they have no business having children," Brinkley muttered, stabbing another square shape into the cake. A cake she had been up all night baking and icing, after Chase had fallen asleep with his computer.

"Here, why don't I help you with that ..." Mary offered, nudging Brinkley aside.

"I got it," Brinkley snapped.

"Brinkley, sweetie, go enjoy yourself," said Mary.

The offer was too hard to resist. Brinkley surrendered the knife with grace and gratitude – at least she hoped it appeared that way, even though what she really felt was exhaustion and eagerness – and walked away from the cake table altogether.

It was only a few steps until Brinkley bumped into her mother-in-law, Betty, who sure enough had a martini in her hand. Betty was an adorable sixty-year-old woman with a platinum-blonde bob and a laugh that reminded Brinkley of champagne and bubble baths. Betty rarely drank, but when she did, it was always a martini.

"Oh, Brinkley!" Betty cheered, swooping Brinkley into a hug.

"Come here, my child! I feel like you've been running around all day – we've barely gotten to talk. Where's your drink?" Betty looked around. "You deserve a drink. This party is amazing, and I know it didn't magically appear." Betty leaned towards Brinkley, drops of her martini spilling over the side of the glass as she whispered, "And I know my son was not the one who pulled this off."

Brinkley studied her mother-in-law, with her wrinkles framing her smile, reminding everyone of all the laughter cherished inside. It gave Brinkley hope that maybe one year she, too, would be able to accept and display her own age.

Betty's hair was straight today, only curling at the ends to frame her pointy chin. In Betty's long, somehow stainless, white maxi dress adorned with pictures of leopards, Brinkley felt as if she were staring at an angel, and she didn't care if that angel was a bit tipsy.

Without warning or hesitation, Brinkley's eyes began to water. "I'm sorry," her voice cracked as she fanned her face to get her emotions under control. "I feel like I really needed to hear that."

With a bright smile, Betty stretched her arms for another hug. "Come here," she soothed, patting Brinkley's back. After a few seconds, Betty leaned away but kept her hands on Brinkley's shoulders. She looked into her eyes. "I know I saw you after the funeral, but if there's anything you need ..."

"Thank you." Brinkley nodded for the hundredth time today. It seemed everyone at this party had heard about Nana's passing.

If she were being honest, Brinkley needed a lot. Starting with a day away from her kids, a trip to the spa, a bottle of wine, and a pound of pasta. All to herself. But Chase's parents already did so much to help with the kids. Brinkley couldn't find it in herself to ask for more. Besides, pasta contained too many carbs and Brinkley was really trying to shed the rest of her baby weight ...

So instead of asking for help, Brinkley had been trying to grieve her nana, her final grandparent to pass, by herself. But while trying to process and grieve, she was on full-time mom duty trying to keep her daughters alive while answering the bottomless hole of questions Lily asked about where, exactly, Nana had gone.

Brinkley had read somewhere that butterflies were a symbol for the human soul. It seemed like a beautiful, comforting idea to share with a five-year-old. So, she had told Lily every time she saw a butterfly, it was as if Nana were saying hi.

The problem was, Lily's five-year-old self hadn't perfected the art of discerning between coping mechanisms and reality, so she quite literally seemed to believe Nana had turned into a butterfly.

Not just a butterfly, but every ... single ... butterfly.

"Nana! Mom, I found Nana!" Lily would scream any time anything with a pulse and a pair of wings would fly by. Daisy was starting to pick up on this trend and would often join her older sister's frenzy.

The worst part was the kids from summer camp were starting to notice. Even today, at Lily's own birthday, Brinkley had overheard a little snot-nose kid snickering to his friend, "She actually thinks her nana's a butterfly."

But Lily appeared to get so much joy out of this tale, how could Brinkley refine it now?

"My prayers have been with you and your family this whole week," Betty's bubbly voice pulled Brinkley back to the party. "So seriously, Brinkley, whether it's groceries, or you just want a little 'me' time, feel free to reach out. I would be happy to babysit my grandbabies."

"Thank you," Brinkley said, but her mind was distracted again, scanning the party to make sure all the kids had a piece of cake and all the guests looked entertained.

Chapter 16

Avery grabbed a beer from the cooler and scanned Brinkley's backyard for a familiar face.

Her nieces were near the birthday cake table, displaying big pouts and puppy dog eyes to Chase. Brinkley was nearby talking to her mother-in-law, who was swaying on the grass with a martini in hand. Avery's eyes continued inspecting. Kids were throwing their bodies with abandon in the bounce house, and, as Avery's focus was drawn towards it, she recognized the sound of a familiar laugh.

Squinting and clutching her cold beer, Avery waltzed to the bounce house. As she weaved her way through adults and children, she spotted Elizabeth, in her typical blazer – this time pastel pink – standing next to John, who was dressed in a paint-splattered T-shirt and jeans.

The laugh emanating from the bounce house drew Avery closer like a moth to a flame.

"Is that ..."

"Mom," Elizabeth finished with a nod. Her hair was slicked into a low bun today, her hands busy smoothing over invisible strands of frizz.

Avery peered through the mesh of the bounce house and sure enough spotted her mother, flying through the air.

"Avery!" Mama Donna squealed. "Avery, look! I'm flying!"

"She's going to break a hip," Avery said to Elizabeth, who was observing their mother with a stoic expression.

"I know. I told her," Elizabeth confirmed in her monotone.

"She'll be careful," said John. "She's awakening her inner child. Let her have fun."

He raised his beer for a cheer, but the sisters stared.

"Does Brinkley know this is happening?" Avery asked. "Does she have insurance for this kind of thing?"

"I'm not sure ..." Elizabeth tilted her head at the bounce house and took a sip of her red wine.

"Girls!" Their mother was giggling now. Giggling. As if she were one of the five-year-olds.

"That bounce house is changing her," said Avery.

"Girls, you need to come in and give it a try!"

"We're okay, Mom," said Elizabeth and raised her wine cup towards the inflated house.

"I'm comin' in, Mama Donna!" John called.

"What?" Elizabeth exclaimed.

"Hold my beer," he said, slipping his bottle into Elizabeth's free hand before lunging.

All the kids cheered as he entered.

"Jesus ..." Elizabeth breathed.

Avery watched as this tall, muscular man was now flying through a bounce house. His ear-length, wavy hair whipped in the wind with every jump.

"This is so inappropriate," Elizabeth muttered, with John's beer in one hand and her wine in the other.

Avery glanced around. More adults did appear to crowd around the house either for a show or to protect their children. One wrong landing and John could surely break some unfortunate kid's bone.

Avery looked towards the birthday cake table for Brinkley, but saw her dad and his fiancée instead.

Even from this distance, Sin's lips looked as though she had used Brinkley's balloon pump to plump her pout. Avery looked from her dad, who was canoodling his nose against his fiancée's, to her mom, who was jumping and giggling for all the world to see. Both of them had positioned themselves to be in direct view of each other.

It was all starting to make sense.

"John is going to pop that house," Elizabeth hissed.

"Have you said hi to Dad yet?"

"Ugh. No," Elizabeth groaned, taking another sip of her wine. "When I saw him, I was with Mother, so ..."

"Right." Avery put her hand on Elizabeth's shoulder. "Well, you enjoy the show, and I'm going to go say hi."

As Avery walked away, she could hear Elizabeth yell, "John, Mom, this is absolutely ridiculous. Get out. Get *out*, John!"

Hidden among the crowd of families she didn't know, Avery lingered in her anonymity for a moment to take a long swig of her beer. When she got closer to her father and Sin, he erupted into a smile and open arms. Avery couldn't help but smile back.

"Oh, hey! Look who's here," he said, leaning in for a hug. She got squeezed against his chest, as Avery's father was a whole foot taller than her. Avery remembered when she was a little girl, seeing her father as taller than the other dads, giving her an odd sense of pride, as if his height were enough to protect her and one day she would be able to reach him. As she got older, her father's build only reminded her of how short she was.

She pulled away from the hug. "Hi, Dad. Hi, Sin."

"Well, a few more months and you'll be calling her step-mom," her father said with a chuckle. He raised his fiancée's hand to wave the large diamond in the sunlight, or perhaps quite literally in Avery's face. An engagement ring that cost more than a year of college tuition.

"Wait a second – a few months?" Avery said once the diamond was out of her face and she could process his words. "Did you guys pick a date?"

"Yes, and our venue is absolutely stunning – you're going to love it," Sin sang in her soft, baby-like voice. She tucked a strand of hair behind her ear to show off another diamond, this time in the form of an earring.

There's another year of college I never attended, Avery thought.

This whole party was beginning to make her feel a bit nauseous. Her mother bouncing in a bounce house that just happened to be in full view of her ex-husband. The blood diamonds glittering before her in the late afternoon sun. The one-too-many beers she had drunk to calm her nerves – what, exactly, Avery's nerves were from she had no idea, considering her only role was to show up to a birthday party.

Yet it was requiring all her strength not to allow herself to faint.

"Oh no, Avery, did you get another tattoo?" her dad groaned, pulling Avery's arm to inspect the small, simple mountain tattoo near her elbow.

"No," said Avery, studying her father's weathered face as he inspected her arm. "I got this one years ago. I actually got it to remind me of our old camping—"

"You're too broke for tattoos! Don't waste your money on any more," her father commanded.

Avery withdrew her arm. "I pay all my bills, Dad."

"Yeah, but I've seen your car—"

Another thing I've paid for myself.

"I think you have other things you should be spending your money on," he said, raising his beer bottle to his lips.

Avery crossed her arms and watched her father take another sip of his drink.

"I want to have you and your sisters come for dinner soon," he said, rubbing his dark, graying beard with a crooked smile. Her father had gone bald many years ago, and he liked to joke that he hadn't gone bald, but his thick head of hair had simply found new settlement across his jaw, closer to the food and the drinks.

It wasn't a very funny joke.

"A nice Fourth of July barbeque, maybe," he said, rubbing his fingers through the thick strands of his beard.

"Yes, I would love some bonding time with you girls," Sin said. "Our wedding date is going to be here before we know it, so I think we all should get to know one another more."

"I think we have a good understanding of one another." Avery shrugged, glaring at the sparkling diamonds adorning Sin's body. "Wait," Avery said, shaking her head. "You said you're getting married in a few months? Isn't Elizabeth's wedding in a few months?"

"Yeah, it's not the same date. I know her date, don't worry," her father said.

Before Avery could question further, Sin's baby voice interrupted her thoughts.

"Oh, by the way," Sin started, her usually tan face looking more orange in the sun, "I'm so sorry about your grandmother. Brinkley told us she passed. I'm just so sorry."

Avery nodded and looked towards her father, but he offered nothing. "You never liked Nana. Did you, Dad?"

His eyes grew wide beneath his overgrown, dark eyebrows. "What? Me? I mean, I feel bad she passed ..."

"When you and Mom were getting divorced, you told her you hated her entire family."

"What? No. No, I would never say that."

"Oh, sweetie," said Sin, her plump lips landing in a pout. "Some-times parents say a lot of crazy things during a divorce."

Avery did not know if she wanted to laugh or scream at this woman, who was no more than a few years older than her, for calling her "sweetie" and trying to talk Avery through the process of divorce. A divorce that Sin hadn't been forced to witness, but was now going to benefit from.

"Oh, don't I know it," Avery muttered with a loose smile, but her tone did not come off as light as she had hoped. Her head was buzzing. She looked at the nearly empty beer bottle in her hand. "Well, would you look at that, I'm out of a drink."

Offering one nod to her dad, one nod to Sin, Avery was about to walk away when her father gently grabbed her arm.

"I thought Nana was controlling."

Well, maybe because you were always out of control, Avery thought, but said nothing.

"Over everything. She was one of those people who seemed terrified of what would happen if she wasn't in control," he said, but released her arm. "And I was never like that, you know?"

Avery tried lingering in their eye contact, as if she would understand more through their stare, but her father was already looking away, greeting another middle-aged couple he had apparently met before.

With another nod, Avery marched forwards, past the cooler and into the cluster of sycamore trees in Brinkley's backyard. Once she was partially hidden from the party, her pace slowed. She made her way to the treehouse Chase had built for the girls a year ago, climbing up the few rings of the ladder to enter the small wooden structure.

What she didn't realize was that a little pair of amber eyes had been following her.

Chapter 17

"What are you doing up here?" a squeaky voice asked.

Avery closed her hand around the unlit joint and crawled to the entrance of the treehouse to peer at her niece below. Lily's face was painted like a tiger. The birthday crown she had worn all afternoon was left in the dirt as she began climbing the wooden rungs of the ladder.

"How'd you know I was here?" said Avery. "Isn't this a little high to climb by yourself?"

"Oh, please," Lily huffed. "It's only a few steps. Anyway, I watched you walk here. Why are you here?"

"Because I needed space. Does your mom know you're out here? You should go back to your party."

"But this is my tree house," Lily said as she reached the top of the ladder and crawled inside. She swiped her little hands against each other to remove any flecks of dirt. "Can't I hang with you? I don't want to go back to the party. Daisy blew out all my birthday candles."

"Oh yeah, girl, I saw that. I'm sorry," said Avery.

With her arms crossed and lips pouted, Lily made it clear she needed more than a simple apology.

"I'm sure your dad relit the candles so you would get a turn too, didn't he?"

"So? It still made me sad," said Lily, the squeakiness that was usually in her voice replaced by softness.

Avery looked at her niece's puppy-dog eyes looking back at her for answers. Lily was now five, and her ability to form memories, and therefore grudges, was only going to increase with every birthday. Until, one year, she'd learn how to have memories without holding the bitterness that came with them.

Good luck, kid, Avery thought, *I'm twenty-six and still waiting for that year.*

"You can hang with me," Avery finally agreed.

Just as fast as she said the words, her niece picked up a cushion from the corner of the treehouse and sat next to Avery.

"I think you should let the birthday candle thing slide, though," Avery said. "Your face looks like a tiger right now. That stuff's not cheap."

"Auntie A, what are you talking about?"

"Your parents love you, Lily. A lot. And it's not just because they hired face painters for your birthday. Or because you have a bounce house bigger than my apartment. Or because your wardrobe costs more than my rent—"

"Okay, Auntie A, I think I might go back to the party," Lily said.

Avery didn't know if Lily was leaving because she understood, or because she was sick of this weird aunt always making comments about her rent.

"Wait," Avery said, "before you go, can I ask for a favor?"

"Sure!" Lily cheered, sitting up straighter. She was still at the age when favors were fun.

"Can you get me a match? Or a lighter? Like a lighter for candles. But do not play with it, okay?"

"Are you gonna burn down my tree house?" Lily shrieked, her eyes almost bulging out of her head.

"Shh! You can keep your tree house. I just need a lighter."

"What do you need it for?" said Lily, crossing her arms again.

"To light something."

Lily raised an eyebrow.

"Oh, don't give me that look. I need to light something only grown-ups can know about."

Lily looked Avery up and down before lunging towards her, her tiger face leading the way.

"What's that in your hand?" Her eyes were pressed so close to Avery's, it made them blur into one big alien eyeball.

"It's nothing!" Avery leaned backwards to escape her niece's alien eye.

"Oh, no! Auntie A, do you smoke? My mom says people who smoke die! Is this why we're really having a party? Are you dying?"

"What? Lily, why would you have a party if I'm dying?" said Avery, her eyes as wide as her niece's. "Look, this isn't a cigarette. It's a ... miniature candle." Avery held the joint in front of her niece for a second as if to prove it wasn't a cigarette, before slipping it back into the pocket of her romper.

"Ew, why does it smell like a skunk? That's a really gross candle, Auntie A. My mommy has really good-smelling candles." Lily's eyes brightened for a moment. "Hey, I have an idea! You can take one of our candles."

Avery smiled at her niece, who always tried sending Avery home with something from their house. Sometimes Avery wondered if Lily could smell her financial desperation.

"Hey, wait a second ..." Lily began, squinting her eyes. "That didn't look like a candle ..."

"Why don't we both head back to the party?" Avery suggested, but just as the last syllable left her tongue, Lily was screaming her blood-curdling scream.

"Mom! Auntie A is smoking! Help, help!"

"You're going to scare your mom, Lily!" Avery said more strongly than she usually spoke to her niece, causing Lily to pause from her screams.

"Auntie A, I'm going to ask one more time. Do you smoke?" Lily demanded.

Avery looked into her eyes. "Yes," she admitted. "But I would never smoke in front of you. Because I shouldn't."

Maybe it was the way the sunlight shone through the window of the tree house and into her niece's eyes, but it looked like Lily was glowing. All kids ever seemed to want was the truth. They didn't judge, not in the earliest years. They hadn't fully learned how yet. Instead, Lily seemed to appreciate the glimpses of adult honesty. As if these glimpses confirmed a creeping suspicion that, as a child, she had a lot more keys to living than the adults ever had.

Avery peered down the ladder of the tree house, waiting for someone to appear, to see why a child was screaming "*help*". Sure enough, Brinkley was sprinting to the tree house, shrieking her daughter's name.

Now Avery knew who Lily inherited that shriek from.

"Lily!" Brinkley came into view of the tree house entrance looking like a ravaged animal. Her eyes were wide, her chest heaving with shallow breaths. "Lily, baby, you scared me."

"I told Daddy I was coming to see—"

"I know," Brinkley was still trying to catch her breath. "But then some drunk douche bag dad said he thought he heard a little girl yelling 'help'—"

"Was it our dad?" Avery chuckled.

Brinkley was bent over, clutching her stomach. "Like, if you hear a child yelling for help, why wouldn't you go fucking help? What if this was an emergency?"

"I'm sorry, Mommy," said Lily, apparently understanding her current position and letting her mother's bad word slide. "I just found out Aunt Avery smokes."

Avery felt her jaw drop and her eyes bulge as she glared at her niece.

"What?" Brinkley demanded.

When Avery snapped her head towards her sister still standing on the ground below, it looked as if Brinkley had stopped breathing again.

"I would never do it in front of her," Avery said.

"It's a kid's birthday party, Avery. *My* kid's."

"Girl, that's why I needed to smoke," Avery said with a laugh, then saw Brinkley's frantic face. "Look, I came through your woods because I didn't want anyone to see me. I didn't think Lily would leave her party to hang with me." Avery shrugged. "Though it did make me feel kind of special." *Until she ratted me out.* "Honestly, I'm sorry. I thought I'd be able to come out here and have a moment alone."

Brinkley rolled her eyes. "You didn't go to your car, Avery, you came to my daughter's tree house."

"I didn't think hot-boxing my car was a smart place to smoke when we have the entire outdoors available," Avery said before descending the ladder.

"What's hot-boxing?" Lily wondered.

Nostrils flared, Brinkley narrowed her eyes at Avery.

"It's ... when a box gets really hot from ... the sun," Avery tried.

Lily scrunched her face.

"Lily, follow your aunt Avery and come down, please," Brinkley said before her daughter could ask any more questions. "No more tree house today. You have an entire bounce house over there."

"Okay, I'm sorry, Mommy."

"Also, Cynthia and Grandude are getting ready to leave and want to say goodbye to you."

Now Avery's face scrunched. "Are you guys still entertaining that name?"

"Well," said Brinkley, "when he found out mom was getting called Mama Donna, 'grandpa' wasn't appealing to him any more."

"You mean Sin?" Lily's squeaky voice snapped Brinkley and Avery's attention towards her as she reached the dirt ground. She looked at them with her hand on her hip and an eyebrow cocked in the air.

"What? Her name is Cynthia, Lily," Brinkley corrected.

"Well, Mama Donna told me she calls her Sin because she's done a lot of sinning," Lily explained, then tilted her head. "Mom, what's a sin?"

"We need to start monitoring what we say around her," Brinkley whispered to Avery, before taking Lily's hand in her own and leading the way back to the party. She looked at her daughter. "Listen, we're going to call her Cynthia. Now, when Grandude and Cynthia come to say goodbye—"

"I will say goodbye back," Lily finished.

"Why are you bothering making an effort with this one?" Avery whispered to her sister as they walked through the trees. "She's his third girlfriend in like, one year."

"First fiancée though."

"They got engaged after three months of dating, and announced their engagement like, what? Weeks after Elizabeth's?" Avery whispered, trying to talk fast before they were around other people again. "I swear Dad saw how much attention Elizabeth got for her engagement and needed to make something all about him. That's what he and Mom always do. It's always about them."

"Mommy, you're walking really slow. Grandude's by the birthday cake. Can I go say goodbye now?" said Lily.

"Sure, honey, go ahead."

Brinkley tracked her daughter's every move as she skipped through the party. Once Lily was by Grandude's side, Brinkley stopped walking

99

and faced her sister.

"Look, Cynthia's our dad's fiancée now. I'm trying to be nice because I have to be nice. We both have to play nice if we want to continue a relationship with our dad at all."

Avery began scratching the tattoos on her arm. "I don't know if the relationship I have with him is worth playing nice any more. I don't know if it ever was."

After a few quiet steps along the grass, Brinkley spoke.

"I understand," she said. "But he's Lily's grandfather and she loves him. It's not really about what I want, any more."

Brinkley glanced at the party and then at the ground with a sigh.

Without saying a word, Avery took her sister's hand in hers and led the way.

Chapter 18

A wall made of pastel-pink roses and white lettering saying "Oh Baby" was erected on the Astors' backyard stone patio, displayed proudly behind the long rows of rectangular tables seating over one hundred and fifty baby shower guests. Beautiful bouquets of pinks and creams lined the table, along with white tealights set in candle holders shaped like baby cradles. Waiters, dressed in suits even though it was late June, surrounded the table, ready to refill the guests' glasses with almost every sip they took.

Jordan, the VIP mommy-to-be, was seated at the head of the table wearing a flowy white dress complete with the words "Future Mommy" hand-sewn across the back in pink calligraphy. Her shoulder-length, freshly blown-out brown-blonde hair was adorned with a white flower crown.

Elizabeth was seated at the other end of the table, readjusting in her pink velvet chair.

Smiles and laughter filled the air, but Elizabeth needed an Advil. No, she needed a Xanax.

Elizabeth worked five days a week as a CPA. The weekends were supposed to be her days. Her two days to do as she pleased. Yet the last two weekends had been hijacked by Nana's death, may she rest in peace, and this weekend had been devoted to her niece's birthday party, and now this – her future sister-in-law's baby shower.

And the baby shower was beautiful, really. The sky was a brilliant shade of blue and there was not a cloud in sight. The white outdoor tent Mrs. Astor had ordered came equipped with air conditioners so everyone could enjoy the baby shower outside without having to actually deal with being outside. Yet no amount of air conditioning or specialized cocktails, aptly named "Jordan Juice" and "Mommy Mimosa", could save Elizabeth from the company she found herself in – Lena, Ivy, and Clementine were Jordan's three best friends Elizabeth had met once before, at Jordan's wedding a few years ago, and had never wanted to see again.

Yet here she was. Assigned to a seat next to all of them.

"I went to one wedding that served s'mores during cocktail hour," Clementine began, her long manicured fingernails wrapping around her glass of Sangria. "Like, how tacky is that? The marshmallows got all over my manicure."

Lena, Clementine, and Ivy had been discussing the dos and don'ts of wedding planning for – Elizabeth glanced at her phone – two hours. They had offered their unsolicited advice and opinions through Elizabeth's two glasses of Jordan Juice, plate of bruschetta, entrée of cauliflower steak, and now, as Elizabeth stared at the pink sorbet in her bowl, they were going to continue through dessert.

"I'm sorry, but that's just rude," Ivy declared. "I'll never forget this one wedding I went to … The *butter* was *hard*." She leaned back in her chair, her face full of disgust.

"Ew," Clementine gasped.

"I went to a wedding where the groom's dick was hard," said Lena and shrugged as her round face nodded at everyone. "I swear. He had a boner during his vows. All the bridesmaids confirmed."

For Christ's sake. Have any of you been to a wedding you've actually enjoyed? Elizabeth wanted to ask. She was nearly finished her third glass of Jordan Juice and had had enough of the Ladies Who Lunch.

Perhaps it was the alcohol, or the summer weather, or the conversation she found herself in, but Elizabeth felt her face growing hot. Burning hot. She had always loved attending weddings, whether it was a grand ball or a simple celebration. Of course, she had been to weddings where the weather, or food, or speeches were not to her liking. But in her mind, going to a wedding was entering someone else's fantasy. So, you show up to celebrate, and when the food tastes like shit, it's your one night to lie and say it was fantastic.

Yet over the years, it seemed no matter what wedding she went to, no matter how much time or money the bride and groom had invested, there were always guests who found flaws, latched on to them, and complained. Elizabeth never understood these guests. Now she realized she had spent the last two hours with them.

As she listened to Lena, Clementine, and Ivy's egos drone on and on, she realized the modern wedding, at least to these kinds of guests, wasn't a celebration of love. It was a performance to showcase one's social status and perfection. Or to tear others' down. With a buzzing head, she reached for her glass of Sangria, but it was empty again. Sure enough, one waiter raced over to refill.

"Same drink, Ma'am?" the waiter asked, his posture so straight he looked like a sophisticated robot.

"Yes, please, thank you so much, Justin," she said with more than a hint of desperation in her voice.

"Hello, beautiful ladies," Jordan's voice suddenly cooed. Her hands were rubbing her belly as she stepped towards them, making her rounds. "How is everything over here?"

"It's good." Clementine smiled. "We've been giving Elizabeth all our tips for wedding planning."

"Oh, that's amazing. Yes, give her all your advice," Jordan said, still rubbing her belly with a smile. "She only has a few more months to settle everything, and with my baby coming, I've had no time to guide her, you know."

"Well, even with the baby coming, you, your family, and your friends have offered more than enough, so, don't even worry about it," said Elizabeth, her voice falling flat. She plastered a smile on her face, but as she forced the smile, she felt as if all her drinks were hitting her at once. "Please excuse me," she said, "I need to go pee."

Chapter 19

I t had been crowded for a Thursday night at the bar, Avery considered with pleasure. The last call had been made, doors locked, glassware and bar tools washed and put away, and alcohol dated. All that was left was counting tips, and Avery and her co-worker, Ethan, were huddled together, counting the bills one by one. After a few slow weeks, both were praying for a decent break.

"Two hundred and seventy-two dollars," Ethan said, with neither a smile nor a frown. "One hundred and thirty-six dollars each. There were a lot of ones in that stack."

"At least it's better than it's been," Avery said, stuffing her share into her wallet.

"Better than it's been? We had so many drunken fools tonight," Ethan snorted, fiddling with the silver ring of his eyebrow piercing before rolling his eyes. "I can't wait until I graduate my graphic design program and move out West. Then at least I'll be dealing with rich, Silicon Valley fools."

"I could never live out West," Izzy said, shaking her head. "When I'm in a bad mood, I want to be in a bad mood without the sunshine and a bunch of plastic smiles glaring back at me."

"Well, maybe you wouldn't be in a bad mood if there weren't so many crusty people around here," said Ethan. "I can't even order a coffee without getting attitude. Maybe it would be nice to get a smile every now and then, even if it is fake, you know?"

"No." Avery shook her head. "I'm on Izzy's side with this one. Philly is the only place I feel safe to reveal my true emotions in public."

"Yeah, unless your true emotions involve supporting a different sports team."

"I admire the loyalty," Izzy shrugged.

Ethan shook his head. "Whatever. I'll have my degree in a year, and I know you two will be begging to visit."

"Key word is 'visit'," said Izzy, taking a sip of her white wine, which still had condensation on the glass. "Why was it crowded tonight?"

Sometimes Izzy visited Avery at the bar after nannying for a family, the Johnsons, who lived in one of the well-kept, redbrick townhomes in Society Hill, a few minutes' walk to the bar. After meeting them through a babysitting app, Izzy had been nannying the Johnsons' only child for years every summer, watching their now seven-year-old during date nights and random days. Even though Izzy had a full-time job as an elementary school teacher, she nannied during her time off to help pay her student loans faster.

One day a few years ago, Avery had taken a detour from her usual route to work to drop Izzy off at the home. Mostly she wanted to see what a place called Society Hill would look like, and she found herself walking along a redbrick sidewalk, shaded beneath a canopy of city trees. It seemed every other house in this neighborhood held vibrant flowerbeds whose plants poured from each window. Avery remembered staring at the flowerbeds, so lush against the redbrick, and found herself wondering, just for a moment, if the people inside were happy with their life.

According to Izzy, the Johnsons were kind and generous. They would gift Izzy an extra check at the end of the summer and often invite her to stay for their family dinner, which, according to Izzy, no matter what was planned, the family always made sure to eat together. The child was, for the most part, quiet and well mannered. Izzy said professional family portraits hung on almost every wall. Avery wondered if she would ever be able to enjoy a life like that.

Avery thought of her own childhood of sitting at a vacant dinner table. Her older sisters would often be watching a show in the other room, trying to use the volume of the TV to drown the sound of her parents' yelling upstairs, only to later be yelled at to turn the noise down. But she also thought of the moments spent in her mother's bedroom, when her father was working into all hours of the night, or had left for the weekend, and her mother would let Avery and her sisters stay awake as long as they wanted. Or needed. They would sit at the edge of their mother's bed, and talk about everything – religion, stories from school, aspirations for their futures. Avery couldn't remember details of those conversations now, but those nights felt like the best gifts in the whole world, when her and her loved ones felt free to expose parts of themselves normally kept hidden – all of their thoughts and worries, but also all of their dreams, and for a night each of them would realize that no matter how unsettled life could feel, they would always have each other.

And so, Avery wondered if she would be able to enjoy a life like the Johnsons. Not attain one but enjoy one. There was an addictive beauty Avery had found in a more unpredictable life.

"Usually, this place is as dead as the people who come," Izzy added under her breath, and then Avery noticed her friend's eyes scrutinizing her. "What are you thinking about?"

"Nothing, just lost in thought ..." Avery shook her head. "What do you mean this place is usually as dead as the people who come?"

"That's just when Avery's working," Ethan said with a snicker.

"What?"

"Anytime I share a shift with you, the older crowd comes. They love you," Ethan said, and raised his eyebrows.

"Oh, come on. I'm only BFFs with one older customer. I'm not responsible for the entire crowd."

"There's Raymond, the history professor. Rosie and Joanne, the couple who always ask which Sunday brunches you're working. Then there's that old man with the eye patch, that lady who always wears bright pink lipstick that smears all over our glasses—"

"Ugh, Sofia. I wish she would figure that lipstick situation out. I told her to try a lip stain …"

Ethan tilted his chin down, staring at her.

"This is starting to sound a little creepy," said Izzy, clutching her glass of white wine. "Do you have a thing for old people, Avery? Tell us now."

Ethan laughed.

"Listen. They are the grandparents I never had, and they are lovely," said Avery, standing up straighter. "They give me advice, tell me stories; Rosie and Joanne always shower me with compliments and tip well. And do you know that Raymond has not missed a single birthday of mine since coming here?" Avery raised her eyebrows at her co-worker and best friend. "Every Wednesday that's closest to my birthday, Raymond comes into the bar with a card and a small gift. My own father doesn't even know when my birthday is! One time my dad texted me '*Happy Birthday*' and it was July. My birthday is in February."

"Okay, this is gettin' a little sad," said Ethan and crouched to dig through the mini fridge behind the bar. "I'm guessing still no peace with your nana's last words?"

"She told you about that too?" Izzy said to Ethan as he pulled two beers out of the fridge. The bar had closed, but whenever their schedules aligned, the three of them always enjoyed a drink after hours.

"Oh yeah …" Ethan nodded before turning to Avery. "Have you ever thought of going to a medium? Even if they're total bullshit, at least they'll tell you what you want to hear."

"What do you mean?"

Ethan cracked open his beer. "Mediums are in the business of closure. If you go to one, they're not going to tell you how much your dead relative hated you. They're going to tell you the words you wish you heard. And if they're good at what they do, it could be healing."

Avery considered this for a moment. "I don't know how something could be healing if it's fake …"

"Well, if it's not healing, at the very least it would be fun," said Ethan.

Avery glanced at Izzy, who shrugged as she gathered her long, dark brown curls into a ponytail. She looked back at Ethan, who was already busy wiping the counter for a final time. "I mean, I'm open to trying anything …"

She imagined sitting around a crystal ball with her sisters. The medium would announce that there had been a mistake, that their nana had meant to say Avery was a wonderful sister and friend whose hard work would one day pay off in an adventurous, exciting future.

Avery let out a breath. "I don't know. I don't even know how I would find one. I wouldn't trust anyone who advertises a gift like that. And if they're not advertising, I have no way of finding them, so …"

"I know a woman," said Izzy. "Mira. My cousin told me about her after my uncle died."

"Well, if this isn't a sign, I don't know what is," Ethan said with a grin.

"Did she seem legit?"

Izzy shrugged. "Never went. Not my thing. But I can ask my cousin if she still has her info."

"Hmm ..." Avery crossed her arms. "I mean, why not?"

Izzy nodded. "I'll ask tomorrow."

Ethan put away his rag and grabbed his beer. "Just so you know," he said, "I have no idea where you're going either, Avery. And I also don't know if you know where you're going. But I think it's fucking fabulous." He raised his beer to hers.

Avery cracked open her can. "Thanks?"

"I don't know if that's what she wants to hear ..." said Izzy, looking between them.

"It's fine," Avery said with an exhale, leading the way to a high-top table at the back of the bar.

"According to my uncle Terry, my nana had a forbidden, pen-pal love affair with some Italian, so who's judging who," Avery said as she brought the beer can to her lips.

"What?" said Izzy.

"God, your nana sounds fabulous," Ethan said.

Avery glared at him.

"What?" Ethan said, wrapping his hands around his beer can as his eyes darted between Izzy and Avery's dirty looks.

"Avery, you know I love you," Ethan started, "but you got to admit ... Your nana was psychological. I hate that you're the unfavored grandchild, but if any of my grandchildren piss me off during my life, last words are the perfect time for revenge."

"Avery didn't do anything wrong to her nana," said Izzy, then put her hand over top Avery's. "Girl, don't listen to him."

"No, I'm intrigued," Avery said. "You think she said those things to hurt me?"

"Well, she certainly didn't tell you them to make you feel good ..."

"That's what I thought! Yet my whole family has been trying to convince me it's one big misunderstanding."

"Oh, honey, well of course they are," Ethan said. "Why would they question sweet little old Nana when she's always praised them?"

"Exactly!" said Avery, pointing her finger across the table at Ethan.

"But you know what? I don't think her honesty with you is a bad thing."

Avery dropped her hand. People who weren't experiencing a tragedy were always trying to give one a positive twist.

Ethan continued, "Especially when it hurts, it makes you ... reevaluate. And sometimes we need a good kick in the ass to do that."

"What are you telling me I need to reevaluate?"

"I don't know," he said and shrugged. "I have my own shit. Only you can figure that out." Ethan eyed Avery down as he chugged his beer.

"What's with the so-called forbidden pen pal?" said Izzy.

"Oh ... After the funeral, Elizabeth and I were talking to our uncle Terry, and Elizabeth brought up the gift Nana gave her, some priceless coin pouch or whatever ... My nana told Elizabeth she had purchased the coin pouch all by herself. Uncle Terry swore that's not what happened," Avery explained, leaning into the table as if sharing a secret even though no one else was in the bar to hear it. "Uncle Terry told us the coin pouch was a gift from an Italian man my nana met in Rome. Apparently, when Nana came back from Italy, she and this man would exchange love letters even," Avery paused for dramatic effect, "when she was married to my grandpa."

"I knew it!" Ethan cheered. "Your nana is fabulous."

Avery was about to laugh, but Izzy snapped her head towards him.

"Why would that make anyone fabulous?" Izzy asked. "She had a husband and family."

Ethan glanced at Avery before looking at Izzy. "I was just joking ..."

"It didn't sound like you were," Izzy said, looking into her wine with raised eyebrows.

"Izzy?" said Avery. "Is everything okay with you and Tyler?"

Her friend didn't respond, just took a sip of her wine.

"Izzy," Avery pressed.

Tyler was a guy Izzy had met a year ago − the first guy in a long time, perhaps ever, whom Izzy had seemed able to trust and open up to.

"Everything's fine." Izzy met Avery's eyes and shook her head. "I'm just not desperate to stay exclusive with him any more. It's all good. I'm much happier to move on from that mess."

"I mean, I never considered you desperate to be exclusive with him," said Avery. "And I wouldn't call it a mess. I mean, you and Tyler have been hooking up for a year and have so much chemistry, it—"

"Let's stop talking about it, okay?" Izzy said, staring at Avery with her jaw set.

Ethan's eyes darted between the two friends.

"So back to your nana's forbidden love affair ..." he egged on.

"Yes, let's get back to that," Izzy muttered, but took a sip of her wine.

"You know, I was a little conflicted about my nana having an affair, too," Avery said, but kept her eyes on Izzy. "Elizabeth doesn't even believe it's real ... Um ..."

Izzy was fiddling with the gold bangle on her wrist while Ethan was staring at Avery, hungry for more.

"If it helps, it's not like I was close with my grandpa," Avery said. "He was cool, but I never felt like their marriage was, you know ... livin' the dream. My mom basically grew up in a patriarchy and my nana waited on him hand and foot, so ..."

"Jeez, Avery, I knew you had daddy issues but now you have granddaddy issues too?" Ethan said.

"That's usually how it works, Ethan. My parents' issues didn't pop up out of nowhere."

"Demons get passed down," Izzy said, still looking down.

"Okay, I take it back," said Ethan, looking at Izzy. "Her nana is not fabulous. She is one big hussy—"

"Jeez, Ethan," Avery said.

"Well, how dare she have an affair with an Italian man over snail mail when she had dinner to cook and shoes to shine for your grandpa?"

Avery laughed, and glanced at Izzy. The corners of Izzy's lips curled. "Anyway, who knows if it's true. We'll never know now."

"Why would Terry lie about it?" Izzy said, finally raising her eyes.

"I don't know, but Elizabeth is convinced he did. He and Nana had a weird relationship. So maybe he's just bitter?"

"Damn, your family sounds twisted," Ethan said almost as a whisper.

"What does Brinkley think about all of this?" Izzy wondered. "Does she believe your uncle?"

"Honestly?" said Avery, feeling her eyebrow raise as she spoke the word. "I didn't bother bringing it up to Brinkley. Sometimes she tries so hard to keep the peace, and what brings her peace seems to be changing ever since she had kids. So I don't even know what she'd believe. I can't trust it."

"Kids are demons," muttered Ethan.

"Well what does your mom say about it?" Izzy asked, then released a chuckle. "Good ol' Mama Donna."

"Oh, I don't know. Elizabeth is usually her mouthpiece, so I assumed they'd have the same reaction."

"You have to ask Mama Donna about this," Ethan said. "I'm intrigued."

"Yeah," Avery said, tilting her head and losing her gaze to something not in the room. "Yeah, maybe I will."

They talked into the early morning hours, while the moon was still out, and the sun not yet risen. When Avery and Izzy left the bar, however, Izzy said she was going to meet up with Tyler. After the tension in the bar, Avery didn't want to question it. Instead, she ordered a ride, wondering when they had reached this point in their friendship when they were hesitant to question each other about the decisions they were making in life, and whether it signified a healthy or destructive part of growing up. But who was she to question anyone on how they were living their life, when they were the ones who had to sleep with themselves at night.

The entire car ride, her thoughts swirled with questions and memories and worries. She hadn't realized the driver had made it to her apartment until he raised his voice.

"Miss, you're home," he said with a glare, and tapped the back of the passenger seat for good measure.

When Avery tucked herself into bed, she couldn't fall asleep. She tried, lying there with her eyes and blinds closed, trying to block out the artificial city light by placing an old T-shirt over her eyes. But she was still swirling with consciousness. Memories had a way of popping in and out of her mind all the time, though the reasons for their appearances were not always understood. As she lay in her darkened bedroom, with the signs of early dawn beginning to transform the world outside her window, a particular memory couldn't get out of her head.

A memory from high school. Avery had visited her nana's house with her mom, though she couldn't remember where her sisters were. Perhaps college, or their own apartments. Avery had been sitting in the small kitchen of Nana's house, the smells of spices filling the air. Nana's house had always smelled like the spices of homemade cooking. Avery remembered because it was a smell she had craved while growing up in her own home.

Beads of sweat had formed on Nana's face as she had chopped, boiled, and cooked. Avery remembered those beads, glistening against the rising steam of whatever was brewing in the large silver pot. Noise from the TV had floated through the house, into the kitchen. TV always seemed to be the background noise to Nana's cooking, but it was never on a channel Nana chose.

Avery had been observing Nana, who had remained focused on the task at hand. At one point, she had looked at Nana and said, "You and Grandpa must really love each other."

All she remembered was her nana snapping a lid on one of the pots and locking eyes with Avery. "This isn't love."

Three words. They hadn't meant anything more than confusion at first. At least not on the conscious level. But here Avery was, more than a decade later, thinking about them into the early hours of morning.

Chapter 20

There was not a cloud in sight today, Brinkley noted with a glance at the intense blue sky above. A bead of sweat formed on her forehead, matting her blonde hair to her face. A small canopy of trees offered shade as she and her father walked along the cement trail.

When Richard had called this morning, Brinkley was in the middle of getting ready for her daily morning walk. She had just purchased a new, self-help audiobook, *How to Fill Your Glass When Your Life is in a Perpetual Drought* and was excited to let its wisdom wash over her. But it had been a long time since Brinkley had been able to spend one-on-one time with her dad, and since she didn't know the next time she'd get the chance to see him sans Sin, she'd invited her father on her walk.

"You know, that was a really fun kid's party," her father said now, smoothing over his thick, salt-and-pepper colored beard as he walked. "You and Chase did a great job."

"Thank you," Brinkley said. "I mean, I planned and executed everything. But yeah, I couldn't have done it without Chase." *Even though I literally did do it without him.*

"Of course," said Richard. "Chase is a great guy. He seems to work really hard for his family."

"Yeah, he does," said Brinkley, sucking in a breath as she looked at the spotless sky above. When her father didn't add anything, Brinkley said the line she felt everyone was thinking these days: "I'm lucky to have him."

"And it's good you recognize that," Richard said and nodded. "You know, Chase kind of reminds me of me when I was younger."

Oh, here we go, Brinkley thought as she felt her lips press tighter together.

"I also worked like a dog for my family – for you guys," Richard said, now combing his fingers through his graying beard. "Too bad your mother never appreciated it. She loved spending the money, of course, but always had to start a fight over my work ethic. Made things miserable."

"Well," Brinkley said with a nervous smile, "I don't think it was the work she had a problem with, Dad."

When her father didn't say anything, Brinkley continued: "I mean, I think it was more so the extracurricular activities you involved yourself in ..."

Brinkley stopped herself when she saw her father's jaw twitch. After all, the sun was out, the sky was blue, and she wasn't in the mood to start unpacking whose fault it was that her parents' marriage had failed. Especially since they were both pretty awful to each other.

But her father wasn't ready to let it go. "What's that supposed to mean?" he demanded.

"What? Nothing," she said. "Anyway, how's ... um... How's life?"

"It's good," he said, but there was a sharp edge in his voice.

Brinkley would have to try harder to change the subject that quickly.

"Okay, so I have a question," Brinkley tried, keeping her eyes on the cement below.

Richard waited.

"If you had to write something short and sweet about me," Brinkley began, her short ponytail swaying with every step, "what would it say?"

Her father crinkled his eyebrows. "What's this for?"

"For fun!"

"Uh ..." Richard cleared his throat. "I don't know."

Brinkley's smile slipped. "Well ... Why don't you know?"

"I would say ..." Richard tried again. "You're a great mom, great daughter, and you married a great guy," he said with a shrug, pausing for a moment before his eyes lit up. "How'd I do?"

Brinkley stared wide-eyed at her father, but he was too busy wiping the sweat from the top of his bald head to offer any more words.

"Okay, then," she said under her breath, trying to switch her focus to the steps she was taking. Her hopes had not been high for her father's response, anyway. Maybe she should ask her sisters next time. No, they would just make a joke out of it. "Lily and Daisy will be excited to see you when we get them from summer camp," Brinkley said eventually.

"Oh, that's a shame," Richard said, rubbing the back of his head now. "I have to leave after this walk."

"Oh," Brinkley said, her face falling as she continued to look at the sidewalk beneath their feet.

"Yeah, I gotta go shopping for a ferret after this."

"What?"

"Yeah, Sin's been asking for a ferret."

"Dad, you're probably allergic to ferrets," said Brinkley. "You're allergic to anything with fur. Like, deathly allergic. And what kind of adult requests a ferret, of all pets?"

"I'll be okay," he said.

"You weren't okay when I was twelve years old, begging for a dog," said Brinkley. "And I wanted a Maltese! At least Maltese are hypoallergenic. Now you're about to get a ferret?"

"Sin wants a ferret," Richard repeated with a shrug. "Said she had one when she was a little girl – Starlight – and has missed it ever since. They're great companion animals, you know."

"You sound like you've joined a cult."

"Oh, don't start with that." Richard rolled his eyes. "I'm a grown man, Brinkley. I'll pick Lily and Daisy up from camp another time."

With heavy sigh, Brinkley continued to walk.

"Anyway, how's your ... mother doing?" Richard asked, but refused to look at Brinkley. "Saw her at Lily's party. She's not dating anyone, is she?"

"Why are you asking this?" Brinkley wondered aloud.

"At Lily's party she went into the bounce house," he said. "She seemed a bit giddy, no?"

"I think she was just happy, Dad. It was her granddaughter's birthday party," said Brinkley. "Anyway, can we not talk about Mom?"

"Why not?"

"Because why do you want to know if she's dating? You two are divorced! Beyond that, you're engaged now, Dad!"

"Well she is your mother," Richard snapped. "We had a family together, so why can't I ask about her? Is she complaining about me to you girls again?"

"No!" Brinkley groaned before composing herself. "You two always ask about each other, you know. To be honest, it's exhausting. At this point just get back together and I'll throw you a grand fortieth anniversary party."

"Are you kidding me?" Richard asked, stopping in his tracks so he could stare at Brinkley with disgust. "I could never get back with your mother. I have never met anyone who's treated me better than Sin."

"Sin is trying to kill you with a ferret!" Brinkley said, the volume of her own voice causing her to pause and look around for any nosy neighbors.

One man in a baseball cap nodded at her as he passed.

She plastered a smile onto her face. "Hey, how are ya?"

Once he was a good yard away, Brinkley's smile disappeared, and she narrowed her eyes at her father. Her father, however, had resumed walking and was yards ahead.

"Dad," she called, her breath heavy once she caught up to him. Maybe she needed to turn these walks into runs, if she'd ever have a chance of shedding this three-year-old baby weight. "I know Sin is your fiancée," Brinkley said and scrunched her face, "so I'm sorry if I offended you. But honestly, I don't know if Sin is out for your best—"

"Oh, Sin and I booked a wedding venue, by the way," he said, as if he hadn't been listening.

"You ... booked a wedding venue?" Brinkley repeated, a small laugh escaping her lips.

"Yep. In a few months we'll be married."

Brinkley's meager laugh dissolved through the air as a shadow crossed her face. "A few months?"

"Yeah, and Lily and Daisy will be flower girls."

"They will?" Her gaze swept back to the ground. "Wait, isn't Elizabeth and John's wedding in a few months? Lily and Daisy are going to have quite the year."

"Yeah, I know their date, don't worry. It's not the same date," Richard said, waving his hand as if to shoo her words away.

"Okay ..."

"Is your mother bringing a plus-one to Elizabeth's?"

"Okay, slow down. How did we go from talking about ferrets, to weddings, to Mother again?"

"I was just asking a question, Brinkley. No need to get defensive. So ... is she?"

Brinkley closed her eyes, groaning in her mind as she wondered why she ever gave up her audiobook for this.

Chapter 21

"I booked an appointment to go see a medium," Avery said, her smile wide, stopping to stare at each family member seated on the couch of Brinkley's living room. It was a Wednesday afternoon, and usually Avery would be at her apartment, getting ready for her afternoon shift at the bar, but Elizabeth had texted everyone that she had taken a sick day at work and wanted to hang out. At first, Avery was concerned. Elizabeth never wanted to hang out with anyone, let alone sacrifice a sick day to do so. But when Elizabeth specified she didn't want to discuss anything involving weddings, work, or children, Avery understood that Elizabeth's nerves were probably maxed out from too much time wedding planning, working a job she didn't like, and one too many events celebrating children.

Also, Elizabeth hadn't mentioned anything about grief, death, and family secrets, so Avery assumed those topics were still on the table. Now that her family was gathered, it seemed as good a time as any for Avery to extend the invitation to her appointment with the medium.

Brinkley wrinkled her eyebrows. Elizabeth set her phone down.

Mama Donna rolled her eyes. "Oh, Avery, mediums aren't real."

"Well, Mother, I happen to have a lot of questions for Nana."

"Is this still about what she said when she was dying? You really need to let that go. She was a wonderful Nana to you, Avery. To all of you."

"No, Mother," said Avery, sitting up straighter. "This is about her hidden love affair she had while she was married to Grandpa."

"What?" Mama Donna gasped.

"What are you talking about?" Brinkley asked, her face twisted into disgust – as much as it could be because of the Botox – as she glared at Avery.

Before Avery could answer, Elizabeth jumped to the defense. "Uncle Terry was drunk and told us that Nana met someone while she was in Italy."

"But Nana went to Italy before she was even engaged," Brinkley said, her face still twisted. "So how would that be an affair?"

"Well, apparently," Elizabeth said, and glared at Avery before looking back at Brinkley, "Nana exchanged letters with this person even when she was married to Grandpa."

Elizabeth rolled her eyes with a sigh. She began to smooth over the roots of her long dark brown hair. "This is according to Uncle Terry, though. I mean, come on."

"But why would he say that?" Brinkley spat, her face twisting further.

Avery waited for their mother to jump to Nana's defense, but Mama Donna kept her eyes cast downwards and leaned back into the couch.

"Even for Uncle Terry, that's a messed-up thing to say," Brinkley said.

"What do you mean 'even for Uncle Terry'?" Avery shot back. "He's a nice guy!"

"He's crazy." Elizabeth rolled her eyes.

"I am waiting for those eyeballs to roll right out of your head," Avery snapped.

"I don't think Nana would've done that to Grandpa," Brinkley argued. "She was so heartbroken when he died."

As the back-and-forth continued in the background, Avery felt the rising nausea, and she couldn't tell if it was from the second iced coffee she had chugged before coming to Brinkley's, or from feeling like she was living on a different planet than everyone in the room. The feeling was all too familiar. Years of memories flooded Avery's brain: Elizabeth doing anything to take Mama Donna's side, as if that were enough to protect their mother from the trauma of a marriage gone wrong, and Brinkley doing all she could to see the best in people, to protect any feeling of peace. But one memory was louder than the others, refusing to get lost in the storm.

Avery could still picture the bright red color bleeding from Temple University's application webpage, her cursor blinking but everything beside it was left blank.

"Have you talked to your father?" her mother had inquired, her tone already poisoned by stress.

"Yes, Mom. Multiple times. He repeated that I'm young and stupid, and it doesn't matter how hard I work, because I'll never become anything with a journalism degree. He made it clear he's never going to cosign a loan, let alone help me pay for college."

"Then I don't know why you're torturing yourself on a college website, Avery. Your father is the one making all the money. He's always been the one with the money," her mother continued, and Avery could hear her mother's footsteps pacing as her voice trembled. "I've sacrificed my whole life raising you, Avery. I don't know what to do. My hands are tied."

"You could help me get a loan," said Avery, still staring at the cursor trapped in its own blank space.

"Oh, Avery," her mother had responded, her lip no longer trembling. "You're so young, you have no idea how the world works. As much as I disagree with your father, I agree with him on this—you're not going to amount to anything with that kind of degree."

"I want to pursue journalism, Mom. I've wanted to pursue it since I can remember and you of all people used to encourage it. Used to tell me you'd love to raise a daughter who made a career and life for herself—"

"Things were different then, Avery! You were a child. You were a child, and now it's time to grow up."

Her mother had continued to vomit all her fears of what Avery would amount to in one heavy blur, but all Avery had done was close her mouth, look at her mother, and say, "Okay."

She didn't know why it was all she could say at the time, considering within minutes she had called her sisters, her voice unrecognizable as she'd tried to breathe while recalling everything that had happened.

"Avery, Mom has been through enough in her life," she remembered Elizabeth saying with a tired sigh, as if she hadn't slept. "Can't you respect her and stop being so damn difficult for like, one year? Last year it was your tattoo, and the year before that it was your nose piercing and coming home like a drunken, underage mess. She's trying to guide you into making a sensible decision that will affect the rest of your life. You need to respect her."

"I understand you have dreams, Avery ..." Brinkley's words felt like a mockery now. "But maybe Mom and Dad are trying to do what's best for you." There hadn't even been a break for Avery to respond, before Brinkley had gone on to say, "They're both going through a lot. I think you need to calm down, choose the major they'll at least help you get a loan for, and pursue what you want on the side. That's what Elizabeth and I had to do, and we're doing fine."

"Yeah," Avery remembered saying. But she had never meant it. Brinkley and Elizabeth had chosen the majors their parents demanded, but they had never needed to pay anything back. Avery would essentially be taking on debt to spend the rest of her life paying for someone else's dream.

But Avery had wanted the conversation to end, so she had uttered the word of agreement and bitten her tongue.

Now Avery ached at the decision of her younger self. Once upon a time, this memory had emboldened Avery to continue pursuing her path. But as the years had ticked by, and her family had continued moving on with their lives, Avery couldn't help but wonder if her parents had seen the truth: that she had been young, and stupid, and now would never amount to anything, after all.

And every time she wondered about the truth of those words, she became more resentful that those ideas had been planted in her mind, and she had let them grow wild.

"What are you thinking about?" Brinkley asked, arms crossed as her stare recaptured Avery's attention.

"Nothing—"

"It doesn't look like nothing," said Brinkley.

Avery forced her jaw to relax, and added a shrug. "Just thinking of funerals."

Brinkley almost seemed to shudder as she looked towards her ceiling. "Ugh, I know. I'll never forget Nana's screams at Grandpa's funeral." She shuddered again. "I hate funerals."

"I mean, feeling heartbroken when someone you know dies is pretty normal, Brinkley," Avery said. "It's not exactly evidence that she didn't have an emotional affair."

"What are you talking about? They loved each other!" said Elizabeth.

"Yeah, they were soulmates!" Brinkley said, lunging forwards.

Avery eyed the rose quartz ring on Brinkley's finger. Ethan's voice popped into her head: *Why would they question sweet little old Nana when she's always praised them?* Avery wanted to be done with letting other people tell her what to believe and what to feel. Her eyes focused on their mother, who was now fiddling with an invisible thread on her shirt. "You're awfully quiet, Mom."

"Yeah, Mom, tell her Uncle Terry is crazy!" said Elizabeth.

"I don't know why he told you that," was all their mother said. She was shaking her head, but her voice was quiet. "My brother and my mother never had a good relationship."

"But why not?" said Avery.

"Uh, because he's made a lot of bad life choices that hurt Nana," Elizabeth said.

"What makes a choice bad, Elizabeth?" said Avery.

"Disappearing for years and then showing up with a baby one Christmas Eve would be pretty traumatic for any mother, don't you think?"

"Okay, that's, like, the only evidence you have against him," said Avery.

"It's pretty big evidence, Avery," Elizabeth said, flipping her long ponytail over her shoulder.

"As I've said before, something must have driven him away. People don't just run away from their family when everything is peachy keen," said Avery.

"I thought Cousin Jessie showed up on Easter ..." Brinkley interjected.

Avery's gaze swept towards their mother, but Mama Donna changed the subject, as she always did. It was occurring to Avery that, no matter how often her family got together, the content of the conversations had changed over the years. Lately, everyone seemed quick to divert and distract from the topics that made them uncomfortable.

"Avery, I don't understand your obsession with Nana now. You didn't care this much when she was alive," Mama Donna said, her eyes looking at everything except Avery.

"What's that supposed to mean?" Avery asked, feeling the muscles of her forehead straining as her eyebrows drew together. She narrowed her eyes at her mother, whose mouth had already closed with a shrug.

"I think she means exactly what she said," Elizabeth said.

"Okay, I feel like we should talk about something else," said Brinkley.

"Oh, here she goes again," Mama Donna groaned. "The Convo Police. We can't talk about anything around this girl."

"Well, Lily and Daisy are napping upstairs right now," Brinkley said. "Sorry that I don't want my daughters waking up to a screaming match the way I used to when I was little."

"Oh, you know what – " Mama Donna rolled her eyes. "Time to blame me for all your issues. You know, one day you girls are going to have to grow up and take responsibility for yourselves."

"I do take responsibility!" Brinkley shouted. "That's why I'm trying not to repeat your and Dad's mistakes!"

Avery looked around the room, wondering if anyone was going to point out that Brinkley had fallen into the trap of now causing the very thing she wanted to avoid. No one did.

Avery crossed her arms. "Anyway," she said, still eyeing each family member, "the appointment with the medium is next Saturday at six pm. Who's in and who's out?"

"Avery, why would you want to mess with that stuff?" Mama Donna said. "I don't think it's good. You don't know what evil spirits are lurking."

"Well, Mother, I can't get straight answers from the living, so I'm turning to the dead."

"Oh please, you're turning to a medium. They're not dead. They're just phony."

"You said it's next Saturday?" Brinkley asked, scrolling through her phone.

"Yes, six pm."

"Ugh, another weekend taken from me," Elizabeth muttered.

"I mean, you don't have to come …" Avery said. *In fact, please don't.*

"No wait!" Elizabeth suddenly said, sitting straighter. "I forgot – next weekend I was supposed to meet Mrs. Astor to change the itinerary of my wedding."

"What are you changing?" said Brinkley.

"John and I wanted to cut our cake in private instead of making it a big show for everyone, but I have a feeling she's not going to let that happen," Elizabeth said with raised eyebrows. "Four hundred people must bear witness to John and my symbolic first task as husband and wife. But whatever, this is the perfect excuse to miss the meeting! She can just email me the damn itinerary."

Avery blinked. "Are you, like, forced to see the Astors every weekend? Is that, like, part of your prenup or something?"

"They enjoy getting involved with our wedding planning—"

"Sounds like the Astors are planning the whole thing," Mama Donna said with a snort.

"They are the ones paying for it, so yeah," Elizabeth snapped, "they are planning the whole damn thing."

"Oh, is that supposed to be some sort of dig, Elizabeth?" said Mama Donna. "Maybe if I had gotten a real job, instead of devoting my whole life to raising you kids, I would be able to contribute. Why isn't your asshole father paying for anything? He's made it clear he has enough money with Sin parading that diamond all over town."

Elizabeth groaned. "Mom, we just talked about this at your house. I'm not getting into it again."

But Mama Donna's wild eyes were searching her other daughters'. "Do you girls think your father deserves a plus-one to Elizabeth's wedding? It's bad enough I'll have to see his family there – now I'll have to see his new fiancée, too!"

"Here we go," Avery muttered.

"Ooh, next Saturday I can't," Brinkley broke in, looking up from her phone. "Sorry."

"Now where are you going?" Mama Donna asked, craning her neck towards her daughter.

"Chase is taking the girls and me to the Bahamas." Brinkley smiled, but her eyes remained glued to her phone. "It's just for a long weekend."

"Oh, Brinkley, you live such a dreamy life," Mama Donna said, twirling her hair around her finger while looking at the ground. "Chase is such a great husband – your father never did stuff like that for me."

"Thanks," Brinkley said, but Avery noticed that her usual light and bright voice fell flat.

"Aren't you supposed to wait ninety days after a death before talking to a medium?" Elizabeth asked.

"When I called her, she said different spirits channel in different ways," said Avery.

"Sounds like something someone money hungry would say," Mama Donna muttered.

"Okay, Mom's disinvited," Avery declared.

"You can't disinvite your mother," Mama Donna gasped.

"You don't even want to come! You've been dissing it ever since I brought it up!" Avery heard her voice getting louder, but that did not hinder her. "You know what," she shouted as she rose from the couch, "you're all disinvited!" Before she could overthink, Avery grabbed her car keys from the end table and started walking away.

"What the hell is her problem!" Mama Donna said to the group as if Avery weren't in the same room.

"What's her problem?" Now Brinkley's voice was rising. "I think she's the smartest of us all! I'm ready to disinvite all of you from my house, too!"

"Oh, don't be ridiculous, Brinkley." Mama Donna rolled her eyes.

Elizabeth rose from the couch. "Okay, everyone just sit down for a minute."

Avery put her hand on her hip and eyed the time on her phone.

"I'm talking to you, too, Avery," Elizabeth said, staring at her sister.

"I don't have time to sit any more. I have to go to work."

"Are you going to see that pervert today?" said Mama Donna.

"What?" Brinkley said.

Mama Donna leaned away from the couch. "She didn't tell you? There's an old guy who visits her every Wednesday at work. He's visited her for years. Is that not weird? Tell her that's weird. We don't know who this guy is! He could be a total creep."

Brinkley rolled her eyes. "He could also be really nice."

"Oh, please, Brinkley. You would not be comfortable if an old man tried befriending Lily or Daisy."

"They're five and three. Avery is twenty-six," Brinkley shot back.

"Okay, first off, Mom, his name is Raymond. And he's not a pervert. He's my friend."

"Your friend?" Mama Donna said. "You said he was in his eighties, Avery! Is this about your father?"

"What? Why would this have anything to do with Dad?" Avery asked.

Mama Donna's eyes were becoming glossy with tears. "You girls never had a good father figure. I just worry ... how it's affected you. I worry you're going to make bad choices to fill that void."

"You know what, Mother," Avery said, each word short, "maybe I do have daddy issues. I have daddy issues and granddaddy issues, and you know what else I have? Mama and Nana issues. And on top of that, I also have my own issues!" Avery could feel her breath trapped in her chest, breaking free with every word. "If you and Dad are *so* concerned about me and my issues, stop *using* them to fit with your *own* narrative of what happened in *my* childhood!" With each word she yelled, she felt her veins bulging from her neck. It didn't sound like her voice. It didn't even feel as if it were coming from her. At the same time, it felt like it came from the deepest part of her. A part she had long denied herself to feel, fearful of the damage it would inflict on her identity, her relationships.

Elizabeth was rubbing her mom's back, who was curled into the couch with reddened eyes and a clutched chest. "Why are you speaking like this to me, Avery? I am your mother. I tried my best."

Avery felt her chest rise and fall with every breath. "Everybody wants to act like they're trying their best, Mom. No one can apologize for the fact that their best is fucking painful."

The last thing Avery heard when she stormed out of Brinkley's house was her mother's voice sob, "I don't know what is wrong with that one."

Avery felt her jaw tighten, but also felt something else.

Something had reawakened.

Chapter 22

"Okay, so which chapter are we talking about today?" Jennifer asked the book club group, running her fingers through her straight, glossy hair.

"Hmm ..." Brinkley pretended to be interested as she flipped through the pages of the murder mystery her book club had chosen.

Once a week, Brinkley and a few of her "mom friends", Jennifer, Stacey, and Olivia, would get together for book club. Brinkley had met them a few years ago through the private preschool where they all sent their children. The three women had bonded over their love for their kids, wine, and reality television. Not to mention their similar schedules and shared zip code.

It had been Brinkley's idea to start the book club. Between all the play dates, soccer games, dance recitals, and birthday parties she saw these women at, Brinkley thought a book club would be a fun way to spend time together without their children as the focus. Lately, however, Brinkley had been neglecting her reading. Sometimes she would read synopses online so she could contribute something to the conversation, but this week she hadn't gathered enough energy to do so.

"Girls, before we talk about the book," Stacey, a mom with long, wavy blonde hair and baby blue eyes began, "can we talk about what happened on *Getting Drunk and Yelling* last night?"

Getting Drunk and Yelling was the newest reality show that followed a group of strangers forced to be friends by their one shared mutual friend. There were a lot of parties attended, a lot of drinks served, and a lot of yelling.

"Oh my gosh, I could not believe it!" Jennifer gasped. "Cassie is such an asshole."

"Speaking of reality TV," Olivia chimed in, tucking her brown curls behind her ears before leaning into the group, "has anyone tried eating their own placenta?"

"Liv, what does that have to do with reality TV?" said Jennifer.

"I thought one of the cast members gave it a try last season," said Olivia with a one-shouldered shrug and leaned away.

"No, sweetie," Stacey corrected, patting Olivia's knee.

Brinkley noticed her eyes switching between all three women as she heard her heart beating faster, the blood rushing up her throat and into her eardrums.

"Should we end book club early today?"

All three pairs of eyes turned towards her.

"End book club early? Brinkley, sweetie, what's going on?" Stacey chirped.

Brinkley felt her eyebrows attempt to wrinkle, but her injections kept her face still. "I mean, nothing's going on, I just ..." Brinkley covered her mouth with her glass of wine and took a gulp. When she set her glass down, the three women were still staring at her. "I don't know. Maybe with the girls in summer camp, and Chase's business taking off, I think I've just had a stressful week ..." Brinkley trailed off, her heart beating faster as none of the women stepped in to sympathize. "I don't know, I also can't seem to shed this baby weight—"

"Aw, sweetie, you should come to my Pilates class! You would love it," Stacey cooed, then added, "I mean, obviously you look great, but if you're unhappy with your weight, that's what's important."

"One hundred percent." Olivia nodded. "And aren't you about to go on vacation? Sometimes I get stressed before a getaway."

"You do?" said Brinkley.

"I do," Olivia reassured. "All the packing is so annoying. Not to mention scheduling the car service, making sure each nanny is ready to go, finding everyone's passports, chartering the private plane, ugh ..." She rolled her eyes and took a sip of her rosé.

Olivia had been born with a silver spoon, containing caviar, in her mouth, and had married a partner of almost equal net worth. Rumors were that Olivia and her husband lived separate lives – their house was sure as hell big enough to do so, anyway – and their marriage had been less about love and more about two dynasties joining forces.

But in Brinkley's mind, unhappy people would always create rumors about happy people, and when Olivia showed up to every gathering with her fit physique, dressed in the season's newest designer clothes, with an army of nannies by her side and a face full of perfected makeup sans bags or dark circles, Brinkley wondered if Olivia had more secrets to a happy life than most people.

Or maybe she just had way more money.

"Once you get there," Olivia soothed, placing her hand on Brinkley's knee, "you'll have such a relaxing time. I promise you." Olivia appeared to think for a moment before adding, "I mean, I know you don't bring nannies on vacations, which is also probably why you're stressed, but at least Chase is good with the kids. Even without a nanny, I'm sure you'll be able to enjoy plenty of you time."

"Wait, did you girls see how Chase was playing with the girls at Lily's birthday party?" Jennifer said with a hand over her heart. "It was so precious."

Except for when he let Lily disappear into the woods and I found her nearly smoking a joint with her aunt, Brinkley thought through a tight smile.

"Yeah," Brinkley said, and wondered if anyone else could hear her voice falling. "Yeah, he's just the best – it's just been a hectic week."

"Oh sweetie, we've all been there," Stacey said with a nod.

"How have things been since your nana ..." Jennifer trailed off. "I know we didn't really get to talk at Lily's party ..."

"It really was such a fun party, by the way," said Stacey. "Mama Donna is hysterical."

"Yeah, try growing up with her." Brinkley let out a nervous laugh and took another gulp of her wine. She set the glass down with a sigh. "Anyway, things have been ..." Brinkley looked around the group. "Weird. If I'm being honest."

"Oh, well that's to be expected – that's all part of the mourning process," Stacey tried to assure her.

"Yeah, I mean it would be even weirder if things were normal, you know?" Jennifer agreed.

"After my grandma died, I inherited so much money and it was honestly so hard to spend any of it the first week," Olivia said. The girls looked at Olivia with tilted heads. "What?" Olivia asked, taking another sip of her rosé. "It was. But, I mean, it gets easier every day."

"Well, thank you all ..." Brinkley said and tried to offer a smile. "Yeah, I mean my nana was old, so it was expected. I'm fine." She chuckled as she picked up her glass of rosé. "We're all fine, we're good. The vacation will be good."

Later that night, after the book club meeting, and after giving Lily and Daisy a bath and tucking them into bed, Brinkley found herself glaring at her reflection in her new one-piece bathing suit.

All she could see were stretchmarks and cellulite. She wanted to cry.

Chase came into view of the mirror, still in his business suit, and eyed his wife.

"You look," he said as he came up behind her, wrapping his arms around her, "sexy. I cannot wait—"

"Stop," Brinkley said, nudging him away and disappearing into their walk-in closet.

"What?" Chase said.

"I'm just not in the mood," Brinkley muttered, and began changing out of the swimsuit and into an old, oversized gray sweatsuit.

Chase came into the doorway of their closet. "Was it something I did?"

"I'm just not in the mood," Brinkley said again, refusing to make eye contact with him.

"Well, you looked hot," Chase said. "Make sure you pack that one."

"Yeah, definitely," Brinkley said and sighed. "Did you even start packing yet?"

Chase began to undo his tie. "I was planning to do it tomorrow."

"Chase, we leave in two days. Why are you always last minute with things?"

"Um ..." Chase's eyebrows gathered in confusion as he began to undo the buttons of his crisp white shirt. "Because I've been working like crazy all week? It's a weekend getaway, Brinkley. It's not going to take long for me to pack."

"Oh right, because you only need to worry about packing for yourself."

"Okay, what is that supposed to mean?"

"It means," Brinkley said, hearing the edge enter her voice even though she didn't know whether this argument was justified, "what I said."

Chase blinked. "What?"

"Never mind," Brinkley said, racing out of their closet before reappearing. "It means, Chase, that I'm the one who's always in charge of getting the girls ready. While you're out there making a name for yourself and getting hailed as some kind of hero—"

"Brinkley, who is hailing me as a hero?"

"I'm the one in here, doing the invisible work!" Brinkley felt her eyes grow wider as she threw her hands in the air.

"I'm … I'm …" she said, her fists balled, ready to raise a finger for each bullet point she made, "organizing our finances and budgets, cooking, giving our girls bath-time, story time, play time, not to mention play dates, sometimes with families I don't even like—"

"You know we can ask my mother or the nanny to come more often—"

"I don't want to ask them to come more often!" Brinkley said. "I want to raise my own kids!"

"Please keep your voice down, Brinkley, before you wake *up* our kids."

"Oh, so now you're the expert on raising our children—"

"Brinkley, I'm not trying to fight with you—"

"What would it matter if they woke up, anyway? I would be the one taking care of them while you go watch *Property Piece,* or *Real Estate Royals*—"

"Okay, I have never watched *Real Estate Royals* in my entire life," said Chase.

"Oh, whatever!" Brinkley yelled, raising her hands in the air once more and then narrowing her eyes at her husband. "Stop trying to change the subject."

"I don't know what the subject is!" Chase yelled. His eyes were now wide.

They lingered in their stare for a moment, their mouths a thin line.

"Look," he said, his voice clear and firm, "I know I have been working insane hours lately—"

"Uh, you think?"

"Brinkley, I said I know."

Brinkley rolled her eyes, realizing she didn't know what the hell he had said. Her heart was still beating with anger.

"But that's why I booked us this vacation," he said, his voice softer. "I know we've been stressed. We used to never fight like this, and lately it feels like it's all we do—"

Brinkley opened her mouth, but Chase continued, "Look, we have every reason to be stressed with everything going on." He took a step closer, as if testing the waters. When Brinkley didn't pull away, he said, "This getaway will be a nice reset."

A breath escaped Brinkley's lips.

"And I promise," he said and bowed his head towards her, "when we're on that Caribbean Island, my work phone will be completely off."

"Really?" Brinkley needed to hear him confirm it. For a moment, she even considered calling their lawyer to create a legal document.

"Yes, really," he said. "I promise."

Brinkley wanted to smile at this admission, but she couldn't remember a time when Chase was just hers, without interruption. She didn't even know what that would feel like any more. They had met at an age when their minds had tricked them into feeling grown-up, with their adult jobs and changing tastes. But in the grand scheme of life, Brinkley could now see they had been little more than children. Children in their mid-to-late twenties with nothing tangible tying them to their past, and a whole life of possibility waiting for them ahead.

They had met in the city, at a bar called Time. It had a live jazz band, and clocks of various designs and sizes filled every wall closing in on them, reminding them of their own imagined ideas of age. There was a bar that played techno music upstairs, and Brinkley had really arrived to go there with her group of friends. But when her and her friends had heard a live band, they'd agreed to stay downstairs for one drink. Looking back, it reminded Brinkley of people playing dress-up for an adult world they were still trying to understand and become accepted into.

Brinkley would never forget the dimples on Chase's clean-shaven face as he asked to buy her a drink. The way his body language, from his straight yet relaxed posture, and his easy grin conveyed confidence and knowledge. She'd learned that he was a few years older than her, working as a real estate agent in the city, with aspirations to open his own agency. When he'd asked about Brinkley's life, he had kept his eyes glued to hers, asking the usual questions like where she was from and what she did for a living, but also what she hoped to get out of life, and if she ever got tired of living in the city.

Her answers had been simple back then. She'd wanted happiness, eventually a family, and now that he mentioned it, she did get tired of the noisy streets and the litter strewn across concrete. Brinkley could remember feeling her heartbeat as she spoke, sometimes needing to take a sip of her drink so her words wouldn't come out jumbled. They had talked until last call, though they'd never ordered more than two drinks. Brinkley's friends had eventually emerged from upstairs, long after Chase's own group had left for somewhere new, their smiles bright and hair sweaty. Before she went home, Chase had typed his number into her phone, leaving their fate in her hands.

They'd gotten engaged within two years.

Sounds of little feet racing across their hardwood floor echoed through the hallway, pulling Brinkley back to the present

"Mommy!" Daisy wailed, appearing in the doorway with tears formed in her eyes. "Daddy? I had the bad dream about Jell-O again."

"Jell-O?" Chase said.

"Yeah," Brinkley sighed, "she's been having nightmares about

Jell-O ever since her preschool's end-of-the-year party. They served Jell-O jigglers and Daisy cried for an hour. I think the wiggling freaked her out."

Brinkley walked to Daisy and got on her knees. "Come here, baby," she said, "it was just a dream. You can snuggle in our bed tonight."

"Again?" Chase said in a whisper. "Brinkley, it's Jell-O."

Brinkley shot her husband a look. "It's a Jell-O *monster*, Chase, and it haunts our daughter."

Daisy skipped to their king-sized bed and tucked herself in.

"She's playing you," he whispered.

"No, Chase, she's scared," Brinkley said. "You were working during her end-of-the-year party. You didn't have to see the terror in her eyes when her teacher handed her the Jell-O. But I did."

"Maybe we should make some and force her to eat it," said Chase. "Make her realize there's nothing to be afraid of."

"I'm not going to re-traumatize our child, Chase!"

"Our child can't grow up being scared of Jell-O, Brinkley."

"Mommy?" Daisy's little voice chirped from the bed. "Can you turn off the lights and bring me a nighttime snack please?"

Brinkley pressed her lips together.

"She's playing you," Chase repeated.

Chapter 23

T he door of the medium's house was painted a deep navy, chipping at the bottom to reveal the lightly colored wood it once was. The outside was painted white brick, standing in contrast to the redbrick houses surrounding it. Other than the differing colors, however, there were no crystals, wind chimes, or anything else to discern the medium from her neighbors.

"Can you slow down?" Elizabeth called, clicking along the cobblestone road in her strappy, nude-colored block heels.

Avery maintained her station at the bottom of the stone steps, but looked at her sister. "Why did you wear heels in the city? I told you we'd be walking."

"Yeah, you said walking, Avery. Not hiking across Philadelphia."

"It was a few blocks," Avery muttered.

"Actually …" Elizabeth pulled out her phone and looked at the screen. "It was almost two miles."

"Well, welcome to the city," Avery breathed, turning to face the night-blue door once more.

After Avery's blow-up at Brinkley's, Elizabeth had called and asked, no, pleaded, to be re-invited to the appointment with Mira, the medium. Something about not wanting to go to an appointment with her in-laws. Avery didn't understand why Elizabeth couldn't tell her in-laws she simply didn't want to go to these appointments. At least make up a fake excuse. But, like the good sister she was, Avery had agreed for Elizabeth to come. Yet, with every whine Elizabeth made, the more regret Avery felt.

"You know, I'm kind of glad her house looks like a regular old house of the neighborhood," Avery found herself thinking out loud as Elizabeth joined her at the bottom of the stone steps. "Makes me feel like she's more legit."

"Really?" Elizabeth tilted her head. "See, I'm kind of pissed. I wanted the full experience – tarot cards, crystal balls, cats... I don't know."

Just as Avery was about to climb the few steps, Elizabeth stopped her. "Hold on a sec," Elizabeth said, waving her phone at Avery. "Mom's calling."

"You don't have to answer it now—"

"Hey, Mom," said Elizabeth, her phone already against her ear. "We're at the medium's house ... I'm with Avery ... Mom, you said you didn't want to come ..."

Avery inhaled through her nose, exhaled through her mouth.

"Yes, Mom, she disinvited all of us ... I gave her a call after and was re-invited." Elizabeth raised her eyes towards Avery. "No, I don't think she was purposefully leaving you out."

"We have to go," Avery mouthed.

"You want to talk to her?"

Avery began ferociously shaking her head.

"Okay." Elizabeth pressed the phone against Avery's ear.

When Avery's mouth dropped, Elizabeth shrugged.

"Avery, I am your mother. Why are you leaving me out of plans?"

"You didn't want to come!" Avery hissed into the phone.

"Oh, come on, Avery. Just because I don't want to go to a medium doesn't mean I want to miss out on seeing my daughters."

A groan escaped Avery's lips, into the humid summer air. "Which one is it, Mom?"

"I want to be invited—"

"You were invited! You didn't want to come!"

"But then you re-invited Elizabeth and not me!"

"Mother, our appointment is about to start, and I don't like the energy you're giving. I'm about to connect with the dead, for crying out loud."

"Oh, don't use the dead as an excuse—"

"I'll talk to you later," Avery sang, and hung up the phone with a firm tap.

Elizabeth was scowling at her.

"What?" Avery asked, handing back the phone.

"Did you just hang up on her?"

"Yes. The woman talks in circles. Sometimes it makes me feel like I'm on a bad acid trip riding a merry-go-round."

Elizabeth rolled her eyes. "You would know what that's like."

"Yes, I would," Avery said. "And I would also know when to get the hell off."

"What's that supposed to mean?"

Opening and then closing her mouth, Avery looked back at the night-blue door and decided not to jump down that rabbit hole. She began to ascend the old stone steps.

"We need to get to our appointment," she said instead. "I hope this lady hasn't been watching us, or else she probably already knows we're whack jobs."

"Well, she's the weirdo for not having a sign, or a cat, or anything to signal her gift," Elizabeth said as she followed. "I mean, if you could talk to the dead, wouldn't you want to advertise something about that?"

Avery eyed the gold crescent moon hanging next to the doorbell, as if cradling it. "No, I don't think I would …"

Both sisters remained standing, and staring, at the door.

"Are you going to ring the doorbell?" Elizabeth whispered.

"It's a test," Avery hissed. "Shouldn't she know we're here?"

"Oh my gosh," Elizabeth groaned, pressing the doorbell.

Avery cleared her throat. Elizabeth smoothed over her low ponytail.

The door slid open without a sound. An old woman with a crinkled tan face and long, white hair stood in the entrance. A bony finger rested at her lips as she stepped aside to let them in.

When Avery walked in, she could either go up the stairs or enter what looked to be the medium's office. Which actually kind of looked like Avery's bedroom, with the badly plastered walling and cushions for seats. The room was bare, with only a large, circular table featured in the center, with brass legs and a dark wooden top. Unfortunately for Elizabeth, there were no crystal balls or tarot cards. The table offered nothing except a small, cube-shaped tissue box. Velvet, circular cushions surrounded it in earth tones. Tapestries of mandalas in neutral colors were used as curtains, but other than that, the white weathered walls remained bare.

Avery looked past the bare table, towards the other doorway of the room, but strings of navy-blue beads blocked her view. A calico cat emerged from the beads, prancing to its owner, Mira, the medium, and greeting Avery and Elizabeth with a rub.

Elizabeth dropped to her knees to scratch its ear. Avery sneezed. *Oh great,* she thought, feeling another sneeze forming in her nostrils. *Nana is already here, using my allergies to kill me.*

"Welcome."

Avery jumped at the sound of the woman's high-pitched voice behind her. Somehow this woman, with all her signs of aging, and supposed ability to speak to spirits, had the voice of a lighthearted child.

"Please, please have a sweet," the woman said, and then giggled to herself. "Oh, pardon me, that was Charles speaking. I meant to say 'seat'. But I do have sweets if you like."

Raising an eyebrow, Avery eyed the empty room. *Maybe speaking to the dead would be better for a different day,* she considered.

"And Charles is ..." Avery felt the palms of her hand grow sweaty.

"Dead, yes," Mira the medium confirmed with bright eyes before disappearing through the blue beaded doorway.

Elizabeth, who was still on the ground showering the demon cat with her love, looked at Avery with the corners of her lips curled. "It's starting," she mouthed with a smile and a thumbs -up.

Avery was starting to feel a little dizzy.

"Here, child."

Avery's shoulders shuddered at the childlike voice again. Mira had her wrinkled arms extended towards her, holding a glass bowl full of dark chocolates in her hands.

"Take some. From Charles," Mira encouraged.

Avery took one look at the bowl and shook her head. *I am not getting drugged today,* she thought with another sneeze.

Elizabeth, on the other hand, was helping herself to a handful.

"Please, please, have a seat," Mira squeaked, fluffing the earth-toned floor cushions.

Before the invitation could even finish leaving Mira's lips, Elizabeth seated herself on a green-colored cushion, the cat snuggling into her lap.

She waved her hands at Avery. "Come on."

"Yes, come," Mira said.

"So ... who's Charles?" Elizabeth asked as she popped another chocolate into her mouth.

"Oh, he's just a spirit who likes to visit. He used to live in this neighborhood and gets lonely sometimes, but he's harmless," Mira said. "At least, he has been."

Avery felt her eyes bulge as she eyed her sister, but Elizabeth's gaze was intent on the medium, who was seated happily on her cushion, chin lifted.

"Have you ever met any that aren't?" Avery asked slowly, feeling each individual heartbeat in her chest. Mira just smiled at Avery with crooked teeth.

Despite her nausea, Avery's legs carried her to join the table. This was, after all, her idea. She tried to breathe through her nerves as she sat on the cushion farthest from Elizabeth and the cat she was allergic to.

The medium sat between the sisters, pausing to lock eyes with each of them. Avery could see that her eyes had no color. Just a blank shade of gray.

"So, you both want to do the session together? I always like to double check before beginning."

"Do you do individual sessions?" Elizabeth asked.

If this girl leaves me now... Avery snapped her head towards Elizabeth. "She offers individual sessions, but I scheduled us for a group."

"Oh." Elizabeth crinkled her nose. "Why?"

"It's not too late to switch!" Mira assured, clapping her hands together.

"Because," Avery stated, searching for appropriate words as she looked at the medium and then at her sister, "I wasn't exactly Nana's favorite at the end, so ..." She cleared her throat and looked at the medium with a nervous smile. "I don't think I should be alone when we wake her up or whatever."

Mira said nothing. Only looked at both sisters with a smile.

"Fine." Elizabeth shrugged, still petting the cat who had now fallen asleep on her lap.

"Okay, so my name is Mira," the medium chirped in her little girl voice. "For this reading all you have to do is sit back and listen to the messages being sent through me. If the message is significant to you, you can speak up and ask further questions. Sometimes it takes a while to understand the meaning of a message. Things that once seemed unmeaningful can end up making sense later in life."

Avery felt the words wash over her tense muscles.

"Do you girls need water or anything? Or are we ready to invite the spirit in?"

Now that she mentioned it, Avery's throat was feeling dry ...

"We're ready!" Elizabeth said with a wide smile. "Let 'em in!"

"Okay." The old woman swallowed something in her throat and closed her eyes.

A few minutes of silence passed as the medium sat upright on her clay-colored cushion. Her fingers were intertwined, palms facing up, as if she were holding a bowl in her lap. Her long, white hair brushed against her wrists. A peaceful expression spread through her face.

Then her expression changed. All the wrinkles twisted together, her eyebrows nearly touching each other.

Nana's arrived, Avery thought on seeing the horrified expression.

"I am seeing a woman," Mira said, her soft voice cutting through the silence she had created.

"Nana!" said Elizabeth. "Nana, you're seeing our nana," Elizabeth kept saying, her usually monotone voice becoming strained as she welled up with tears. "Hi, Nana!" She even waved.

Great. Now she knows we're looking for our nana and we'll never know if she's legit.

Mira opened her gray eyes, but they were fixed on somewhere far away. "She wants to show me something." The light from Mira's window was shining directly on her face as she looked. "Oh, okay," she said to no one in particular. "She is showing me a few things. A few ... boxes?"

"Boxes?" said Elizabeth.

"Yes, a box maybe for moving, or a present—"

"Oh my gosh!" Elizabeth sat up straighter, clutching her hand over her mouth. "Our nana gave us each a present before she passed."

"But they weren't in a box ..." Avery countered, trying to communicate with her glare: *Stop feeding this lady information.*

"Yeah, but they were a present," Elizabeth said, clearly not receiving Avery's message, and then looked at the medium. "Avery wasn't a fan of my nana's present to her. Does Nana have anything to say about that?"

Avery nearly threw up her hands.

The medium paused, her hands still positioned in her lap as if she were holding something unseen. Suddenly, she snapped her head to Avery, latching her pale gray gaze onto Avery's eyes. Her voice that had been high-pitched and childlike took on a deeper quality:

"Sometimes spirits ... and people ... have an easier time communicating through symbols."

Avery felt her face growing sweaty, her heat beating faster, as the medium's stare lingered.

"I mean, my nana used some words to communicate, too. But Avery wasn't a fan of those either," said Elizabeth.

Mira continued concentrating on Avery's eyes. After what felt like a full minute, the medium broke the stare and turned to Elizabeth. "Your nana said she loves and misses you."

Avery lifted her chin and breathed in, ready to receive her words of closure, even if this medium was full of it.

Instead, Elizabeth and the medium started discussing the meaning of the number four, and other vague objects.

Avery remained on her cushion with her mouth agape as she watched Elizabeth dab her tears and blow her nose at the medium's sweeping, delicious claims like, "Your nana wants you to know she's proud of you both," and "Your nana says she will always be with you, watching over you".

Ethan was right: this lady was in the business of closure. Avery tried keeping her heart open to the words, trying to accept them for herself even though she didn't believe they were coming from her nana, but she felt nothing. There wasn't sadness. But there wasn't closure.

The words the medium was saying were so disconnected from what Avery had been feeling, it was as if she were watching a TV show. A TV show she had tried to put on for distraction or entertainment, but upon watching, realized it did nothing for her soul. Elizabeth, on the other hand, was having a full-blown encounter. Her face was puffy and streaked with trails of tears as she listened to words she considered true.

"So," Mira's little voice piped up after offering forty-five minutes of vague descriptions and statements, "before we say goodbye to your nana's spirit, are there any last messages you'd like me to pass along?"

Avery straightened her spine. "Yes, actually," she said, and felt her heart begin to beat faster. "Can you ask my nana why she said those last words to me?"

It was the same question Avery had asked her nana's journal not too long ago, and she was still waiting for an answer.

The medium paused, her face still illuminated by the sun, but the sun was lower now, the light softer. With a nod to nothing Avery could perceive, Mira's eyes met hers. "She's telling me to tell you that she said those last words ... because she loves you."

How convenient.

"And you, my child?" Mira asked, taking Elizabeth's hand in her own.

"Wait, I have one more!" Avery said, raising a hand in the air as if she were in class.

Both heads turned toward her.

"Did she ever fall in love ... or perhaps lust is more appropriate for this situation—"

"Are you serious?" Elizabeth said with her tear-streaked face.

"Yes, I am," Avery said, then looked at the medium. "Did she ever fall in love or lust with an Italian man named Francesco?"

As the medium performed her routine pause, Avery's eyes remained studying Elizabeth.

"Your nana just started laughing," Mira said, and began to laugh too.

Avery watched as Elizabeth's eyebrows furrowed.

"She said, 'Oh, dear child, I've loved many people in my life,'" Mira concluded with a giggle and a squeak.

"That's a ... very safe response," Avery muttered under her breath.

"Huh—" Elizabeth started, but the medium cut her off.

It was time to say their goodbyes.

Chapter 24

"Well, that was ... not enlightening," Avery muttered into the humid, early evening air once she and Elizabeth were a few blocks from the medium's house.

Elizabeth stopped in her tracks, feeling her face grow hot. "What? What do you mean? Mira knew so much about Nana."

"Like what?" Avery had stopped too.

"Like the presents she got us! And her birthday being in April!"

"Okay, the medium never specified anything about presents. She said the word 'boxes' and you started feeding her all this information—"

"I was not feeding her—"

"And the medium didn't know Nana's birthday was in April, Elizabeth. She said the number four, and once again, you made that connection."

"Avery, out of all the numbers Mira could have said, she said four."

"Okay, and with *any* number said there'd be a way to connect it to *something*," Avery countered, standing up straighter. "Shout out a number right now. I'll connect it to Nana."

"Avery, I'm not doing this," Elizabeth said and tried to resume their walk, but Avery was standing her ground.

"Why not?"

Elizabeth turned to face Avery again. "Because ..." But she stopped her explanation from going any further, feeling her face grow warm beneath the late sun. They had left Mira's house in good spirits – at least, Elizabeth had been in good spirits – so Elizabeth was willing to drop this argument. It was more important to her to cling to the sliver of good emotion left.

But her sister wasn't willing to do the same.

Elizabeth wasn't surprised. One of Elizabeth's first life memories was holding Avery as a baby. She had been so excited to meet her younger sister, feel her soft skin and kiss her chubby cheeks. But all Avery did was cry, and cry, and cry, as if regretting her life before it had even begun. Even though Avery had been adored as a child, doted on by two older sisters and clearly favored by their mother as "the baby of the family", there was always something churning in Avery's mind, making her snap at random times. Elizabeth would never forget the time she'd eaten Avery's pizza slice. Whenever they were younger and their family ordered pizza, Mama Donna would save the last pepperoni slice for Avery, because it was "the baby's" favorite. Never mind that Elizabeth also loved pepperoni, years before Avery even knew what a damn pepperoni was. The last slice always went to Avery. Well, Elizabeth would never forget the night she had had enough of this nonsense and had "accidentally" eaten the last slice. Avery threw a tantrum, as if all the times that she *had* gotten the last slice could be washed away with enough tears. Donna had the nerve to back Avery up, yelling at Elizabeth for breaking ridiculous pizza rules.

And now, twenty-six years later, Avery was still throwing tantrums, angry that their innocent Nana had no longer played into it while on her deathbed. Of course their Nana would gift Elizabeth a beautiful coin pouch and offer kind parting words – Elizabeth and John had visited their Nana for tea and cookies the first Sunday every month.

And that was on top of visiting her every holiday, birthday, and random family gathering, not to mention calling to make sure her electricity was still working during storms. Meanwhile, Avery lived in her bubble in the city, visiting their nana during the obligatory holiday, with that dazed look in her eye and no words to explain what she was thinking inside.

"Because you know I'm right?" said Avery, drawing Elizabeth out of her memories. "That whole appointment was vague."

Elizabeth fought the urge to roll her eyes. "Why did you invite everyone to see a medium if you weren't willing to have an open mind?"

"I actually disinvited everyone," said Avery. "And I did have an open mind. I still do! My open mind is telling me that whatever that medium said had nothing to do with me, or you, or Nana. Is that okay with you? Am I allowed to have my own experience and perspective in life?"

"Okay, what is this actually about?" Elizabeth said, feeling her frown deepening.

"I want you to let me have my own mind! You shove your perspective down my throat about Mom, Nana, Uncle Terry—"

"If you made half the effort to see the good in Nana as you do with Uncle Terry, maybe you and Nana wouldn't have had such a strained relationship," Elizabeth fought back, feeling her cheeks flush.

"What are you talking about? I went to holidays, birthdays ..."

With an eyebrow cocked in the air, Elizabeth crossed her arms and stared at Avery as she trailed off.

"This is stupid, Elizabeth," Avery finally said. "I should be allowed to have my own beliefs about people without it turning into an argument."

"Are you insane? You're the one who started this argument! If you didn't believe in Mira, why did you take my turn at the end? I had more questions to ask Nana and you completely hijacked my turn so you could ask about Francesco—"

"Nana wasn't actually there, Elizabeth! She's dead!" Avery stopped shouting, her face flushed. Elizabeth could see beads of sweat glistening on her forehead as she pushed a piece of her wavy, caramel-brown hair out of her eyes with a heavy breath.

Elizabeth felt her teeth clench as she stared at her sister, who now had her arms crossed, staring back.

"I don't get you," Avery said, her voice now soft. "You have no problem believing in a stranger who says she can speak to the dead, but you can't consider that there might be some truth to what Uncle Terry said? Why would he make that up, Elizabeth? And what's the big deal if Nana did have a harmless affair?"

"*No* affair is harmless!" Elizabeth felt her voice getting louder than she would have liked. She looked around as she tried recollecting herself, making sure the sidewalk was still deserted. "You of all people should know that, after what we've been through with our parents."

"Nana's marriage was not the same as our parents'—"

"And I don't understand what Uncle Terry's *lies* have to do with Mira," Elizabeth said, her forceful voice taking over her little sister's. "And I don't understand why you're so *obsessed* with believing Nana had an affair. It's like you can't stand the fact she was a good human."

"No, Elizabeth ..." Avery's voice was rising again. She breathed. "No ..." Avery tried again; her voice was more controlled this time. "You've blindly taken Mom and Nana's side all your life. You took Mom's side in the divorce and didn't talk to your own father for years—"

"Look at what our dad was doing, then! How he was acting!" A memory of coming home with her mother one night, while her parents had been in the thick of divorce, fighting over the house, only to hear her father's voice and a woman laughing in the basement, hijacked Elizabeth's mind, making the world around her feel like a dizzy dream. Her mother had left imprints on Elizabeth's wrists from gripping her, to pull her back outside and into the car. Elizabeth and Mama Donna had spent that night at Nana's house, while Avery had missed the whole thing, already at a sleepover with her friends.

"It's not like our mom or Nana was perfect either, though!" Avery snapped. "But you still took *Mom's* side. You got the degree she wanted you to get, you believed anything she wanted you to believe in—"

"Mom wanted me to have a stable job, Avery," Elizabeth spat, and she could feel the red splotches of anger taking over her face. "She wanted to make sure I'd be financially independent, so I would never have to end up like her!"

"You're a shell of yourself, Elizabeth!" Avery's eyes flashed as they locked onto Elizabeth's. "You've become a shell of yourself to please Mom, and I see you doing it with your future in-laws, too!"

And yet I still don't crack under pressure like you, Elizabeth heard her thoughts scream. It's not like Avery had been the only one to deal with fallout from the divorce. Elizabeth had been in high school when it began, and yet she had managed to take care of her mother, her little sister, and herself in the process. Once upon a time, Elizabeth had covered for Avery's decisions. There were a few nights she'd pick her little sister up from drinking too much just to make sure she'd get home safe, and almost every night, no matter what was going on in Elizabeth's life, she'd make sure her phone was on loud in case Avery or their mother called with a crisis.

Until one night, when Elizabeth had been visiting from college and had walked in on Avery giving herself a tattoo. That's when she'd known that she had had enough. Worried about what this news would do to their mother, who was still enraged over the nose piercing Avery had given herself a year earlier, Elizabeth hadn't told on Avery. But she'd tossed and turned for weeks with the secret. Yet even those weeks of worry had gone to waste as Avery had made no effort to try to hide the tattoo, anyway. After a few weeks of wearing long sleeves, her little sister had come to the dinner table in a tank top, the botched pen displayed proudly on her forearm, and Elizabeth hadn't been able to prepare herself for their mother's ensuing shriek.

Avery was throwing her hands in the air now, but words kept pouring out of her as she stepped closer, too fast for Elizabeth to react. "The way you give up your control to the Astors – it's like you put your worth in this select group of people and then just … just … become who they want you to be to please them! Without—" Avery breathed, leaning away to stand straight again. "Without even bothering to consider who you're actually pleasing."

There were no tears forming in Elizabeth's eyes, but her whole world felt filled with static. Before Elizabeth could remove herself, could walk away without looking back, Avery drilled more words into her head.

"And so *of course* you'll trust some stranger … Some old lady who keeps comments vague and nice, so you never have to question who your favorite grandparent really was—"

Elizabeth felt her mouth curl into distaste as she glared at her sister.

"I would bet everything I have, that if the medium said *anything* against Nana, you would not have been so quick to believe in her."

Every muscle in Elizabeth's body tensed as the heavy evening air lingered between them.

"I came to this thing because of you, Avery," Elizabeth finally said, her voice quiet in the empty neighborhood. "And now you're just bitter because you didn't get whatever the hell you were looking for, and I did."

Without a sound or expression, Avery just shook her head.

"I came here looking for something that might help me heal, Elizabeth," Avery said through gritted teeth. "And no, I did not get it. Because I'm self-aware enough to realize healing is not going to come from someone who's already dead."

The two sisters glared at each other.

"I'm not mad at you, Elizabeth," Avery said, but her voice still sounded harsh.

Elizabeth opened her mouth, but she realized she had no words as Avery continued her attack.

"I just think you've traded your own perspective of life, for the one other people have fed you."

John had always described anger as a fire, but as Elizabeth stood on the cement sidewalk, wordless, she felt as if she were made of jagged stone. Nothing was moving any more. Not even the contents of her mind.

But there was no relief in this kind of heavy stillness.

"Do you even know what you want out of life any more—"

"I can't help it, Avery," Elizabeth said, knowing she was no longer choosing her words, but not willing to stop herself from saying them. "I can't help it if you were a disappointment to Mom and Nana, and I wasn't. So stop taking your bitterness out on me."

Once the words left Elizabeth's mouth, she felt she could see her sister clearer.

"I *am* bitter," Avery said, her chin held in the air. "But you know what? At least that bitterness forces me to do something about it. You're just on autopilot, living under everyone else's control ... Even when they're dead."

"Says someone who is bitter," Elizabeth muttered.

An expression crossed Avery's face that Elizabeth didn't quite understand. It appeared to be a look of recognition, though what Avery was recognizing, Elizabeth was unsure.

Without a further word, Avery turned on the heels of her sneakers and walked away.

Elizabeth didn't follow her. For a moment, she remained motionless, looking up at the deepening sky. Even though the sun was still shining, the manmade lights of the buildings had begun casting the city in a hazy glow. After a few silent minutes on the sidewalk, empty except for pieces of shattered glass that reflected all the saturated hues of summer, she wandered along the streets, past the intimidating skyscrapers, and returned to her car to drive home.

Chapter 25

The Bahamian sun glinted off the delicate gold band of Brinkley's rose quartz ring as she reached for her piña colada. *I wonder how that visit to the medium is going,* Brinkley thought as she sipped the creamy coconut drink.

Last week, after Avery had screamed at their mother and stormed out of Brinkley's house like a deranged animal, Elizabeth had whined that she didn't want to be disinvited from the medium. While Elizabeth had been whining, Mama Donna had been complaining about how unstable and ungrateful Avery was, bringing up the time Avery had got caught underage drinking. Instead of apologizing, Avery had looked Mama Donna straight in the eyes and said, "Brinkley and Elizabeth used to underage drink, too. They were just better at hiding it." Which wasn't exactly a lie, but when Mama Donna retold the story, both Elizabeth and Brinkley had remained silent, even after all this time.

Mama Donna had also droned on about the time, just a few years ago, when the family had agreed to celebrate Christmas together – Richard and Mama Donna and Richard's girlfriend all willing to bite their tongues and play nice for a night – and Avery had gifted the three of them a knife "to cut the tension". Personally, Brinkley found that memory hysterical, but Mama Donna had added it to the category of examples when Avery had been in the wrong.

The dynamics of Brinkley's family often reminded her of politics. The alliances, the power shifts, the bribes – the more she thought about it, the more she realized she didn't want to think about it at all. After all, the sun was shining, the waves were crashing, and her husband had taken over parental duties the past three hours, taking the girls for a swim in the pool, and now a walk along the shoreline to search for seashells. Ever since her and Chase's mini argument about packing and parenting, Brinkley had noticed Chase offering her more breaks from the girls during this trip.

And she was going to milk it for all it was worth, Brinkley thought as she pushed her Prada sunglasses up the bridge of her nose.

After readjusting her swim cover-up, Brinkley leaned into the lounge chair underneath the cabana they had rented and fluttered her eyes closed. Just as the sounds of tourists faded, and her breathing slowed, she felt her phone vibrating at the end of her feet.

No ... was all her brain could think, but it kept vibrating. *What if it's an emergency,* the thought flashed through her brain.

She pictured her mom in hysterics. Or her father calling from some kind of hostage situation orchestrated by Sin. Or maybe Elizabeth had finally snapped and called off her wedding – the possibilities seemed to multiply with each vibration.

Groaning, Brinkley sat up and fumbled through her beach bag. *Avery* flashed across the screen. She clicked *Ignore* and leaned back in her seat.

A twinge of guilt tugged at her, but Brinkley decided she would hear about Avery's trip to the medium when her vacation was over.

Besides, if Brinkley was being honest, she wasn't entirely sure what answers Avery was looking for, anyway. So what if their nana didn't know where Avery had been or where she was going. All this time, Brinkley had assumed that Avery had no idea where she was going, either. Between Avery's various, temporary jobs as a nanny, waitress, and now bartender, not to mention Avery's love of weed and camping, Brinkley figured Avery enjoyed keeping her path open, no direction to limit her.

Although, with every year Avery spent in that tiny little apartment, Brinkley wondered if Avery's life was more limited than Brinkley realized.

Before Brinkley could contemplate for too long, her phone vibrated again. With another groan, she fished her phone out of her beach bag.

"Hi, sorry to bother you …" It was Avery's voice, but she was sobbing. "When you're having fun …" Another sob. "In the sun …" Another sob. "And all—"

Brinkley shot up from her chair. "Avery! What happened? Breathe. Just try to breathe."

Avery kept heaving into the phone. "Okay," she sobbed, and it took a few moments until her voice sounded calm. "Okay," Avery said again. "I'm sorry. Is this a bad time?"

Depends on what this is all about.

"Of course not!" Brinkley said. "What happened?"

"Me and Elizabeth went to the medium tonight …"

Brinkley could hear Avery's voice crack.

This is gonna be a while … Brinkley started drifting out of the conversation. Her family's emotions were running high these days, and keeping up with it all was quite honestly giving her a headache.

She watched her daughters make drip sandcastles with their dad. She waved at them when they caught her staring. *Gosh, they're so cute from afar,* she thought as she smiled. *You would never know Daisy ripped off Lily's Barbie doll head this morning …*

"And then Elizabeth said I'm a disappointment to Mom and Nana!" Avery finished with a cry.

"Wait, what?" Brinkley tuned back in.

"Yeah, because I told her she just wants to prove that Nana and Mom are wonderful people. And then she told me I'm just bitter and a disappointment to Mom and Nana."

"Really?" Brinkley gasped. "Okay, you know you're not a disappointment to Mom and Nana—"

"Do I?" Avery sniffled.

"Avery, of course you're not – don't let Elizabeth get to you. And honestly, who cares if you are? You are a kind, hardworking human being. That shouldn't be a disappointment to anyone."

"It was to Nana!"

Brinkley looked at her daughters laughing and splashing ankle-deep in the crystal-clear Caribbean Ocean.

"You know what I think you need? A vacation," Brinkley suggested. "Everyone's emotions are running high, we're all feeling a bit sensitive ... Have you gone camping recently? You used to love camping."

"I can't even remember the last time I went," Avery said with a sniff. "Maybe two years?"

"Two years? Girl, get off this phone, go pack a bag, and call in sick to work this weekend. You are going to go camp and clear your mind."

Brinkley could hear rustling on the other end of the phone before her sister sighed. "Okay. Maybe you're right."

"Good. Now call me if you need anything else. But like, only if you really need me."

"Honey!" she heard her husband call from the water.

Before Brinkley could respond, Lily was running towards her screaming "Mommy, Daisy has diarrhea. She pooped! It's dripping in the sand!"

"Oh Lord, I have to go," Brinkley said, eyeing her surroundings. "The whole beach hates us now."

"What hap—"

"Avery?" Brinkley interrupted.

"Yes?"

"Try to forget what Elizabeth said. She's been bitter ever since she got engaged. I think the Astors bought her soul or something. You're not a disappointment."

"See, it's funny you say she's bitter because she's the one who called me bitter—"

"It's called projecting, Avery."

"Mommy, we need wipes!" Lily kept screaming even though she was only a couple feet away.

"Look, Daisy just took a shit in the sand. I have to go."

Chapter 26

Elizabeth slammed the front door of her and John's one-story cabin.

"How'd it go?" John said. He was hunched over their kitchen counter with a chip in hand, frozen on its path to the dip.

"It went great. Fucking fantastic," she said, flinging the refrigerator door open. "Avery's not going to be a bridesmaid any more."

"What happened?" The chip remained in John's hand, hovering over the dip.

"Nothing, it's fine. She wants me to do things my way, so I'm doing things my way and disinviting her from my bridal party."

As she scanned the contents of the refrigerator, she could feel John's gaze analyzing her every micromovement. But as soon as she made her selection of Tofurky, John cleared his throat.

"Speaking of bridesmaids ..." he began, finally popping the chip into his mouth and leaning into the counter. He swiped his hands together to remove the invisible crumbs. "My sister called."

Elizabeth ripped off the plastic and used her bare teeth to tear a chunk of the vegetarian deli slices. "I swear to God, John, if this is about canapés—"

"She wanted to know when you're available for a bachelorette party."

"What? I told everyone I didn't want a bachelorette party. Multiple times," Elizabeth said as she chewed.

"She said everyone wants a bachelorette party."

"Well, did you tell her I don't?"

"I did, but she said she already planned something—"

"What?" said Elizabeth, a piece of Tofurky falling from her open mouth.

"She already put a deposit on the resort—"

"Resort? What the hell did she plan?" she demanded, hoping John's sister had booked a hotel on a tropical beach somewhere. Even though she knew that beach would be filled with branded bridal gear, plastic dicks, and grown ass women drinking past their limit. She shuddered. Elizabeth didn't like babysitting babies, let alone adults.

"She said she was talking with Lena, Ivy, and Clementine—"

"Why? John, I don't even know those girls, let alone like them!"

John tilted his head. "How do you not like someone you don't know?"

Elizabeth felt every fiber of her being grow hot, as if the very essence of herself was about to erupt into flames. "Maybe you would understand if you were a woman and forced to go to bridal and baby showers every other weekend, sitting next to people who just gossip for hours and talk about high-top tables this, hard butter and dicks that!"

John squinted at her, nodding along, but it only made Elizabeth's temperature hotter.

"But you don't understand, because even though it's *your* sister, you're a man! So, while I'm there smiling and nodding at the stupid shit that pops out of people's mouths, you get to spend your Sundays doing whatever the hell you please. Society respects that *you* have better things to do with your money and time, but me? Oh, hell no!"

John nodded and opened his mouth, but Elizabeth's tongue was on fire now. "John, what did they plan and why did they plan something for me I don't want?"

"Jordan said she was talking to the trio and they all agreed it was sad you didn't want one. So, they planned to kidnap you in the middle of the night, put you on a plane, and you'd wake up in Cabo."

"What!"

"That's why she needed to run it by me. She needed to make sure they'd do it on a weekend you'd be home and I wouldn't call the cops."

"John, is she insane? I tell her I don't want a bachelorette, so she plans to kidnap and force me into one?"

"She said if you didn't want one, kidnapping was the only way."

"Or she could respect my wishes!" Elizabeth said, slamming the pile of Tofurky onto the counter before rubbing her temples. "Your sister is pregnant! Why does *she* even want to go to a bachelorette party?"

"Well, it's an alcohol-free resort, Liz."

"So, just to be clear ... I'm going to be kidnapped ... taken to another country ... and won't be able to drink?" Elizabeth almost chuckled, it was too absurd. At least it took care of the whole babysitting-grown-adults problem. Still, it wasn't enough to make Elizabeth want a bachelorette. It would just be another assault on her energy, paycheck, and time.

Elizabeth eyed John. "Tell me you shut this down so fast."

"I told her I would at least talk to you—"

"Why would you do that?"

"That's what she said!"

"Well, why didn't you just confirm I didn't want one?"

"I didn't know what to do!" Now John was raising his voice, his arms stretched by his side as he puffed his chest. "She put me on the spot! Said she had the whole itinerary planned and everything. Crystal cleanses in the morning, aloe vera baths in the afternoon—"

"Now she's going to blame me if this thing gets canceled," Elizabeth said, then corrected, "*when* this thing gets canceled."

"Darling, I'm sorry, I didn't know what to do ..." John's voice was pleading with her. He walked over to cup Elizabeth's face between his hands.

"Don't 'darling', me, John," she said, recoiling from his touch as she tore another piece of Tofurky with her teeth. "You know what you need to do? You need to grow up!"

"Why are you turning on me like this?" he said. "What did that medium do to you?"

"What did that medium do to me? What did your sister do to you? Your parents are one thing, John, but to be scared of your sister, too?"

"I'm not scared of her!"

"Yes, you are – you're scared."

"You're scared, Elizabeth! You're scared!"

She rolled her eyes. "Of what, John? Please tell me your psycho-analysis. I'm so intrigued."

But Elizabeth could feel John's eyes studying her, so she interrupted his words before he could admit them. "I had a really bad day, John," she sighed, setting her pile of half-eaten Tofurky on their wooden kitchen counter. "This isn't even about your sister," she admitted, rubbing the space between her eyes, then said, "I mean, it kind of is, because she's ready to kidnap me to Cabo, but I don't have the energy to keep arguing. There's enough happening in my life."

John paused, his eyes darting around as if looking for the trap. "Do you want to talk about it?"

Elizabeth looked through the kitchen window, into their sunroom. The twinkle lights were on.

"No." She sighed, walking to the light switch to turn them off. "I just need to get some sleep."

After a few steps towards the bedroom, she raced back to the kitchen, her pointer finger jabbing in John's direction. "But I swear, if I get kidnapped in the middle of the night, you will be sorry. Shut this down, John. Shut. It. Down."

Chapter 27

"You're going camping *alone*? What if you get murdered, Avery? I thought this camping phase of yours was over!" Mama Donna was practically in hysterics as Avery searched through her mother's garage for her old camping gear.

Mama Donna nudged Izzy with her elbow. "Izzy, tell her it's not safe!"

Avery remained focused on sorting through the contents of the bin she had just pulled out. Knowing her mother would react like this, Avery had begged Izzy to come with her so she wouldn't have to face Mama Donna's interrogation alone. If only Avery could afford a bigger apartment. Then she would never have to keep anything stored at her mother's house, and her mother would never have to know what Avery was up to. She could go get murdered in the mountains in peace. *Maybe Brinkley could store a few bins of mine in that three-car garage of hers ...*

Izzy offered her biggest smile and a small shake of her head. "For better or worse, Avery will always do what she wants," she said, and put her hand on Mama Donna's shoulder. "At least you know you raised a strong woman." As an elementary-school teacher, Izzy had years of practice de-escalating irrational parents.

"Yes, and it was never a phase, Mom," said Avery, pulling out an old scarf and then dropping it back into the bin. "It's a lifelong passion. And I have been failing to fulfill it the past couple years."

"Listen, I read the news. There are so many articles about hikers who go on these trails and end up dead. They go out there, think they're gonna have a good time, and end up dead, just like that. They're usually female. Of course."

"Well damn," said Izzy.

"A-ha!" Avery cheered as she fished her stainless-steel wine glass out of the bin and raised it above her head in victory. "Found something!"

"Oh great, Avery, so you're going to the middle of the woods, alone, to get drunk. I mean, Izzy, is this not the craziest thing you've heard? Who does this?"

"Mom, I'm not trying to ski down Mount Everest. I'm going camping. On a campground. It's a very private campground, yes, but there will still be people around ... somewhere."

"You think I trust those people on a campground? My father always said 'Never trust anyone—'"

"Except Jesus Christ," Avery finished. "Yes, I know. He had trust issues."

Avery pulled out another bin.

"He was wise, Avery. He survived a war," Mama Donna snapped, and began to twirl a strand of hair around her finger. "Is this trip about Nana?"

Avery paused from her search to look into her mother's eyes. "I just need a vacation, Mom."

"Oh, don't be ridiculous. It's not like you're going to the Bahamas with your family like Brinkley. Camping alone is just ridiculous. If you want a vacation, save up for an actual vacation. A vacation *with* somebody."

"Mama Donna," Izzy cut in, "I don't understand your daughter's love of sleeping outdoors, either. The campground bathrooms are dirty. The tents smell like feet. I'm always scared of bugs crawling up my vag—"

"Ew," Avery looked at Izzy. "Where are you going with this? And what tent were you in that smells like feet?"

Izzy pursed her lips at Avery before turning back to Donna. "But we love Avery, so we must support what Avery loves, even if we don't understand it. Right?"

"No, Izzy, not if she's going to die!"

"I'm not going to die," Avery muttered, spotting her sleeping bag and tent. "Look what I found!" she sang and began dancing with her tent sack cradled in her arms like a baby.

With a sigh and a roll of her eyes, Mama Donna looked at her daughter. "You know what, whatever. If you want to go camping alone, that's your choice. At your funeral I'll just tell everyone: My daughter lived a short life. She said she'd rather get eaten by a bear than listen to her mother."

"Sounds like a beautiful eulogy for me, Mom," Avery said and pulled out another bin.

"You sure you can't go with her, Izzy?"

"Mom!" Avery snapped. "Izzy already told you she's busy—"

"She's a teacher! Isn't it summertime right now?" Mama Donna turned towards Izzy. "Don't teachers get summers off?"

"Her life doesn't revolve around me!"

"Yeah, I'm sorry, Mama Donna, but I'm too grown to babysit other grown people," Izzy said with a shrug. A half-smirk began to appear on her face. "Now if you want to pay me ..."

Mama Donna and Izzy chuckled together.

"I'm sorry sweetie, you're right," Mama Donna agreed. "What are your plans this weekend?"

"I'm actually going on a date," Izzy said with a smile.

"Wait, what?" Avery said, snapping her head towards her friend. "You didn't tell me that. With who?!"

"I mean, it's not with anyone new ..." Izzy shrugged.

"Oh, is it with that nice boy Tyler?" Donna cooed.

"How do you know Tyler?" Avery snapped her head at her mom.

"Izzy didn't tell you? I ran into her and Tyler at the supermarket the other day."

"Uh, no, the last time we talked I thought you and Tyler were ... fizzling."

"Well, things change. We talked, and ..." Izzy raised her eyes to meet Avery's. "I want to give him a second chance."

"But you were just talking about how you weren't desperate to be exclusive—"

"And I'm still not."

Avery silently studied her friend, but Izzy's face remained stoic.

"Are you sure this is going to make you happy?" Avery said. "I mean, last we talked you acted like you were happy to move on, but then you slept over his apartment, which was confusing – are you even giving yourself a chance to move on?"

"Oh, Avery, she's allowed to change her mind," Mama Donna interjected. "Second chances are good. Everyone deserves one."

"Okay, my mom stayed in her dysfunctional marriage for decades before leaving, so maybe don't take relationship advice from her," Avery said flatly.

"Avery!" Izzy gasped. "Don't talk to your mom like that. That's not right."

"I knew I always loved you," Mama Donna said to Izzy.

"I was just pointing something out, Mom. You don't even know if Tyler's good for her and you're already encouraging a second chance."

"I trust Izzy's judgment, and as a friend, you should too," Mama Donna scolded.

173

Avery looked at her friend and then her mother. Both were glaring at her, their lips frozen in a line.

"Look, it was just a shock to hear after our last conversation." Avery began to put the bins back into place. "But it's fine," she said, struggling to lift one overhead but turning away from her mother's attempt to help. "I want to go on this trip alone anyway. No, I *need* to go alone."

"How are you getting off work?" her mom asked.

"I have off Friday and Saturday, and I'm calling in sick Sunday and Monday. Maybe Tuesday if the weather is nice. I have the flu. Ethan said he'd cover for me."

"Oh, you can't do that, Avery, you need this job to pay your bills!"

"Mom," Avery said, her voice clipped, and if her smile got any tighter it was going to snap, "you and Dad have not paid for so much as toothpaste since I turned eighteen. Maybe even sixteen. The last time I called off work was a year ago, for strep throat. So, you worry about your bills, and I'll worry about mine. If you tell me what to do or how to feel one more time, I will snap."

"Avery, are you all right?" Mama Donna asked, tilting her head at her daughter. "The past few times I've seen you, you've been so ... angry."

Avery took a long inhale through her nose and exhaled a loud sigh. She did it again, and now Izzy was even looking at her, wide-eyed.

"Are you okay?" Izzy asked.

"I am angry," Avery said, each word clear as she looked at both of them. "I have been angry for a long time."

"Oh, here we go," Mama Donna groaned, but Avery wasn't letting her off the hook that fast.

"The only difference now is," Avery glanced at the faded scars on her wrist before locking eyes with her mom, "I'm not taking it out on myself any more. So, if you don't want to see me angry," she smiled another tight smile, "look away."

"I don't see how taking it out on your mother is going to do any good either, Avery," Mama Donna said and broke their gaze so she could stare at the ground.

Perhaps she's right, Avery considered as she felt the guilt of her earlier words setting in.

"I'm sorry," she said, crossing her own arms. "I don't mean to take anything out on you—"

"You can be so mean to me, Avery," was all Mama Donna said, her voice quiet. "I get blamed for everything."

They stood in the silence of Avery's cut-off apology. She looked at her mother, whose eyes looked forlorn. The guilt used to torment Avery, feeling as though she had done something to hurt her mother, and her mother would never forgive her. For a while, Avery tried everything in her power to prove her love. If her mom and dad were fighting, she wouldn't speak to her father. If her mom didn't want to be alone for the night, she would cancel plans with friends to keep her company. If her mother and her got into an argument, Avery would apologize even as her mother's words antagonized her own mind.

Dropping her arms to her sides, Avery sucked in a heavy breath. "I'm sorry, Mom," she tried again, and allowed her guilt to bubble from her heart and into the words she spoke. "I love you."

Mama Donna raised her eyes to Avery's. "If you loved me, you would be nicer to me."

It was then that Avery realized the real source of her guilt wasn't over anything she had said or done. As Avery stood in the silence now, staring into her mother's eyes, she realized her guilt had provided the illusion of control – if everything was Avery's fault, it was in her power to fix it – but that's all it was, an illusion.

The real problem, Avery considered as she allowed her arms to fall to her sides, was trying to cope with the realization that her mother didn't trust how deeply her own daughter loved her. When her mother was in pain like this, it was hard not to steal a slice of that emotion, to try to lighten the weight of that burden.

But there was no fix for someone else's pain.

No matter how many years Avery filled with apologies, no matter how much guilt she felt or how carefully she chose her words, Avery had not been able to fix or lighten the load of her mother's life. She had only weighed down her own.

"Avery?" Izzy waved her hand.

Avery shook her head out of her thoughts and looked at her friend.

"I have to head back to nanny soon. Would you like to respond to your mother before we go, or—"

"I don't think she does, Izzy, it's fine," Mama Donna said, looking at the garage floor. "She was probably just replaying all the reasons I'm a terrible mother."

"Actually no, I wasn't, Mom." Avery shook her head. "Those aren't my thoughts and I hate that you put that on me."

The wrinkles around Mama Donna's mouth came to a pause as her lips pressed shut. For a brief moment, she raised her eyes to look at her daughter before casting her gaze back to the ground.

"We both have tried our best," Avery said into the damp garage air, her voice clear. "And I'm sorry my best can be painful. You don't need to forgive me, but I am sorry for my part. I love you."

Almost imperceptibly, Mama Donna's lips curled at the edges. Then she shifted her weight and looked away, the soft smile disappearing as quickly as it had come.

"I love you too, Avery. More than anything in this world. That's why I don't want you to go camping and get kidnapped—"

"Oh, you two are so cute," Izzy said, unfazed. Over the years, she had witnessed countless arguments in Avery's family. "Let's hug!"

Chapter 28

The sunset stained the evening sky in brilliant hues of orange and red. Warm evening air surrounded Brinkley in a hug as soft, intoxicating sounds of the breeze whispered through the palm trees. On her balcony chair of the hotel room, still in her plush white hotel robe with her damp waves pulled in a messy bun, Brinkley tried her best to take it all in. Yet she couldn't stop spinning the rose quartz ring around and around her finger.

All her senses drifted her into a memory of her and Chase's first vacation together, to Puerto Rico, before their engagement, and children. Before their house on the Main Line, when Brinkley still had her apartment in the city, but most of her clothes and products had been kept at Chase's. The memory still made her body jittery, filled with that nervous energy that seemed harder and harder to experience every year.

One night, Chase had scheduled them for a canoe ride in Puerto Mosquito, Mosquito Bay. Brinkley had been confused why they couldn't go during the day, let alone why they were going at all, but Chase had insisted. When they'd arrived, the tour guide had led them through a short trail of trees, no more than a lamp lighting their way to the canoes bobbing gently in the water. Chase had taken her hand to help her into their canoe. Brinkley's laugh, as she'd fumbled her way in, had sounded like an intruder in the night.

But when Brinkley had dipped her paddle into the water, every submerged part had glowed ethereal, angelic hues of blue, as if some mystical force existed beneath. She'd looked at Chase, her eyes wide but her cheekbones hurting from its smile, and he had offered his dimpled, easy grin. "It's a bioluminescent bay," he had explained, as if that was enough. At the time, Brinkley hadn't known a place like this existed, let alone could exist on planet earth. They had paddled through the mangrove swamp, beneath the ceiling of trees, with their tour guide leading the way and a handful of other tourists paddling close behind, into a clearing, where countless stars glimmered above, and everything glowed below. And Brinkley remembered wanting to clutch Chase's hand, jump into the bay, and exist in that feeling with him for eternity.

They had gone home that night laughing like two teenagers who felt comfortable together for the first time. Talking about the canoe ride, their whole trip, what the rest of their life could be like experiencing the world together. How they would raise a family in such a world.

It had sounded so easy in their fantasies.

Just as the sun began to submerge itself into the ocean for the night, the sound of the balcony door rolling open startled her. Brinkley snapped around to see Chase, two glasses full of red wine in each hand.

"You scared me," she breathed.

Chase raised an eyebrow from behind his rectangular reading glasses. "Who else would it be?"

"I don't know, I ..." Brinkley stood to help her husband close the door. "I wasn't thinking, I guess. Where's Lily and Daisy?"

A smile, bright against his tanned skin, spread across her husband's face.

"I read two pages of their bedtime book and they passed out," he said. "Too much fun in the sun, I guess."

"Lucky you!" Brinkley said as she accepted one of the wine glasses. "I usually have to read the same book ten times before they even consider sleep."

"Maybe we should install a pool in our backyard. It would help get their energy out."

"It's a drowning waiting to happen."

"Nah, we'll put a fence around it," said Chase. "Besides, Lily was like a fish in the water today. One more year of swim lessons and Daisy will be, too."

Brinkley felt her heart sink at this remark as another warm breeze whispered through the trees.

"Do you remember Lily's first swim lesson?" Brinkley heard herself ask.

"Of course I do," said Chase, raising the glass of wine to his lips. He paused before taking a sip. "We were so nervous."

"Yet she jumped right in."

"Then she cried."

"No, Chase, Lily bawled," Brinkley said and laughed. "For the entire lesson. She cried so hard, you wanted to call the whole thing off. Keep Lily in floaties forever."

"I didn't like to see her so scared!" Chase defended with a laugh. "I was worried the instructor didn't know what she was doing."

As the first stars of the night began to appear, the last of the sun dipping beneath the ocean, Brinkley felt her smile fade. "Now you don't have patience for Daisy's fears of the Jell-O monster."

"Being afraid of Jell-O is a bit different than being afraid of drowning, no?"

Brinkley fell silent.

Raising their glasses to their lips, both took a sip and then stared across their balcony, into the unknown of the night as the world continued to darken with every minute.

"Well," Chase said, sucking in a breath. His voice felt loud after the quiet they had found themselves in. "The girls seem to be having a blast on this trip ..."

"They do," Brinkley said, and then tried to make her voice light-hearted again. "Although after Daisy's diarrhea," she added with a laugh, "I don't think we can show our faces on the beach tomorrow."

"Oh, man ..." Chase chuckled, but Brinkley could tell it wasn't the kind of laugh that gave him dimples. "Maybe we'll stick to a pool day tomorrow. Although Daisy seems to be fine now."

"Yeah," Brinkley nodded, "she does."

Brinkley could feel Chase studying her.

"But what about you?" he asked.

"Me?" Brinkley scrunched her nose.

"Between your nana's passing, and the craziness of Lily's birthday party, plus everything going on with my business ... I can't tell if this trip came at the best or worst time."

"Well, we just got here a day ago ..." Brinkley began to answer, but her voice was uneasy. "I mean, it's been a beautiful family vacation," she said. "The girls are having the best time, and it's always nice escaping with you. How could I complain?" Brinkley looked at her husband for an answer, but he just smiled.

"Well, I'm glad," Chase said eventually, raising his glass to toast. "You deserve this."

Brinkley tried to look into her husband's eyes when he said this, to feel the truth of those words, but the sun had disappeared from the sky and the shadows had encircled them.

"Thank you for saying that," she said, fighting the urge to ask him to say it again.

"Of course, Brinkley. I mean it."

"You deserve this too, you know," she said, even though he

probably did know, because all those years of hard work were paying off through a growing, successful business, a family who loved him, and friends who admired him.

"Well, thank you," he said with a yawn, and raised his glass once more to cheer hers. They were silent for a few minutes, sitting on their balcony chairs.

"So," Brinkley broke the silence with a quiet voice, "your work phone is really off?"

"Yes." Chase yawned again as he took another gulp of wine. "I'm a man of my word."

"I know ..." Brinkley trailed off, searching for the words she wanted to say as she stared at the twinkling stars in the sky.

A formless emotion spread through Brinkley, and because it was formless, she did not know the words to describe it. It was a feeling she had been wanting to share with her husband, to let him in on her innermost world and current secrets, if not out of love than at least out of the desire to no longer experience this empty feeling alone, without him.

"I know you've been working really hard for our family," she started, hoping the right words would bless her if she showed them she was willing to try, "and I know I've been, impatient, with all your work stuff lately. I just ..." Her gaze traveled from the glittering sky, towards the ocean. Its movement could no longer be seen in the dark, but the crashing waves could be heard. "I've always wanted to become a mother and raise a family," she said, her voice quiet even in the hushed night, "and, you've helped provide me with more than I could ever ask for—"

The sound of snoring interrupted Brinkley. She turned her head and sure enough saw Chase, asleep on the balcony chair.

I worry it's not enough.

There they were, the words to describe her feeling. They had made themselves known in her mind, but her husband was no longer awake to hear them at the moment she was finally ready to admit them.

Something is missing from my life.

The sound of crashing waves filled the air, and Brinkley kept twirling her rose quartz ring around and around her finger.

Chapter 29

The blue light emanating from Elizabeth's computer screen felt as if it were burning through her cornea, right to the depths of her soul.

Ding. Another email came through.

Elizabeth leaned her elbows against her desk and brought the tips of her manicured fingers to her temples. She could see her two-carat, oval-cut diamond bulging off her ring finger as she massaged her head. She brought the ring in front of her view. It had looked so exciting, so sparkly, when John had first slipped it on her finger.

Around six months ago, on a Saturday morning after a rather long and stressful week of work, Elizabeth had woken up to the sight of roses making a trail to her and John's backyard, dotting the remnants of melting snow with their deep red hue. Elizabeth followed the trail to where John was seated on a wooden tree stump by their fire pit, the ever-changing flames offering warmth in the frosty winter air. The fire pit was one of Elizabeth's favorite places, where her and John would often sit beneath a starry sky and talk about the world, losing track of time.

When he'd heard her walk through the back door, he had swiveled around, a smile spread across his face, creating deep crinkles in the corner of his eyes. He draped a heavy blanket over her that they had bought years ago, from an independent artist during one of their first trips together. She would never forget the shakiness in John's voice as he'd dived into his monologue, sharing all the reasons why he loved her. Little wrinkles had creased between his thick dark eyebrows as he had taken one knee on the ground, asking her to spend the rest of her life with him, to become his wife.

The early morning rays had illuminated the depths of his eyes as he had spoken. She hadn't been able to look away from him, not even for one glance, even though the whole moment had made her feel like she was entering euphoria, as the flames of the fire continued to flicker their heat Elizabeth and John's way.

Yet what had once seemed romantic now felt ominous as she stared at the ring.

Elizabeth found herself longing for that first feeling of their engagement, wishing they had given themselves time to revel in the moment before it had become a memory.

But they had both been over the moon, so of course she had called her family while John had called his to confirm her answer. Everyone already knew she would say yes. They had been together for ten years, and they were smitten with each other.

Still, the longer Elizabeth stared at the sparkling ring claiming her finger, she couldn't help but feel as if another, unseen part of her existence had been hijacked. Taken over by decor, guest lists, and glittering things.

"Elizabeth?" Her administrative assistant, Val, was standing in the doorway of Elizabeth's office.

"Yes?" Elizabeth said, tucking her hands back into her lap.

"Mrs. Astor is on the phone. I tried calling you, but it went straight to voicemail."

For a reason, Elizabeth thought.

As if she could read minds, Val added, "She said it was a slight emergency, so I wanted to let you know."

"Oh my gosh ... Um, okay, send her through."

Was Jordan going into early labor? Elizabeth wondered with a slight panic rising into her beating heart.

Before it could finish its first ring, Elizabeth snatched the phone. "Hello? Is everything okay?"

"Hello, Liz," Mrs. Astor greeted, her voice as calm as ever. "Yes, I am okay, just wanted to make sure I got through. I'm at the florist—"

What psychopath fakes an emergency, was all Elizabeth could think as she smoothed over her hair. It was pulled into a low bun today, so there was not much smoothing she could do.

"You're where?"

"I'm at the florist!"

"What florist?"

"That florist I was telling you about ... in Rittenhouse. Francois is his name. Anyway, I know him because my Jordan used him as the florist for her wedding. He does the best work. You would be thrilled if you could see these bouquets right now. They're stunning."

Elizabeth could feel her face growing hot. "Um, okay?"

"Shall I set up an appointment with him? You and John need to start finalizing what color schemes and flower species you'd like for the wedding. I'm getting a bit worried that you aren't booking these vendors in time—"

The warmth in Elizabeth's face started spreading throughout her collarbone.

"Our wedding is three months away," she said, pressing the phone tighter against her ear. "Some people plan weddings in like a month. We have plenty of time to book vendors—"

"Not good ones, darling. You both are lucky I can pull the strings. Anyway, is there a date that works best for you?"

"I'm actually at work right now – can we discuss this later?"

"Elizabeth, Francois is a popular and in-demand florist. I'm going to go ahead and book us an appointment. If we need to cancel, we can always reschedule."

"You know, John and I haven't done much research yet on which florist we want to use—"

"You're free on weekends, right?" Mrs. Astor interrupted.

"For the most part—"

"Perfect. I'll get us the first available weekend appointment," Mrs. Astor said. "And look, I know you originally said you wanted emerald green in the wedding scheme, but a late summer, early fall wedding is perfect for muted green and beige tones. With maybe splashes of cream. We don't want it to look tacky, you know."

Elizabeth began banging her head on the edge of her desk.

"All right, well I'll get this handled. Enjoy work, and we'll talk later."

Click.

After a few moments of silence, Elizabeth raised her head, but an endless stream of unanswered emails stared back at her.

She let out a long, loud groan, but it wasn't loud enough to block the voice in her head: *You're a shell of yourself.*

Chapter 30

"I can't believe you told Avery, of all people, to go book herself a camping trip. Alone," Mama Donna said, setting her fork down with a *clink*.

"Okay, I never told her to go alone," Brinkley said.

It had been one day since Brinkley had arrived home from her mini getaway and she was already longing to go back. The second their plane had landed, Chase had turned on his work phone, bombarded with unanswered emails and texts. Lily and Daisy had been thrown off their schedules and were therefore annoyed about absolutely everything. The weather was too hot, they were bored of all their toys, they were starving but disgusted by every snack – and why did the mansion they live in not have a pool or ocean in the backyard?

By the time they'd reached their house, Brinkley had been so fed up with the whining, she'd ended up packing trash bags full of her daughters' newest toys and explaining the importance of gratitude and giving. The girls, of course, had lost their minds on seeing their toys confiscated. The toys were now gifted to a women's shelter.

So, when Brinkley received a call from her mother about meeting at a restaurant during Elizabeth's lunch break today, Brinkley had thought it would be a fun way to decompress. Her daughters were back at summer camp – bless those overworked and underpaid counselors

– and her husband sure as hell wouldn't be seen anytime soon, so Brinkley was excited to catch up with her family. Mainly, she wanted to show off her vacation glow and hear Elizabeth's side of the story about her and Avery's visit to the medium.

Not even twenty minutes in, and Brinkley regretted her decision to come.

"Well, now she's camping alone and I am worried sick," Mama Donna droned on as she sipped her iced lemon water. "I mean, it's Avery, Brinkley, of all people—"

"Why do you keep saying, 'Avery of all people'?" Brinkley interjected with a scrunched nose, tilting her head at her mother. "Avery's the only one in this family who still loves camping. Obviously, I'd tell her, of all people, to go do it."

"Okay, but you know she can be a little risk-taker," said Mama Donna. "It makes me nervous. She's only five feet and thinks she can climb a mountain alone? Someone could snatch her right up and shove her in their pack. It happens all the time!"

Brinkley couldn't help but laugh, it was so absurd.

With a roll of her eyes and a shrug, Mama Donna muttered, "You know what, I blame your father for this. He used to love camping."

"Yeah, we know," Brinkley murmured, glancing back at her half-eaten vegetable wrap. It looked so neglected, sitting alone on her plate, but after all those sugary piña coladas in the Bahamas, Brinkley had a new rule of only eating half her meals. Despite this, she decided to take another bite. A vegetable wrap could not have that many calories. Then again one could never know the grams of sugar lurking in a dressing these days ...

She dropped the wrap on her plate and tried to imagine how good it would feel to be able to fit in her skinny jeans again. No vegetable would be worth that victory.

Although, if she couldn't eat vegetables guilt-free, where would she draw the line? Was vegetable guilt a sign she was developing a more serious eating disorder?

Had she lost her damn mind?

Brinkley picked up the wrap again and took another bite. She needed to be a good role model to her daughters and that definitely included eating vegetables guilt-free, dressing be damned.

Besides, she could walk off the sugar later.

"Your father always took you girls camping," Mama Donna continued, interrupting Brinkley's internal battle.

"I remember," Elizabeth muttered.

Brinkley looked at Elizabeth, who had been quiet the entire lunch, but Elizabeth kept her head down. She looked back at her mother, but Mama Donna had already moved on from the topic, busy picking at a piece of spinach stuck between her teeth.

"Camping with Dad was fun," Brinkley said, trying to remember the days of childhood before the accused affair and relentless fighting. All the memories seemed tainted with too much knowledge now.

"Too bad you started forbidding us from going with him," Brinkley added, not because she wanted to hurt her mother, but because she herself was still hurt by the memories now flashing through her mind.

"Oh, Brinkley, don't be ridiculous. I never forbid you girls from anything," Mama Donna said as she held her phone's camera in front of her face to help her release the piece of spinach.

"Mom, yes, you did," Brinkley said. "I'll never forget our vicious fights when I was younger, because Dad wanted to take us camping, and I wanted to go." Brinkley felt her heart pounding as she could see Elizabeth's head turn towards her. Their mother opened her mouth to protest, but Brinkley had more to say. "You and Dad were fighting all the time, and you told me that if I went, I was taking his side after he betrayed his family—"

"Brinkley, this did not happen! You are lying—"

189

"I remember it too," Elizabeth interrupted, but her voice was quiet and lifeless.

Now Mama Donna's eyes were wide, staring at Elizabeth. "Well whatever I said — if I said anything — must have not been that bad, because *Avery* continued to go camping with her father."

"Avery's a different breed," Elizabeth muttered. "That girl will fight her way through anything without getting tired."

Brinkley wrinkled her eyebrows at her sister, but Elizabeth was quick to add:

"Look, I'm not trying to blame you, Mom," Elizabeth sighed. "I understand." She looked at Brinkley. "And you should, too. Why do you think Dad planned a fun camping trip for us right after his affair?"

"Because he always planned fun camping trips for us—"

"No, Brinkley," Elizabeth said with a sigh, as if running out of patience. "He knew what he did, and he knew what he was doing. He wanted us to believe him and not Mom, hoping a camping trip was enough to win us over."

"Or he wanted to maintain a healthy relationship with us—" Before Brinkley could even finish her sentence, Elizabeth changed the subject:

"Anyway, can we stop talking about Avery? The girl isn't even here."

"Oh, you just wait until you're a mom, Liz," said Mama Donna, apparently finished with denying her daughters' childhoods.

"I don't want to be one," said Elizabeth.

Mama Donna ignored her and looked at Brinkley. "Aren't I right? How would you feel if little Lily said she was going to pack her things and camp alone in the mountains?"

"Well, Lily is five, so ..." Brinkley trailed off, but kept glaring at her mother.

Mama Donna shook her head. "You girls, you'll just never get it."

"Where is Avery, anyway? Did she already leave?" Elizabeth asked.

Brinkley could feel Elizabeth's gaze burning through her.

"Why are you looking at me?" Brinkley finally asked, keeping her eyes focused on her three-fourths eaten wrap. "I just got back from vacation."

"You're probably the first one Avery called when it happened," Elizabeth said.

"When what happened?" Mama Donna asked. "What did I miss?"

"You're not missing anything," said Brinkley.

"Avery and I got into a fight after seeing the medium," Elizabeth said.

"What! Why? See, I told you mediums are no good."

"The medium was great. Avery was the problem," said Elizabeth, now stabbing her fork through her strawberry salad.

"Well, what happened?" Mama Donna demanded. "Is that why Avery didn't come today? She told me she had work, but usually she doesn't work this time on a Tuesday."

"No, she really is working today," Brinkley said. "Someone called out of work and she wanted to pick up extra shifts before her camping trip."

"Yeah right," Elizabeth said, stabbing her fork through another strawberry. "You'd lie for Avery. She probably didn't come because of our fight."

Brinkley rolled her eyes. "There's nothing to lie about, Elizabeth. Avery told me she's working, so I believe she's working. You give her a call if you don't believe it."

"I don't want to call her," said Elizabeth.

"Can someone please tell me what this damn fight was about?" Mama Donna smacked the table, causing the dishes and utensils to jump.

Brinkley scanned the restaurant to make sure the other diners weren't aware of the drama happening at their table. One elderly man was side-eyeing Brinkley, probably soaking in his entertainment for the day. Brinkley looked at her mother with wide eyes and an open mouth. "Okay, calm down, Mother."

"Well then explain what happened already!"

Sitting straighter, Elizabeth cleared her throat. "After the medium, Avery flipped out at me. Out of nowhere."

"Is that girl all right? She seems so angry lately ..."

"Elizabeth, why don't you tell us what the fight was about," said Brinkley.

"Basically ..." Elizabeth appeared to think for a moment before explaining. "She was mad I enjoyed the medium and she didn't."

"Really?" said Brinkley. "That's all?"

Elizabeth shoveled a forkful of salad into her mouth. "Well," she began, covering her mouth as she chewed and talked, "she said she couldn't understand why I would believe a medium over Uncle Terry. Then called me a shell of myself." Elizabeth looked at her mother and then at her sister as she finished chewing. "Like ... what does that even mean? I'm not a shell of myself."

Brinkley continued to bite her tongue.

"Uncle Terry?" Mama Donna broke in, saying his name as a question. Her face was contorted as she appeared to be searching her own mind for a connection, an explanation. "What does he have to do with any of this? Has he been in contact with you girls again?"

Now Elizabeth's face was the confused one as she dabbed her mouth with her white cloth napkin. "In contact? What?" she said. "No, we spoke to Uncle Terry after the funeral – Mom, we told you this. He made up that story about Nana and some Italian lover, remember?"

"I'm confused," said Brinkley. "What does Uncle Terry, or Nana's supposed lover, have to do with you and Avery fighting at the medium's?"

"I just told you!" Elizabeth said. "Avery's obsessed with believing Nana had an affair and is mad I don't. I think she only went to the medium to confirm the affair, and was pissed off when the medium didn't, because it *didn't actually happen.*"

Elizabeth flipped her ponytail over her shoulder. Their mother remained silent.

"Elizabeth," Brinkley began, raising an eyebrow as she observed her sister, "you don't think Avery's anger had anything to do with – oh, I don't know – you telling her she was a disappointment to Mom and Nana?"

Mama Donna gasped.

Now Elizabeth was the one rolling her eyes. "I knew she called you."

"Elizabeth, you didn't tell her that, did you?" Mama Donna said, sounding breathless.

"Mom, you've told her she's a disappointment yourself," Elizabeth said.

"What? Elizabeth, I would never say that about one of my children—"

"Well, you said it about Avery," Elizabeth said with a shrug.

"Yeah, Mom, you can't sit there and keep acting like you don't remember these things," said Brinkley. "You've said Avery's a disappointment multiple times."

"You mean when she refused to go to college? I was terrified for her. I wanted her to fulfill her potential ..." Their mother's voice cracked as her eyes welled with tears.

"Yet you and Dad offered no financial support to help her get there. That makes sense."

"We were going through a divorce, Brinkley. We lost a lot of money."

"And you both kept a lot of money," Brinkley countered.

"Brinkley, why are you starting with me?" Mama Donna pleaded, her voice becoming high-pitched. "Your father's the one with all the money, showering every girlfriend of the month with expensive gifts. Is anyone yelling at him about Avery's college?"

"Look, Mom," Elizabeth leaned into the table, "we're not saying what you said was wrong—"

"Even though it was," Brinkley added.

"We're just saying you've definitely told Avery she's a disappointment before, so, in the heat of the moment I repeated it."

"But that's an awful thing to repeat," Mama Donna said, and a few tears slipped from her eyes, down her cheeks, and into her spinach wrap. "It's not like I actually meant it. She just, she was so difficult during those years. She never listened to me. Nothing I said got through to her—"

"Mom, it's fine," said Elizabeth. "I don't think Avery is suffering from any emotional scars. Even after I repeated it, she just looked at me with her blank face, unaffected." Elizabeth stabbed through another strawberry. "She said pretty messed-up things to me too, if anyone cares. Like calling me a shell of myself." When no one responded, Elizabeth said, "Besides, she's more pissed off that I don't believe our crazy uncle than anything else."

Their mother was shaking her leg so hard, the table began to shake, too.

"Girls," she said, just as Brinkley was getting ready to yell at her mother to control her leg, "I have something to tell you."

Chapter 31

"Our finest pale ale," Avery announced, setting the beer glass on the coaster in front of Uncle Terry.

"Thanks, kid," he said, running his hand through his thinning hair. He peered at Avery. "You know, I was surprised you called me to come down. I don't think you've ever called me."

"And I don't think you've ever come down," Avery said.

"We should change that," he said, and reached for his beer. "We both live in the city – it seems silly we don't see each other more often. I mean, we're family."

"Let's change it," Avery said, knowing it was one of those promises that would never be kept. "So how are you doing? I haven't seen you since the funeral."

"I'm all right, keepin' busy, you know." Uncle Terry sighed. "How are you?"

Avery felt her lips spread into a soft smile. "I'm all right, too," she said, watching her uncle taste his beer.

Avery looked at the end of the bar for a moment to make sure the other two guests in this place didn't need anything. Their beer glasses were half-full, their eyes glued to the game playing on the TV.

She looked back at her uncle.

"I have a question ... Do you remember telling me and Elizabeth about a man named Francesco?"

"Oh yeah, I did," he said, tangling his fingers through his beard. "Why?"

"Well, I was ... intrigued ... by the story. I want to know more," Avery said, watching as her uncle took another sip of his beer. When he set his glass on the coaster, she continued, "Recently I went to a medium for answers, and it made me realize that the answers I'm looking for are pretty specific."

Her uncle looked at her from under his bushy eyebrows. "Um, okay. What answers you lookin' for?"

"I guess I just want to hear the story, you know. I mean, this whole time I've known Nana as a nana, if that makes sense? And now I've been reflecting on some memories and stuff, and I'm realizing that she has, like, a whole life I have no idea about."

Avery glanced at the ground before meeting her uncle's eyes. "I want to know how you know about ... Francesco ... and why it was hidden from everyone else."

After a minute of peering at her from beneath his eyebrows, Uncle Terry released a huff and leaned into the wooden bar counter. "Can I smoke in here?"

"Um, no, I thought that was outlawed."

"Real bars you can," he grumbled, then leaned back on his barstool and looked at her. "Your know your nana used to keep a journal ..."

"Wait, what?" Avery felt all of her senses narrow onto her uncle Terry as she waited for him to repeat something else, to confirm she had misheard.

"Yeah, she kept a few journals—"

"What! Since when? Why didn't she tell me that?"

"She didn't want anyone to know, Avery."

Avery felt as if the room were spinning around her. The image of her nana, lying on those sterile white sheets, her hand outstretched with that smooth, tan leather journal, solidified itself in her mind.

"She had them hidden in a box on the top shelf of her closet. When I was little, I used to be in the room with her, watching her write. And then she would shut the journal, tiptoe to her closet and store it away ..."

Avery was trying to focus on every word her uncle uttered, but the memory in her mind continued to grow in detail. Her nana's labored breath as she spoke, her clouded eyes that scrutinized Avery.

"One day I got curious," he said. "So I went to the box, and I read them."

How dare you, Avery thought, feeling the panic of imagining someone reading her own journals from when she was younger. Everything was in there. Her private inner world.

As if reading her mind, he added, "Now that I'm older, I know it wasn't right. I think it destroyed our relationship. We couldn't look at each other the same, you know?" He sucked in a breath, his eyes cast downwards. "There was a lot in there that Nana never talked to anyone about, and never wanted to talk to anyone about." He let out a long, deep sigh. "Francesco and the coin pouch were just one of the stories."

"There were others?" Avery said, feeling her own breath get caught in her chest. "Like other lovers?"

"Well, no, no other stories like that, no." Uncle Terry shook his head. "Francesco was the only man, other than Grandpa, that she wrote about. But there were stories about other things."

"Like what?"

Uncle Terry frowned as he spoke. "She wrote a lot about her parents being strict and controlling. Always pressurin' her to get married and have children, even though she wanted to see the world, become a teacher ..."

"She never told me any of this," Avery said, feeling and hearing her anger rise from the pit of her stomach and up her throat.

Uncle Terry's gaze got lost in the liquid of his drink. "There were also stories of Grandpa being controlling, and distant – some things were in there that were hard to read as a kid, you know?" He took a sip of his beer. "There wasn't much in there that we couldn't have seen with our own two eyes. My parents were always polite to each other. My grandparents always overbearing. But after reading the journals," he shook his head again, "it was impossible not to see it." A chuckle escaped his lips as he smoothed over his belly. "And of course, me and my big mouth had to confront not only Nana about all of it, but Grandpa, Aunt Carol." He raised his eyes to meet Avery's. "Your mom, too."

"I had a feeling my mom knew about it," Avery said, shaking her head. "When I brought it up, she was so quiet. And when my mom is quiet, it's always a sign she's hiding something."

"Yep," Uncle Terry said, pressing his lips together for a moment.

"But why wouldn't my mom just tell me about it?"

"Your mom and Aunt Carol were furious at your nana and me. Furious at me for bringing the harsh truth into their perfect denial. And furious at Nana for giving her emotions to a man who wasn't our dad. But it didn't take too long for them to sweep it under the rug."

He sighed, and took another sip of his beer before clearing his throat. "My dad was furious, though. I was afraid he and Nana were gonna separate, but people didn't do that back then." He let out a long exhale through his mouth. "Nope, people just kept living in the same house as strangers. And the problem with Nana was, she loved putting up fronts to people. Her childhood was idyllic. Her parents supportive. Her husband unflawed." He paused, his gaze searching for something outside of the bar window. "I think part of her grew to hate me, for seeing right through it."

Avery felt her muscles tense. "I can see that ..."

198

The wrinkles around Uncle Terry's eyes fell. He was watching the people passing outside, as Avery had done so many times before.

"Nana ended up throwing away all her journals," he finally said. "She burned all the letters from Francesco, right in front of me, my sisters, and our dad. I could never tell if she was trying to prove her loyalty to us, or if she wanted us to witness the pain on her face as she tossed each letter into the fireplace. Force us to see what we had done, since we had forced her."

Avery imagined someone reading all her journals from when she was younger. She would never be able to look at them the same. Journals that once contained the mysteries of being alive would now be books filled with secrets that could be judged by eyes not living the life inside.

Avery would have ripped up the pages, jumbling all the words into an unreadable, forgettable regret, too.

"I don't think she ever kept one again," Uncle Terry said. His gaze was still lost in the window to the outside world.

"Yeah, I mean ..." Avery trailed off, finishing the words in her mind: *How could she?*

"But even without the journals ..." Uncle Terry's lips pressed together for a moment. "I never let her keep up the front. I would always remark, 'That's not how it happened', or 'Are you sure', if she told a story that didn't match what I had read—"

"Yeah," Avery said, her word more like a whisper as she followed his gaze towards the window. "Yeah, I remember you making comments like that. At holidays and stuff. Always drove Elizabeth mad."

Uncle Terry shifted in his barstool to look at Avery. "I wanted my mom to come clean. Be honest about her life. It was a much more fascinating life than she let on. But now ..." He trailed off, his gaze getting lost with his words. "Now she's gone. And she never did tell anyone about Francesco, or her parents' control, or the truth about how she felt in her marriage." He looked down at his drink. "And I'm starting to realize it was never my story to tell. It was hers, and she wanted to die without telling it."

Avery could see her uncle's lips press down as his wrinkles deepened.

"All the years she was alive, I put a strain on our relationship, and for what? Because I was angry at her for loving a fantasy instead of my dad? Because I was nosy and wanted to blab everything?"

"Or maybe you were just ..." Avery scanned her mind for sympathy, for the right words to say. But she had no idea what the right words were. "Young. And confused," she finally said. "We all make questionable choices and we don't always know what to do with them. Sometimes we learn, but sometimes not."

Uncle Terry remained silent.

"Sometimes life feels so complex, no one knows what to do." Avery shrugged, shaking her head. "It's not like Nana's truth is the only truth." Avery felt the weight of this settle into her stomach. "I mean, clearly her truth is not the only truth," Avery said, "after what you just told me."

The corners of his mouth curled, so she pressed on.

"Nana's life is intertwined with yours, and the rest of her family, and it's intertwined with mine and the rest of the grandchildren, so you know what? I'm happy that you're able to share another side of her story."

Avery had Uncle Terry's focus now.

"I am," she confirmed.

When Uncle Terry didn't offer a response, Avery looked at her hands and pretended she was interested in her cuticles. "I've been carrying a lot of guilt myself. About Nana."

"Really?"

"Yeah. Me and her ... We became distant over the years. When Nana was ... dying ... she had nice things to say to my sisters. Gifted them with objects she still seemed to cherish, even during her last moments of life."

"And when she got to you?"

"She gifted me a journal, actually," Avery said, a small laugh edging its way into the admission. She shook her head. "She basically said she bought it and didn't want it, though. It was empty except for two words, '*Dear Self*'."

"Ah ..." A slow smile spread across Uncle Terry's face. "That's how she started all her entries."

"I never knew she kept a journal before." Avery was still shaking her head. "She gifted me one and didn't offer a hint as to why. Didn't even tell me she used to keep one—"

"I'm surprised your mom didn't at least tell you."

Avery shrugged. "Sometimes my mom likes keeping up fronts, too," she said with a large inhale to slow her beating heart. "To admit my nana used to keep a journal would risk more questions being asked, and my mom avoids questions she doesn't like the answers to."

"I guess everyone picks up some tendencies from their parents."

"Yeah ..." Avery nodded, and was about to check on her customers, but there was a nagging question in her mind. "I just wish I knew what her intentions were with my gift. Why give me a journal if she regretted keeping one? I don't understand."

"Maybe she regretted throwing hers away." Uncle Terry took another gulp of his beer before setting his glass down and letting out a breath. "Maybe she didn't know what else to give. I don't know if you'll ever find an answer, kid. So just create one you like."

"Hmm," Avery thought aloud, and she felt her shoulders relax, if only for a moment.

They both looked out the window, at all of the people passing by.

Chapter 32

"What do you need to tell us, Mother?" Elizabeth demanded, her chin pointed down as she glared at Mama Donna, who was uncrossing and re-crossing her legs until she decided on a position.

"Uncle Terry was telling the truth."

Elizabeth's fork fell to the floor in multiple clatters. Brinkley looked at her sister, whose usually flawless face began developing splotches of maroon all along her cheeks and neck.

"What?" was all Elizabeth spat.

"Nana did meet someone when she was in Italy," their mother said, her lips drawing into a line. "She wasn't married when she met him. She hadn't even met Grandpa at that point—"

"Oh my God," Elizabeth blurted out. "Oh my *God*," she repeated, this time throwing her white cloth napkin onto the table.

"And when she did get married?" Brinkley trailed off, trying to put the pieces of information together.

"They still wrote to each other, but they didn't meet up or anything – well, not that I know of," Mama Donna said, looking into her wrap as she shook her head. "I mean, they were both married and living in separate countries—"

"Francesco was married too? Why would they keep writing to each other!" Elizabeth said, too loudly for Brinkley's liking. More than just the elderly man would be staring at them now. "How could she do that to Grandpa, to her family! To Francesco's family!"

"The heart wants what it wants, I guess," Brinkley said, trying and failing to imagine her sweet, little nana having an emotional affair. Perhaps Nana and Francesco had become close friends, and the letters were a big misunderstanding, Brinkley tried to convince herself. But Mama Donna continued to add details.

"Look, Elizabeth, I was upset when I found out too. I didn't even want to tell you. And Nana was scared of what you girls would think if you ever found out – that's why I was surprised she gifted you that pouch!" Mama Donna looked into something in the distance with gritted teeth. "I could kill my brother."

"Wait," Elizabeth snapped, "my pouch *is* from a lover?"

Brinkley slouched in her seat and scanned the restaurant, making awkward eye contact with the hostess who glanced their way. She sunk further into the booth.

"Elizabeth, why are you getting so upset about this?" Mama Donna asked. "Francesco mailed the pouch to her as a gift. It was very special to Nana."

"What? She didn't even get it while she was in Italy?"

"Well, it's from Italy. Francesco had the pouch made for her and mailed it as a gift with one of his letters. This is all according to Nana's journal—"

"Nana kept a journal?" Brinkley said. "Does Avery know?"

But their mother's eyes were trained on Elizabeth. The splotches on Elizabeth's cheeks spread across her temples.

"I thought Nana was this independent woman, buying that coin pouch with her own money, as a gift to herself ..." Tears welled in Elizabeth's eyes. "Now I'm finding out my gift was really from a lover? I'm about to get married! Why would she gift me that?"

Brinkley's eyes were darting between Elizabeth and her mother. "Elizabeth, I don't think Nana gifted you the pouch to comment on your own relationship, I just think—"

Elizabeth cut Brinkley off, her eyes piercing the rose quartz ring. "Oh yeah, Brinkley? How would you feel if you found out this ring wasn't from Grandpa, but from an affair with a man Nana never even talked about named *Francesco*?"

Brinkley snatched her ring closer to her and looked at her mom.

"Don't worry, Nana was telling the truth about that one," Mama Donna said, nodding towards Brinkley's ring before looking back at Elizabeth. "Please get a hold of yourself. You're starting to make a scene."

"You haven't seen a scene yet, Mother!" Elizabeth shrieked. "Avery was right – all my life, I've defended you and Nana with no question. Do you know how many times I've fought with Avery defending you? Meanwhile, Nana was somebody's mistress!"

"Or somebody's pen pal," Brinkley whispered, trying to soften her family's voices in the process.

"Look, my mother and father loved each other, but there was never any passion in their relationship—"

"What do you mean?" said Brinkley, eyeing her mother with a disgusted look. "She and Grandpa loved each other."

"Of course they did, but who knows how many mistresses my father could've had—"

"What!" Elizabeth and Brinkley both shrieked.

"Okay, could we keep it down," Mama Donna asked, scanning the restaurant. "I like coming here for lunch and I don't need the staff knowing about my parents' affairs."

"What is even happening?" It sounded to Brinkley as if Elizabeth had started to hyperventilate. "All this time we were brought up to believe Nana and Grandpa had this great marriage, and now that they're both dead we're finding out they had affairs? What, were they like swingers or something?"

"Elizabeth, don't be dramatic. They were not swingers—"

"So, they were cheaters? Like that's any better, Mother!" Elizabeth hissed.

"Look, girls, I don't know why you're getting so worked up about this," Mama Donna said, picking up her spinach wrap to resume eating. "I admit, I was upset when I was younger," she said as she chewed, "but Nana broke it off with her lover as soon as she got caught, and the older I get, the more I realize, no family is perfect."

"I thought Nana and Grandpa were loyal, and devoted, and oh, I don't know, loved each other," Elizabeth said. "My whole life has been a lie!"

"Elizabeth, you're acting a bit naïve about this. They did love each other. In their own way," Mama Donna said. "Nana was an adventurous woman before marrying my father. And he was a good father and all, but ..." Mama Donna shrugged, using her hands to shoo away the sentiment. "He was also controlling. And Nana waited on him for everything."

Now the maroon splotches were draining from Elizabeth's face, along with the rest of her color.

But Mama Donna continued, "If harmless love letters gave my mother some passion, why not let her have it? Gosh, sometimes I wish I had started an emotional affair while I was married. Maybe it would have been easier to deal with your father's affairs if I had had a few of my own."

"Well thanks, Mom, thanks a lot for that beautiful marital advice." Elizabeth blew her nose into the napkin. "Did Grandpa ever find out?"

"Oh my gosh, yeah. All thanks to my brother, of course ..." Mama Donna rolled her eyes. "He could never keep his mouth shut."

"How did Uncle Terry find out?" Brinkley asked. Her heart was thudding so hard, she could hear it in her ears. "And does Uncle Terry believe Nana and Grandpa had passion for each other?"

Mama Donna looked at both of them, from Elizabeth's pale face, to Brinkley's trembling hands. She leaned into the table.

"So, your Uncle Terry knows quite a few things about your nana ..."

Chapter 33

Elizabeth stormed through the front door of her and John's cabin. John was seated in his upholstered armchair, a glass of whiskey in one hand, a pile of papers filled with black smudges and crossed out sentences in the other. Elizabeth had experienced this scene many times before, and knew it meant John was reading a draft of one of his chapters. Usually, Elizabeth would offer encouraging words or ask to read his work. This time, Elizabeth was on a mission and was not going to let the sight of her future husband or his work get in her way.

"Darling?" he asked, his eyebrow raised as she stomped past him, into their bedroom.

"Darling?" he called after her, but it was no use. Elizabeth's mind was too distracted by the task at hand to bother answering him.

Flinging open the wardrobe doors, Elizabeth began feeling around until she pulled out the crimson-red leather pouch her nana had gifted her and chucked it across the room.

When she looked up from her rage, John's body was blocking the doorway, eyebrow still raised.

"Tough day at work? It's not tax season, is it?"

"John, tax season ended in April!" she yelled. "It's July!"

"Okay ..." John wrinkled his eyebrows and seemed to tip-toe across the room. Keeping his eyes on her, he bent down and lifted the pouch between his fingers. "So, do you want to talk about why you threw this across our bedroom? Isn't this your nana's pouch?"

"Yes," Elizabeth said, crossing her arms. "But no, I don't care to talk about it."

John tilted his head, his eyes studying her for a moment before he took a seat at the edge of their bed. "Okay, well ... would you like some good news?"

Elizabeth stared at him.

"I called my sister, and you will no longer be kidnapped to Cabo. I was clear and firm, Elizabeth."

"Your good news is that I won't be kidnapped by your family? Shouldn't that be a given?"

"Well, Jordan mentioned that ... maybe ... a better time to throw you a proper bachelorette would be after her baby is born. I tried to explain that you will never want one, but she insisted you might feel differently after —"

"So instead of putting an end to the problem now, you displaced it onto our future selves ..."

"I will make sure you don't get kidnapped to Cabo, Elizabeth. Not now, not ever. I promise."

"That's great, John," Elizabeth muttered, but it was all she could respond before John revealed more:

"Also, my mother called."

Elizabeth felt her heart skip a beat.

"She's wondering when we're going to reschedule the meeting to finalize the itinerary for our wedding—"

A loud groan escaped Elizabeth's lips. She rocked her head back to look at their wooden beamed ceiling, as if cursing the heavens.

"I don't know, John. Can't she send the itinerary in an email?"

"Well, they want to make sure we're happy with what they've

planned—"

"What does it matter if we're not happy with what they've planned?" Elizabeth snapped. "It's not like anything will change! We can save ourselves a bunch of time by telling them to email us the schedule, and we'll be sure to show up on time and go along with the program."

"Okay, what is going on?"

Elizabeth looked away from the ceiling, towards their bird feeder outside, and muttered, "I should never have gone to the medium. Now Avery and I are fighting, and I was the one who was wrong."

"Well ..." John began, and when Elizabeth looked at the crease between his brows, she could tell he was scanning his mind for the correct words.

"Just say it, John," Elizabeth said. After her visit to the medium, she had briefly told John about her fight with Avery. His suggestion was to call her younger sister and work things out. To "create space" for their differing viewpoints. At the time, Elizabeth had been too stubborn, too confident in her own beliefs to care about creating space for her sister's.

Now she just felt stupid.

"It's never too late to call your sister," John said, his eyes locked onto Elizabeth's. The gray flecks matched the overcast sky outside. "Everyone's been wrong at multiple points in their lives. Just call her and admit your mistake. Problem solved. But what, exactly, were you wrong about?"

"No, John, not problem solved!" Elizabeth said, wanting to shake him from his seat at the edge of the bed. For someone who obsessed over every word and detail in his books, John was always ready to oversimplify the realities of life. "I just discovered my nana is not who she claimed, who I *believed* she was! I can't exactly hop on the phone right now and apologize to Avery. I'm still in shock, John.

Shock."

"Darling ... what happened? Start from the beginning."

Elizabeth looked at her fiancé, who was always eager to listen, to help. She felt her shoulders drop as she exhaled a breath.

"Growing up, Avery and I always disagreed—"

"Maybe a summary?" John suggested.

With a clenched jaw, and flared nostrils, Elizabeth glared at him.

"I'm sorry, I want to help, I really do, but maybe in a time-efficient way." John's thick eyebrows wrinkled together as he studied Elizabeth's reactions to his words. "You've told me so many details of your childhood, I could write a whole book about it." He tilted his head at the wooden floor beneath them. "Maybe I should write a book about it ..."

"John, you can't exploit my troubled childhood! Are you insane?"

"No, Elizabeth, I'm sorry," John stammered, lingering on the bed as he looked up at her. "It was a silly idea. I don't even know if anyone would want to read about something so ... tragic," he concluded, but then quickly mumbled, "Although it could make for a great tragic comedy..."

"Oh my gosh," Elizabeth breathed, bringing her hand to her aching forehead. "John, can you get out of your writer world and come back to the real world, please? I am in shock over the events that transpired today, and I kinda need some support!"

"Right. Of course. I'm sorry," John said, nodding to his own words. "So, what happened?"

Releasing a loud breath, Elizabeth turned her body to face John. "So, you already know about that crazy story Uncle Terry told about Nana and a man named ..." Elizabeth felt the name stuck in her throat, she couldn't bear to utter it again.

"Francesco?" John finished for her.

"Yeah." She cleared her throat. "Well, at lunch today my mother admitted it was all true."

John raised his eyebrows, but the rest of his face remained still.

Elizabeth narrowed her eyes at him. "Why don't you seem shocked?"

"Well," John bowed his head, shielding his eyes toward the wooden floor beneath them, "I never thought it was untrue ..."

"This whole time you believed my uncle?"

"Why are you so upset by that?"

"Because you acted like that pouch was a beautiful gift, John! How could you think it's a beautiful gift if you believed it was from a lover?"

"One does not cancel out the other?"

"Oh my gosh!" Elizabeth shrieked, feeling the veins bulge from her neck. "If you ever got a lover, John, I would burn you and your writing studio to the ground."

"What?" John's eyes widened. "Elizabeth, take a deep breath and come sit with me, please."

Shaking her head, Elizabeth was pacing across their bedroom now.

"Elizabeth, *you* are my lover," John declared, the depth of his voice stopping Elizabeth from her zoo-like pace, but only for a brief moment.

"John, you said she gifted me that coin pouch because I'm an independent woman—"

"Well, I'm a writer, Liz. I create stories in my head all the time," John explained with a shrug. "Doesn't mean you should listen to them."

With a groan, Elizabeth rolled her eyes. "You're going to be my husband, John! I want to be able to listen to you!"

"Well, I think you should listen to yourself—"

"I tried!" she yelled. "Turns out, I'm not that great of a person to listen to, either. I thought my nana was an angel, John. A faithful angel. Turns out, Uncle Terry and Avery were right all along! My nana was—"

"Human," John finished, his eyes locked onto Elizabeth's. "A human, just like you, and just like me. It's not fair to compare her to other standards."

Something was caught in Elizabeth's throat as she stared at her fiancé now. She had to bite her lip to stop it from trembling.

"Still, John," she said, collapsing next to him on their bed, "even for human standards, I never expected her to be a ... a cheater. Even if the affair wasn't physical. It was emotional — somehow that seems worse. I could never do that to you. To anyone. She should've divorced Grandpa if that's how she felt."

"Elizabeth ..." John took her chin between his hands. "You are judging your nana based on your experiences."

Elizabeth blinked. "So?"

"Imagine if you were born into a different time, with a different set of parents, and found yourself in a different kind of relationship ..."

Feeling her body cool at her fiancé's words, Elizabeth found herself nodding along, even though she wasn't sure how this sentiment would end.

"We shouldn't judge others for lives we've never lived," he said, letting go of her face and taking her hands. "I mean, it's not like she's going to end up in history books," he added with a shrug. "She just got mixed up in her own life. It happens to all of us."

"But why would she gift me a pouch from her lover, John?" Elizabeth whispered, withdrawing her hand. "We're about to get married. I don't want a gift from her affair!"

There was laughter in John's eyes, as if the shades of blue were overtaking the gray.

"Elizabeth, maybe it's not so literal," he said, reaching for her hand again. "Yes, we are getting married, but maybe in your nana's eyes, what we share is much more than being husband and wife. She seemed to want much more out of her marriage," he said, giving her hand a squeeze. "Maybe she looks at us as though we're more like lovers."

Allowing her hand to slip into John's, Elizabeth considered this rebranding of her gift.

"How do I know this is not another one of your stories you're just telling me to make me feel better?"

"Elizabeth, everything we tell ourselves is a story," he said. "Just listen to the one that feels right for you."

Chapter 34

"*I'm freeeee to cliiimb, freee to cliiimb ... My nana was a liar and it's all riiiiight ...*"

Avery was driving along the highway, belting out her made-up tune from the depths of her soul. Her car radio had been broken for years, and after hours of driving to the mountains of West Virginia, she needed to provide her own entertainment.

Every verse grew louder.

"*Now Nana's in heaaaven, and she's got some skeeeletons ...*"

Her windows were rolled down and her frizzy hair whipped in the wind as she sang.

Her phone started ringing.

"*I wonder who she'll choose to see, her lover or her huuubby,*" Avery continued singing, but her phone's ring was relentless, throwing her off-key.

She cleared her throat, and without taking her eyes off the road, tried feeling for her phone. When she glanced at the screen, she saw the name "Richard" flashing.

"Why is he calling me?" she asked aloud, even though she was driving alone. Her dad never called her. She sucked in a breath and accepted the call.

"Avery!" Richard's voice cheered. "It's me, Dad."

"Yeah, I know. How are you?"

"I'm good. Just wanted to tell you to come over at two o'clock tomorrow."

"What?"

"I'm having a barbeque at two o'clock tomorrow, for Fourth of July weekend."

"Oh, I didn't know that was, like, an actual plan."

"What do you mean? I told you at Lily's birthday party."

"And then I never heard from you again, so I didn't think it was still happening. Sorry, Dad, I'm actually on my way to the mountains for the weekend."

"You're what?"

Even over the sounds of the highway wind, Avery could hear the disgust in his voice.

"I'm on my way to the mountains. You're calling, the mountains are calling ... I feel so popular these days."

"Are you high?"

"What? No, I'm just happy."

"You know what, Avery, I'm getting tired of this. Every time I host something, you make a million excuses not to come."

"I'm not making a million excuses, Dad. I'm telling you one," she said, gripping the phone with all her strength because she felt the conversation escalating and predicted she was two sentences away from chucking it out the window.

"I bet if your mother was having everyone over, you'd be sure to show up."

"If Mother was hosting anything while I was driving to the mountains, I wouldn't, because I'd be driving to the mountains," Avery said.

"You're going to the mountains, Avery? Really? How convenient that it's on the same day as my barbeque."

"Yeah, I'm going camping," Avery said, pressing the phone into her ear. "You used to take us camping, remember?"

"Yeah, until your mother took that from me, too."

"Right, yeah, I remember that," Avery said, but her eyes were focused on the mountains growing against the highway ahead. "Good old childhood memories, huh?"

There was a pause.

"My barbeque is tomorrow at two o'clock. I expect to see you there."

Avery couldn't help but laugh as the mountains around her continued growing in size and depth. "I told you. I'm on my way to the mountains. This isn't some excuse to get out of your barbeque, Dad. This is my life."

His voice became sinister when he spoke now. It always happened in a flash – that tone – disorienting the people it spoke to as they tried to retrace what had been triggered, where the conversation had gone wrong. The voice reminded Avery of memories she had once been afraid of. The times when her mother would push him too hard, make one too many accusations about his late nights at the office, or use her words to degrade his character, and her parents' arguments would transform from one of words, to one with discordant sounds happening behind slammed doors. It was always a conflicting combination of relief and torment, when her father would pack his bags and leave for a hotel, often after he and her mother had changed into conservative clothing, her mother with a face full of fresh makeup, and together, her parents would sweep the shattered glass or tape over the newest hole in the wall.

"The Poconos are two hours away," he spat. "You can turn your shit car around and make it to my barbeque on time. I have an important announcement to tell everyone and I expect you there."

Avery felt the force of anger expand through her body, rising through her chest. For years, her father's anger had intimidated her into submission. He was a different human when he was happy, when things went his way. Avery had grown up never wanting to say or do anything that would set him off.

But the thing about anger, she realized now, is that it's transformative, and it infects the very people who obey.

"You can expect me," she said, ignoring the tremor in her voice. "But I won't be there. I've had enough, Dad."

From the driver seat of her so-called "shit" car, with the hum of the highway and the world passing before her eyes, Avery didn't offer her father a chance to respond. She hung up and placed her phone in the cupholder.

Chapter 35

"Your skin is going to love this exfoliation," Brinkley's esthetician of many years, Aimi, cooed as Brinkley lay back on a chair with a warm towel draped across her face. "Especially after all that time in the sun during your vacation. Where'd you go again? Fiji?"

"Um, no ... The Caribbean."

"Ugh, right. I can't keep up with all my privileged clients," Aimi said. "Was it amazing?"

"Yeah," said Brinkley, "it was, it really was. The girls had the best time, but ..." Brinkley cleared her throat. "Do you ever feel like something is ... missing ... in your life?"

"Every paycheck," Aimi snorted to herself. Brinkley made a mental note to tip extra today.

"Right," she said, and tried closing her eyes beneath the towel, but the complete darkness only made the ambient music playing seem more apparent and obnoxious.

"But I think I know what you mean," Aimi said, her hands leaving Brinkley's face for a moment.

"You do?" Brinkley asked, hopeful.

"Yeah, I do. Before I met Noah – that hot psychiatrist I was telling you about – I always felt like something was missing in my life. Turns out it was antidepressants."

Brinkley tilted her head, causing the towel to droop below her eye. Aimi reset its position. "Really?"

"Yep. All those years of feeling hollow inside and getting panic attacks – turns out it's not the only way to live. You just have to pop a pill every day."

"Well, that's great," Brinkley said, but even underneath the comfort of spa sheets and the aroma of soothing essential oils, she felt her senses deflate. "So, you took antidepressants and realized ... nothing is missing from your life?"

"Pretty much," Aimi said, and now removed the towel in replacement of thick steam. "Or ... maybe something is? I don't know. I don't consider those questions any more."

"I see ..."

"Why? You think you want a prescription? Noah can hook you up."

Brinkley could hear the tinkering sounds of Aimi mixing a face potion together.

"Um, that's okay," Brinkley began, although the thought of being able to feel complete with the pop of a pill was tempting. "What does it feel like?"

"Taking Prozac? It feels like I'm more level. Like I can get through a day of work without invasive thoughts or a panic attack taking over," Aimi said. "Other than that, I don't really notice much."

"That sounds kind of nice."

"Yeah ..." Aimi sighed. "But everyone's different. I don't want to be on it forever, you know?" Before Brinkley could respond, Aimi continued, "Anyway, why do you ask? Is everything good with you and Chase?"

"Yeah," Brinkley said, but the silence that followed made her feel self-conscious. "I don't know ... He's a wonderful father. And he's a wonderful husband. I mean, we just had a great vacation together."

"Well, there must be a reason you're here *after* the vacation, saying something's missing from your life."

"I know," Brinkley said, her voice quiet against the ambient music. "I just don't know what it is."

"Is the spark gone? You have two little ones running around with a husband who's building a business. I can't imagine the strain that would put on my relationship."

"I mean, we still have sex ..."

"Like what, once a month?" Aimi said, and her fingers moved softly across Brinkley's face in slow, circular motions. "Maybe you both need a day away from the kids and experience something new together." There was a pause before Aimi gasped. "Wait, I think I have some Molly in my purse! You two should do that together, then you'll really fall back in love."

"Why do you have Molly in your purse?" Brinkley's eyelids flew open.

Aimi dropped the damp cloth overtop Brinkley's eyes again. "Don't judge me, it's from the concert Noah took me to last weekend."

"That's very ... kind of you, but I don't think taking MDMA with my husband is what we need right now."

"No, you're right," Aimi agreed, and began to massage Brinkley's shoulders. "Sometimes we just get bored in our routines. Maybe you need a break."

"I had a break. I just got back from vacation."

"Oh, right," Aimi said, and her hands paused their massage for a moment. "Well, maybe you need another one. Alone. No husband, no kids. Just you, a glass of wine and some alone time."

Brinkley pondered this as her friend's hands continued to massage her skin, and then wondered at what point she had begun considering her esthetician her friend. Shouldn't there be someone she could share these feelings with, other than a woman still working for her on the clock? For as close as she considered herself with her sisters, and as much time as she spent with her mom friends, why was her esthetician, a woman she saw no more than an hour every month, the only person she felt comfortable admitting her truth to?

"Maybe you're right," Brinkley sighed, and tried settling deeper into the facial chair. "Things have been ... confusing, lately ... after my nana died."

"Oh right!" Aimi gasped. "I'm so sorry about that."

"It's okay, really," Brinkley said, but could feel more words on the tip of her tongue, begging to be released. "It's just, recently I found out some ... secrets ... about her, my nana. And it's only added to the confusion. I think."

"Ooh, secrets? What happened?"

"Oh nothing, I just, I found out my nana had an affair," Brinkley said before she could stop herself. "A love letter affair, not like a physical affair ... Well, I guess you can never be totally sure if it got physical, but, the man lived in Italy, so ..." When Aimi did not offer to fill the awkward silence, Brinkley finished, "Probably wasn't physical."

"Well, a lover from abroad, that's kind of cool," Aimi said as her hands moved swiftly across Brinkley's skin.

"Yeah, apparently my grandfather found out. Eventually. And they decided to stay married, so ... I guess that proves true love."

"Yeah, although in that day and age, who knows," Aimi said. "People stayed in horrible marriages all the time. People still do!"

Brinkley felt her body begin to sweat beneath the spa's towel.

"Good point, I guess," she said, thinking of the ring safely stored in her jewelry drawer at home. It felt too scandalous to wear at the moment. "You know, before my nana passed, she gifted me this beautiful ring my grandpa had gotten for her ..."

"That's a special gift!"

"Is it though?" Brinkley said. "At first, I believed it was this beautiful symbol of love she had given because she believed in my marriage, but now ..."

"Now you're wondering if your nana ever really loved your grandpa, or if her heart was with her lover abroad?" Aimi finished.

"Yeah ... Ow!" Brinkley said as Aimi began to dig out her blackheads.

"Sorry, girl, your skin seems more stressed than usual."

"That's because it is," Brinkley muttered.

"Well hey, I still think your ring is a symbol of love," Aimi said.

"You do?"

"Yeah, I mean, life is long. Shit happens. Your nana raised a whole family with your grandpa, so that's what's real. The other guy ... Now that's just a fling, a fantasy."

"Yeah ..." Brinkley said.

Images of a beautiful, heartbroken young Nana writing love letters to a man who wasn't their grandpa had made a home in her mind.

Still, Brinkley sighed. "That's true ..."

Chapter 36

After an hour of re-reading instructions and tinkering with equipment, Avery stepped back to admire her work. Her two-person, mustard-yellow tent stood like a proud little triangle. The tent had been purchased when Avery was in high school, when she could fall into depression's grips and still latch on to a sliver of hope that there was a future worth surviving for. A future filled with possibility and adventure. Now she understood what a blessing it was to even have that.

Avery circled around now, trying her best to adjust her eyes to dusk's light to check for any errors. It was no use. She fumbled through her backpack and switched on her headlamp for help. One of the guy ropes that secured her tent to the ground looked too lax. She bent to the ground, dirt getting underneath her fingernails as she pulled the peg from the earth and tugged the string tighter. Since she'd forgotten to pack a hammer, she grabbed the jagged rock she had found nearby and tapped the peg in place.

With a sigh of tired triumph, Avery looked at the cloudy evening sky. She felt a bit reckless in the dark. Somewhere between her father's call and setting up her campsite, her plan to drive hours away from home, and to camp in the West Virginia mountains, alone, had transformed from a great idea of the heart to a foolish one of the mind.

When Avery had been stuck in her small city apartment, the trappings of her modern life had been so apparent to her; it was a never-ending stream of work, conversations, and commitments. Not to mention all the confusion and anger that seemed to creep its way into her family's dynamics following Nana's death. It seemed everyone was grieving, but no one was grieving together. Each member of her family was trapped in their own story, trying to find where Nana's life and death belonged in it.

You're a disappointment.

The old words of her family members hijacked her thoughts, but it wasn't in their voices any more. It was in her voice, and she could hear herself loud and clear alone in the night.

Fat raindrops began to fall from the sky, shattering on her head and every nearby twig. Avery felt something in the depths of her stomach churning. It made her dizzy. *What am I doing here?* was all she could think.

Because she was alone, in a campsite hidden by towering trees, she looked up at the falling clouds and asked the question out loud.

"What am I doing here?"

Chapter 37

"What are we doing here?" Elizabeth asked John as they walked across the bakery's parking lot.

"What do you mean? We're going to watch my parents taste wedding cake," John said, his eyes focused on the small, redbrick building that looked more like a house than a bakery. He smoothed over his hair, even though it was already gelled to the side without a loose strand in sight.

"Okay, well, we have my dad's barbeque right after, so it seems like a lot to pack in. Especially when we already picked a wedding cake," Elizabeth said. "A delicious wedding cake, by the way, that we both agreed on months ago." She tried to keep up with John's tense stride while she was in strappy nude-colored wedges. "Besides, is it even a cake tasting if the bride and groom aren't going to taste it?"

John stopped walking and faced his fiancée. "I already told you, my family is worried about having a dairy-free wedding cake. They want to make sure the guests enjoy it, too."

"Well yeah, I want our guests to enjoy it too, but don't you think your parents should try the one we picked before assuming people won't like it? And don't you think they should have brought this up months ago, when we were actually planning the menu? I mean, to switch it so last minute feels sneaky."

"I don't know, Elizabeth. My family is trying to help, okay?"

"Whatever."

"Why did you agree to come to this cake tasting if you have a problem with it?"

"I don't know, John. Maybe I've had time to actually consider how our wedding is being handled. It seems like we're shells of ourselves."

"What?"

"We're the only ones compromising on decisions for *our* wedding," Elizabeth said. "The last time we discussed our wedding cake, you agreed that we didn't need to have dairy in it. I don't want our wedding cake to originate from the crime of a baby being stolen from her mother, just so humans can make some kind of fucked-up cake with the mother's milk."

"Well, we can have two wedding cakes."

"John, when we discussed our menu, we agreed we didn't want food that came from animals. I mean, if your family wants to pay for a separate wedding cake, fine. But what's next? A rack of ribs passed around after we say 'I do'?"

John remained silent.

"Oh my fucking gosh," Elizabeth said, and could feel her face turn to fire. "Oh my gosh – they're trying to change our whole menu, aren't they?"

Just as John began to nod, Elizabeth heard a shrill voice call from behind: "Hello darlings!" A muscle in Elizabeth's jaw twitched as Mrs. Astor approached, leaning in for double air kisses.

"Hello, Mother," John greeted with a hug, "Father."

"Well, what are you doing out here?" Mrs. Astor said. "Have you met the baker yet? He's the nicest little old man."

"He took good care of our Jordan's wedding," Mr. Astor confirmed, his posture straight as always, and his hair gelled to the side like John's, though his receding hairline was becoming more apparent every year.

Elizabeth had always thought John inherited hints of the best genes from each of his parents – his mother's full head of healthy hair and her mesmerizing, jewel-toned eyes, but his father's tall, broad build, and voice that had as much depth as an A-list actor. Though, where John's personality came from, was entirely his own creation.

"Well," John said with a smile on his face, but Elizabeth could hear the impatience in his voice. "Let's get on with it, then."

As everyone began filing towards the front door of the bakery, Elizabeth tugged the sleeve of John's button-down shirt.

"We can discuss it later," he muttered to Elizabeth. His parents were only a few steps ahead.

"John, I don't know what you told your parents, but we are not serving ribs, or any other body part of a dead animal at our wedding," she hissed, stopping in her tracks. "I do not want death being served on the day that's supposed to celebrate love and life. *Our* love and life."

"Keep your voice down! You're starting to act like one of those crazy vegans."

"You know what, when we gave up meat, I did think full-on vegans were a little crazy. But the more I live, the more I wonder if it's the *world* that's crazy, John," Elizabeth spat. "Female cows are being forced to get pregnant and have their babies *stolen* from them so that humans can put the milk in wedding cakes that all the guests are going to complain about anyway!"

As her in-laws opened the door of the dairy-filled bakery with John close behind, Elizabeth felt every fiber of her being tense.

"I need to go home," Elizabeth heard a voice say. When all eyes turned towards her, she realized the voice she had heard was her own. "I'm sorry ..." she began. "I feel really nauseous, and I need to go home. John, the keys please?"

The faint lines in John's face grew deeper. Keeping his eyes on Elizabeth, he fished the car keys out of his pocket and handed them over.

She had to yank the keys from his fingers, he was gripping onto them so tight.

"Oh no!" Mrs. Astor clasped her hand over her heart. "I did hear a stomach bug was going around. Do you want John to go home with you? My husband and I can handle selecting the cake."

Elizabeth kept her lips pressed shut at Mrs. Astor's nerve to offer her the services of Elizabeth's own fiancé. John remained still, his hands glued inside his pockets. His eyes were trying to negotiate with Elizabeth, the ends of his eyebrows sagging in desperation, but his mouth remained closed. Elizabeth wanted to laugh, or maybe scream and cry, at the irony of her future husband remaining so clear about everyone else's lives, yet unable to face his own story. The story of a boy who had been born into a family who could provide him anything, help his wildest dreams come true with their professional connections and lavish checks mailed every few years. Yet, with the same ease, his family could snatch it away at any moment. And now all that boy wanted was to start a new life as a man, but it would always be within the cage he had learned to depend on the comfort of.

Without a further second wasted, Elizabeth clutched the keys in her hand and looked at Mrs. Astor, who had the corners of her mouth curled. "That's all right, you can keep him," she said.

With a tight smile, Elizabeth turned on her wedges and stalked across the parking lot, to her slick black car she had chosen with her own money.

Chapter 38

"Where's Avery?" were the first two words that came out of Richard's mouth when his other daughters entered the front door of his house.

"Hi to you too, Dad," Elizabeth said, her voice flat as she appeared to clutch the casserole dish she had brought even tighter. "The drive was long – a lot of traffic. Thanks for asking."

Richard looked at Brinkley from beneath his dark, overgrown eyebrows. "What's her problem?" he asked, even though Elizabeth was standing right there.

"Um ..." Brinkley paused to glance at her sister. Elizabeth looked as though she were trying to cast a hex on their father with her intense gaze. "There was a lot of traffic."

"Yeah, and my in-laws want to serve dead animals at John and my wedding," Elizabeth added.

Brinkley had listened to Elizabeth's in-law drama the entire ride over. She had never felt more grateful for Chase's family then after hearing the horrors of what lurked behind the double wooden doors of the Astors' estate.

"Oh, thank goodness," their dad said. "A plant-based menu would have been terrible. The guests need their meat."

"Then why," Elizabeth's smile was as tight as her words, "did you ask me to bring my *meat-free* potato casserole?"

"I mean, I've enjoyed the things you've cooked, but people don't go to a nice wedding to eat tofu, Elizabeth."

Elizabeth's face developed splotches that were a shade of red Brinkley hadn't seen on her sister before. Except, perhaps at lunch a few days ago, when Elizabeth had learned about Nana's emotional affair ...

"Am I the only one who thought people attend weddings to celebrate the bride and groom?"

Richard chuckled. "Just let it go. A little lamb chop won't kill you."

"No, Dad, but it kills the lamb. Vegetables won't kill *you*. In fact," Elizabeth was nearly snarling as she stepped towards her father, "it would help your high cholesterol you always complain about and maybe even your bitter heart."

In one flash, Brinkley watched her sister raise the casserole dish over her head and bring it down with a smash on her father's black-and-white tiled floor.

"What the hell is wrong with you!" her father shouted, his eyeballs looking as though they were ready to pop out of his head and roll right into the mess.

Elizabeth stood in the broken glass for a moment, her collarbones jutting against the fabric of her cream-colored blouse. Her blouse that was now splattered with yellow casserole pieces.

Before anyone could see her cry, she raced towards the bathroom, her beautiful, long ponytail swaying with her steps.

"I don't know what the hell her deal is," said Richard.

Brinkley's mouth was open, but no words came out.

"She's cleaning this up," he added before walking away.

For a moment, Brinkley's gaze got lost in the mess of potato pieces and shattered glass.

What the hell ... she thought as she stared. *I asked Chase's parents to babysit for this?*

The truth was, Brinkley could have brought her kids to this barbeque. They would have been overjoyed to see their grandude. But then the process of getting here would have become a production, which was especially hard to deal with when Chase was working. Not to mention, once getting here, her girls would never want to leave, which made getting home a whole other production. Brinkley wanted this barbeque to happen like a hit-and-run. A small obligation to check off before she could enjoy the rest of her Saturday in peace.

As she tiptoed around the fragmented glass and food pieces, she couldn't help but feel that her children were better behaved than the adults in her life.

When she approached the large bathroom door, heavy sobs could be heard from the other side. The kind of sobs that made it hard to breathe, to even exist.

Brinkley nudged the door as gently as she could and took her thirty-year-old sister into her arms.

"I'm—under—so—much—stress," Elizabeth managed to say in between sobs, her chest rising and falling against Brinkley's embrace.

"Oh, honey," Brinkley said, releasing the hug. "What's going on? You can't let him get to you like that."

"But he can be horrible. He's not contributing a cent to our wedding, but he has the nerve to insult the kind of food I want? He hasn't even given it a try!" Elizabeth's sobs had slowed as she spoke, but now were beginning to pick up again. "He's my dad. What is his problem?"

"Unfortunately, a lot of things." Brinkley sighed. "He likes things his way. And hey, you like having things your way, too. That's just how people are." Brinkley squeezed Elizabeth's hands in hers. "You have to stay strong in what you want and not let people get to you, okay?"

At least you know what you want.

"That's easier said than done, Brinkley, when other people are the ones paying for the whole ordeal."

"Why don't you try having a conversation with the Astors and find a compromise that works for both of you?"

"Because, Brinkley, they don't know the meaning of compromise. This isn't just a fad diet John and I are trying out for a year. This has been our life for *years*. I compromised on the wedding venue, the photographer, the guest count, the guest list, not to mention I've listened to all the unsolicited advice with grace, as much grace as I can muster, anyway—"

"Okay, where are you going with this?"

"My point is ..." Elizabeth looked at Brinkley, her tears were wiped away and replaced with bloodshot eyes. "I've compromised a lot. Not just for this wedding but my entire life. For one night, John and my *wedding* night, I want the people who love me and John to just respect us for one thing. I don't want to compromise on this one thing, Brinkley. For One. Damn. Night."

As Elizabeth's body began to tremble, her voice sounded as if it came from the deepest place in her throat. "One night is all I am asking for, for these people – these people who are supposed to love us, by the way – to just respect me, and John. Our choices."

She sank further onto the black-and-white tiled bathroom floor, her hands covering her face as her body shook with sobs. "Why is that so hard for people to do?"

Watching her sister's hunched body shaking on a bathroom floor, Brinkley knew she had to do something. She grabbed a handful of tissues and crouched so her eyes were level with Elizabeth's.

"Listen to me," she said, and gripped her sister's shoulder. "This is your life."

Elizabeth looked at her through reddened eyes.

"Your life, Elizabeth. Stop asking for just one night of it."

A wave of calm seemed to wash over Elizabeth as she continued to look into Brinkley's eyes and took a deep breath.

"Now listen," Brinkley said, "we are going to get off this floor, clean up that casserole, and then we can either get the hell out of here, or stay to find out what train-wreck announcement Dad has for us this time."

The last time their father had invited his daughters over for an "announcement" was a few months after Elizabeth had gotten engaged to John.

Their dad's announcement? He was also engaged – to his girlfriend of a few months. And wait until they saw the ring! Brinkley would never forget the look on her sisters' faces when Cynthia – Sin – had flashed the bulging diamond of her engagement ring. Avery had seen her college tuition, and Elizabeth had seen the price of her wedding, two things their father had refused his daughters, sparkling on the ring finger of his newest flavor of the year.

The flavor of Sin was a bitter one, indeed.

Brinkley remembered going to bed that night thanking her lucky stars she had grown up before the divorce had turned their father sour towards his role as the provider. Growing up, he had ensured meals were on the table, the lights stayed on, and the family could take a vacation every now and then. When the divorce was announced, Brinkley had been in college, long after her father had made it clear she'd be able to graduate without debt, and though she did have to major in business, Brinkley had developed an interest in her classes easily.

While Elizabeth and Avery had been living at home, making it clear they favored their mother's side – though Avery was often a wildcard who could snap at either parent at any moment – Brinkley had been at college, assuming the role of peacemaker. It never sat well with Elizabeth or Mama Donna, but choosing neither side was the only

YOU DON'T KNOW NANA

control Brinkley felt she had in the disintegration of her family as she knew it. And the smile her father would give every time she came around, his whole face lit with hope, made the disagreements with her sister and mother worth it.

So, when Brinkley had announced her engagement to Chase, it hadn't been a question of whether her father would pay. But as the years ticked by, with Elizabeth and Avery slow to come back around, often choosing to spend holidays with their mother while Brinkley split her time, Brinkley could see the years wear him down. More wrinkles around his mouth, deepening themselves into a semi-permanent frown. Brinkley was excited when Elizabeth had wanted to introduce her new boyfriend, John, to Richard, thinking it was the first step towards peace. But Richard had extended a stiff hand towards John, and the conversation that night had felt jagged and awkward. It was then that Brinkley had realized that some wrinkles were too deep to hide.

Brinkley glanced in the bathroom's oval mirror, checking to make sure her forehead was still smooth, as if the memory itself could age her. With her reflection's smooth reassurance, Brinkley walked to the hallway closet to collect paper towels, a broom, and a dustpan. When she walked out of the closet, she saw Elizabeth crouched against the shattered dish, picking up the big pieces of glass with her bare hands.

They were cleaning up the mess, but Brinkley felt a pit in her stomach.

Chapter 39

Streams of sunlight had woken Avery this morning. Her body felt stiff from sleeping on the floor of her tent, and her hair was matted to her forehead in the summer heat. Once she unzipped her tent to reveal rows of evergreens, and allowed their pine scent to expand her lungs, she felt as though a tonic were easing her aching muscles and clearing her mind. It lasted a few moments, but it had been so long since she had felt clarity, a few moments felt like a gift.

What am I doing here?

It was the question she had gone to bed and woken up with, but she found it easier to answer in the sunlight.

She had come here to hike. Avery had spent weeks asking unsolvable questions and agonizing over possible answers. Now, she was alone in the mountains. There was no greater place to learn how to let go, when there was a whole mountain to climb. One didn't reach the summit by holding on to excess baggage.

After gathering her gear, which consisted of a small backpack, trail mix, a peanut butter banana sandwich, plenty of water, a headlamp, and a map, Avery embarked on the trail that would take her miles up a mountain, to a scenic overlook at the highest point in West Virginia. She'd be able to see the expanse of sprawling Appalachian Mountains.

After years of no practice, she was nervous to take on such a long hike. But she also felt she had nothing to lose from trying.

After following the music of a trickling stream for miles, Avery came to a fork in the trail. One path continued to follow the melodic water. The other path led into a dense cluster of evergreen trees. When Avery was younger, she used to pick the path that "felt" right. The one she was more drawn to. She'd end up getting lost in various forests until some kind hiker would give her proper instructions or she would get sick of wandering and use her map to get back on track. *No wonder my mom thinks I'm gonna get murdered out here,* she thought with a chuckle as she reflected on the memories of getting lost now.

There were no signs or trail markers visible from this fork. There hadn't been many the entire hike, and when she did stumble on one, each looked more run-down than the last. After a few minutes of studying her surroundings, she picked the trail that led upwards, away from the moving stream, into the dense cluster of the forest. Following the stream meant following the flow of water, so she knew if she wanted to climb the mountain, she would have to start climbing opposite of where the water flowed.

Tightening her backpack, Avery began the ascent into the forest. The trail was much darker under the shadows of the trees. For a moment she looked up, but all she saw was a rich green ceiling of overlapping pine needles. Grabbing a swig of water from the bottle in the side pocket of her backpack, she followed the slight curve in the trail and stumbled on space.

Avery's chest rose as she inhaled, but the forest was quiet. It was quite literally taking her breath away; she didn't want a single sound to disturb the moment.

There were no more trees guarding the trail. All that consumed her gaze was a meadow of wildflowers and rolling hills of the Appalachian Mountains, stretching for miles underneath an angry gray sky. The trail of the forest seemed to end, or perhaps transform, into a footpath of this hushed, vast meadow.

With her breath still full, Avery waited in the shelter of the forest for a moment. Her gaze swept across the open space, and she felt her foot take a step. A bird released itself from its hiding spot in the canopy, its small brown wings flapping against the overcast sky before finding shelter in another tree.

Releasing her breath in a slow, quiet movement, she felt her chest relax towards her heart and she began to follow the skinny footpath of the meadow. Wildflowers, in vibrant brushstrokes of orange, pink, and purple lined the path she walked. The more she searched for wildflowers, the more her eyes spotted them.

Her legs grew heavier as she neared the middle of the meadow. She looked around, for any sign of an animal or fellow hiker, but she was alone.

Yet she did not feel alone. In the silent space of wildflowers, tall grasses, and evergreens, she could feel her own presence with her, guiding every step she took.

Chapter 40

The shade from their father's redbrick house offered cool relief from the July sun. It was Cynthia's suggestion to eat outside. So here they were, outside, Brinkley and Richard in charge of setting the table while Cynthia was nowhere to be found. Elizabeth remained seated in the uncomfortable patio chair, swatting at a mosquito.

"Thank you for, uh, cleaning that mess up," Richard said, clearing his throat after he put down the tray of burgers.

Elizabeth felt her cheeks flush in embarrassment. Her father was obviously referring to the casserole she had purposely shattered on his tiled floor just an hour earlier. At the time, anger had surged through her body, possessing her muscles and mind to release the casserole dish into the air. In the moment, it had felt sickeningly satisfying to shatter that dish. But once that moment had passed and the anger was released, Elizabeth had been left with the same emotions she had come to Richard's house with – stress and shame. Not to mention a giant mess.

Clearing her throat, Elizabeth nodded at her father. "Yeah, uh, of course."

Part of her wanted to apologize for overreacting to his comment about plant-based food. The other part of her, however, was desperate for him – for anyone – to understand her reaction.

Before she could make up her mind, Richard had already moved on.

"It's a shame your partners couldn't make it," he said, just as he assumed his seat at the head of the table. "And where are my grandbabies?"

"Lily and Daisy are with Chase's parents today," Brinkley said, taking the spot between Richard and Elizabeth. "Chase had back-to-back appointments all day, so he couldn't make it." Brinkley smiled tightly. "Business is booming."

"That's great! You're lucky you married a hard worker, you know."

I told John if he came I'd chop his balls off, so... Elizabeth reflected as she sipped her chilled glass of Chardonnay.

"I was always working when I was married to your mother," Richard was grumbling now. "Always just trying to provide for you guys."

"Uh huh," Brinkley said, drawing out the word. "So you've told us." She coughed.

Elizabeth was too drained from the day to stick up for her mother the way she usually did. Instead, she stared at her father, who was seated at the head of his long, empty table in his big, vacant backyard.

The backyard patio was stunning, though, she had to admit, with its various shades of redbrick contrasted against deep green ivy that climbed up the walls of his house. The patio overlooked her father's rose garden, which surrounded a plain circular fountain against a backdrop of tall shoots of Juniper trees.

Roses were her mother's favorite flower. Elizabeth always found it curious her father had planted a whole garden of them, but her father's voice chopped through her thoughts.

"And where's my future son-in-law?"

"Also working," Elizabeth lied.

"Isn't John a writer? Can't he choose his own hours?" The irritation had become even more apparent in Richard's voice now. "The last time we talked, you said he'd come."

"John is an artist, Dad. He can't choose when inspiration comes."

She had to bite her tongue – it was such a blatant lie. Most days, John was on a strict schedule, waking up at the crack of dawn and staying in his studio till dusk, creating and deleting and transforming the scenes of his stories whether the inspiration came or not. Today, however, he had agreed to make an exception to his schedule so he could attend this barbeque. Still, her father would never know the process of writing a book, so it seemed too easy and convenient of a lie for Elizabeth to pass up, to help her avoid having to explain what had really occurred at the bakery.

"Okay ..." Richard said the word slowly. "And where's Avery? I set up this whole barbeque and no one comes?"

"I didn't know we were considered no one," Elizabeth muttered and took another sip of her Chardonnay.

"Avery's camping," Brinkley said. "She needed a getaway. I think things have been ... hard ... for her, since Nana died."

"She's actually camping?" Richard said, scratching his beard. "I thought that was an excuse."

Before Elizabeth could ask him what he meant, Sin's baby voice cut through the air:

"Are you all waiting for me?" she said as she stepped onto the patio, a long, fluffy animal cradled in her hands. "You didn't have to do that!"

Elizabeth took one look at the furry animal, one look at her glass of Chardonnay, and began to chug. After a few gulps, she snapped her head towards her father. "Whose animal is that? And *what* is that?"

Sin clutched her bedazzled floor-length, turquoise-blue shawl tighter as she floated towards the patio table. "It's our ferret, Daisy!"

"Yeah ..." Richard smiled and then sneezed. "We wanted to name her after our grandbaby."

"You mean my *daughter*?" Brinkley said, and Elizabeth noticed beads of sweat beginning to form on her sister's forehead. "I don't know how I feel about that."

"Dad, aren't you deathly allergic to animals?" Elizabeth said just as Richard sneezed again.

"Ah, I have medication," Richard shook his head, his eyes watering as he rubbed them. "I'm fine."

Sin hovered over the table. "It smells delicious, Richard! Now what did we make ... burgers and hot dogs?"

Richard sneezed again.

"Maybe we should put the ferret inside," Brinkley suggested.

"Or in a shelter!" Elizabeth said. "We're going to have to call an ambulance by the end of this dinner."

"Oh, Daisy, it's okay," Sin said, making her voice sound even more like a baby's when she talked to the animal. "Not everyone can handle your cuteness."

When another sneeze escaped Richard's nose, he looked at Sin and nodded. "Maybe it's best," he agreed.

"Oh, Richard, come on," Sin said, her plump lips forming a pout. "I'll sit at the other end of the table. You'll be fine."

Without further argument, Sin sat at the opposite end of the table with Daisy the ferret latching onto her shoulder, trying to crawl – or escape, except for its owner's hands gripping its slim body.

"Um, I don't think he will be fine, *Sin*," Elizabeth said, glaring at the weasel just as her father released another sneeze. "That thing is going to kill him."

"No, Daisy's a sweet little girl," Sin said as she smoothed her hands over the ferret's fur. "Isn't that right, Daisy?"

"That's not how allergies work," Elizabeth said, leaning a bit too menacingly towards Sin as she felt her face twist in disgust.

"What other names were you two entertaining?" Brinkley wondered aloud.

"Enough!" Richard bellowed, his bloodshot eyes glaring at everyone seated. "It's time to eat. I've been barbequing all afternoon and I'm starving."

Richard's voice had always had a unique quality to Elizabeth. There was something soft about his tone, but lurking beneath the softness was a guttural rasp struggling to be heard. Elizabeth always wondered if it was from the years he used to smoke, or the years he'd lose his temper.

Everyone at the table held their breath as they eyed one another, the plates of food between them.

"I'm starving too," Brinkley said, her voice quiet. "This looks great. Thanks for grilling, Dad."

"Yes, thank you," Sin said, looking around the table. "Did anyone make a side dish?"

"I mean, I made a potato casserole, but ..." Elizabeth gulped the rest of her wine instead of finishing the sentence.

"The patties in front of Elizabeth are all hers," Richard grumbled, but looked at Elizabeth with a relaxed face. "I made sure they're plant-based, don't worry. Hope I grilled them okay."

Elizabeth felt her jaw soften. "Thank you." She grabbed the bottle of wine sitting between her and Brinkley and poured herself another glass. *I might as well put a straw in this bottle,* she thought, eyeing the ferret, whose little claws were still latching onto the sequins of Sin's shawl.

"Where's Avery?" Sin wondered with a pout. "We have special news for everyone."

"Why is everyone so concerned about Avery!" Elizabeth snapped, setting the bottle down with a *thunk.*

"She's camping," Brinkley said and checked the time on her phone.

"What's the announcement?"

"Is she still ... What is she doing this time around?" said Richard.

"Oh, stop it, Richard," Sin giggled, tucking a strand of her hair behind her ears.

Elizabeth felt her eyes drawn to the obnoxious diamond sparkling on her future stepmother's finger. She pictured what wedding planning would be like if she didn't need to rely on the Astors' money, if she had a father who treated his daughters as well as he treated his girlfriends.

Of course, Elizabeth and John could bring their finances together, dip into their savings, and afford their own wedding, sans ballroom and four hundred guests. But the Astors had insisted on paying, presenting the offer as a wonderful opportunity to save money for an unforgettable honeymoon, or "whatever they so wished". The offer had been too good to pass up, the Astors too insistent to be swayed, and Elizabeth never wanted to put financial pressure on John, as he was trying to follow up "his life's biggest success" with his next book. Now deposits had been placed, a photographer and fourteen-piece wedding band booked, a dairy-free cake selected, and a dairy-filled wedding cake about to be added to the menu.

As Elizabeth sat at the long, rectangular table, the seat across from her haunting her with its emptiness, she tried to trace her way back to how she had gotten so deep into planning a wedding she now despised.

"Yes, Avery's still a bartender," Brinkley said. "She's been doing it for a few years, you know. I think she should open her own bar one day. She's great at engaging with people."

Elizabeth eyed Richard, who was resting his chin on his thumb, his fingers balled into a fist.

"I don't know," he said, but his voice was quiet against the chatter of the birds. "I don't know with that one."

"Neither did Nana," Elizabeth snorted. "Maybe it's the one thing you two have ever agreed on."

Though she couldn't see the details of her father's eyes from where she was sitting, they looked like a murky glass, lost in thought about a past that would never be explained or confessed.

"While we're all here and not throwing casseroles," Brinkley said and side-eyed Elizabeth, then leaned onto the table with her elbows, "what's the exciting announcement you have for us?"

Richard glanced at Sin, and Elizabeth noticed him give her a furtive smile.

"I mean, we wanted Avery here, but who knows when we'll see her next, so ..." Richard looked at his daughters, his eyes gleaming in the sunlight. "We booked a venue and date for our wedding."

"Oh! Congrats," Brinkley said and raised her water glass to their dad.

"That's exciting," said Elizabeth, her voice flatter than usual as she took more gulps of her wine.

"Thank you," said Sin, and repositioned the ferret, whose eyes were wide and claws spread – as if equally confused and terrified about his presence at this dinner – to her other shoulder. "The venue is gorgeous."

Elizabeth found herself still nodding along. "When's the big day?"

"September twentieth," their father said, and finally began to assemble his burger.

Elizabeth stopped nodding. She could still hear the chatter of the birds, could still see Brinkley's eyes widen and sense Sin's stare, but it all seemed faraway, distant.

"September twentieth?" Elizabeth repeated, her heart beating faster. "Of ... Of what year?"

The only thing that did feel clear to Elizabeth was her father as he squeezed ketchup onto his burger and tore through a bite.

"This year. Couple months away."

She imagined pelting her father with the uneaten hot dogs one by one until there were none left. But even her imagination couldn't bring her joy.

"You mean ... right when John and I are getting married? Dad, September twentieth is ..."

There was a tremble in her voice when she spoke, making it sound as though she were laughing, because her options were to either laugh or have a mental breakdown. Which would be her second one of the day, so Elizabeth chose laughter.

"That's right. The Thursday before your wedding. I figured it would make travel easier for everyone – you know, all the cousins, aunts, and uncles. Everyone's so spread out these days and not everyone likes to travel – this way they can just make an extended weekend out of it."

Elizabeth could feel Brinkley and Sin's eyes studying her, but her father's words were all she could hear.

Then she heard her own voice speak.

"Dad," it said, but it was all she could bring herself to say.

Her father kept eating his burger.

"If your side of the family doesn't want to travel twice in one year," Elizabeth began, her heart beating so fast her chest was starting to hurt, "I'm sure they would travel for you and Sin the year after—"

"No, we're not waiting that long," he said, and squeezed more ketchup out of the bottle.

"Why?"

"You don't want to be bride buddies with me?" Sin cocked her head back in a laugh. "You don't want to go wedding dress shopping and menu tasting together?"

"Hey now, don't go tasting with her," Richard chuckled. "She wants to make the whole thing plant-based."

"Oh, Richard!" Sin laughed.

Elizabeth looked at Brinkley, who was staring back at her, while biting her lip, her eyes wide with compassion.

She looked back at her father, who was still busy eating his burger.

Still, Elizabeth tried to find the words. "I don't think John and I will be comfortable with you getting married *two days* before us ... I mean, is that really necessary?"

Richard dropped his burger onto the plate and snapped his head to face Elizabeth.

"Let me make one thing clear, Elizabeth," he said, placing his elbows on the table, and clasping his hands together. It felt as if his eyes could pierce through a part of her, but Elizabeth wasn't sure which part. "The venue is booked. I didn't invite you here for a discussion. I invited you here to celebrate. You and John don't own the month of September, Elizabeth, and other than my family, we won't share too many of the same guests. So why," he said, leaning forwards, his gaze locked on her, "are you making our date a problem?"

There was a pause. Even the ferret was still.

"Maybe you both should discuss this another time. Maybe privately ..."

As Brinkley's voice cut in, Elizabeth could feel the sound of the singing birds and trickling fountain come back into focus.

"There's nothing more to discuss, but sure," Richard said, his voice firm.

Why are you making our date a problem? Elizabeth considered. She felt there was an answer to his question, but in her newfound numbness, nothing about her wedding seemed worth the fight any more.

Chapter 41

The dark clouds that had once been forming and transforming in the sky were now unified as one overcast, texture-less gray cloud Avery seemed unable to escape.

Rocks lined each side of the trail with short, leafy shrubs scattered throughout. Clusters of spruce trees, of various ages, and a coral-shaped, mint-green moss Avery had never seen before, could be spotted every few feet. Every now and then, a bare, sinister-looking tree with thick, straggly branches would mark its place on the open mountaintop.

Avery missed the music of the stream. Without it, she was left with the narrative of her mind. As she walked along the rocky terrain, she was thinking of her adolescence – of when she was fifteen years old in the passenger seat of her father's dark silver car, driving home after a fun camping trip. Avery hadn't known it then, but it would be the last camping trip they would take together.

If only she had known, she considered now, replaying the phone conversation Avery had had with her father only yesterday, when he had told her to "turn her shit car around". If she had known it would have been her last camping trip with him, she would have done more to soak that weekend in.

Then again, maybe she would have done a lot of things differently.

Kept her mouth shut instead of being so quick to speak her mind. Sometimes it felt like her adolescence was an endless battle of pleading with her parents to be nicer to each other one week, only to be angry and yelling at them both the next. Though she had fought with her father more. During the divorce, he had refused to leave the house, stumbling home drunk, often with a nasty monologue about the world for anyone willing to listen. Avery would retreat to her room. Rather than continuing to love someone who was making those decisions, Avery had let the fights with her father dwindle into a cold indifference. He would write her cards every Christmas, cementing his love for her in writing, and Avery had accepted each one, but offered nothing in return. Not a hint of love or sympathy.

After a few years, her father had stopped writing her cards. At the time, Avery felt he had done the bare minimum. Surely salvaging a relationship with a child should be worth more than a few years' try. Now, Avery couldn't think of those nights he stumbled home, or those words written in the cards, without feeling a stab of the imagined pain her father must have been experiencing alone.

And had any of it been worth it? Had her arguments, her anger, or her indifference helped either parent become more understanding of the other side? Or had it created a wedge between them all, and trained Avery to bury her feelings in her adult life, until there were too many to bury and she exploded.

But it protected you, a part of her mind shot back, as Avery forced her tired legs to continue climbing up the rocky trail.

It protected me, she tried to accept the thought, but her heart still beat fast. She forced a short exhale through her nose and continued putting one foot in front of the other.

While offering this mental confessional to the mountain, Avery also had to admit she'd probably wait to get that nose piercing and forearm tattoo for when she was of age, instead of doing it herself. At the time, her family had acted like she was rebelling for attention. In reality, she had wanted to decorate her body with things that brought her joy in a world that was constantly trying to tell her how to look and feel about herself. But the way her family had reacted to it, the way her parents had seemed to take it so personally, made Avery burn with shame.

Maybe if she had done these things differently, had shared less of her mind and hidden more of herself, then she and her father would still be able to go camping together, and have different conversations on the phone.

Then you would be happy, wouldn't you? The corners of her mouth curled in a smug smile from realizing the ridiculousness of her regrets. But her mind was quick to pull her back into memory.

It was always quick to drag her back.

Her father had seemed particularly happy during their last camping trip. On their way home, he had been smiling, allowing her to listen to her favorite songs on the radio and turning up the volume when his favorites came on. When her dad was that happy, with his smile spilling into his eyes, Avery had sworn she knew what love between a parent and child was supposed to feel like.

As Avery walked along the mountain now, she couldn't remember what song was playing on the radio when they'd pulled into the driveway. All she remembered was the sharp tone that had escaped his lips.

"What the fuck," he'd barked when they drove up to the garage. Avery's nana and grandpa were in their driveway, helping her mother load boxes of belongings into the trunk of her minivan. Avery remembered the way her father had kicked open his car door. She thought he had broken it off. The way he had stormed towards her mother, Nana, and Grandpa as if they were strangers stealing from his house.

His hard work paid for those things, her father had yelled.

Her hard work put all those things to good use, her mom had screamed.

Avery remembered making eye contact with Nana as they remained standing in the driveway of their daughter and son-in-law's house. Their hands had been full, their bodies still. While looking Avery's way, Nana had offered her a smile, a box still clutched in her grip. *How could she smile? Why would she smile?*

Avery had wondered about it then, and still didn't know the answers as she walked along the rocky trail now. At the time, it had seemed almost offensive for Nana to stand there, smiling, while her parents had screamed at each other in the driveway. It had felt as though Nana's smile was giving her blessing to the chaos that had infiltrated Avery's home.

Maybe Nana's smile had been innocent, coming from a desire to help. But at the time, all Avery had known was that she couldn't bear witness to yet another fight.

Instead, Avery had gotten out of the car and stepped between her parents, had tried de-escalating the argument like she had attempted so many times before. But this time she had been on her father's side, ready to argue on behalf of his getting blindsided. That's when Nana had pulled her away from her mother and father.

"Don't get involved in adult arguments," Nana had scolded Avery. "And *never* go against your mother like that. Go inside. Everything is fine." Here was Nana, one of the few people Avery trusted, standing in her parents' shared driveway, telling Avery not to get involved in an argument she was already involved in, whether she spoke up or not. Her parents were screaming at each other, using pots and pans as substitutes for their real issues as their fifteen-year-old daughter watched from the window inside.

This wasn't the only time her grandparents had hushed her, forbidding her from getting involved or speaking up. Her grandparents had been too focused on the fragile state her mother was in during that time to consider the enduring effect it would have on their granddaughter. They'd loved Avery, of course, but they hadn't wanted to hear what she had to say.

It hadn't taken long for Avery to realize that in this divorce, no one – not even her grandparents – was going to be on her side. No one was going to let her speak and no one was going to speak for her. Her parents would spend years fighting over her custody, but through the arguments, it became harder to figure out what they were fighting over any more.

Exhaling the memory, Avery forced her body to continue stepping up the rocky terrain. As she climbed, she realized her grandparents may never have had a clue about the inner demons of depression Avery was inheriting during that time. But a young mind is often confident, especially when the self-esteem is weak, so Avery didn't smile at her nana then, and didn't return calls later or make visits beyond ones she was forced to. And she'd made it clear, with the scowl on her face and the silence in the air, every time she was visiting out of force.

Nana loved to put up fronts, Uncle Terry's words reminded her. She pictured Nana's smile again, as Nana clutched the box of belongings that didn't belong to her. Avery tried to picture the smile from her nana's point of view.

Everything is fine, her nana had claimed during a time in Avery's life when nothing had felt fine.

I don't know where you've been. I don't know where you're going ...

You never wanted to know where I was, Avery wanted to scream at the angry clouds above. *You only wanted people to live in your lies.*

Fat rain droplets began to fall, creating dark marks on the rocks of the trail. Avery released a heavy exhale, trying to calm her tense muscles.

Now her grandparents were all dead, somewhere else. Or nowhere. Her father's father had abandoned his family when her father was in middle school, so Avery never got to meet him. He often haunted her memories as a sad, lost soul.

Sometimes he was something much darker.

Avery's father's mother had raised him, juggling different jobs while trying to raise a family. They'd developed a close bond, but Avery had never got to witness it, because life had taken its toll, and she had had a heart attack before Avery was born. Avery's dad didn't remark on his past often, but when he did, his mother's presence always pervaded his memories. Sometimes her father would retell the story of how his mother had learned to sew just so he could have a new suit to the dance. The story would end as abruptly as it had begun, her father never a fan of living with ghosts. Yet his abrupt ending of his mother's memory only made Avery wonder if he was reliving his mother's death over and over again. Never granting himself permission to linger, to say the goodbyes he had been denied.

Mama Donna's parents had died within a couple years of each other. When Avery had stood by her grandpa in his final days, not once had he mentioned her growing distance over the years. She had been touched by his generous heart, assuming his silence about her distance was representative of his unconditional love and forgiveness.

Yet, as her footsteps became heavier and sloppier, causing her to stumble along the stone trail that was becoming slick with rain droplets, another thought haunted her mind.

How naïve to think silence means forgiveness.

Because Avery was lost in thought, the parking lot at the top of the mountain seemed to come out of nowhere, even though her whole day of hiking had led her here.

"What the ..." she breathed, nearly tripping on to the smooth black tar of the road.

One car was parked there. Avery spotted a sign next to it that read:

"Welcome to the Top of Mountain State. Highest point in West Virginia. Elevation 4863 feet. Observation Tower 900 feet."

Before hiking, Avery had known there was a road that led to a parking lot at the top of this mountain. It had been paved years ago, to make the Observation Tower more accessible to people who couldn't, or didn't want to, climb a mountain. Still, as Avery looked past the sign and across the vacant lot now, she felt as if nothing could have prepared her for the strange feeling of entering a paved road after spending the whole day hiking the wilderness to get here.

The observation tower was a humble structure elevated above the spruce trees so people could get a fantastic, clear view of the rugged Appalachian Mountains. Even though Avery had worked for this view, this moment, she couldn't see even a few feet in front of her.

She was quite literally stuck in a cloud.

She began to feel dizzy when a woman with long braids started to emerge from the clouds surrounding the trail to the observation tower.

"Excuse me!" Avery walked towards the woman. "Were you just at the observation tower? Can you see anything through this cloud?"

"Nah, afraid not," said the woman, and Avery could see the woman had a delicate gold nose ring as she neared. The woman pulled the keys out of her black rain jacket and the headlights of the only parked car lit up, though muffled by the cloud.

"Did you ..." the woman looked at her with a raised eyebrow. "Did you hike all the way up here in this weather?"

"Yeah," Avery said, observing the misty haze that seemed to be closing in on them by the minute.

"Did you know you could have driven?"

"Yeah," Avery said with a nod. "I wanted to hike, for some reason."

"Cool," the woman said, pulling the hood of her black rain jacket over her head as the raindrops fell more frequently. "How'd you like it?"

"It was ..." Avery took a moment to think, though all the thoughts that had been running through her mind had left an empty yet foggy space behind them now that she was put on the spot. "Hard," she concluded, too tired to try to think of any more words. She looked around her, trying to envision the scene of the sprawling mountains that the cloud was blocking. "I did it for the mountain view, but ..."

"Can't control the weather."

"Can't control a lot of things."

"Well, congrats." The woman offered a soft smile. "You made it anyway."

Avery felt her eyebrow twitch at this admission.

The woman walked towards her car. "Hey, you need a ride back down or anything?" she said, pausing by her car door.

"That's okay," Avery said. "I think I have a few miles left in me."

Avery looked back at the trail. At all the steps she would need to retrace. Without giving herself time to back out, she pulled her headlamp from her backpack.

She was going to hike until her feet were weary and her mind was still.

Chapter 42

After Richard's barbeque, Elizabeth felt drained of emotion. By the time Brinkley dropped her off at home, making her swear she would call if she needed anything – as if Elizabeth would ever take someone up on that offer – Elizabeth could no longer support herself and felt her body collapse behind her closed front door.

She took a few breaths, feeling the emptiness that pervaded her and John's cabin.

After sitting in her own numbness, watching the sun coat the earth in its golden light and elongate the shadows of the trees outside, Elizabeth picked herself up. She cut across her and John's backyard, past their fire pit, to the shed they had transformed into John's writing studio.

Psychedelic rock was blaring from the shed, and Elizabeth felt its vibrations with each step she took.

Through the crack of the parted doors, Elizabeth could see her husband's forearm covered in ink. His back was hunched over his notebook, his dark brown locks undone from the gelled comb over he had styled earlier this morning to meet his parents.

As she watched his hands glide along the paper beneath him, bringing life onto a blank space, Elizabeth felt a tug in her heart.

All she wanted was to forget their disagreement over wedding cakes and menus. Or whatever that disagreement had been about. She was willing to let it all go, just to be held in the security of her fiancé's arms.

She tapped on the large shed door. Usually, John hated being disturbed while in the middle of writing, but this was an exception. This was for making up.

She began smoothing her fingers through her long ponytail, thinking of how nice it was going to feel to exchange apologies, or perhaps skip the apology in exchange for a kiss. She would have her friend – her future husband – back, and they would make fun of his parents' choice of wedding cake and her father's ridiculous wedding date.

But John didn't come to the door. And the more she thought, the harder it was to imagine the humor.

I mean, what was there to laugh at? Elizabeth considered.

Haha, your parents liked the vanilla cake? How did I guess? Oh, and my father is getting married two days before us. To a woman who is going to kill him with a ferret and collect all the money in his will! How hilarious, let's laugh some more!

With wrinkled eyebrows, she knocked on the shed door once more and waited.

And waited.

Peering through the crack, she could see her husband still hunched over his work, his head bobbing, his writing hand moving with the rhythm of the music.

She shoved the door open.

"Hello?" She waved her hand in front of his face.

With wide eyes and wild hair, John looked up.

"What?" he shouted over the music.

Elizabeth rolled her eyes and jabbed her finger onto speaker's power button. "I've been waiting outside, knocking, the past ten minutes,

John," she said.

John looked directly in her eyes. "Why? The door was open."

Elizabeth pursed her lips.

Looking Elizabeth up and down and raising his eyebrows, John said, "Well, now that you're here, may I offer you a glass of wine?"

"I need one," Elizabeth muttered.

"It's been out here a bit, so it's probably warm by now," he said, pouring a glass of deep red liquid. He glanced at her with a subtle smirk. "Just don't tell my parents."

"Disobeying your parents' proper rules?" Elizabeth raised an eyebrow. "Are you trying to seduce me?" *And is it pathetic if it's working?* she wondered.

"I mean, I'm always trying to seduce you," John said as he handed Elizabeth the delicate stem of the glass. He took a step closer and said, "You just don't let me."

"Yes, I do," she said, but rolled her eyes and pressed the glass to her lips just as he leaned in for a kiss.

With raised eyebrows, John took a step back.

Elizabeth looked at him. "What?" she asked, even though he hadn't spoken. John opened his mouth to speak, and then closed it.

"Okay, maybe recently I've had some trouble getting in the mood, but I've been under a lot of stress, John,"

Still, John remained silent. The empty space lingering between them allowed the memories of the last twenty-four hours, as well as the past six months of their engagement, to possess her brain once again. All the bookings and bills that had to go through the Astors, appointments they had had to attend, the once-exciting but now dull conversations about venues, food, decor, dates ...

Head spinning, Elizabeth felt the unwanted truth rise from her chest, up her throat.

"My dad announced he's getting married the Thursday before our wedding."

John leaned his head back to observe her as she chugged her glass of warm red wine.

"Wait ... What?" he said, when she brought her half-empty glass down.

Apparently, he needed her to repeat it. Yet Elizabeth couldn't bring herself to say it again, so she offered a nod. "Yep."

"And this isn't one of his weird, cruel jokes he likes to do to make himself feel powerful? Like when I asked for your hand in marriage and he told me to get a real job?"

"Nope. I mean, maybe it is, but he's actually playing it out this time," Elizabeth said, feeling her hand tremble as she brought the glass of wine back to her lips. "As if he didn't do enough damage during my childhood, now he's trying to infiltrate my adulthood, too. He and Sin already put the deposit on the venue and everything."

"But why? Why would he want to get married *two days* before his daughter?"

"He said it'd be easier for all the cousins, aunts, uncles to be there." Elizabeth shook her head as she took another gulp of wine. Her heart was beating as fast as it had been when her father first made the announcement. She began pacing around the shed.

"My dad said his family doesn't like traveling twice in one year, or some bullshit like that? I don't know. His whole family is spread out, so he figured people could make an extended weekend out of it ..."

"Then why doesn't he postpone his wedding a year? Or two! This is his second wedding – what's his rush?"

"I don't know, John. He said he doesn't want to wait that long—"

"Is he a toddler? What does he mean he doesn't want to wait that long? He barely knows Sin! Maybe that's a sign he *should* wait that long."

"I don't know, John. He just said he doesn't want to," Elizabeth repeated, bringing her fingertips to her forehead as she continued to pace.

"He doesn't want to ..." John nodded as he repeated the words, but there was a strain in his calm voice.

"What?" Elizabeth stopped in her tracks, snapping her attention to John, who was now crossing his arms.

"I guess that's how you and your family handle things. When you don't want to do something, you just don't do it. You just ... take the keys and drive the car," he said, adding under his breath, "figuratively and literally."

Elizabeth narrowed her eyes at John. "Is this about me leaving you at the bakery?"

"Yes, it's about the bakery."

"Then just say it's about the bakery, John. Don't speak in riddles trying to compare me to my *dad*."

"I just *said* it was about the bakery." John let out a long breath, his broad chest deflating. "While we're on the subject of ... difficult parents – you hurt me when you left me *alone* with mine, Liz."

"Okay, let's just chill on the dramatics for a sec," Elizabeth said. "I left you alone, John, after you dropped the *bombshell* that your parents want to change our whole wedding menu after we spent *months* selecting one!" Now Elizabeth's voice was the one getting loud. "And there was no reason for us to be there in the first place! Do you know how ridiculous it is that your parents wanted us to *watch* them eat *our* wedding cake?"

"Not this again—"

"You're the one who brought it up!"

"I just wanted you to know I was hurt, Elizabeth. Am I allowed to have feelings? Or are you trying to condition me into toxic masculinity just like my father!"

"Oh my gosh." She rolled her eyes and heard herself let out a laugh

— a mangled, twisted laugh — at the ridiculousness of his statement. "As if I don't hear enough about your feelings! Every month there's a new one you're 'exploring' for your art. I hear about you, and your feelings, and your work, *all* the time!"

"Darling," he said, letting out a long breath through his nostrils.

"You want to know *my* feelings, John?"

"Yes, Elizabeth! Yes, I do. It's like ... It's like your heart has been Fort Knox the past few months and all the old keys don't seem to work any more—"

"You are *literally* controlled by your entire family!" she shouted, feeling her armpits begin to sweat as she lunged her upper body towards him. "I knew your parents were powerful, but holy shit, John, it's like they take people's heads and fill them with air—"

With a gaping mouth, he recoiled from her words, but she pressed on.

"How many family gatherings do we need to go to, John? How many humblebrags do we need to hear?" Elizabeth began to pace across the shed again.

"I thought you enjoyed the gatherings!" he shouted.

"In the beginning, I did! When we started dating, I was twenty years old, John. I barely had a voice or self-esteem of my own."

Even though her face was flushed and her voice raspy, Elizabeth couldn't have shoved the words back down her throat if she had wanted to. The key to her heart had apparently been found, and she was ready to unleash its contents all over the floor of her fiancé's writing studio.

"I was *desperate* for your family to like me, but I'm thirty now, John! I have my own mind – a mind they never bother to ask about, by the way – and I don't want to spend my few days off work to watch your parents eat wedding cake—"

"I thought we were talking about my family's gatherings! Now we're back on the wedding cake?"

"We're talking about it all, John! I've spent ten years – a whole *decade* – listening to your family shove unsolicited advice down my throat and I have had *enough*!"

"Well, do you think it's how I want to spend my days, Elizabeth? You don't think I'd rather spend that time writing, or making love to you? I go because I want my trust fund, Liz. We've talked about this. We just need to suck it up now, so we can live a better life later!" he shouted, his face growing red.

"Later may never come, John! Our life keeps ticking by and we may never create a life outside your parents' cage!" She slammed the studio door behind her as she left.

"Elizabeth!" she heard John call. "Elizabeth! You can be mad at me all you want, but don't take it out on my studio!"

"Shut up, John," she yelled across their backyard. "Kill me off in your next book because *I'm dead inside.*"

Chapter 43

"Sounds of Nature" filled Brinkley's Calcutta marble bathroom as she soaked in a bubble bath of her free-standing, white porcelain tub. Lily and Daisy had been tucked into bed an hour ago, and Chase was still working in their bedroom next door, so Brinkley decided to take Aimi's advice and treat herself to some relaxing alone time. This was her first time bathing in the tub since she and Chase had purchased the house years ago.

She tried leaning her head back with one full breath, but her neck grew sore within seconds. The towel she had placed between her neck and the curved edge of the tub was not enough. Perhaps she needed to buy a bathtub pillow.

Or something.

Flickering, unscented candles lined her bathroom's white marble vanity. They were supposed to keep the room washed in romantic light. Yet all Brinkley could think about as she eyed the flickering flames now was what a fire hazard bath time had become. Had she really needed to light twenty candles? The more she stared, the more she realized the flickering light was giving her a headache.

She looked back at the bubbles with a huff, but the bubbles weren't fascinating, either.

Fluttering her eyes closed, she tried to become one with the sounds of a forest playing from her phone. The sound of birds chirping was her last straw. With a loud sigh, she stood from the tub, but her movement was too fast, too sloppy for the slippery porcelain, and she fell on her butt in one swift motion.

"Ouch!" she yelped, her voice echoing through the bathroom as her bubble bath transformed into a blood bath.

During her fall from grace, Brinkley must have swiped a chunk of her butt on the tub's faucet, creating a thick gash in her right butt cheek.

"Ouch," she repeated, this time encased in heavy sobs.

"Are you okay?" Chase was in the bathroom, his rectangular glasses framing his panicked eyes. "What happened? Is that blood?"

"My butt, my butt, my butt," Brinkley heaved, her hand reaching to put pressure on the wound.

"What happened?" Chase said as he tried to catch his breath. He held out a towel.

"Not our white towels!" Brinkley shrieked.

"Sorry!" Chase grabbed a beige one.

Oh whatever.

Brinkley snatched the towel and took her husband's hand to help her out of the tub.

"I tried getting out of the tub and slipped," Brinkley cried, her butt throbbing. "I think my butt cheek was cut on the faucet."

Sure enough, when she looked at the bathtub's faucet, it was covered in blood.

"Do you need stitches?" said Chase.

"I am not getting stitches on my ass, Chase."

"You might need them!"

She limped over to the mirror to look at the gash. Bad idea. She covered the gruesome scene with the towel again.

"I need a Band-Aid."

Chase was already sifting through their vanity drawers. Before he finished pulling the band-aid out, Brinkley had seized it from his hands.

"Chase, this size is for a paper cut!" she said, throwing the band-aid back at him.

"Right, sorry," he said, and began riffling through the drawers again.

She snatched the larger-sized band-aid from him. The last thing she needed was her husband to see her butt like this after he had already witnessed what had happened to her body during birth.

"I can put it on," he said.

"Thanks, but I got it," she said. When he didn't move, she widened her eyes at him. "Can I have some privacy? I'd like to at least try to keep our passion alive, before we end up like my nana and grandpa!"

"What? Brinkley, there will always be passion—"

"Chase!"

"Okay, jeez," Chase muttered, and left her alone.

Her reflection in the mirror stared back at her. Brinkley sighed. At least her face looked fresh from her facial. She ripped open the bandage and twisted her body so she could see her butt in the mirror. Dripping blood and cellulite stared back at her. Dropping her towel, Brinkley took a moment to stare at her new, naked body. Its stretch marks, its larger, curvier shape since birth. For a moment, she actually appreciated her new curves, her fuller boobs and butt.

Then she imagined all the other bodies out there, the bodies with a thin waist and voluptuous curves. A flat stomach with somehow big boobs. She tried sending self-love to her insecurities. Tried imagining her stretch marks as tiger stripes, but it was damn near impossible when it didn't feel like her body any more.

It didn't even feel like anyone else's body. At least, not anyone on the movies she watched, the ads she saw, the billboards she drove by.

Not really. She couldn't even find a body that resembled hers in her family or friend group.

Who did this body belong to?

Brinkley wet a paper towel and dabbed at the blood starting to stain her skin. With another sigh, she placed the bandage over her wound.

When she had given birth to her daughters, she'd felt as if they were little puzzle pieces she had never realized had been missing from her life. Even with all the morning sickness, body changes, and life adjustments, Brinkley couldn't – didn't even want to – imagine what her life would be like without them.

Now her family felt complete, but the puzzle of her life suddenly felt as if it had come undone. Chase and Brinkley were more than comfortable with their income, and fulfilled with the size of their family. As she rewrapped herself into a new towel, she wondered what else could possibly be missing. She had her health, and her loved ones had their health. She had the most beautiful, loving family, and a husband who supported and provided for them.

Since she couldn't find any flaws on her own, she grabbed her phone. After turning off her nature playlist, she enlisted the internet for help. She knew it was silly, but she wanted an answer and she wanted it now, so she typed: *I feel like something is missing in my life.*

And into the internet hole she went.

Chapter 44

A very tossed and turned in the humid summer night.

She loved nature, she truly did, but did the crickets have to chirp this loud? It's not like they were at a damn rave. With a sigh, she sat up from her sleeping bag and began to scratch the tattoos on her arms. She smacked her forearm, feeling the sting of a bug bite. The crickets continued chirping.

Nature was not interested in her inner melodrama.

Avery released a long breath into the loud night, the sound of it like a heavy crashing wave dispersing through sand. She unzipped her tent to peer outside, but everything was bathed in shadows.

Tucking herself back into her tent and zipping it closed, she felt alone. And scared. She looked through the darkness encircling her. There was nothing to distract her and no safer place to go when she was alone, in a forest, in the middle of the night.

She rustled around her backpack for her headlamp and felt the smooth, worn edges of Nana's journal. Her hand moved past the object and kept feeling for her headlamp until it was in her grasp.

With her tent now lit and nothing else to do, Avery couldn't stop thinking about the journal. She had brought it just in case she was ready to give it one more look, or perhaps write in it one more time.

Pulling it out, she noticed the slightly fraying edges of the cover, and the small, darker-colored creases that formed against the tan, smooth leather. Before she could convince herself otherwise, she took the long leather string that held it shut and began to unwrap. Even though she knew what it said inside, she took a deep breath before peeling the cover open.

But when she opened to the yellowed front page, only one thought came to mind. *You brought the wrong journal.*

She hadn't actually brought the wrong journal – *Dear Self* was still scribbled in Nana's sprawling cursive – but when Avery read the words now, she couldn't shake an overwhelming desire to have a journal of her own again. One that contained her own thoughts and stories.

Avery continued studying the two words: *Dear Self.* During all those years of ferociously writing memories, thoughts, fears, and desires, Avery had been too young to comprehend that all the time she had kept a journal, she had really been writing to more than just a book. All those years, she *had* been writing to a part of herself. But what part of her had she been writing to?

Still staring at her Nana's handwriting, Avery realized she hadn't bothered to study this physical imprint of her Nana before. Her Nana wrote the *D* and the *S* with large curves and swirls, making those letters look grander against the other, smaller letters that followed behind. The handwriting was legible, but on closer inspection Avery realized it was a mix of cursive and print; each letter flowed into the next, but in their own, haphazard way, as if her Nana had scribbled those words quickly, with no time to waste. As if there was something urgent she had wanted to say, and this piece of paper was the only place she could actually say it.

And yet, the rest of the page remained empty.

Avery released a sigh. Nana could have taken her time beginning this entry, and all of Avery's ideas about her handwriting could be nothing more than a projection.

I wrote in one page and knew it wasn't for me ...

A thickness formed in her chest as she thought of Uncle Terry violating Nana's inner world, causing Nana to lose trust in the writing process. Avery knew all too well what losing trust in writing felt like. She had let years slip by without a pen, because she thought she didn't have anything new to say. The depressing and the joyful, the exciting and mundane parts of life all seemed to blend into an endless cycle no longer worth documenting.

Yet, as the journal grew heavy in her hands, the desire for a pen consumed her. She placed the book on the floor of her tent and rustled through her backpack until she found one. She flipped to the question she had written days before.

Why did you choose those last words for me before you died?

Without hesitating, she flipped to a new, blank page. Whether it was the lack of sleep, the inevitable boredom of camping alone, or the energy of the forest, Avery was compelled to try answering this question again. At the very least, she wanted to document these emotions, this night.

When the ink touched the paper, the workings of her mind man-ifested into words, flowing just as easily as it had when she was younger. As if no time had passed at all.

But so many years *had* passed, and as Avery wrote, she forgot about time as she got lost and found in memories throughout the years. Moving into the city with unknown naivete and still-unfulfilled dreams, holding her nieces for the first time and realizing there was a whole storage of love inside her she hadn't known existed, finding out that it was sometimes easier to feel safe with strangers, like Raymond and Ethan, than the people she knew, and realizing she had what it took to survive and take care of herself, even on the sleepless nights when all her memories felt like hauntings.

As the words glided out of her mind, through her hands, and onto the paper, Avery felt as if she were witnessing those memories with a new a perspective, a new presence. And this perspective, she realized as she recounted those sleepless nights, had been through a lot, so it had a lot to teach her.

She filled pages and pages with her words. She detailed the memories that came during her hike – of Nana's smile, her parents' anger, and how, as a teenager, she thought those memories would fade as she got older, but they were more alive than ever. She admitted that it was hard for her brain to tell time.

Finally, she documented those confusing last moments with Nana.

I don't know where you've been. I don't know where you're going. I don't even know if you know where you're going.

There.

She sat upright, reading and re-reading those last words. They looked much smaller on paper compared to the space they claimed in her mind.

When she was finished, her hand was aching and the joint near her finger was inflamed from the pressure of the pen. She used her index finger to smooth over the last page of the entry carefully, as if too strong a touch would crumble these written confessions.

Avery thought of her hike earlier in the day, when she had been beneath a storm cloud amid a sea of wildflowers. It had stirred the sensation that she was not alone and had never been alone. Through it all, Avery had always been with herself. And so far, she realized, as she stared at the memories she had just written, she had gotten herself through everything.

The crickets were still chirping. Avery wrapped her nana's journal shut and lay down to drift into her dreams.

Chapter 45

"**M**om!" the squeaky voice of Daisy's best friend, Olive, shouted. "Mom! I pooped!"

Olive's mother, Olivia, leaned her elbows onto Brinkley's white marble island with a groan and buried her head in her hands, making her long curls cascade down her arms.

"Why did my nannies have to go on strike?"

"I'm sorry, Liv," Brinkley said as she looked at the bowl of chips and then settled on a carrot stick to dip into hummus. "Did they give any reason?"

Olivia had called Brinkley early that morning to complain that her nannies were going on strike. Last Brinkley checked, Olivia had a whole army of nannies at her disposal, one for each of her three children that had been with the family since each child's birth. So Brinkley was confused, and quite frankly a bit scared, that all of them had gone on strike. Was Olivia's husband a pervert? Did she get herself involved in something shady – perhaps money laundering? Or were Olivia and her husband just terrible employers?

The desperate fear had been in Olivia's voice, though, so Brinkley hadn't wasted time asking questions before suggesting a playdate between Daisy and Olive.

When Olivia dropped Olive off, however, Brinkley knew something else must be up. Her friend's usually flawless makeup was replaced with dark circles under her eyes, her designer clothes swapped with a baggy, neutral-toned sweat suit (it still looked designer, though), and Olivia's usually smooth voice was entering pitches and tones Brinkley hadn't heard from her friend before.

"Mom!" Olive shrieked, breaking through Brinkley's thoughts.

"Just a minute, sweetheart!" Olivia called, and then rolled her eyes, looking at Brinkley. "I don't know how you do it with two little ones. Ever since my nannies went on strike, I feel like I'm struggling to keep Olive alive. I'm lucky the twins are ten, you know?"

"Speaking of your nannies going on strike, did they give a reason?" Brinkley said. The last thing she needed was the FBI breaking down her doors to capture her friend.

Olivia reached for the bowl of carrots sitting on the white marble island between them. She dipped one in hummus and took a crunchy bite as she explained, "They want more money, healthcare, paid time off – like, can I tell them to take a number? Everyone in Brian and my life want more money."

A wave of relief washed over Brinkley.

"Well ..." Brinkley felt as though she were tiptoeing as she spoke. "They have been with your family for a while, and you did say they take good care of your kids—"

"So? Isn't minimum wage enough? I mean, I'm going through a lot in my life right now, how greedy can these people get?"

Brinkley's jaw dropped. "You pay your nannies minimum wage?"

"Mom!" Olive shrieked again, presumably still stuck on the toilet.

With her jaw still dropped, Brinkley shifted her gaze in the direction of the bathroom and then back at her friend.

"Yeah." Olivia chomped on her carrot. "Trust me, I thought it was low, too, but Brian says we all have to start somewhere."

"Wait, wasn't Brian born into money?"

"Yeah, but his parents had to build that wealth." Olivia shrugged. "Of course, Brian's not the one dealing with the kids when all the nannies go on strike. I swear, if I wasn't pregnant, I'd divorce him today."

"*Mom! Mom! Mom!*" Olive's screeches echoed through Brinkley's tall ceilings. "Wait, what?" Brinkley said.

"I'm coming, sweetheart!" Olivia yelled and then leaned back on her elbows. "Sometimes I wonder if I birthed a demon," she said as she shook her head, ignoring the baby and marital bombshell she just dropped.

"The other day we were watching *The Little Mermaid,* and Olive cried about Ariel killing Ursula." Olivia continued to nibble on the carrot as she spoke. "I'm not kidding you, she cried and said Ariel was the evil one. Is that not alarming?"

"Maybe Olive has a deeper sense of empathy than most?" Brinkley offered. "Anyway, you're pregnant? Do you actually want to divorce Brian?"

"*Mom!*" the shriek was loud and rattling.

"Do you want me to—" Brinkley began.

"Ugh, no, I'll get her," Olivia said, and rounded the corner of the kitchen to get into the bathroom.

The thought of divorce made Brinkley clammy as she considered her own parents' divorce. The fighting, the division, the different roles each child was forced to play. But she also thought of her parents married and fighting. The misery of living in a tense, constantly unhappy household.

Her thoughts trailed to Chase, his face always illuminated by a blue screen, his voice quiet. The more she tried imagining his voice, the more distant the memory of it became. It made her want to grab her children into a great big hug.

Padding her way across her kitchen island and into her daughters' playroom, Brinkley called for her daughters the second she entered the room.

"Mommy!" Lily and Daisy beamed in unison, their eyes brightening on seeing their mom enter.

Lily dropped her puppet and ran to hug her mother, Daisy trailing close behind. They latched on to her as she dropped to her knees to come to eye level with them. With every year that passed, Brinkley felt her heart overfill and then break every time her daughters greeted her like this.

It all goes so fast, everyone who ever had a kid always had to remind her.

As she squeezed her daughters against her chest, Brinkley tried her best to take it all in. She always considered the playroom the best spot in the house. Its glittering, pastel- colored wallpaper was adorned with textured butterflies that appeared to flutter across the wall. In one corner sat a wooden kitchen set that was next to a wooden tool set, with a rack of superhero, princess, and animal costumes in between. The other corner had a gray indoor fort, filled with comfy pillows and snuggly stuffed animals. It stood next to a wall lined with children's books and an art easel.

Brinkley continued to squeeze her daughters, breathing in the lavender scent of their baby shampoo, feeling their little hands clutching her close.

The moment didn't last long.

"Help!" Olivia's cry broke through their smiles. "Olive stuffed way too much toilet paper into the toilet and now it's overflowing!" she screamed from the bathroom. "Oh my gosh, there's a turd on the tile! I'm so sorry. I need a towel! Olive, we are never going to be invited back."

Even Lily and Daisy's faces were scrunched in disgust as they looked at their mother for leadership.

"Coming," Brinkley called.

Kids were gross when they weren't your own.

With Olive in a fresh pair of Daisy's clothes and the bathroom scrubbed clean, Olivia and Brinkley decided to move the play date outside.

Brinkley set down a bowl of chips and guacamole on the table between them and then lowered herself into her chair, trying to conceal the jab of pain that shot through her butt after sitting. She checked on her bathtub-butt-cheek wound every day, and there was a bruise in shades of dark purple, lime green, and hints of blue hugging the crusty red scab. In other words, it was healing, but it still looked nasty, and still ached whenever Brinkley wanted to take a seat. "I am so sorry about that," Olivia repeated for the one hundredth time, and Brinkley thought her friend had somehow heard about the fall, but then Olivia added, "Olive is potty-trained for the most part – at least, my nannies were supposed to potty-train her – but I'm learning that she still uses a whole roll of toilet paper to wipe herself. If I knew she had to go number two, I would've never left her alone."

"It's okay. A couple more years and she'll be able to handle it all by herself. It'll go by fast," Brinkley said, watching Lily push her little sister on the swing. She remembered when Lily had been too small to even stand, and she and Chase would have to give her gentle pushes in the baby swing.

"A couple years can be a long time," Olivia groaned.

Brinkley continued looking at the playset. The baby swing was empty now.

"So ..." Brinkley's voice trailed off in the quiet afternoon heat as she debated what was too intrusive to ask. For all the years of friendship they had shared – for all the gatherings, and gossip, and book analyses – the walls of distance between them was more apparent than ever.

As if reading her mind, Olivia spoke. "So I'm pregnant," she declared again, keeping her eyes focused on their daughters. "Found out last week. It's terrible timing. I can't be pregnant right now."

"Maybe ..." Brinkley shrugged, pausing before regurgitating the lie she wasn't sure she believed in. "Maybe it's happening right now for a reason."

"Do you really believe that?"

Brinkley opened her mouth to speak and then closed it. "I don't know," Brinkley finally admitted. "But it doesn't seem like a bad idea to believe in." She turned to face her friend, to look into her eyes. "What's going on?"

"Nothing new. I just feel spread thin, which is ridiculous, I know, because I have all this money, and help, and whatever. But I do. I feel spread thin," Olivia confessed, her gaze transfixed by something in the distance before she snapped back to Brinkley. "And that makes me feel incompetent, you know? Like, if I can't handle my life, whose life could I handle?"

Brinkley followed her friend's gaze back to the playset, where their daughters were swinging high in the sky.

"Sometimes I just find myself lying awake at night, wondering, is this all there is?" Olivia was looking at Brinkley now, the whites of her eyes reddened, contrasting against the dark hazel shades of her iris. "I mean really," she continued, something pleading in her voice. "Is this all there is?"

Feeling her heart fall, Brinkley never felt closer yet more distant from her friend. It felt as if she were talking to someone different from the Olivia she thought she had known. Had the signs of unhappiness always been there, masked by the designer clothes and makeup? Or was her friend so blessed, so catered to all her life, that having to take care of a child was all it took to send her spiraling?

"Sometimes I feel like we've all been sold a fake dream," Olivia was saying now, her gaze once again lost on something in the distance. "I have the house, the family, the money ... but it's not enough. I can't bring another child into this world ..."

Brinkley found herself brainstorming ways to divert the conversation to a different topic. In a world that had become devoid of sharing raw emotions with each other, Brinkley was unsure how to respond. But when Brinkley looked at her friend, all she saw was a human who was hurting, who had probably been hurting, and had grown tired of pretending pain wasn't part of her perfect life.

"I get those feelings too, sometimes," Brinkley said.

"You do?"

"I do. Sometimes it feels like something must be wrong with me for feeling that way, but ..." Brinkley sucked in a breath, watching her girls laughing and giggling as they climbed up the slide. "Maybe it's just part of being human. No matter how lucky people think your life is."

Olivia appeared to mull this over.

"Maybe being human is just ... hard. Sometimes." Once the words left Brinkley's lips, she felt the weight of their truth lift. "Maybe you don't need a bigger reason for your feelings than that."

Brinkley thought of her nana then, and the rose quartz ring that was still tucked safely away in Brinkley's vanity drawer. She wondered if Nana had felt these feelings, too. *Is this all there is?* Were those love letters Nana's way of coping with a life that didn't entirely fulfill her, even though society had convinced her it should?

"Well," Olivia's voice broke through Brinkley's thoughts, "maybe you're right. I'm sure having to quit amphetamines cold turkey isn't helping, either—"

"Wait, what?"

"Yeah, now that I'm pregnant, I shouldn't take amphetamines. Gosh, I'm going to gain so much weight!"

"You have ADHD?"

"No, girl, I take them so I'm not hungry."

Brinkley felt her eyes bulge. "But ... is that even safe?"

"Who cares? It keeps me fit, gives me energy. Just when I lost all my baby weight from Olive, this new baby is going to ruin it all."

"Liv, that can't be healthy!"

"I know, I know," Olivia said, and waved her hand in the air. "I just ... I wasn't planning on taking them forever. Just as long as I needed to lose weight. The pills make me feel good, more confident, and capable. Is that so bad?"

"Well, when you put it like that, no ... But ..."

It was then that Brinkley realized the very friend she had admired and compared herself to, the friend who seemed to have it all and was always put together, was just an illusion. A figment of her own imagination.

No one knew what happened behind closed doors.

"But why do we need to be a certain weight, and have a certain amount of energy ... to feel confident and capable?" Brinkley heard herself say. "I think we *have* been sold a fake dream, Liv. And I think we need to wake up."

Chapter 46

The sunlight streamed through Elizabeth's bedroom window and woke her.

She squinted at the heap of her and John's clothes sprinkled on the floor like breadcrumbs leading to bed, flashbacks of the previous night filling her mind. After their fight, John had entered their house with a bouquet of flowers and weeds he'd picked from their wooded backyard. He'd apologized, declared he wanted to marry her, and didn't care about the extraneous details that would get him there. No matter how important his family made every single detail seem.

He wanted to stand by her side as her husband-to-be, her man, and get through the stress of wedding planning together.

Elizabeth hadn't even cared what he was saying at that point. Standing in their bedroom doorway with a bouquet he had picked himself, from the backyard he had proposed to her in, the backyard they would continue building a life on, she had been more than ready to kiss and make up.

She snuggled her naked body into the covers and closed her eyes to reimagine their night, but smells of coffee coming from the kitchen filled her senses. John loved his coffee strong.

Before Elizabeth had time to gather herself to join him for a cup,

John appeared in the doorway. A wooden breakfast tray was in his hands complete with tofu scramble, burnt toast with jelly, and a vintage white porcelain cup they had found at a flea market years ago filled with espresso.

"What's all this?" Elizabeth asked, smiling.

"I've been thinking a lot about our anger and our love yesterday," he said, his broad shoulders blocking their doorway before stepping fully inside.

"Okay ..."

He set the tray overtop their comforter and sat next to Elizabeth. "And I think," he said, placing his hand on Elizabeth's thigh, "I think we're experiencing something worth exploring ..."

"Um, okay ..."

"I think we should just do it—"

"Do what?"

"Elope."

It took a minute for Elizabeth to process those two words. "Wait, you're serious?"

"Yes, Elizabeth."

They remained in eye contact, but his didn't have a hint of humor in them.

"What are we doing?" he said.

Elizabeth tilted her head. She hadn't even had coffee yet. Her fingers took the dainty espresso cup in her hand and shot the liquid back.

"What are we doing?" he repeated, his voice deeper this time. "Stressing about cakes and dates and guests and flowers? For what? For whom? We can run off, have an adventure and not even tell anyone until it's all done."

Elizabeth felt her eyebrows raise, but her eyes remained glued to John.

"I asked you to marry me because I wanted *you*." He was on both his knees now, clasping her hands in his. "Yet ever since we've been engaged, we've been stressed, we've been disappointed – I can't even write a goddamn paragraph that's not trash, I'm so creatively blocked by the madness."

His eyes were intent on hers, the sunlight illuminating them to make the blue shade more vibrant than usual.

"Elizabeth Rose," he declared, his deep voice commanding the air, "You are the light that illuminates my words—"

Elizabeth felt her smile fade as she looked at the ceiling. "See, that's putting you at the center and me in a supporting role—"

"First draft." He shook his head, and an earnest smile appeared on his face. It reminded her of the same look he'd given when he was down on one knee, asking her to marry him. She imagined for a moment being able to take that moment back. Or re-experience it in a new, everlasting way. "If you really want a traditional wedding, I am all in. But, Elizabeth," he paused and nodded towards her, "all I need is you."

"This is all very sweet, John," she said, stroking his cheek with her hand. "But there's no way your parents will let us elope."

"I don't care. Don't you see, Elizabeth? I don't care any more. I woke up and realized I've been an author of other characters' lives, yet never my own."

"Yeah, like you literally woke up and realized all this," Elizabeth said, trying to resist the temptation of canceling their giant wedding. But the idea had already implanted itself in her mind. "There's no way you'll still get your trust fund if we elope."

"Elizabeth." He had his hands on both her shoulders. "You were right."

Elizabeth felt herself sit straighter, and let him continue.

"I have had that trust hung over my head for thirty years. Every five years I get another sprinkle of it, as if I'm … I'm some kind of rabbit with a carrot hung over his nose," he said with flared nostrils.

John rose to his feet and began pacing their bedroom. "And every year," he said, "if I begin to do something – anything – my parents disapprove of, they wave that trust in my face and remind me who's in charge. Remember the pig roast, Elizabeth?"

"Yes," Elizabeth said, having flashbacks of when she and John had been forced to attend the Astors' pig roast after John had declared he was no longer going to consume meat.

Mr. Astor had not been happy with John's new decision, no matter how many coral reefs and forests, not to mention animals and humans, a vegetarian diet could save. Mr. Astor believed real men ate meat. So, when John had been firm in his new relationship to food, Mr. Astor had thrown a pig roast. When Elizabeth and John had voiced their discomfort about attending, sure enough, the trust had been brought up. Subtly. But clearly.

The memory made Elizabeth's blood boil.

"I don't want to be a rabbit any more!" John said. "I want to be a man."

"A broke man?" Elizabeth asked even though the pig roast memory made her shudder.

"Liz …" John was on both his knees again, his eyes pleading. "Are you happy?"

Elizabeth brought her eyebrows together. "Um …"

"Are you happy?"

They stared at each other. Elizabeth felt her airways constrict and muscles tense as she tried to suppress her tears. He carefully tucked a strand of her hair behind her ears.

"I told you, you were right. We're in a cage."

"Well yeah, but it has four hundred thread count sheets and Champagne and—"

John was ready to confront his story. Only yesterday, it was all Elizabeth thought she had wanted – for him to recognize the power of his autonomy, and how his family had managed to keep that autonomy in the palm of their hands. But now that he was ready to take his power back, Elizabeth felt her own nerves flushing through her body. It was easier to confront their situation while knowing John would keep them stuck. Now that he was ready to fling the doors of their metaphorical cage wide open, Elizabeth was forced to face the fact that John had not been the only one keeping them there.

"But it's a cage," said John, his voice clear and firm. "I'll stay in it as long as you want to, but I think there's so much more we could experience. On our terms."

No words could make it past Elizabeth's constricted throat as she remained sitting upright, trying to process what John was proposing. It was different to his first proposal – there was no sparkling ring, no expensive Champagne, no one left who they felt like sharing this moment with. But the actual proposal was the same – he wanted to share the rest of his life with her.

A wave of calm spread from her chest throughout her body as she let her fiancé embrace her still-naked body in his arms.

"Picture it," he said, his voice muffled from his lips being pressed against her hair. "A private ceremony somewhere, just me and you … No one to impress, no one to entertain or cater to. No small talk, going from table to table to greet every guest. Just us, Liz. Just us, beneath the sky …"

Elizabeth closed her eyes, listening to his promise. She imagined an intimate dinner under a blanket of stars, the sound of the ocean soothing their senses. The more she imagined it, the more the foggy chatter of her mind seemed to lift. For the first time since getting engaged, the wedding she now visualized filled her heart with meaning. With love.

There was still a tugging in her heart at the thought of not having her sisters there and fear of the Astors' reaction. Perhaps terror. But after their effort of trying to follow the traditional route, the thought of throwing a wedding to please everyone except her and John felt much worse.

After all, all she wanted to do – all she had ever wanted to do – was marry the man who had been the love of her life. The one who had been by her side, through all of life's ups and downs, the past decade. John was the one who made her laugh during life's monotony, who helped her dream beyond traditional dreams and work through her fears when she wanted to run away from them. After Elizabeth had grown up in a broken home, disillusioned with love and marriage, John had appeared in her life. And through the years of his consistent love, John was the one who made Elizabeth believe in concepts like soul mates and happily ever afters. Somewhere along the wedding planning process they had lost their way, but as John kept her secure in his arms, sharing his vision with her, Elizabeth felt she had found the wedding worth fighting for.

"If you're serious about this," she said, "I don't want to do it in secret."

"So, let's tell people," John agreed. "Let's tell everyone. We have nothing to hide."

Elizabeth breathed, and in that breath, she noticed all the tension and stress she had been carrying throughout their engagement was released. Even if it was only for a moment, she finally felt aligned with herself and her relationship, and she couldn't remember the last time things had felt this right.

Chapter 47

Avery's voice was droning on in the background, raving about her recent camping trip while Brinkley washed a delicate wine glass in her large, farmhouse-style sink. *Avery hiked a whole mountain and had gotten stuck in a rain cloud! It was all for the best though.* Brinkley forgot why. *The mountains made Avery realize how insignificant yet significant everything is!* Brinkley didn't entirely understand that one, but was too tired to ask for an explanation. Even the chirping crickets played some kind of important role ... Brinkley couldn't keep up. She was happy her sister had enjoyed the trip, but nothing about Avery's descriptions sounded enjoyable.

This morning, not wanting to experience the day alone, Brinkley had invited Avery over for some sister time. Lily and Daisy were at summer camp, Chase was at work, and Brinkley wanted to take a break from her mom friends. She was still processing Olivia's last visit, wondering who else was an illusion in her life. Yet every time she wondered about others, she kept thinking of herself. Her own illusion of herself whom she had crafted and perfected and presented to the world.

As Brinkley's hand moved across the glass, encasing it in soapy suds, Avery was talking about some kind of meadow, as if the girl was starring in a remake of *The Sound of Music* or something. Brinkley's mind drifted further into itself.

I think we need to wake up, Liv ...

Brinkley thought of Chase, who had worked late last night. The blue glow of his computer screen haunted her dreams. Sometimes she'd have a recurring nightmare of tossing his computer right out of their big bedroom window. In her dream, she'd watch it fall and smash on their landscaped grass, and then she and her husband would be forced to look at their broken reflection in all the little pieces on the ground—

A clatter of actual glass broke through her thoughts. She felt something in her stomach churning as she stared at the broken glass in her hand. Blood, a brilliant red hue, separated into various branches as it dripped down her hand to join the rest of the shatters in the sink.

Brinkley stared as Avery rushed over.

"Brinkley!" Avery gasped. "What the hell? Are you okay?"

Brinkley continued staring at the dripping waterfall of blood. *Not again,* was all she could think. Her butt was still in the process of healing, and now this?

Avery immediately started riffling through the cabinet under the sink before finding a brown paper bag. She threw the big chunks of glass inside.

The red blood began traveling towards the drain.

"Brinkley, you're bleeding! Go get bandage or something! Is any glass stuck in your hand? Are you okay?"

"Sorry," Brinkley muttered. She placed what was left of the broken glass she was holding into the brown paper bag.

"Why are you apologizing? What happened?" said Avery. "Do you need stitches?"

"No," Brinkley said, but just as she said it, she felt the sting of the cut on her palm.

She brought her hand to her face to search for any microscopic pieces stuck inside.

Avery snatched Brinkley's hand to examine for herself.

"Okay …" she said, "I'll take care of the glass in the sink. Go wash your hands and get a band-aid."

Brinkley nodded, still unsure how that had happened. As she entered her powder room and washed the blood from her hands, she concluded that their wine glasses were too delicate. She had put them on her and Chase's wedding registry years ago, when she was still in her early twenties, before children and the stresses of daily life had weighed her down. Thicker glass was more her speed these days. This would not have happened with thicker glass.

She searched through her powder room cabinets and pulled out a pack of Dinosaur- themed band-aids. Daisy had picked them out months ago.

We need to get thicker glasses, she continued repeating the thought as she smacked the band-aid on.

When she rejoined Avery in the kitchen, who was still hunched over the sink, probably scanning for any more pieces, Brinkley was ready to set up snacks for the two of them to share. Avery's voice stopped her in her tracks to the pantry.

"Brinkley, what happened?"

Brinkley looked at Avery, who was no longer hunched over the sink, but staring right at her.

"I don't know?" Brinkley said, crossing her arms. "I always thought I liked wine glasses that felt delicate and dainty, but I think we picked ones that are a little too fragile. I mean, it broke right in my hand!"

Avery seemed to shift her weight away from Brinkley as she surveyed her.

"Brinkley," she said. "Is everything okay?"

"Yes ..." Brinkley felt her words getting trapped in her throat. "Yes, I was just washing the glass, and zoned out and it was too fragile." She held up her dinosaur-patched hand. "Clearly. Anyway, did you want white or red wine—"

"What were you thinking about?" Avery pressed.

"I don't know, nothing," Brinkley said, uncrossing her arms and racing back to the pantry.

Brinkley took a moment to linger in the privacy of the pantry closet, away from Avery's scrutinizing eyes. Organic snacks of every shape and size stared back at her. She kept looking through the packaging and labels but forgot what she had come into the pantry for. Her hands snatched a bag of chips and a jar of salsa. When she returned to the kitchen, Avery was already seated at the large marble island between them.

"Are you sure everything's okay?"

"Yes, Avery, I'm allowed to have an accident—"

"Okay, but you just broke a wine glass with your bare hands as if you're the Incredible Hulk or something—"

"I told you, they're fragile glasses!"

"You've never broken one before ..." Avery shrugged. "It was the way you stopped afterwards ... The way you just stared ..."

Brinkley glanced at her knuckles, which were white from clutching the jar. She relaxed her grip and shoved the snack onto the island with a huff before taking a seat next to Avery.

"I don't know," she said, looking at the ground. "I don't know what's wrong."

Brinkley could feel Avery eyeing her. Finally, Avery got up, pulled two unbroken glasses from the cabinet, took a bottle of Pinot Grigio from the wine fridge, and poured them each a full glass.

"Start talking," Avery said as she screwed the wine cap back on the bottle.

"It's going to sound crazy," Brinkley said, becoming increasingly self-conscious of the marble, the space, the luxury of her kitchen and entire house as she sat across from her sister who lived paycheck to paycheck. She glanced once more at Avery, but Avery was sitting still, her eyes focused on nothing but Brinkley. "Lately I just feel like something is missing from my life," she confessed, and then immediately added, "And I know that's ridiculous to say. I know I've been lucky in so many ways—"

"That's not ridiculous," Avery said with a shake of her head and a sip of her wine. Brinkley blinked, but Avery didn't offer anything else.

"I just feel like ..." Now Brinkley was the one trying to provide herself with an explanation. "I'm healthy, all my loved ones are healthy. My children are blessings. My nanny isn't on strike. I have a husband who provides us all with an amazing life – like, we are a really lucky family."

When Avery did not agree or disagree, Brinkley felt the need to press on.

"Is there something wrong with me," she said, noticing a tremble in her voice, "that after all of that I still feel like something is missing from my life?"

"Well, do you think something is wrong with you?"

"I don't know. Am I just being ungrateful, or too greedy with life or something?"

Brinkley's gaze got lost in the design of the white marble. The way the gray shades looked like unmoving waves against a white sea. She sighed.

"Everyone is always telling me how lucky I am, and I can't tell if it's true, or if it's just an illusion I've fed into."

"Well, if you don't feel lucky right now, who are you going to listen to? Yourself or them?"

"It's just hard to feel like I can listen to myself," Brinkley said, looking back into her sister's eyes, "when I don't even know why I'm feeling this way. The other day I was so desperate, I went to the internet to ask what's missing from my life. How pathetic is that?"

"Okay, well, there's your first problem. You think a search engine knows you and your life better than you do?"

Too embarrassed to continue making eye contact, Brinkley pretended to be fascinated by the grout on her kitchen's white tile floor.

Avery didn't fill the silence.

"I guess I ... I didn't think of it like that," Brinkley admitted.

"Look, I don't care how beautiful your house, or how perfect your skin is—"

Brinkley released a small laugh.

"You're allowed to feel the way you feel. In fact, you're feeling it for a reason," Avery said.

"Yeah," Brinkley said, feeling her heart beat faster. "I guess you're right. I probably just need to exercise more or something. Start to feel like myself again."

But she could feel Avery's eyes studying her.

"You think exercise is going to solve this?" Avery said, her eyes now glaring at the band-aid on Brinkley's hand.

"I don't know, we'll see," Brinkley said with a shrug. "Anyway, you were telling me about your camping trip?" When Avery didn't immediately engage with her change of topic, Brinkley tried again. "Oh, and did you hear about dad's wedding date?"

Chapter 48

"What about Bali?" Elizabeth called from her and John's sunroom.

It was a breezy July day, allowing the wind chimes to fill the room with soothing notes. Elizabeth remained snuggled in a blanket on their outdoor couch, imagining different places where they could elope.

"Bali?" John called from their kitchen, which shared a window to their sunroom. He was preparing a pasta dish for them to celebrate their new wedding plans.

After spending a few long days weighing the pros and cons of a traditional wedding with a private one, both had decided, once and for all, to cancel their traditional wedding and have a private ceremony, just the two of them. At this point, the only pros they could come up with for having a traditional wedding were to ensure another sprinkle of John's trust would arrive on his thirty-fifth birthday, and to not make anyone angry.

Yet they had spent their whole lives trying not to anger certain people, and it hadn't been working out for them. Private ceremony it would be, but they hadn't told anyone yet. Wanting to give themselves at least a week to enjoy this moment in their relationship, they were celebrating in secret.

Elizabeth stretched from her fingertips through her toes with a smile. She extended her ring finger in front of her, admiring the gold band that surrounded the flawless oval diamond. It reflected the light of the late summer sun, sending soft-colored glimmers across her surroundings. Who knew wedding planning could be so fun and romantic, when other people's money and neuroses weren't involved.

"That would be incredible," John said as the aroma of fresh tomatoes, onions, and garlic wafted into the sunroom. "Perhaps as a honeymoon? I'm thinking our ceremony should be somewhere closer. Somewhere we've been before." He emerged in their sunroom, wooden spoon in hand, and grinned at her. "How do you feel about getting married in Maine?"

"John, that's the first place you took me!" Elizabeth said, recalling their first vacation together. She didn't remember in which season they had gone, but she remembered a clean chill in the air, John's arms always snuggling her into his body, as they'd walked amid rocky shores and evergreens on the beach. They had talked about so many things during those walks, but the conversations she remembered were the ones about their dreams, usually shared beneath a blanket and a bottle of red wine. It was the trip when John had opened up about wanting more out of life. After growing up with almost anything money could by, John was tired of looking around him and still seeing fake smiles and lying eyes. He wanted to travel the world, not curate a vacation, but actually travel. Become familiar with strangers, learn how to communicate in different languages, experience places with eyes that did not yet belong to him. Elizabeth had opened up about wanting to be happy, but never knowing how to get there.

John had reassured her that there was more to being alive than being happy. He found purpose in every emotion. Elizabeth had become captivated by John and his words, and it was then, on the rocky shores of Maine with the Atlantic waves crashing nearby, when she had known there would be a lot of different people in the world who could promise many different lives, but she wanted the one with John by her side. Maine would be the poetic place to fulfill that past moment and begin their future.

"I know it is," John said with a chuckle. "That's why I suggested it."

"John, it's perfect."

Before she could continue talking about their plans, Elizabeth's phone vibrated in her lap. She saw "Avery" flashing on the screen. Her heart was beating faster, but she would not let her sister, or anyone for that matter, ruin this moment. So, she stole a breath, silenced her phone, and looked back at John. "Should we rent the same house from our first trip?"

He looked her up and down and raised an eyebrow. "The one with the hot tub?"

"Yes, the one with the hot tub." She leaned onto her elbows, but her phone started vibrating again.

"Avery" flashed on her screen.

John eyed the phone. He picked it up and placed it in Elizabeth's hand. "Answer it. I'll hold that thought and finish up dinner."

"But I don't want—"

"She's your sister," he said, his voice firm. "And she was right about your uncle Terry. Just admit you were wrong so you can both move on."

Elizabeth watched her husband's body until he disappeared through the door. Taking a long breath, she looked back at her sister's name flashing on the screen. Perhaps now *would* be a good time to make up. After all, she was about to start the next chapter of her life. She didn't want to carry baggage from the past into her blissful new future.

Besides, it wasn't as if Avery had said anything wrong, Elizabeth considered. Hurtful, yes. But sometimes hurtful truths were what people needed to hear, to help them wake up from their lies.

Elizabeth brought the phone to her ear.

"Hello?"

"Hey, Liz. It's Avery."

Wrinkling her eyebrows, Elizabeth said, "I know, Avery. I have caller ID. We're in the twenty-first century."

"Right, well, I didn't know if you deleted my number or anything," Avery said, her words fast.

"I know your number by heart, Avery."

"Right. Well, I just wanted to call and say I heard about Dad's wedding date. I don't like quoting Mama Donna that much, but ... what an asshole."

A smile spread across Elizabeth's face as she continued admiring her ring.

"Well, thank you," she said. "But it's okay, really. I think it's happening for the best."

"Wow!" Avery said, and Elizabeth could hear the shock in her sister's voice. "Good for you."

A long silence followed, as both sisters seemed to be holding their breath.

"I actually called to say something else, too ..."

Here it was, the apology Avery had probably spent the last couple of weeks crafting. It had been the longest the sisters had gone without talking since possibly forever. Little did Avery know Elizabeth had been considering an apology of her own.

"Uncle Terry was telling the truth about Nana," Avery said. "I found out the whole story, and mom can back it up."

Elizabeth's jaw dropped. "Wait, you called to tell me *that*?"

"Yeah, I wanted to tell you first."

"How sweet of you, Avery." Elizabeth rolled her eyes.

"What? We got into a huge fight over it, so I did some digging. I figured we deserve to know who's right and who's wrong so we can both move on," Avery said.

The sound of an ambulance traveled through the phone. "Where are you?" Elizabeth said.

"What's that?" Avery said loudly, but her voice was muffled by the second round of sirens.

Elizabeth waited for the alarms to fade. "Is everything okay over there?"

"What? Yeah, what do you mean?"

"It sounded like five ambulances just blasted next to your ear."

"Oh yeah, that's just the city. Anyway, I also called because ... I'm sorry," Avery admitted. "I said hurtful things after our visit to the medium, and ... you're my sister, and I just want to see you happy. But the way I went about it was not right. I thought about you a lot during camping ..."

"You did?" Elizabeth asked, feeling her heart warm at this admission.

"Well, I thought about a lot of things," Avery added.

Elizabeth waited, but apparently Avery's apology was finished.

"Well, thank you," she said. "I'm sorry, too. Telling you that you're a disappointment to Mom and Nana was awful of me. I should have never repeated that, Avery." The reception was either bad, or Avery was remaining silent on the other end. "Because it's not even true," Elizabeth said, and she felt her throat tighten as her guilt settled into her heart. Though Avery had come into this world throwing tantrums, she had witnessed a lot at a young age, and Elizabeth hadn't always chosen to defend her little sister in childhood. The least she could do was step it up in adulthood. "I really am sorry."

"Well, Mom said it, so ... it could very well be true for her," Avery said with an audible sigh. "But it's just an opinion. An opinion I just don't want to share, you know?"

There was another moment of silence as Elizabeth continued to feel the weight of her own words.

"And you shouldn't share that opinion," Elizabeth said, her voice forceful. "When I said it, I was a disappointment to *myself*, Avery, and I projected that onto you. The same way Mom and Nana did when they told you that."

A silence that felt like an hour passed as the two sisters lingered in their separate places, connected by something unseen.

"Well ... thank you," Avery broke the silence, but her voice was quiet.

"Besides," Elizabeth said, finally feeling empowered enough to come clean. "Mom told me all about Nana and her documented love affair with Francesco, so ... you were right to believe Uncle Terry. Nana is no better than you or any of us. She's human, after all."

"Wait, Mom already told you?"

"Yeah. When Brinkley got back from the Bahamas we went to lunch, and Mama Donna spilled the beans."

"Wow."

"I know."

"So, she told you how Nana used to keep journals? And how Uncle Terry read all of them?"

"Yeah," Elizabeth started, then felt her eyebrows furrow. "Wait, so how did you find out?"

"Like I said, I did some digging. I invited Uncle Terry to the bar. We talked about everything."

Elizabeth leaned back into her patio couch and smoothed over the blanket covering her legs.

"I was so quick to write him off," she said, shaking her head. "And all for who? I feel stupid for how mad I got. I was under so much stress I wasn't dealing with—"

"So maybe it was for yourself," Avery said, and Elizabeth could almost hear the shrug in her sister's voice. "You're about to get married, and Mom and Dad didn't exactly share a marriage to believe in. It's okay to want proof that marriage isn't a mistake."

A breeze floated through the screens of the sunroom, creating more music through the air.

"But I hope one day you realize you don't need proof any more," Avery said. "You and John have already created something special with each other."

Elizabeth looked through the window of the sunroom that peeked into the kitchen, where John was stirring the pasta. A curly strand of his hair fell in front of his face as he hunched over the pot, deep in concentration as if he was literally trying to pour his love into the food.

"Thank you," said Elizabeth. "I think we do realize it. We've been caught up in the wrong things the past few months, but—"

"It happens to everyone," Avery finished. "But the truth will always set you free, or some shit like that, right?"

Elizabeth felt her cheekbones rise in a smile. "Yeah, Avery. That's exactly how the saying goes."

"Anyway, I have to run to work. Love you."

"Love you, too."

Chapter 49

"Why can't you reschedule?" Brinkley demanded as she stabbed a small diamond stud through her ear. "Isn't creating your own schedule the whole point of being your own boss? John and Elizabeth *never* invite people over for dinner. This is a special event!"

"It doesn't work like that, Brinkley," Chase said as he selected a tie from their walk-in closet. "This is a major deal for me. For us. I can't tell one of our highest-income clients I need to reschedule the showing."

"Right." Brinkley clenched her jaw as she stabbed another diamond stud through her other ear. "Of course."

"What's wrong?"

"You already know what's wrong!" Brinkley said, storming out of their walk-in closet.

"I don't, Brinkley." Chase appeared in the bedroom. "That's why I'm asking."

It seemed absurd to Brinkley that her own husband would be so oblivious to how his constant work schedule was affecting his wife, his family. Still, her husband's admission made Brinkley's irritation soften as she thought of her last get-together with Olivia. Maybe Brinkley, after spending years in a zip code full of pretty appearances, had internalized more than she ever thought. Perhaps she, like so many of the adults around her, had simply become a master of concealing her own emotions, even to her husband.

"I'm just stressed, Chase. You're always working," she said, collapsing on their king-sized bed. "I've had to take care of the girls, take care of our house – do you know how many things I've had to show up to alone?"

"I understand work has been crazy," Chase said. "But I'm doing it for us. For our family. In a few years it will all pay off."

Perhaps it was his matter-of-fact tone, or the way he seemed to blame his work, instead of reflect on his own choices, that made Brinkley's heart drop. As she sat on their bed, Brinkley felt the room around her grow into a neutral-toned blur as her eyes narrowed onto her husband.

"A few years," Brinkley repeated, her voice detached from herself.

Chase's eyes searched hers as he combed through his hair. "What?" His voice was quiet.

Brinkley opened her mouth and then closed it.

"What?" he pressed.

"I know marriage is about sacrifice," she began, letting her gaze fall to the plush white carpet beneath them. "But I don't know how much longer I can keep sacrificing my happiness for your work, Chase."

"Wait ..." Chase paused, shifting his weight. "Are you serious?"

Brinkley raised her eyes to meet his gaze.

"Brinkley, what are you sacrificing?"

"I already told you!" she said, rising from their bed with her hands in the air. "I'm not happy, Chase!"

"Brinkley, you enjoy living in this big house, going on vacations, throwing over-the-top parties—"

"Don't you dare throw those things in my face, Chase," she said, glaring at him with flared nostrils.

"Well, do you not? Those things cost money, Brinkley. A lot of money."

"Oh, don't patronize me about money, Chase!" she shouted, feeling her heart beat in a rhythm she only recognized when she was angry. "You enjoy working eighty hours a week and building a name for yourself, while I, your wife, handle everything behind closed doors!"

Her hands were still flailing in the air as she stepped towards him. "I didn't marry you for this kind of lifestyle, Chase, so don't you dare—"

"But you sure as hell enjoy the benefits of it!" he said, his face flushed with anger.

It could be scary sometimes, to realize how deeply one phrase could cut. How quickly one argument could erupt and create a scar that would take more time to heal than it did to create.

Brinkley felt every muscle of her being tense as she glared at him through blurry eyes.

"Fuck you," she spat.

"Brinkley—"

"No, Chase. Fuck. You." She didn't recognize her voice when she snarled the words.

"Brinkley, I'm sorry ..." Chase tried stepping towards her as her vision blurred into tears. She clenched her jaw tighter, as if that would help hold her emotions back. "It came out wrong..." he was saying, but Brinkley's whole world felt dizzy as she recoiled from his touch.

"I married you because I wanted a life with you," she said, her voice trembling. She collapsed on their king-sized bed and took deep breaths to prevent her tears from falling. "But this ..." she tried, clenching her jaw once again as she shook her head. "We're not even sharing a life any more, Chase."

Through watery eyes, she looked at her husband, who remained standing a few feet from her, his shoulders hunched.

"Brinkley ..." Chase opened his mouth, but she saw him glance at his watch. "Brinkley, I don't even know what to say."

The urge to cry faded as Brinkley listened to his words.

"I know things have been hectic as hell, but I'm telling you, it will all pay off—"

"I know," Brinkley muttered, her eyes stuck in a trance on their walk-in closet. "You've told me that promise many times."

Chase released a sigh and tried to sit next to her on their bed. But Brinkley remained in her position, not moving towards or away from him.

"I mean," he said, "your family is always getting together. I promise I'll make sure I'm at the next dinner or whatever. But the reality is, someone needs to pay for the mortgage on this house, and the girls' dance lessons, and private preschool, and—"

"I know, Chase. I'm the one who pays all those bills, remember? I handle all of our finances, paperwork, car repairs, cooking, child-care—"

"Yeah, we both do a lot to help this family function," Chase said, reaching out to touch her leg, but Brinkley remained lifeless.

"Why is our marriage a problem today of all days? It's not like I'm missing Lily's graduation, or anyone's wedding. I'm missing a family dinner, Brinkley. A *last-minute* one. And I'm missing it for an important work event. When she still didn't answer, Chase pressed on: "Why is that such a problem? Do we need to hire a full-time nanny? What do you need, Brinkley?"

Before Brinkley could continue arguing, the sound of Daisy's shriek echoed through their house.

"Daisy!" Brinkley gasped, thundering down the hallway into the girls' shared bedroom. Daisy was collapsed on the floor in a puddle of tears.

"I didn't do it, Mom. I didn't do anything!" Lily shouted.

Brinkley eyed Lily as she scooped Daisy off the floor. Daisy was in

300

full sobs, her little finger pointing at her sister Lily.

"She put gum in my hair!" Daisy wailed.

"What the ..." Brinkley breathed, but sure enough, a wad of pink bubblegum was tangled in a handful of Daisy's ringlets.

"Where did the gum come from, Lily?"

"I didn't do it!" Lily shouted, just as Chase appeared in the girls' bedroom doorway.

"What's going on?" he said in his "stern dad" tone.

"It's a little too late for you to be the knight-in-shining-armor, Chase," Brinkley snapped. "I can handle it."

"I know you can handle it," Chase said, but entered the bedroom. "I want to help you handle it."

Brinkley rolled her eyes. She wasn't in the mood to work as a team.

"Okay, okay, I'm sorry!" Lily said, as if she had been involved in an hour of interrogation, and threw her body to the floor. "It was me." Lily's forearm collapsed over her forehead. "I put bubblegum in Daisy's hair. She wasn't sharing!"

Brinkley could see Daisy glaring at Lily with beady eyes.

"Where did you get the bubblegum?" Chase demanded. "You know you're not allowed to have any without asking permission."

Of course, Lily put on her big puppy dog eyes as she tilted her chin down. *Here we go,* Brinkley thought, eyeing her husband and her daughter.

"I'm really sorry. I found it in the pantry. I wanted to practice ... chewing ..." Lily explained, her voice full of dramatic remorse.

"Baby, it's okay. We just want you to be safe—" Chase began, but Brinkley stepped in.

"You know you're not allowed to chew bubblegum, Lily. You could choke and get seriously hurt or die," Brinkley said.

After all, Brinkley would be the one having to conduct the Heimlich on her daughters while Chase was at work. The headlines would read

"Terrible Mother Allowed her Child to Choke on Bubblegum. Handsome Husband and Father of the Year Came Home to Heartbreak."

Lily's eyeballs grew so wide, it snapped Brinkley out of her thoughts.

"I could die?" Lily cried.

"Well, honey, you could get seriously hurt—" Chase tried, but Brinkley wasn't having any of it.

"No, Chase. While you're out showing houses and I'm here juggling a million different tasks, if Lily sneaks into the pantry, and eats food she's not supposed to, she could choke, and she could die."

Brinkley looked at Lily. "And we don't want that to happen to you, Lily. You and Daisy are the most important things in your daddy and my life, and we need to keep you safe. Okay?"

"Okay, Mommy, I'm sorry," Lily said with a pout. "I promise I won't do it again."

"What about my hair?" Daisy wailed.

"I'll get the scissors," Chase said, and began to get up.

"What!" Daisy's shriek stopped him midway.

"Way to go," Brinkley snapped at her husband.

"What? We need to cut it out."

"Not my hair! Cut Lily's hair!" Daisy pointed her finger at her sister as she screamed.

"Maybe that's fair?" Chase said, looking at Brinkley for leadership.

"What!" Now Lily was the one shrieking. "Don't chop off my beautiful hair!"

"Thanks," Brinkley hissed as Chase just stood there with his hands out as if to say, *What do you want me to do?*

It was times like these when Brinkley wondered what the hell people were thinking when they walked down the aisle and promised the rest of their lives to another human being.

Brinkley cleared her throat and looked at both her girls. "We are not going to chop off anyone's hair. Lily, do you see how upset your sister is from having gum in her hair?"

"Yes." Lily's puppy dog eyes returned. "I'm so, so sorry, Daisy. Next time just share—"

"Lily," Brinkley cut her off and glared at her daughter.

"It was not nice of me to stick gum in your hair. I'm really sorry, Daisy. I will not do it again," Lily said.

Daisy was playing hardball this afternoon and, without a smile or change of expression, snapped her head away from sister.

"I think she needs some time," Brinkley told Lily.

With Daisy still scooped in her arms, Brinkley carried her daughter down the stairs and placed her in a kitchen seat.

Chase followed close behind. "What can I help with?" he asked once Brinkley entered their kitchen pantry.

"We're fine, Chase. Just forget it. I got it," she said, and grabbed a jar of peanut butter. "Just go to your showing or whatever."

"Brinkley ..." Chase pulled Brinkley's arm for a moment, staring at her through his thick lashes. "Why won't you let me help?"

Brinkley looked at him, silent. She couldn't find an answer, so she shoved the jar of peanut butter into his hands. "Here, then. Scoop some onto the gum and let it sit for a few minutes before washing it out. I'm going to finish getting ready for John and Elizabeth's." She glanced through the doorway of the pantry, at the clock on their stove, and groaned. "I'm already late. When's your mom coming for the girls?"

"Should be here any minute. Just go, I'll stay with the girls until my mom gets here." "What about your showing?"

"I have more time than you," he said.

They lingered in their stare, and Brinkley could see Daisy already fiddling with her hair, trying to release it from the bubblegum's grip but probably only making it worse.

"Fine ..." She sighed, then added, "Thank you."

Before she was out of the pantry, he clutched her hand. "We'll talk after?"

"Sure. Yeah," Brinkley said. "Whenever you're not working."

"Should I try to swing by after the showing?"

She rolled her eyes.

"What?"

"We both know how that goes, Chase. You never make it."

Chase pressed his lips together and released her hand from his.

Chapter 50

"Oh, I'm so glad the weather was nice so we could keep the top down. The drive to their house is gorgeous," Avery's mother cooed. "Look at all these trees! You don't see neighborhoods like this any more. Everything is so developed these days. It makes me sick."

Avery was in the passenger seat of her mother's white Mustang. Mama Donna had traded her old SUV for the convertible the week after Avery's father had announced his engagement to Sin.

They were driving along the quiet, wooded road to Elizabeth and John's house. Elizabeth and John had invited Brinkley, Chase, Avery, and their mother over for dinner, though they'd refused to give any reason why, which had immediately made Avery suspicious.

John didn't like having people "invade his creative space" when he was in the middle of writing a book. For a minute, Avery entertained the idea that her sister could be pregnant, but that seemed absurd considering neither of them wanted kids now, probably ever.

Could her brain not get more creative than a pregnancy? *Think,* Avery commanded herself, *other major life events Western society celebrates ...*

Elizabeth and John were already engaged, already homeowners, almost definitely not pregnant ...

Oh my gosh, Elizabeth finally quit her boring ass job and won't be so mean any more—

"And I'm just so happy you and Elizabeth made up," her mother said.

"Wait, what? How did you know about our fight?"

"Elizabeth told me. At lunch. You were on that mountain." Mama Donna slammed on the brakes on reaching a stop sign, only to accelerate again.

"Of course she did," Avery muttered.

"Well, what's the problem with that?" Mama Donna said. "I am your mother. I should know when my children are fighting. Why don't *you* ever come to me with these things?"

"What things?"

"Things, Avery, things!" Mama Donna slammed on the brakes at another stop sign before re-accelerating. "You don't tell me anything about your life."

Avery didn't even have a chance to think before her mother was crying in the driver's seat.

"Jesus, Mom, do you need me to drive?"

"I'm fine," her mother said. "You know I didn't mean it, right? You know you're—"

"You just missed their driveway."

"Oh, shit!" said Mama Donna, slamming on the brakes once again.

"Do you even have a driver's license?" Avery wondered aloud.

The car started reversing along the quiet road.

"This is ridiculous," Mama Donna muttered, sniffling the remnants of her snot. "I always miss their driveway. Who makes a driveway this hidden?"

Yet the convertible was speeding along, right up the hill where Elizabeth and John's one-story cabin sat.

"What were you trying to say before you started crying? Do I even want to know?" Avery said as they flew past the tall trees lining the driveway.

"I was saying ..." Mama Donna parked the car, her chin lifted even though she couldn't meet Avery's eyes. "I didn't mean it. About you being a disappointment to me and Nana." She gathered her purse and let herself out of the car. "I mean, maybe I said it at the time because you were being defiant and rude—"

"Mom," Avery interrupted. "I can sit here and label all the ways I viewed you during that time, too. But I think we've done that to each other enough over the years."

Her mom shifted her weight onto her other foot. "What are you saying, Avery?"

"I'm saying you don't need to apologize for whatever you said back then." Avery let herself out of the car. "I finally don't need one."

With pursed lips, her mother walked past Avery, towards the front door. "Well then, if you don't need your mother's apology, fine. That's just fine," Mama Donna muttered, her words punctuating every step.

Avery felt a sideways smirk spread across her face as she listened to the ramblings, following her mother one step at a time.

Chapter 51

Everyone was gathered in Elizabeth and John's sunroom. The summer evening sun had begun to descend, shadowing the room and the tree-filled backyard into a cool darkness.

Elizabeth flicked on the twinkle lights that zigzagged across the ceiling, creating manmade stars for her guests to enjoy before joining her husband on one of their outdoor couches.

"So," Elizabeth began with a smile as she made eye contact with each guest, "thank you all for coming."

A breeze swept through the sunroom, the wind chimes creating soft music that now drifted through the refreshing night air.

"You're about to announce something, aren't you?" Avery said with one foot shaking up and down. "I knew this couldn't just be for dinner."

"Wait, what?" Brinkley sat straighter in her chair and looked at John and Elizabeth. "You have an announcement? I thought this was just, like, a special dinner."

Brinkley could practically feel the migraine setting in. *Enough with these damn announcements,* she thought. *Just call me next time.*

But John was looking at Avery with an expression that resembled a child after someone tells him the tooth fairy isn't real. "Wait, what gave it away?" he said.

"Come on, John. Inviting us to your house when you're in the middle of writing a book?" said Avery. "When I showed up unannounced during book two, you chased me out with a stick." Brinkley watched as Avery tilted her head, appearing to think for a moment before admitting, "And you know what, I always thought the character you killed off in your book resembled me, so is there any truth to that or …"

"I don't decide what characters you are, Avery. You do," said John.

Brinkley watched as John dropped to his knees to come eye level with Elizabeth. "Now it's ruined."

"Hun, it's not ruined," Elizabeth tried to assure him.

"Did I … ruin something?" Avery said, wincing.

John ignored her and continued to whisper to Elizabeth. "I really wanted to, you know, have that element of surprise. Total surprise. And now they already know something is coming." Brinkley swore she saw John side-eye Avery.

"Looks like someone's going to die again in book three," Brinkley muttered.

"Well," Elizabeth said, smoothing her hands over John's shoulders before her eyes seemed to light up, "think of it as a plot twist!"

"A plot twist?" John repeated in a whisper.

Brinkley was straining to hear every word of their not-private private conversation.

"Okay, yeah," he said before sitting back on the sunroom's couch.

"You've always been perceptive, Avery," John noted and then cleared his throat. His deep voice acted like a magnet drawing everyone's attention. "We do, in fact, have an announcement."

"Well, get on with it already," said Mama Donna. "I'm hungry. You two aren't moving, are you? I love this little cabin in the woods. You'll never find another house like it. Not nearby—"

"We're eloping!" Elizabeth blurted out before bursting into a fit of giggles. "But we're telling you guys. We're not inviting you guys, because no one is invited, but we've decided to tell everyone! Why keep what we want a secret?"

She was still giggling, but maybe it was sobbing, Brinkley thought, because she hadn't seen Elizabeth laugh like this in a long time. Perhaps ever.

"So, it's not really eloping," John took over. "It's more like killing the demon that was our traditional wedding and replacing it with a marvel of love."

"Oh, don't be ridiculous!" Mama Donna said, her voice reaching that pitch that always made Brinkley's heart pound faster. "Is this about your asshole father and his selfish new wedding date?"

"Honestly," Avery started, her mouth open as she seemed to collect her thoughts, "I think this is maybe the best idea you two have ever had ..."

"What!" Mama Donna gasped. "How could you say that? Elizabeth is my daughter, and John is the son I never had! I need to be at their wedding!"

"Yeah, why would you say that, Avery?" said John. "Book three needs to be the best idea I've ever had!"

Avery slunk down in her seat.

Elizabeth gained control of her laughter and was now looking at their mother. "Mom, you have complained since we got engaged about having to see Dad and Sin at our wedding."

Another, bigger smile took over Elizabeth's face. "But now you don't have to worry. I solved your problem! You're welcome."

"Oh, come on, Elizabeth. Obviously, I don't want to see your father – or anyone left in his life – but it's not worth canceling your wedding over," Mama Donna argued, twirling a strand of hair around and around her finger. "You two already booked a venue! A beautiful venue that people would die for, and you don't even have to pay for it.

Do you know how lucky you two are?"

"Maybe they don't feel lucky, Mom," Brinkley said, even though she herself was still processing the news.

But no one seemed to consider Brinkley's input as Avery was quick to chime in:

"If people would die over Hotel Aurore, they need to reevaluate their life."

"Thank you, Avery!" John said, his palms in prayer but his arms extended towards her.

Brinkley felt as if her eyes were in a four-way ping-pong match.

"Yeah, Mom, John and I have been in a cage," Elizabeth said. Her voice had returned to its usual monotone, but there was still a hint of a smile on her face. "It's a golden cage," she continued, "but it's a cage. And we're breaking out of it."

John grabbed Elizabeth's hand and declared, "Together. We're breaking free together as husband and wife."

"Oh, don't be an idiot," Mama Donna groaned.

Brinkley waited for Elizabeth to fight back, but she and John just smiled at each other, their teeth shining under their manmade, twinkle-lit sky.

For some reason, Brinkley felt her heart beat continue to pick up speed as she stared at her sister and future brother-in-law beaming at each other, their hands clasped in unity. Without being able to resist, she glanced at her phone, but the only message she had received was from Betty, her mother-in-law, with a picture of Lily and Daisy playing house.

Of course, there was no male figure playing house with them, Brinkley considered with bitterness. Her daughters were raising those baby dolls all by themselves. With a wavering smile and a pounding headache, Brinkley put her phone away and looked at the happy couple.

"Are you sure this is what you really want to do?" Brinkley heard herself asking, still feeling the intensity of her heart beat. She didn't know whether her feelings were from sadness at imagining her sister's wedding day happening without her, from wisdom of how difficult marriage can become, or from longing at seeing her sister and John so happy.

"Yes!" John and Elizabeth answered in unison. Now Brinkley's head began to pound.

"Look, traditional weddings are beautiful for ... other people. You know, people who *want* them," Elizabeth began to explain, leaning across her sunroom's coffee table towards Brinkley. "But John and I no longer find meaning in it. And on our wedding day, we don't want to put on a performance for other people."

"Yeah, we're not actors," John added, shaking his head and then, pointing to his heart, said, "I'm a writer. She's an accountant."

"Yeah, and ever since I've been engaged, I've been miserable," Elizabeth said. From the corner of her eye, Brinkley could see Avery nodding along. "I'm finally happy again." Elizabeth squeezed John's hand and looked up at him. "*We're* happy again."

Before Brinkley's tear could finish forming at the inspiration of seeing Elizabeth and John prioritize their relationship's happiness above all else, their mother interrupted.

"Well, isn't that just great, but what do you expect us to do, Liz?" Mama Donna said. "After driving all the way out here, you want us to cheer for your new wedding that none of us are apparently a part of?"

Elizabeth groaned. "See, John, I told you it was weird to bring everyone together to announce this. We should have just texted."

"Texted?" John was repulsed. "No one communicates any more!"

"Yeah, I am your mother, Elizabeth. You don't text your mother news like this!"

"Well, we're damned if we do, damned if we don't then, right?"

Elizabeth said, her voice rising.

Just as Brinkley was about to de-escalate the situation, she saw Elizabeth's shoulders shake as the melody of her laughter returned.

"Well then," Elizabeth said, her laugh lines forming deep creases around her mouth as she threw up her hands, "I guess it doesn't matter what we do."

John's head turned towards Elizabeth with a smile. "It doesn't matter!"

"But it does matter!" Mama Donna argued, and Brinkley could see tears welling in her mother's eyes. "I don't want to miss your wedding."

Even Elizabeth's smile faded at this admission, as her and John's gaze traveled towards Mama Donna. John leaned forwards, bowing his head towards their mother as he studied her with his earnest eyes.

"Donna ..." He said her name with softness. "I know this may seem unsettling. A shock, even. But there's a lot that's been leading up to this. And you will not miss our life, okay?"

Mama Donna remained silent, her thin lips pressing together in secrecy. She continued twirling her strand of hair around her finger, the motion growing faster by the second.

"We are here, and we will always be here," John said, taking his time with each word. "We just want this one day to ourselves, to start our marriage in a way that means something to us. Can you understand that?" When Mama Donna didn't answer, John added, "We haven't even told your ex-husband about our plans. We wanted to tell you first. It would mean a lot to us to have your blessing."

Mama Donna was still silent, but her scowl appeared to relax. After what felt like a full minute of this staring contest, she raised an eyebrow and looked at Elizabeth.

"Is this true?" Mama Donna asked, still twirling her hair around her finger. "You told me before your father? And you really care about my blessing?"

"It's true," said Elizabeth.

Mama Donna let go of her hair and crossed her arms, eyeing them both.

"All right," she finally said, pursing her lips. "I still need time to process all this, but ... if this is what makes you happy, you ... probably have my blessing."

Elizabeth and John looked at each other with pure glee. "We're getting married!" they squealed.

Their joy was so contagious, even Brinkley couldn't help but smile. Though buried beneath the happiness for her sister, and guarded by her smile, there was still a void beating through Brinkley's heart. And she felt terrible for experiencing it during this moment in her sister's life. So she smiled wider, as if her smile could be armor for the unseen feeling she secured inside.

Chapter 52

Avery was seated beside Brinkley under the twinkle lights of John and Elizabeth's sunroom. Their mother had stepped outside to "make a call", which really meant calling her friends to complain about the developments of the evening, while Elizabeth and John had gone inside to finish preparing dinner.

Looking through the sunroom's window that led to the kitchen, Avery watched the happy couple as they seemed to glow while putting last touches on their dishes. The window felt like her own personal portal into a romantic silent film.

She smiled to herself and took a swig of her beer. "Do you think Elizabeth will still be Mom's favorite after eloping?"

"Hmm ..." Brinkley was looking through the window as well. "Probably. Mom will still need someone to gossip about us to." Brinkley sighed. "Plus, she absolutely adores John, so ..."

"True," she said, and then eyed her sister. "Where's Chase again? Working?"

"Yeah." Even though Brinkley's tone had fallen flat, Avery noticed her sister adding a smile as she elaborated: "Chase's agency was hired to sell an expensive, restored property in Rittenhouse, so ..." Brinkley trailed off, taking a sip of her water before flashing another smile. "It's a really exciting time for his company. For us, really. I mean, this will be the most expensive property he's sold to date, so I'm really proud of him."

"Yeah, that's awesome," Avery said, but kept her eyes lingering on her sister. "So how have *you* been?"

"Me?" Brinkley looked at her sister with a scrunched nose. "What, are you still thinking about the broken wine glass?"

"Um ... I wasn't, but now I am—"

"I've been good. I mean, life isn't perfect, obviously, but I've been thinking about what you said and everything ... About feeling things for a reason and all that," Brinkley said, her eyes focused on the window. "And I think I need to do more to honor my feelings, shed some things that no longer serve me—"

"Like what?"

"I mean ..." Brinkley trailed off, looking at her stomach. "Starting with these extra pounds I've gained since having children."

"You really think it's the pounds you need to shed?" Avery challenged.

"Yes!" Brinkley snapped her head towards Avery. "If my weight's not the problem, what are you trying to say is?"

Avery felt her mouth hanging open, but was unsure if she wanted to reveal any of her thoughts. They remained staring at each other until Brinkley leaned back into the couch, focusing her gaze on the window.

"It's been three years since I've had Daisy, and every year I keep saying I'm going to stick to a workout regimen, eat healthy, stay active ..."

A warm night breeze rustled through the sunroom, and the promises Brinkley had made to herself were swept away.

Before Avery could encourage Brinkley to open her heart to the people closest to her, especially herself, Brinkley changed the subject and the moment was lost.

"How could Elizabeth not care about having a wedding?"

Avery could feel a slight crinkle in her eyebrows at this sudden change of topic. "But she will have a wedding ... She'll have the wedding she actually wants."

Brinkley ignored Avery's claim. "She's so ready to do what John wants, but what about what she wants? Do husbands even consider their wives as separate, complete people, or is Elizabeth just another ... another character in a book to him, a book he gets all the praise for, while Elizabeth is the one behind the scenes, actually providing the inspiration?"

Avery looked at Brinkley, but her sister was busy swishing her water around and around as if it were wine.

"Are we still talking about Elizabeth and John?"

"Yes," Brinkley said, glaring at Avery. "Why? I'm just worried about her. About them. I mean, canceling a wedding like this? If they can't handle the pressures of an engagement, how will they handle the pressures of marriage?"

"Okay, just ..." Avery looked back at the sunroom with a nod, carefully considering her next words. "I don't think this private wedding ceremony is only John's idea," she said. "In fact, it seems like the first thing Elizabeth's felt sure about in a long time."

While Brinkley fell silent, Avery stole a breath. Elizabeth and John had disappeared into a different room, out of sight. All that was left to see was an empty kitchen.

"Look," Avery said, turning so her whole body faced Brinkley, "whether their relationship ended now or years later, there would be pain." Avery paused, studying Brinkley, but Brinkley looked lost in her glass of water. "So even if you're worried, let's just see how this adventure helps them grow."

Brinkley's eyes lingered on her glass.

Avery readjusted a pillow and lounged back. "Honestly? I think there's something that's always seemed fleeting about their relationship. They met when they were so young, with so many transitions and changes to go through. Yet here they are, years later, still protecting what they have." After taking a swig from her beer, Avery felt the corners of her mouth curl. "And I think there's something valuable about that. I think they put their passions first, and I think they're going to live an exciting life for it."

"Exciting isn't always happy," Brinkley said under breath. "Or healthy."

"They seem happy and healthy to me, Brinkley," Avery crossed her arms as Brinkley's gaze studied her from the corners of her eye.

"Dinner's ready!" Elizabeth sang into the sunroom before disappearing as fast as she had come.

Brinkley rose from her seat with a sigh. "Well, let's go see if Mom has processed this."

"Yeah," Avery said. She rose from the couch and followed her sister's footsteps into Elizabeth and John's dining room.

Mama Donna was seated at one end of the dark ironwood table, with John at the other end. Elizabeth was smoothing a napkin over her lap, seated next to John. An empty space remained between her and their mother, but Brinkley and Avery took their seats opposite Elizabeth.

The dark wooden walls of the dining room encircled the table. Only the small brass chandelier, with arms sculpted to resemble metal vines, offered romantic light. Even after everyone was seated and napkins were smoothed over laps, the family remained still, silent.

For perhaps the first time ever, Avery considered. She glanced at John, who was observing his guests, particularly Mama Donna, with a slight smile.

They lingered in silence for a moment before Mama Donna readjusted in her seat and eyed John. "You know," she began, letting out a breath, "I was a bit ... taken aback ... by your news earlier, but ..." A big fat tear formed in Mama Donna's eyes. "I know how your father is and you don't want him ruining your day, so—"

"I mean, he's not the only reason—" Elizabeth tried correcting, but Mama Donna charged ahead.

"Hell, I even think you two will have a better time," Mama Donna said, dropping her chin onto her hand. "I'm starting to wonder if my wedding was just a distraction from the asshole I was actually marrying."

Mama Donna's daughters collectively rolled their eyes, but John laughed a deep, belly-driven laugh that reverberated its joy through the room, making Elizabeth and their mother start to laugh, too.

Avery joined in, but she couldn't help noticing Brinkley sitting next to her, checking her phone.

Chapter 53

When Brinkley arrived home from Elizabeth and John's, the girls were already tucked into bed, fast asleep. The blue glow of the TV illuminated her master bedroom with Chase sprawled on their bed, also asleep.

With a sigh, Brinkley tiptoed to her walk-in closet for a pair of pajamas. She climbed her closet's step stool to reach the top shelf where Chase kept all his comfortable old T-shirts. Sometimes when Brinkley felt distant from Chase, either after a fight or a long, busy week, Brinkley liked to fall asleep in his clothes. To feel like a part of him could still be close to her, comforting her.

During her attempt to get her favorite heather-gray one, which required standing on her tiptoes and reaching through her fingertips, she yanked a little too hard and ended up falling to the ground in one loud thump.

"Ouch!" she yelped, rubbing the throb in her right butt cheek – the same cheek she had gashed on the tub only a week ago – as she lay in a ball on the hardwood floor.

She heard Chase stir with a grumble.

Knowing a bruise was about to form, she examined her outer cheek with a wince and waited for her husband to appear to make sure she was okay. Yet the doorway to their walk-in closet remained empty.

Nostrils flared and her jaw tense, she stomped out of the closet with a limp and flicked on the ceiling lights. Chase remained snoring. When she and Chase had first begun dating, Brinkley had loved the way he looked when he slept. His square jaw was always relaxed and the creases that usually lined his forehead faded. The tranquil expression had always made Brinkley wish she could jump into his dreams.

Now, however, his stoic face was making her blood boil. She couldn't remember the last time she got a full night's sleep without Daisy waking her up and crawling into bed. Chase slept through everything, so unless Brinkley woke him up, nighttime duty always fell to her.

Brinkley flicked on the light on his nightstand, and when he still didn't wake up, she began to shove his body. "Chase!" Brinkley snapped. "Chase, wake up."

Eyes still closed, Chase turned away, using his arm to swat the air. As if she were a mosquito.

"Chase, get the hell up!" she yelled, and ripped the covers off in one swift motion. "What?" Chase groaned, rubbing his eyes. "I'm exhausted, Brinkley. What do you want?"

"What do I want?" Brinkley spat. "What do I want?" she repeated, partly because she couldn't believe he didn't know what she wanted and partly because she, herself, did not know.

But she felt she had to finish what she started, so she stormed to his side of the bed. "I want a husband who checks to make sure I'm okay when I fall from the top of the closet!"

Chase barely had his eyes open, but Brinkley wasn't finished. In fact, she was just getting started.

"Why do you keep your T-shirts up there, anyway? You know I like wearing your old T-shirts to bed, and yet you keep them on the top shelf? I'm like five foot four, Chase – how do you expect me to reach them safely?"

Chase's face distorted in disgust as he snatched his rectangular glasses from the nightstand and shoved them on his face. He squinted at his phone and then glared at her.

"Brinkley, it's ten pm. Why are you yelling at me right now?"

"I was trying to get a T-shirt for bed, and I fell, and you—" Brinkley had to adjust her volume so the girls didn't wake up. "You didn't even care," she whispered.

"I was sleeping!" Chase defended, wiping the crusts from his eyes.

"Okay, well our sleeping arrangements aren't working for me any more," Brinkley said with crossed arms.

"Okay ... ?" Chase said, his eyes growing wide, which only made Brinkley angrier. "And why's that?"

"You sleep through everything, Chase! Do you know how many times I've woken up to deal with Daisy wetting the bed, or having a nightmare about the Jell-O monster? And don't even get me *started* on how many times I've woken up because of your obnoxious computer light. Why should I have to sacrifice sleep because *you* don't know how to stop working at an appropriate time?"

Chase opened his mouth, but Brinkley cut him off. "Even when you *do* go to bed early, I still can't fall asleep because you breathe so damn loudly!"

"My breathing? Really?"

"Yes, really, Chase. You should go to a doctor for how loud you breathe at night."

"Okay, I will set up an appointment with a doctor. For breathing."

"Oh, don't be sarcastic with me, Chase."

"Brinkley, I am sorry you fell in the closet. Are you okay?" Chase grumbled. But before Brinkley could answer, he got out of bed with a heavy sigh and disappeared into their closet.

Brinkley felt her heart beat faster with every second he lingered.

Had she gone too far? Was he setting up a bed for himself in the closet?

"Chase?" she finally called. "Are you sleep-walking? This conversation is not over."

He returned with one of his T-shirts and a pair of sweatpants.

"A peace offering," he said as he placed the clothing into her hands.

"Well, I don't want them any more," Brinkley said, because she wasn't ready to let this argument end. "Not after I nearly died trying to get them."

"Okay, I'm going back to bed," Chase said, gathering the covers Brinkley had ripped off his body. "This is ridiculous."

"Of course you are ..." Brinkley rolled her eyes.

"What does that even mean, Brinkley?"

"Before I went to Elizabeth's, you said that we would talk later," Brinkley said, stalking her husband to his side of the bed. "Well, it's later, you're not working, but you're still not ready to talk? I knew you were full of it."

Chase released a long exhale through flared nostrils. His patience was running thin and she knew it.

"I feel like," she finally broke the tense silence, but paused when realizing Chase had finished tucking himself into bed with his back turned towards her.

"Forget it," she said. "I'll sleep in the guest room."

"Brinkley," Chase said, rubbing his eyes before reaching for his glasses again. He put them on and looked at her. "Stop being ridiculous. Just tell me what's wrong."

The dreaded question.

"I don't know, Chase!" she snapped. She felt her eyes wildly searching him, but all she could see was a look of hurt cross his face.

Padding towards her side of the bed, she took a seat.

"We don't do anything any more," she said. "Remember when we first started dating, all the spontaneous little trips and dates we'd go on—"

"We just went to the Bahamas. Was that not good enough?"

Their eyes lingered on each other for a moment before Brinkley released a long, quiet sigh. "Never mind."

The unexpected, quick surrender seemed to work, Brinkley realized, as her husband propped himself up with pillows. He studied her face as if one wrong word could set off an atomic bomb.

"How was dinner?" Chase finally spoke after a stretch of silence. "I'm sorry I couldn't make it."

"John and Elizabeth canceled their wedding," she said, her voice sounding distant from the jumbled thoughts in her mind. "They've decided to have a private ceremony."

"Wait, really?"

Brinkley nodded, replaying the maniacal fit of her sister's giggles with a shudder.

"How do you feel about it ..." Chase tried, and Brinkley could feel his eyes still trying to read her face.

"I mean, as long as my sister's happy, I'm happy, right?" she said with a sigh. "And they both seem very happy, so ..."

"Well, that's good, then," Chase said, his voice a bit too cheerful for Brinkley's lingering mood. "Good for them."

She opened her mouth and then closed it. *Remember when we were happy?*

"Come into bed," Chase pleaded, looking at her.

Without a word, Brinkley turned off their ceiling lights and began changing into the pajamas her husband had retrieved for her. She pulled down the covers to let herself in.

"I wish you'd been with me tonight," she whispered.

"I know, Brinkley, I wish I was too."

They both stared at their high, white ceiling illuminated by the light of their nightstand's lamp.

"Do you really?" she said.

"What do you mean?" Chase said. He rolled onto his side to face her. "Of course I do. I can't wait until this property is sold so we can have more time together again."

"Yeah," Brinkley said, but her gaze was still lost on the ceiling. "Yeah, that would be nice."

"Brinkley ..." He reached his hand for hers, but she didn't clutch his back.

"Did your showing at least go well tonight?"

"Yeah ..." He sighed. He rolled away, retrieving his hand to his chest as he stared at the wall. "Yeah, the buyers seemed interested, so we'll see." When she didn't answer, he continued: "It would be huge. Not only would it earn good commission; it'd keep me on the radar for big sales like that. I mean, it's one of the most expensive properties listed in Philadelphia. It's a big deal."

"Right," Brinkley said.

They lay in their silence.

"I'm proud of you, Chase," she finally added, because no matter what they were experiencing in their life or marriage, it was a sentiment that had always rung true. Over the years, Brinkley and Chase had grown and they were not the same people they had agreed to marry. But through it all, Brinkley was always proud of the man she had chosen, and right now it felt like an important sentiment to hold on to.

"Thank you," Chase said, revealing nothing in his tone, and flicked off the light. Just before Brinkley closed her eyes, he spoke again: "I wouldn't be this successful without you, you know."

"Yeah ... Thank you."

It was a sentiment she had heard many times before. Throughout the years, it was becoming harder and harder to have faith her husband believed it. Probably because it was becoming harder and harder for Brinkley to believe it herself.

Their words faded through the darkness as Chase fell back asleep. But Brinkley remained awake, staring at the darkened ceiling. She pictured her sister with John, how happy they'd both seemed tonight, and thought back to her own engagement with Chase. Sure, she and Chase had experienced wedding planning drama – who didn't – but Brinkley remembered her engagement as a special time, when she and Chase had fallen even more in love with their shared life and had become excited for their future. Their wedding day had ended up feeling even more joyous than imagined or planned. At the time, Brinkley had thought it was a good sign. As if a fairytale wedding foreshadowed a fairytale marriage. Now, as she lay awake in the dark, alone with her thoughts and the sound of her husband's heavy breathing, she didn't know if anything was a foreshadowing. She thought of her friend Olivia, who could also be lying awake in bed, at this moment, worried about her own marriage, her pregnancy, her future.

She thought of her sister Avery, who had rushed back to work after Elizabeth's and was now serving drinks to customers, counting every tip with guarded thoughts and a subdued smile.

She thought of her father, lying with Sin, a woman he tried to use to fill a fear in his heart of not wanting to grow old alone. To do so would force him to face the consequences of how he had treated his loved ones throughout his life.

She thought of her mother, alone in her two-story, three-bedroom house, the only undivided remnant of her divorce. Surely her mother had gone through many nights like this, lying awake in bed, with her husband by her side and her kids a few doors down, yearning for a different life. Until the reality of that life set in.

And Brinkley thought of Nana. All those secrets Nana's heart must have held.

As she thought of all these people, Brinkley wondered if she really knew any of them at all, and if any of them knew her.

Just as she found herself reaching for the rose quartz ring Nana had gifted her, she realized her finger was empty. The ring was still stored in her vanity drawer. Brinkley tiptoed towards her vanity, opened the top drawer, and stared at the ring.

The last words Nana had spoken to her echoed through her jumbled mind:

You are a wonderful mother and wife ... You live such a lucky life. She ran her fingers over the jagged edges of the rose quartz stone. *It was one of the first gifts your grandfather ever got for me ... I've been wearing it ever since.* She pictured Nana's cloudy eyes, her labored breathing. *It's a symbol of love.*

Brinkley felt herself wince. Was this ring a symbol of love? Or was Elizabeth's pouch from Francesco the real symbol? Spending years writing love letters to someone you would never sleep with again seemed like more than lust.

She placed the ring back in the drawer and padded to bed.

Since she was lying alone in the dark, with nothing to distract her now that she had lost her faith in the internet, a thought resurfaced in Brinkley's mind, as if waiting for this alone time to make itself known.

You are allowed to feel the way you feel. In fact, you're feeling it for a reason.

She closed her eyes, and went to sleep.

Chapter 54

I t was an especially slow Wednesday afternoon at the bar, leaving Avery plenty of time to catch up with Raymond. She had updated him on the status of her father's new wedding date, to which he replied in his strained voice:

"Have you wondered what life would be like if your parents weren't the focus?"

Avery tilted her head, but continued drying a beer glass with a dishrag. "Um, what?"

"What if you no longer allowed your parents to become the focus of your stories, your life?" he said.

"Well ..." Avery set the glass down only to replace it with another. "They're not really the focus of my life, you know. But they are my parents and they do provide a lot of ... drama, so ..." Avery trailed off, unable to meet Raymond's gaze.

Before Avery could change the topic, Raymond finished the last of his old-fashioned and looked right at Avery.

"You've told me much about your family," he said, and his squint made his usually soft gaze appear harsh. "What has been going on with you?"

"Nothing, really."

"You're too young and too curious of an individual for that," he said, and she could feel his eyes still on her.

"Well, I went camping, as you know, and ..." She paused from drying another glass. "That was ... healing. Helped me reflect on some things." Avery's eyes seemed to brighten for a moment. "I've actually been thinking about where my next camping trip could be." She was still using the dishrag to dry the glass even though she couldn't see any more water droplets. "I wanted to take a road trip across the country, you know, and visit a bunch of national parks along the way, but I've been thinking, and ... Why wait? Maybe I could start with one little trip at a time, and someday—"

"Good," he cut her off. "When are you quitting this place?"

Avery stopped drying the glass and looked at Raymond. *He must be having a stroke,* she thought, but Raymond remained sitting upright, his face even, arms folded on the bar counter.

"Raymond," she started. "What?"

"Avery, I have been coming to this bar every Wednesday for the past three years. When I first met you, you were a young woman using this place to find your next step in the world. But I'm getting older," he said, "and I don't want to die while you're still working here, unhappy. You know how to connect with people. You understand them. You have emotional experience – maybe too much for your own good. But you have it, and you could do something with it. Something that fulfills you."

Avery felt her heart stiffening with every word he spoke.

"I know it's nice, finally getting comfortable with life," he said. Raymond reached his head towards her, his index finger pointing down, on the counter. "But this bar is not it."

"But ..." Avery stumbled over her thoughts. Starting to feel dizzy and feeling her stomach flip-flop, Avery tried to recall the past three years she had confided in this guy. All this time, she had trusted that he was an open mind, but now, even after she had told him almost everything going on in her life, he was minimizing her job. Just like her family.

But when she looked into his deep-set eyes, which had remained focused on her the entire time, she couldn't help but feel her defenses weaken. His eyes did not reveal anger, or superiority. There was a truth they were trying to convey.

For a moment, she allowed herself to imagine that the man she had trusted for three years was not actually putting her down to intimidate her into a different place. Maybe it was possible that, through all their interactions, he did understand her, at least a sliver of her, and was trying build her up.

To help her get to a happier place.

She felt her chest rise with a breath, but before she could even decide which version of this man to believe in, the man she thought she could trust versus the man who was now telling her what to do with her life, Raymond spoke.

"You have shown me deep kindness, Avery," he said, and Avery could see that his eyes were glossy as he spoke. "Kinder than my grandchildren, even children, have. I want to see you fulfill your potential."

Avery had to break their gaze as her stomach continued to churn. She clutched her dishrag and began to wipe the counter. "Well, thank you ..." she stammered, watching her hands move in circles. "I'll think about it."

Raymond raised his empty glass to her with a nod.

"But just so we're clear," she said, pausing for a moment to meet his gaze once again, "this isn't your way of saying you're dying, right?"

His deep belly chuckle returned. She breathed.

"You're always so worried about my dying! We're all dying, Avery." He wiped a tear from his eyes before his tone became serious again. "That's why I want you to get out of here while you still can."

Avery could feel a shadow cross her face when he said this. She wrinkled her eyebrows at him, but he continued staring right into her eyes.

"Well ... you're not sick or anything, right?"

"I probably have quite a few years left in me," he said.

"Okay," she breathed, looking at the floor as she felt her mouth grow dry, "I just had to ask, you know? I can't handle another person's last words right now."

Raymond didn't laugh.

"I'm okay, Avery," he said once again. "But even if I weren't – you would be able to handle it. You're a lot more resilient than you give yourself credit for."

Avery could still feel his eyes on her, but she couldn't bring herself to meet them.

"Thank you," she said, then looked at the other end of the bar. "Seriously, thank you ... Um, I need to check on my other customers."

Before he could say anything else, she walked away.

Chapter 55

"Do you think your mom will flip a table when we tell her?" Elizabeth whispered as she stepped out of her car. She hooked her arm in John's and together they walked up the beige stone steps.

They were going to enter the Astors' mansion as a united front.

"I hope," John muttered. "It would be the most emotion that woman has shown my whole adult life."

Elizabeth could feel her skin growing hot as they reached the double wooden doors. She considered her fiancé's messy hair, which was nearly touching his shoulders in loose waves. Now that they were standing before the Astors' grand entryway, Elizabeth felt deep regret over John's decision not to use gel.

Before leaving their cabin, John had had a crisis over whether to part and gel his hair as he had always done whenever seeing his family. "My hair will set the tone, Liz," he had argued while getting ready. "I want to set the right tone."

"It's just hair, John," she had yelled after a half-hour had passed with no decision.

"Not to them!" he had called after her. "You don't understand what they're like!"

"John, you seemed to mostly like your family until, like, one week

332

ago. So, you're going to have to chill with the dramatics of how tormented you are," she had said from their bedroom. "I'm the one with the messed-up childhood. Not you."

"Why can't you validate my pain, Liz? Why can't you ever validate my pain?"

Elizabeth remembered how John's words had made her surrender her defenses. They had quickly made up, blaming the argument on the stress of having to tell his parents their new wedding plans.

Now Elizabeth stood at the Astors' double wooden doors, trying to smooth over John's wild hair.

John rang the doorbell. It opened with a creak.

"Well, hello," Mrs. Astor greeted them, her carmine-red lips curling into a smile.

"Hello, Jane." John nodded, and then looked at the ground, walking into the foyer.

Oh, here we go, Elizabeth thought. He was already acting weird.

"John, what happened to your hair?" Mrs. Astor asked.

"This is my hair," he said and continued walking towards the dining room while Elizabeth remained in the doorway.

So much for appearing as a united front.

"Is everything all right with you two?" Mrs. Astor asked Elizabeth in a low voice.

Well, he's not calling me by my first name, Elizabeth thought as she looked at Mrs. Astor with a tight smile. *I'm still his darling.*

But Elizabeth simply tilted her head. "Yes. Why?"

Mrs. Astor leaned away from Elizabeth with widened eyes and a shrug.

"Come on in, darling," she finally said, and propped the front door just wide enough to let Elizabeth through.

The sounds of clinking china and quiet chewing filled the Astors' dining room after they had talked at length about which careers they should encourage Jordan and Jared's unborn baby to pursue. By the end, everyone except Elizabeth and John had agreed that one should stay away from the arts unless they were fine and pursued on the side, technology could be profitable but also tacky, while medicine and law were timeless. Plus, Cousin Peyton and Uncle Bradford would be out of practice by the time this child was of age, and there was always a need for a lawyer and a doctor in the family.

"So," said Jordan, her eyes on Elizabeth and John, who were seated across from her, "you two have been awfully quiet. How is your little cottage in the woods holding up? It's a bit small, no?"

"Not for us, no." Elizabeth shook her head. She and John had purposely purchased a home they could pay off right away, rather than take out a mortgage. Being flashy did not fulfill them, but being debt-free in the woods did.

"What if you want children?" said Jordan.

"We don't," said John.

"You know what you could do," Jordan continued, not hearing him, "you could build an addition. Or even buy the lot next to you and build a new house ... Turn your little one into a guest house. Cottagecore is so trendy these days."

"Yeah?" Elizabeth said, her face beginning to flush as she finished off her wine. "That would be a lovely solution, if I thought our house was a problem." She looked at her husband, her voice cracking. "Honey?"

They had agreed to make their wedding announcement after dinner was served, and it had been served. In fact, quite a bit of time had passed. Yet John kept his eyes focused on the leftover green beans he was stirring with his fork.

"Shall we tell them?" Elizabeth asked through a tight smile.

He took a huge scoop of green beans, which Elizabeth knew was his least favorite vegetable, and shoved them into his mouth.

Elizabeth kicked his shin underneath the table. John choked, grabbing his chest.

"John! Are you okay?" Jordan gasped, nearly lunging across the table, causing her fork to clatter to the ground as John continued to cough.

"Aw, Hun, just let it out," Elizabeth cooed, eyeing his every movement.

"Do you need the Heimlich? I believe Chef Monroe is certified," Mrs. Astor said with her cool, smooth voice.

After one last cough and a few more chews, John took a sip of his water. Then he took another.

He patted his chest.

He cleared his throat.

"Oh, for Christ's sake, John," Mr. Astor grumbled, turning his head towards his son.

Mrs. Astor, though, had not been distracted.

"What did you want to tell us, Johnathan?" she said from her seat at the head of the table. Her lips remained pressed into a straight, red line as she eyed her son. Her elbows rested on the table, fingers clasped into a fist, which only made the moment more intimidating, because Mrs. Astor knew and obeyed the rules of etiquette.

John cleared his throat again.

"Elizabeth and I ..." John's gaze lingered on the floor for a moment before looking at his parents. "We have had a change of wedding plans."

"Is that so?" Mrs. Astor said, her lips still pursed, but her eyes traveled between John and Elizabeth. "Well ... what are they?"

"We are going to cancel our wedding at Hotel Aurore, and just ... get married. Alone. Just us."

Elizabeth swallowed as she watched Mrs. Astor stab John with her glare. But John maintained his eye contact. Elizabeth's eyes couldn't stop darting between them.

"This is a joke," Jordan said before catching Elizabeth's gaze. "Is he joking?"

"No. We are serious," John said, breaking the staring contest with his mother so he could face his sister. "We tried the traditional wedding path, and it never felt right for us. So, we want to do something that does. But we ... We want your guys' blessing," John said, looking back at his mother. "That would mean a lot to us."

"But to not have family there?" Jordan argued. "What is that solving?"

"A lot, apparently," said John.

Elizabeth glanced at Mr. Astor, who was sitting silently at the table, keeping his attention focused on the steak beneath him, even though his eyebrows had gathered into a scowl.

"Hmm," Mrs. Astor said and seemed to sit up straighter. "We'll see."

John snapped his head towards his mother. "We're actually doing it next month."

The look of disdain was written all over Mrs. Astor's cold, twisted face when she heard this. Her forehead was still smooth, but her lips had parted and smudged upwards in distaste.

"Wait, what?" Jordan cried. "What's the rush?"

"Is she pregnant?" Mr. Astor grumbled. "At least she signed the prenup."

"The rush?" John said, a small chuckle escaping his lips. "The rush?"

Elizabeth's stomach was doing flips and tricks as if it were performing in the goddamn Olympics.

"We've been dating for ten years, Jordan," John barked. "What are you talking about, *What's the rush?* That's longer than you and Jared

336

have known each other!"

Jared, quiet as always, appeared to bury his head into his steak.

"Johnathan, keep your voice down," Mrs. Astor hissed.

Instead, John smacked his hands on the dinner table. "And no, Father, we're not pregnant! We're in love."

"I don't know where he came from." Mr. Astor continued scowling as he looked at his wife.

Without even glancing Elizabeth's way, Mrs. Astor grabbed the knife near her plate to continue slicing her steak. *She seems to be enjoying that a little too much,* Elizabeth observed as Mrs. Astor's eyes remained focused on the thick strips she was carving.

"Mom," John said, his voice sharper than his mother's knife. All eyes were drawn to him. He sat up straight, his body facing his mother's direction. The silent pause hovered in the air. "Is there something wrong?" he asked with one thick, dark eyebrow raised.

Mrs. Astor placed a slice of steak in her mouth and chewed, keeping her eyes on her son the whole time.

"No, Johnathan, nothing is wrong," she said, her smooth voice making the hairs on Elizabeth's back rise. "I hope you both have a ... charming time."

The rest of their family, per their routine, followed Mrs. Astor's lead. They ate their steak in silence and did not speak of anything involving John and Elizabeth's new wedding plans.

As Elizabeth tried to finish eating the remnants of her tofu steak and green beans, she couldn't help but steal glances around the table.

The Astors' even temperaments weren't impressing her any more. In fact, they were haunting her.

She looked at her fiancé, his eyes already cast down to the floor, and took his hand in hers with a squeeze.

He squeezed hers back.

Chapter 56

Brinkley, Avery, and Mama Donna were sitting on a satin, ivory-colored sofa of a wedding dress boutique in the city. They were sipping on champagne, oohing and aahing over every dress Elizabeth tried on.

"You look like a mermaid goddess in that one," Avery said of a wedding dress bejeweled with pearls.

"You look like an elegant heiress," Brinkley praised over a dress with a high neckline and low-cut back.

"Not any more," Elizabeth snorted, and cut that dress from her list of possibilities.

"Oh, you look just like me on my wedding day! I love it!" Mama Donna exclaimed over a lace one. "Not my wedding, but I always loved my dress."

"We get it, Mom," said Avery.

Brinkley checked her watch. Their appointment time was coming to an end, and Elizabeth had narrowed her choices to two dresses. She waltzed out of the curtain-veiled dressing room in a sleek, ivory-colored satin dress. It had a cowl neckline with a low-cut back. Thin straps of satin connected the front to the back, adding a touch of sexy elegance.

Elizabeth's dark brown hair, always parted straight down the middle, draped down her back, reflecting all the soft lighting of the boutique with its smooth silkiness. Even the light brown shade of Elizabeth's eyes, as they looked hopefully at her audience, seemed to coordinate perfectly with the look.

"That's the one!" said Brinkley, feeling her eyes grow wet with emotion.

"Oh no, you look like a hussy, Liz," Mama Donna groaned.

The stylist who had been assisting Elizabeth that morning placed her hand over her mouth to shield her laugh.

"A hussy, Mom? Really?" Elizabeth said on her stage, the three large mirrors revealing her from every angle. She used her right hand to hold her hair back as she leaned towards her mother, as if ready to lunge. "This is one of my top two choices. For my *wedding* dress. Do you really need to use that language?"

"I'm sorry ... I'm sorry ..." Mama Donna surrendered her free hand in the air as she sipped her champagne. "I just want to be honest, so you don't look like a hussy in your wedding pictures."

"And your other favorite dress happens to be Mom's favorite, so ..." Avery sipped her champagne as well, eyeing Mama Donna from the corner of her eye. "I think Mom's trying to push her own agenda over there."

"Oh, come on, Avery." Mama Donna rolled her eyes and took another sip of champagne. "We're all giving our opinions! You girls shouldn't invite me if you can't handle my truth."

Elizabeth rolled her eyes just as their mother burst into a mixture of laughter and tears.

"I can remember holding Elizabeth as a little baby, and now," she said, more tears beginning to well in her eyes, replacing the ones she had just wiped away, "now she's all grown up."

"Aw, Mom," Elizabeth beamed from her small stage.

"Okay, can we save the crying for somewhere we're more ...

private?" Avery said, her eyes scanning the boutique.

"Yeah, you never cried like this when we went shopping for my wedding dress," said Brinkley.

The stylist stepped forward. "Did you want to try the lace dress one more time? Our appointment is up ..."

Elizabeth turned to her reflection in the mirror. She smoothed over the already-smooth satin fabric and tilted her chin up. Everyone on the sofa held their breath. The stylist checked her watch again.

"Yes," Elizabeth said. "Yes, let's try the lace dress one more time."

"Oh, you are going to look *stunning*, Elizabeth," Mama Donna cheered as if she were a beauty pageant mother sending her daughter onstage.

"Okay, so the stylist and the store hate us," Brinkley muttered.

"I know." Mama Donna was whispering now. "Did you see how the stylist was checking her watch? They really try to move you along like cattle."

"Okay, well, we have been here for one hour, we're three minutes over our appointment time, and," Brinkley glanced at the changing room before whispering, "Elizabeth has tried on the lace dress three times before this."

Avery and Mama Donna responded with glares.

"What are you saying, Brinkley?" said Mama Donna. "Do you know how much money I'm about to give them for a *dress*? I don't give a flying fart if we're three minutes over, let's be *ten*—"

"Here comes the bride," Avery announced just as the stylist and Elizabeth emerged from the dressing room.

"You look so elegant, Elizabeth," said Mama Donna, tears once again filling her eyes. Brinkley watched as her sister admired herself in the mirror.

"Are you crying?" Avery asked Elizabeth.

Elizabeth laughed, wiping away her tears. "A little bit. It's just so beautiful."

Brinkley felt herself smile. The dress *was* beautiful. A Bardot top, with two little lace sleeves flowing around her biceps. The train was small, also lace, with delicate flower details.

Still, Brinkley preferred the satin one.

"Pick that one, Liz, that's the one," Mama Donna insisted.

"You do look stunning," Brinkley said, but added, "in both of them."

"What do you think?" Elizabeth's eyes were on Avery.

"Pick the one that makes you feel happiest," Avery said.

"Oh, talk about a safe response," Mama Donna complained with a roll of her eyes.

Elizabeth looked down and smoothed over the lace. Everyone on the couch was waiting, holding their breath. She twirled to admire herself in the mirror once more.

"Okay," Elizabeth announced. Her teary eyes had cleared, and she was looking at her family with a bright smile. "This is the dress! I found my wedding dress!"

All three women erupted into cheers and lunged towards Elizabeth with open arms, engulfing her in a tight hug.

After wedding dress shopping, the three sisters and their mother filed into one of Elizabeth's favorite restaurants in the city. Mama Donna had offered to take them somewhere more formal, but Elizabeth had objected.

Now they were all seated at the table of the casual restaurant, a bowl of fresh guacamole and various salsas in the middle. Elizabeth excused herself to go to the bathroom, and had not taken even four steps until their mother leaned in.

"Is anyone else getting sad we'll be missing the wedding?"

"Mom," Brinkley said, ready to change the subject even though she was getting more than a little sad, but Avery cut her off.

"I mean, of course it's sad. I've always wanted to see her and John get married." Avery shrugged, taking a sip of water before adding, "But honestly, her and John seem happy ..." Avery tilted her head. "The joy is back in their eyes."

Just as Mama Donna opened her mouth with a nod, Brinkley saw Elizabeth emerge from the bathroom. "She's coming back," she warned.

Everyone reached for their water.

Elizabeth pulled out her chair, complaining about the line being too long, when their mother blurted out:

"We were just saying we're sad we're going to miss your and John's wedding."

"Mom, don't make her feel bad!" Brinkley hissed.

"No, this is good," Elizabeth said, placing her napkin on her lap as she took her seat with bright eyes and a relaxed smile. "John and I think it's very healthy to let your emotions out. If you don't release them, they become your inner demons, and those demons find a way out one way or another." Her eyes lingered on Brinkley. "It was actually Brinkley's advice that made me realize I needed to take charge of my wedding."

"What?" Mama Donna gasped, her head whipping towards Brinkley with bulging eyes. "First you tell Avery to get lost in the mountains alone, and then you tell Elizabeth to get married alone? What is wrong with you?"

Brinkley felt her jaw hanging open as she stared at Elizabeth. "Okay, why am I always getting the blame?"

"Blame?" Elizabeth said with wrinkled eyebrows, as if she were genuinely confused. "Brinkley, do you remember when you found me crying in Dad's bathroom? After I shattered the casserole dish?"

"Yes, I remember," Brinkley said, looking at Elizabeth. "How could

I forget a potato casserole flying through the air."

"Elizabeth, you shattered a casserole dish?" Mama Donna gasped.

"I did. Like I said, those demons find a way. Anyway," she said, facing Brinkley again, "you reminded me that this is my life, and I shouldn't just ask for one night of it."

"Yeah, I remember ..." Brinkley said, feeling her mother's glare grow more intense by the second. "So ... what? You heard that and decided to cancel your wedding?"

"No, canceling the wedding was John's stroke of genius," Elizabeth quickly corrected. "But hearing it helped snap me out of something. So, thanks."

"Really?" Brinkley said, feeling her voice crack. Gosh, it was becoming so easy for her to cry these days. It made her worry she was becoming her mother. She cleared her throat.

"Aw, you know what," Avery broke in, also looking at Brinkley now, "if it weren't for Brinkley suggesting I go camping, I feel like I wouldn't have gone again. At least not any time soon—"

"Oh, here we go," said Mama Donna, rolling her eyes.

Avery ignored her, her gaze still lingering on Brinkley. Brinkley felt a smile spreading from her heart and across her face. "And that trip meant a lot to me—"

"Now she's just trying to steal my thunder," Elizabeth muttered.

"Give me a break, Elizabeth—"

Brinkley didn't feel the need to de-escalate the situation, her face was beaming with so much pride.

"Anyway," Elizabeth broke in as she pulled a tortilla chip from the stack, "you all should come to John and my bonfire. We have one every month, when John burns all his unwanted work, and then we just ... let ourselves feel whatever we need to feel while we watch. It's pretty magnificent. Not to mention healing."

"Well, what would we burn?" said Avery.

"I mean, you can burn anything. Letters, notes to yourself, receipts – anything you want to let go of."

Avery's usually slumped posture straightened. "When's the next one?"

"The night before we leave for our wedding. We'll have refreshments, food. All you guys have to bring is stuff you want to burn. John and I are ready to start this next chapter of life with a clean slate."

"That does sound healing," Avery mused, but her gaze was focused on somewhere else.

"Will that be the last chance we get to see you before you go?" Brinkley asked, hearing the tremor in her voice as images of Elizabeth in her wedding dress were now flooding her brain. "Before you run off and get married?"

"Oh, Brinkley, are you sad?" Mama Donna said, rubbing Brinkley's back. "See, Elizabeth, we just want to be there to see you." Mama Donna stopped rubbing Brinkley's back as she looked at the bowls of salsa between them. "Also ... I'm supposed to go to Napa next weekend with my girlfriends, so I won't be able to make the bonfire. I'm sorry."

"Dropped like a hot potato," Avery muttered. "But I'll be there."

"Me too," said Brinkley, leaning towards Elizabeth. "The bonfire doesn't sound like my thing, but I'm not going to miss the last chance to see you two off."

With softened eyes, Elizabeth clasped her mother and sister's hands in hers. "I know John and my new wedding plans might be sad for people. I'm going to miss you all so much." Elizabeth surveyed everyone seated around the table before adding with a shrug, "But John and I can't play favorites, and to be frank, I don't know if any of you would have even made the cut." With a bright smile, Elizabeth added, "I'll be sure to send photos!"

"I know, I get it," their mother sighed, twirling a strand of hair around her finger. "Ya know, the priest showed up drunk to my wedding. I swear. He showed up drunk. Should've known then it was an omen."

"That's lovely, Mother," said Avery.

"And you're sure you don't want a little celebration? Nothing big." Mama Donna held up her hands as if someone had accused her of something. "Just a little something with friends and family. Everyone can have fun, give their blessing, and celebrate your love!"

Brinkley's heart tugged at the chance to celebrate her sister getting married. Plus, it would be a family event Chase had to attend.

"Aw, that's beautiful," Elizabeth sang, and then returned to her usual monotone. "No one would pay for it, though."

"I'd pay for it," Brinkley said. When everyone looked at her, she nodded. "I would love to get the chance to celebrate, actually. I can get a plant-based caterer, decorations, maybe an ice sculpture—"

"That's so sweet of you!" Elizabeth said. "But I don't know if John and I want a celebration right now. Especially not a big, over-the-top one. We have a happier time when things are casual."

"I can keep it casual!" Brinkley said, sitting straighter. "A nice, *casual*, backyard barbeque. Maybe we can get a food truck and a photo booth—"

"No, I meant actually casual," Elizabeth clarified. "Like, go to the grocery store, pick up some food and beer, hang some string lights and call it a day."

"Oh, I want the food truck," Mama Donna whined, dropping the strand of hair she had been twirling.

"I can't even be in charge of my *made-up* wedding celebration," Elizabeth said, incredulous. She shook her head. "Anyway, that's all very sweet, Brinkley, but maybe after our wedding. John hasn't been speaking to his family since we told them our new plans, and it's not like we'd care to invite any of our friends last-minute like this."

"Maybe the party would be a good way to bring the Astors together!" Mama Donna tried. "I'm sure they're just shocked like we were. Giving them a chance to at least celebrate you two would probably make them feel better."

"Hah!" Elizabeth laughed, popping a chip, loaded with guacamole and mango salsa, in her mouth. "You have not spent the past decade with them, Mother."

"That's their only son, Elizabeth. They put down payments on vendors for you two! You have to understand if they're a bit upset right now."

"Trust me, Mom, I understand anyone being upset," said Elizabeth. "But they live in a different world than we do. A world where feelings aren't expressed. I mean, when John and I told the Astors our new plans, Mrs. Astor said she hopes we'll have a 'charming time'—"

"Well that's nice," Brinkley tried.

"Nothing about Mrs. Astor's tone or body language matched her words, Brinkley. Yet everyone at the table accepted it anyway and continued to eat their steak in silence. It wasn't nice, it was eerie." Elizabeth looked back at her mother. "And as for the down payments, John assured me his parents will get their money back. They're the Astors, after all. They're so well-connected in this area, no business is going to get in their way. Most of the vendors they booked are owned by their friends."

"The rich get richer," Mama Donna grunted. "That's what my father always told me when I was younger."

"Well, forget the Astors, then! We still want a chance to celebrate you two," Brinkley said, leaning into the table. "And why wouldn't you want to invite friends?"

"John and I have become quite the recluses since his critically acclaimed book," Elizabeth explained. "We keep our group small, and most of the people in it don't have consistent or easy schedules.

They're all *artists.* It will be much more intriguing to run off, get married, and fill our friends in later."

"So, in your life, it's basically just ... you and John, your families, and ... a few friends you probably met through him?" Brinkley said. "Doesn't that make you a bit ... worried?"

"Why would it?" Elizabeth said, and perhaps she really didn't know, because she simply stared at Brinkley, waiting for the answer.

Brinkley looked around before leaning forwards. "What's going to happen when you and John aren't enough for each other any more? You need more people in your life, Elizabeth, to support your marriage."

"Brinkley, we have people," Elizabeth said. "Very inspiring people, might I add. We just don't have an *excess* of people." Elizabeth popped another chip into her mouth, which was already full of food as she spoke. "I don't think it's a bad thing to know when to let things go." Tilting her head, she appeared to mull something over as she chewed. "In fact, maybe you should try it. Make space for new friends. Your perspective on life feels very ... stale."

"Elizabeth," Brinkley snapped, surprised at the edge she heard in her own voice, "what are you going to do when John's done getting to know you? Are you going to be another character left behind in a book, with no one acknowledging *you're* the muse who supported him behind the scenes and helped make it happen?"

Everyone at the table grew silent, their eyes studying Brinkley and Elizabeth, but Elizabeth's gaze was relaxed as she took a minute to consider this.

"Well," she said matter-of-factly, "he'll never be done getting to know me. That's what makes us soul mates. We know how to keep getting to know each other." A secure smile spread across Elizabeth's face as she added, "And it doesn't happen behind the scenes. He's dedicated every book to me."

The words sliced through Brinkley's beating heart.

As Elizabeth continued devouring the bowl of chips between them, spilling on exciting wedding details and raving about the next chapter of life she was about to begin, Brinkley leaned back in her seat, feeling her heavy heartbeat fade into the background of life.

She felt exposed, sitting there, listening to the new developments in her sister's life. After having children, especially after having Daisy, she couldn't remember the last time she and Chase had tried getting to know each other. Actually, she hadn't bothered to think that there was anything left to know.

Nana popped into her head – the secrets a loved one could hold – and a curiosity began to grow.

Chapter 57

"I refuse to go to this bullshit meeting without my future wife!" John's voice trembled as he looked at Elizabeth with a flushed pink face. Even his already-dark hair seemed to have turned a shade darker by the sheer will of his mood.

"Aw, babe ..." Elizabeth tugged at John's fist, which unraveled into a palm. Elizabeth took his hand and placed it on her heart. "I love that you want me there," she said, "but your parents don't want me in your trust fund meeting. I was never going to be involved with the trust anyway." She felt her muscles tense when she heard her own words and added under her breath, "The prenup took care of that."

John's face seemed to soften, but Elizabeth felt the bitterness of past passivity flood her mind. The prenup that offered Elizabeth more money for each child she gave birth to, even though the Astors knew she had never wanted children. It basically equated Elizabeth's worth to the number of children she could bear, as if the only value she could add to their lives were heirs and heiresses to their fucked-up thrones. No one besides John ever acknowledged that, without John's trust fund, Elizabeth was the breadwinner of the household, as John's book royalties continued to dwindle every year. Still, Elizabeth had signed that prenup with no protest, not even a visible scowl on her face.

"You know what," she figured out loud when realizing the absurdity of not attending a meeting that involved her future husband's finances, "maybe I should go. I mean, this is about *our* future. Maybe we should *demand* that I go."

"Yes, Elizabeth, we should."

"I mean, I am going to be your wife. We are going to share the rest of our lives together! Why shouldn't I go to a meeting that's about our finances?"

"Exactly," John agreed with a sharp nod.

"When they threaten to take the trust away from you – and we both know that's what this meeting is about, let's be real – *I'm* going to be the breadwinner and you don't see me running to the bank without you!"

"Elizabeth, yes, that's what I've been saying!"

Elizabeth walked past her husband, clicking her tongue. She stood in front of the screen door to the sunroom and stared through the trunks of the seemingly never-ending trees. She replayed the moment she had signed that prenup over in her head, feeling the scowl she should have shown then deepening across her face now.

"Darling ..." The depth of John's voice snapped Elizabeth's attention back to him. "I'm going to call them and tell them I'm not going. Not unless my soon-to-be wife comes."

"Yes! I am demanding a seat at that stuffy table."

"Yes!" John held his flip-phone in the air as if he were the Statue of Liberty.

"Put it on speaker!"

"Of course." John stabbed each number on the keypad but kept hitting the wrong numbers, and since it was a flip-phone – John refused to get a smart phone – he had to keep hitting the backspace.

"Jesus ..." Elizabeth sighed, watching his struggle.

"What, Liz, I'm under a lot of stress right now."

"When are you going to get a real phone?"

"This is my real phone," he said as he missed another number.

"Why don't you just go to your contacts?"

John stopped typing. He pressed a few buttons and sure enough, pulled up his contacts. The speaker was on. The phone started ringing.

Elizabeth could feel her past selves all smiling and nodding, tugging at her, trying to make her second-guess herself and play nice just as she had been groomed to do all her life. *It's time to smile and nod at me, bitches,* she found herself thinking as the phone rang.

"Hello, Johnathan," Mrs. Astor's tired voice answered the phone. She sounded even more chilling over speakerphone.

"Hello, Mother." John looked around their kitchen before speaking again. "I got your message about having a meeting about my trust ..." He glanced at Elizabeth, who offered two thumbs-up. "And that Elizabeth shouldn't join me. You know that Elizabeth and I are sharing our future together, right?"

"I'm just trying to protect her, Johnathan," his mother said with an audible sigh. "Your father doesn't think you're stable enough to inherit your trust in five years. We can revisit it again when you're forty, depending on where you are in life."

"Father doesn't, or you don't, Mother?" said John.

There was a moment of silence that allowed Elizabeth's heart to lift in hopes of hearing honesty.

"Johnathan, is everything okay with you? You seem a little ... unstable. We have the resources to get you access to the best help."

"I'm stable!" John yelled into the phone.

"Right ..."

Elizabeth smoothed her hand over her husband's back. He cleared his throat.

"I'm just starting to feel ... tired – no, actually, that's a lie. I am exhausted. I am exhausted that any time someone expresses an emotion or idea you don't like, you act like something is wrong with them." His volume remained low, but his tone sounded as though he were a shaken-up soda bottle ready to explode on whatever unfortunate soul turned his cap.

"Johnathan," his mother's even-toned, cool voice said, "don't make this about other people when it's really about you—"

That was all it took for John to shout: "Maybe I am unstable, Mother! Compared to you and Father, everything is unstable! You two are as stoic and chalky as your plaster busts in your library." His wild hair waved frantically in front of his face as he rocked his body forwards and brought his mouth right to the phone. "It's impossible to have an actual conversation with you. Honestly, I'm more connected to my fictional characters than I am to *you*," he finished.

This emotion was also met with a sigh, and even though they couldn't see Mrs. Astor, Elizabeth swore she could hear the woman's eyes roll.

"I'm sorry to hear that, Johnathan," she said, but her tone remained the same.

Elizabeth looked at John as he awaited more to be said, but when nothing came, she saw his slow, resigned blink as he exhaled through his nose.

"When you don't like what I choose, you use the trust fund to control me, and I've had enough. I will not be controlled any more. By you, Father, my trust—"

"Johnathan, it is so sad you're linking money with love. Your father and I are trying to do what's best for you, and we raised you better than this. Of course, we always did have a worry Elizabeth did not come from a proper family—"

Elizabeth felt her jaw drop to the ground, but Mrs. Astor was not finished.

"But we welcomed her with open arms, and now we must deal with the consequences. We're afraid her upbringing has planted some ... ideas ... in your head, and you're not seeing clearly."

"A 'proper' family?! What the hell does that even mean, Mother? I assume growing up in a household devoid of emotion and getting raised by a nanny my whole life is your idea of proper, then," John yelled, still gripping the phone so his knuckles were white. "That is my future wife you are talking about, and it was my idea to elope. Not hers. You have quite literally linked money with love by calling a meeting to re-discuss my trust following the announcement of my new wedding plans."

"Johnathan, please – any correlation between the trust and your wedding is a matter of your own conscience. As I've said, you just seem a bit ... unstable right now. Your father and I don't want to fund instability."

"She is so full of it!" Elizabeth broke in, the rage overriding her logic. As soon as the words left her mouth, her palm smacked itself over her jaw, which was still dangling open.

"Johnathan, am I on speaker phone?"

John looked at Elizabeth with wide eyes. All she could do was shake her head and run from the phone.

"Excuse me for a moment, Mother. I ... have another call." He pressed "mute" and turned to Elizabeth. "What do you want me to do? Do you want to talk to her?"

"Tell her she misheard ..." Elizabeth was violently shaking her head.

"What happened to demanding a seat at the table?"

"It's going to take me some time, okay? That woman is psychological."

"She's powerful, Elizabeth. She was born into power, inherited power, and married power. That does something to a person. It's what I've been trying to tell you all these years."

"Okay, John, well I was not born into power, so excuse me if I got a little blinded by your family's perfect etiquette and polished shoes!"

With a short breath, John unmuted the phone. "Hello, Mother. I'm back. It was ... the doctor."

"Well, I'm glad you are seeing one," Mrs. Astor said with another sigh. "Anyway, Johnathan, I was hoping we'd have a meeting about the new details of your trust; but ... I see that you're very ... angry... with your life right now. Your father and I have always given you everything, and I worry it's only spoiled you. So, why don't you take the time you need, and we can discuss your trust in ... happier times."

Elizabeth was fully prepared to pick her jaw off the ground when it dropped again. She stormed towards her husband as he covered the end of the phone, his eyes searching hers as if to anticipate what she would say next.

"Oh, because us getting married isn't a happy time?" she whisper-yelled.

John brought the phone back to his ear and collected himself, like a true Astor. "Mother, I believe you are mistaken because this is a very happy time. In three weeks, I will be standing before the Atlantic, getting married to the love of my life."

"Okay, Johnathan," Mrs. Astor said. "I can see there is no reasoning with you, so how could I stop you? I hope you both enjoy your trip, before you grow up and understand the foresight you are lacking."

His jaw tightened but his words were smooth. "Goodbye, Mother."

"Goodbye, Johnathan."

John hung up with a smile and walked to embrace Elizabeth, but Elizabeth held her hands up.

"Wait, but is the trust fund meeting still happening? Did we demand a seat for me? Shit, do I still not have a seat?"

"Liz." He said her name as if it were a command and took her into his arms. "It was never a meeting. It was an extortion attempt."

Elizabeth looked at John amusingly, but with furrowed brows.

"We have three weeks left of being engaged," he continued. "We are going to enjoy them on our own terms."

Chapter 58

The restaurant was quiet. Brinkley was sitting across from her husband at their candlelit, two-person table. Chase was still dressed in his business suit, his short hair freshly cut and combed to the side, framing his handsome face.

When Chase had come home from work that day, Brinkley had surprised him with dinner plans at an expensive seafood restaurant in the city while Mama Donna would watch their girls. Wanting to go somewhere special, Brinkley reserved a table at the same restaurant they used to frequent during the honeymoon stage of their marriage. Before kids and a growing business.

Over a couple of glasses of Sauvignon Blanc, Brinkley felt a light-heartedness fill her heart that she had not experienced in a long time. After spending the past couple of weeks in sleepless nights where she had pondered her fate, Brinkley was ready to follow her own advice and take charge of her life. The advice had apparently helped her sisters, and now it was time to help herself.

So instead of waiting for her husband to surprise her with a romantic evening, which he hadn't done in years, Brinkley had put on her Spanx, a tailored black jumpsuit, and her favorite pair of heels, and escaped to the city with her husband.

As she sipped her second glass of white wine, free from parental duties for the night, she wondered if a little date night sans children was all she and her husband needed, after all.

The candle glowed against Chase's face as he leaned forwards, the light illuminating the stubble growing across his jaw. The flickering flame reflected in his soft eyes.

"You look beautiful," he said, the corners of his lips curling into a smile. "What's this surprise for?"

"I suppose wedding dress shopping had me feeling ..." Brinkley shrugged one shoulder forwards as she took another sip of her wine. "Romantic."

"I'll have to thank Elizabeth."

"Besides," she said, setting down her glass, "I realized it's been a while since we ... I don't know. Got to know each other again. Everything's always work, kids, house stuff—"

"Well," Chase said, leaning back into his chair, "what would you like to know?"

"I mean ..." The second he asked the question, Brinkley felt the magic of their night dim. "This isn't one of your work interviews, Chase."

"What do you mean?" Chase leaned forwards again.

"Nothing ..." Brinkley shook her head. She wasn't going to let one unromantic question ruin their whole evening. "I mean, I don't have specific questions for what I want to know about you ... I just thought we could naturally, you know, talk and get to know each other again ..."

"Right," Chase said. "Right, yeah, of course."

After a few silent, awkward moments, Chase cleared his throat and tried again.

"You know," he said, eyeing Brinkley with the candlelight creating a twinkle in his eyes, "this night was a great idea."

"Apparently I'm full of them," Brinkley beamed.

"And I," Chase began, keeping his eyes trained on Brinkley as he reached for something inside his suit pocket, "have a little something for you."

Brinkley felt her own eyes twinkling. "Oh really?" she said, trying to play it cool with a raised eyebrow, as if they were on their first date again. "What kind of surprise?"

Smiling to himself, he pulled out a folded packet of papers and handed it to her.

Plane tickets. It was the first idea that came to Brinkley's mind as she accepted the packet. *Maybe this time without the kids – a spontaneous little trip, like the old days ... But with more money, which is even better, because now we can vacation in one of those huts in the water ...*

With raised eyebrows, Brinkley kept her gaze on Chase as she unfolded the packet. But when she looked down, images of an expensive-looking, modern-styled office intruded on her imagination of swimming with sting rays.

There were pictures of moody-colored walls with slate-colored cabinets and a thin, light wooden desk with sleek, tan leather chairs, brass accents ...

"What is this?" She looked from the images and back at her husband, trying to keep what must have been a horrified expression on her face, neutral.

"Plans for the old nursery," he said with a proud grin. "I've been working with designers the past couple of months to turn the nursery into a home office for us. The girls are only getting older, and I think it's good they keep learning to share a room ..." Chase was talking, but his words sounded like a blurred jumble of sounds as Brinkley watched his mouth move. "I know when I work late it keeps you up at night, so I figured we could use a nice, quiet space to get our work done. You could go through our finances, schedule appointments—"

"Instead of going to bed at a normal time with your wife ... you're going to turn the nursery into an office and ... spend your nights there?" Brinkley took a gulp of her wine.

Just then the server appeared, balancing a large plate of fresh oysters. "Here is your order of oysters," she said, setting the plate between them. "And your lobster mac n' cheese is coming right up."

"That was fast," Brinkley said, eyeing the server. What kind of operation were they running in this so-called upscale restaurant? She pictured a conveyor belt of frozen lobster mac n' cheeses in the back, getting reheated each time a new customer came in.

"Can I get you two anything else?" the server said with a bright smile. "Perhaps more wine or anything?"

"Uh, yes, please." Brinkley smiled, but her eyes were still drilling holes into her husband. "Another glass of Sauv. Thank you."

The server appeared to study Chase for a moment, who in turn was studying the packet of papers in Brinkley's hand with a frown, before skipping off to the kitchen.

Brinkley opened her mouth and then closed it, her gaze falling on the oyster shells. "You're not happy with it," Chase said. Finally. "Is it the style? I was worried it was too modern, but we can find ways to make it more of what you want ..."

Brinkley's gaze fell on the plate of oysters between them. *Do not stab him with the shell. He means well; do not stab him with a shell.*

"Two orders of lobster mac n' cheese!" The server reappeared, startling Brinkley out of her trance. "And a glass of Sauvignon Blanc for the lady."

Brinkley watched as she set the steaming-hot dish in the middle of the table, and the cold glass of wine in front of Brinkley. The young server looked so happy. Brinkley couldn't help but analyze her smooth face and guessed she was in her early twenties. Before the weight of the world would make the wrinkles set in.

Suddenly Brinkley found herself longing for her early twenties.

Never mind the financial insecurities, hangovers, the whole what-is-being-an-adult-and-am-I-doing-it-right panic. Brinkley was craving a hot date night out, with a coma-like hangover in the morning and a cheap, stale bagel for breakfast with nothing to do except binge her favorite shows.

Those days were long gone. Tomorrow Brinkley would have to rise early for Daisy's swim lesson. Oh, and Lily had a play date with Sage and Rosemary, the twins she had met at summer camp, because Brinkley now lived in a world where it was common to name one's child after one's favorite herb. Then again, she had named her daughters after her favorite flowers, so who was she to judge. After dropping Lily off she needed to—

"Can I get you two anything else?" their server asked.

A one-way ticket to Bora Bora.

"We're okay, thank you," Chase said, smiling with his dimples.

Brinkley couldn't remember the last time he had smiled at *her* with dimples.

Once the server was gone, Chase leaned into the table. "If you hate the office, we can scrap the whole idea," he said. "I was just trying to do something nice."

"For who?" Brinkley could see her husband visibly tense at her words. Or maybe it was her tone. She hadn't meant for her words to come out so warlike.

There was silence between them until Chase nodded.

"Right," he muttered. "According to you, I can't do anything right."

Brinkley ignored the tugging in her heart. "I mean an office, Chase? Let's not act like that's really a gift for me."

"Well, do you want to think of something else for that room?" he barked, his voice growing a volume louder than the quiet restaurant. "Just tell me what you want, Brinkley. Tell me, so I can give it to you!"

"Keep your voice down," Brinkley hissed, scanning the room in a self-conscious fury.

"Who was this dinner really for, Brinkley?" Chase pressed, whisper-yelling across the table.

"What are you talking about? It was for us, so we can, oh, I don't know, reconnect and try to remember why we love each other!"

"And you had to book it on a weekday, after one of the longest days of work?" Brinkley felt her jaw drop. *He means well; do not stab him with a shell,* she continued to repeat in her mind.

"Just a second ago you were saying what a great idea this dinner was!" Brinkley said. "Now all of a sudden, because I didn't like your so-called surprise to me, you have to shit all over my surprise to you?"

"This dinner is a great idea," Chase said, leaning menacingly across the table. "For a weekend, Brinkley. I have been in a suit for fourteen hours. You don't think I'm ready for bed?" Brinkley's mouth was hanging open, ready to interrupt, but Chase pressed on. "I put a smile on my face and said this was a great idea because that is the appropriate response to a surprise."

"You just want me to kiss your ass like all your employees do," Brinkley said. "Well, guess what, Chase? I'm not your employee. I am your *wife* – a fact you seem to have forgotten."

"What are you even talking about? Obviously, you're my wife; I wouldn't let anyone else in my life treat me like this!"

"Oh, like what, Chase? All these months I thought you were busy selling the Philadelphia property, the so-called 'biggest sale of your career' —"

"It *is* the biggest sale of my career!"

"Now I'm finding out you've been spending the past few months meeting designers and making plans for our home I had nothing to do with?"

"I wanted to surprise you with something nice!"

Brinkley felt her jaw hanging open, as if mid-sentence, but she couldn't find any words to say, as she suddenly became self-conscious of the other diners around her.

"You know what, this is embarrassing," she said, throwing her cloth napkin on the table. She raised a hand and tried making eye contact with a server. "Excuse me?"

"Brinkley, please put your hand down," Chase murmured through clenched teeth, his face flushed red.

"No. My mother should not have to stay late watching our kids for *this*," Brinkley said, and stood up. "Excuse me? Hello?"

The server, who was in the midst of taking another order, murmured something to her customers before walking over to Brinkley and Chase's table.

"Hi, what—" the server started, her smile already wavering before Brinkley interrupted.

"I'm so sorry, there's been a family emergency ..." Brinkley could see Chase shaking his head as she spoke.

That was all it took.

"You know what, no. My husband is being an ass right now, even though everyone thinks he's so great because he's changed a diaper a few times in his life, so can we get these wrapped up to go?"

The server's jaw dropped.

"Thank you so much," Brinkley said.

"Oh, of ..." The server looked between Brinkley and Chase as she grabbed the plates of food. "Of course! Yeah, sorry about that. I mean—"

"It's not your fault." Brinkley shook her head. "Enjoy your youth."

When the server had taken their plates and disappeared into the kitchen, Brinkley felt the embarrassment of the moment sink in. Creating scenes in restaurants – she really was becoming her mother. She might have even outdone her mother tonight. The thought made her shudder.

Remaining in his seat, his face drained of color, Chase was rubbing his hands across the creases of his forehead, as if in pain.

The packet of papers felt heavy in Brinkley's lap. A mixture of shame and regret churned in her stomach. How spoiled was she, to expect a trip to Bora Bora and then feel disappointment and start a fight over a home renovation, as she stuffed her face with oysters, lobster, and expensive wine?

Then again, how taken for granted was she, for her husband to plan a home renovation without any of her input, and then fold it up in a nice clean packet and call it a surprise for her? Somewhere along the way, Chase must have known the office wasn't a surprise for her. Not really. And if he didn't, well ... that thought was even scarier.

As she mulled this over, Brinkley couldn't tell if she was losing her mind or rediscovering it. Still, with the quiet space between them after their argument in a public space, a place they had once shared happy memories in, she felt her guilt and shame win.

"I'm sorry," she admitted out loud, and her voice felt small in the big restaurant. "All I wanted was to have a nice, romantic evening with you. I've just been ... unhappy ... Our life just ... doesn't seem to be working for me lately." She swallowed air as Chase remained motionless across from her.

He kept his gaze focused on the empty table between them. "Nothing to apologize for," he said, but as he said it, his head was nodding.

Brinkley sucked in a breath through her nostrils, realizing the truth of their interaction. For a while, she had been willing to act as his accomplice and sweep their issues under the carpet. But even the carpet was fraying, lumpy, and uncomfortable now.

She didn't want to live with it any more.

"This isn't the first time I've brought up my unhappiness with our ... our marriage, Chase. I know you want to ignore it, but you need to listen to me. Don't you see? I'm not happy any more," the words poured out of her.

A look of pure hurt crossed his face. "But I ... We ..."

"And I'm realizing it's not about needing a getaway, or a date night, or a renovation." She looked at him through tear-filled eyes. "It's deeper than that, and I am sick – I am so sick – of people trying to convince me otherwise."

His eyes, which always made Brinkley feel warm, were now switching back and forth between hers, trying to make sense of her.

"I know ..." She began to wipe beneath her eyes and swallow back tears. "I know," she said once her voice could have more clarity. "We live a great life. It doesn't make sense. But it's how I feel." Brinkley raised her eyes to meet his. "And it's how I've felt for some time now."

When he didn't say anything, she continued while she still had the courage:

"I want more Chase," she said, and his appearance was blurred through her watery eyes. "And I don't mean more as in a bigger house, or a bigger business, or any of that bullshit. I just mean I want more from ..."

His face looked broken, his cheeks flushing dark shades of a desert. Feeling her own heart breaking at his reflection, Brinkley closed her mouth.

"From what?" he finally asked, his Adam's apple bulging from his neck.

"From this," she said, gesturing at the space between them. "This marriage. This life. It's not enough for me any more. There must be more. This can't be all there is to life."

"But since ... since when?" His mouth hung open.

"The past year." She swallowed, but her mouth was dry.

He blinked, his mouth still hanging open. "Why did you wait so long to tell me?"

"I don't know, Chase," Brinkley admitted, her voice strained. "I felt like I did try telling you, you just didn't want to hear it. So, I tried to ignore it, and then I tried to fix it—"

The server reappeared, a smile plastered on her face as she placed the bill in the middle of the table. Then she regurgitated the phrase said to every customer at the end of every meal: "Thank you both so much, I hope you come again, and I hope you have a wonderful night!" The server offered a slight bow of her head, as Brinkley took the check in silence.

"Maybe we should talk about this later. At home," Chase said with a sigh, leaning into the back of his seat.

"Sure. Yeah," Brinkley said, too depleted to fight for her words to be heard.

Chapter 59

"So yeah, Raymond wants me to quit the bar, but I have no idea what else I should be doing with my life," Avery said, feeling her forehead grow sweaty, her hair becoming even frizzier in the humid air. "At least not for money," she added, trying to tame the frizz into a ponytail before giving up and letting it all loose.

Avery looked at Brinkley for possible wisdom or guidance, but her sister was silent, charging ahead on the trail with narrowed eyes.

"Brinkley?" Avery said. "Were you listening to anything I just said?"

"I told Chase I'm not happy with our marriage any more."

Avery stopped walking. Brinkley had invited her to go for a walk this morning, but she had not expected a bombshell to be dropped.

"You what?"

Brinkley also stopped walking, but she was a few paces ahead of Avery. "What?" she said, turning around. "I've been feeling like something is missing from my life for a while now, and I think you're right – there's a reason I'm feeling this way and I need to confront it." Brinkley began walking again, and Avery had to jog to catch up. "My children are definitely not the issue, finances are great, and it's not like I'm in a job I don't like. In fact, being a mom has been the most rewarding job I've had." Brinkley shook her head as she seemed to tick off the imaginary list for things that constitute a fulfilled life. "It must be my marriage," she concluded. "Chase and his damn business have taken over my life."

"Um ..." Avery felt her eyebrows crinkling together as she tried to process all the information coming her way. "What did Chase say?"

"I don't know ..." Avery saw Brinkley roll her eyes before maintaining her gaze on the trail ahead. "Chase didn't say much. He keeps saying, *'Just tell me what you want'*. Well, maybe what I want is a husband I don't have to spell things out for. Like, why is it my job to find out what's missing in our relationship, and then spell out ways he can fix it?"

Brinkley's pace increased as fast as her words. "Maybe what I want is a husband who prioritizes family over making more and more money every year. A husband who goes to bed with his wife at an appropriate time and doesn't make me go to stupid family gatherings alone. A husband who doesn't turn our nursery into an office!" With flared nostrils and a tense face, Brinkley said, "Maybe that's what I want."

"Okay ..." Avery began, feeling like she needed to tiptoe, but with Brinkley's pace she was still doing more of a light jog. She began to scratch the tattoos on her arm. "Did you tell him all that?"

"Avery, were you listening to me? Why is it my job to spell everything out for him? He knows I'm unhappy – can't he get creative on his own and find ways to solve this?"

"Is he your husband or your therapist?" Avery said, feeling a dizzy spell coming on.

Brinkley glared at her before returning her gaze to the trail.

"I'm sorry, you're my sister and I will always love and support you, but ..." Avery glanced at Brinkley, whose face was still tense, lips pursed in a line, and chose her next words carefully. "But ... is it ... possible ... that you're using your marriage as ... maybe ... an excuse for your own inner turmoil?"

"What are you saying?"

"It just seems like – and please don't get mad at me for saying this – that you're putting a lot of pressure on Chase to fix your problems."

"What?"

"I mean, Chase seems happy with your guys' life. Is it Chase's job to figure out what's missing in the marriage when he doesn't feel like anything is?"

"You know what, I'm so sick of this!" Brinkley stopped walking and threw her hands in the air.

"Sick of what?"

"Everyone letting Chase get away with everything! If he so much as gives his own kids a bath at night, he's father and husband of the year. If he's happy with his life, then it's all my fault if I'm not happy and becomes my job to fix it!" Brinkley shrieked. "That's not fair!"

Avery couldn't help but offer the passers-by an "I'm sorry" smile before looking back at her sister, whose short ponytail was coming undone, sweaty strands of hair dangling in front of her face.

"Well ..." Avery stammered. "I kinda thought that was marriage ..."

"If I was a man making my career dreams come true by day and then transforming into father and husband of the year by night, I'd be damn happy with my life, too!"

"But you just said you enjoy being a mom. So, aren't your dreams coming true, too?"

"I love being a mom, Avery! Are you not listening? I like everything in my life except my marriage right now. At least I think I do. But I don't appreciate everyone taking Chase's side just because he knows how to wipe a butt."

"Wait ... What?" Avery's head was spinning.

"Forget it!" Brinkley snapped.

"Look, I don't know why you're coming to me with marriage stuff,"

Avery said, the skin on her arm red now from her scratching. "I don't have experience with this. I dated one guy who I was really starting to like in my early twenties, and one day I woke up in his bed, had an anxiety attack, and left without ever explaining myself. Couldn't even bring myself to answer his calls after."

Brinkley groaned and charged forwards on the trail.

"And other than that, it's been one failed date after another. At this point, I might just adopt a cat and call it a day—"

"Okay, this is not helping—"

"Why don't you try talking to Elizabeth? Or one of your mom friends, like Olivia or something?"

"Olivia and I have been drifting apart," Brinkley said. "The girl has been addicted to amphetamines, her nannies went on strike, and now she's going through drug withdrawal because she found out she's pregnant with a husband she doesn't even like."

"Wait, what the actual—"

"I can't dump my garbage on top," Brinkley huffed and then explained, "And I don't exactly want to emulate Elizabeth and John's relationship, so why would I go to her for advice?"

"Well, maybe the relationships you judge are the ones you should get to know more about," Avery tried, eyeing her sister from the corner of her eye. When Brinkley didn't respond, Avery added, "The one you have now is clearly not working for you."

"Thanks."

"You said it yourself," Avery muttered with a shrug.

"Next time I swear I'm just going to listen to my audiobook," Brinkley said to the air. "No one's allowed on my walks any more."

They walked the rest of the trail in silence. Even though they shared the same planet, Avery had always assumed Brinkley and her group of friends lived in a different world. A world that was free of the stress, worry, and drama that comes from working a full-time job and still feeling financially insecure. As Avery resumed walking in silence, considering all that Brinkley had just confessed, she realized everyone – no matter how fabulous their house – struggled with something behind the closed front door. The realization haunted and soothed her.

Chapter 60

"I told Chase I was unhappy with our marriage."

Here we go again, Avery thought with a silent groan and set down her fork. Brinkley had broken this news to her only a few days earlier while on a walk together, and had made it apparent she wasn't happy with Avery's advice. Yet now, she was taking Avery's advice by bringing the issue up with Elizabeth, but forcing Avery to be witness to the conversation.

After taking a sip of orange juice, Elizabeth tilted her head and eyed Brinkley.

"Really? I thought your life was perfect."

"Why!" Brinkley cried. "Why does everyone assume that?"

"I don't know, you have really nice in-laws, children who are actually cute. Not to mention a husband who makes enough money so the past ten years of your life haven't been controlled by a trust or a job you hate ..." Elizabeth tapped her finger against her chin, "You're all healthy—"

Brinkley looked as if she wanted to shove her foot in her mouth.

"Plus, you guys always seem happy," Elizabeth added, and scooped a bite of pancake into her mouth. "So, what's the issue?"

"I don't know. Never mind."

"No, I'm genuinely curious. What is your issue?" Elizabeth pressed.

Avery looked at Brinkley, wondering the same thing. She wondered how Brinkley would feel if they swapped places and Brinkley was living alone, in a job that barely paid bills for a beat-up car and a small apartment in the city. Then she wondered how someone being born in a worse-off situation would feel about Avery's own life. Perhaps humans were too adaptive to their circumstances, always getting used to their blessings as if they were a birthright, and always wanting more, as if attaining more would fill the innate void.

"Do you want another baby?" Elizabeth wondered. "I don't know how, but I feel like that's always a source of tension with baby people."

Avery looked at Brinkley and thought of their mother, who had gotten pregnant with Avery after the marriage had already turned toxic. Avery's father had admitted she was her mother's idea, that he was done having children after Elizabeth. It made Avery wonder why her mother had given birth to her, after knowing her husband didn't want to father another child.

Sometimes, Avery thought her mother had hoped Avery would be the solution to the void in her marriage and life. No wonder her mother had called Avery a disappointment – the reason for Avery's very existence had been impossible to fulfill.

Avery shook her head and crossed her arms. "You know Dad didn't even want me? It was all Mom's idea, and I swear she just had me hoping it would fill some kind of void, make her happy again."

Brinkley blinked. "Why would Dad tell you that?"

"I don't know." Avery shrugged. "It's not like he was mad or anything. I think he just felt like being honest."

"That doesn't make it okay!" said Brinkley.

"Yeah, that's messed up!" said Elizabeth, even her usual monotone breaking into a higher pitch.

Avery leaned into the booth, trying to search for that same emotional reaction to her father's old words. After all, she remembered the shame she had felt after hearing them, but now, no emotions came. She sat with this indifference as Elizabeth and Brinkley's attempts at trying to soothe her became background music to her own thoughts. She waited for any hint of bitterness, or anger, or even longing to surface, but none came, and for a flicker of time, she caught herself missing those emotions that had once filled this empty space. Somehow through her adult years, an empty space had become more uncomfortable than angry bitterness.

"What are you thinking about?" Brinkley's eyes were now focused on Avery. "Are you okay?"

Out of instinct, Avery said, "Nothing, just lost in thought."

"You were deep in thought," Brinkley pressed. "You know, Dad has always been a terrible communicator. I'm sure he didn't mean it."

"Yeah, who knows ..." Avery shrugged and began to scratch the tattoos on her arm. Through all the hurtful memories that now appeared in her mind, vying for a chance to cling to her identity and fill the emptiness, Avery breathed. "I think I just brought it up because I don't want you making the same mistake, you know? You can't use a baby to fill some kind of void. I mean, that baby is going to grow up one day and have to deal with the consequences of your choices—"

"Okay, let's stop with the baby talk," Brinkley interjected, the sympathy in her voice replaced with an edge. "Chase and I are both done having children. That's not what's missing."

"Maybe what you need is a vacation," Elizabeth suggested, flipping her long hair over her shoulder. "See the world in a new way."

"I just had a vacation, Elizabeth."

Elizabeth closed her mouth, studying Brinkley for a moment before saying, "How did Chase react when you told him? Does he feel the same way?"

"No, he seemed surprised." Brinkley glared at both her sisters. "Just like both of you. As if it's so absurd that I could want more out of him."

"Girl, you're projecting." Elizabeth rolled her eyes. "I did think your life was perfect. I'm not entirely surprised it's not. It's pretty common to not have a perfect life."

Avery felt herself zoning out of the conversation. She continued to breathe through her thoughts as she questioned the purpose of her existence, the reason her father would admit that specific truth, when she looked towards the diner's doors and she saw their mother making her way to them.

"Did you invite Mama Donna to brunch?" Avery heard herself ask.

Avery couldn't confirm whether it was indeed their mother, as the woman in question was wearing oversized, hot-pink circle sunglasses, and a thin ruby-red shawl covering the top of her head.

"Yes, I invited our mother," Elizabeth said, waving Mama Donna to the table. "And honestly, I don't think it could be better timing with the early midlife crisis Brinkley's in."

"Can we refer to it as a late quarter-life crisis?" Brinkley said and then began to chug her coffee. She set the mug down and dabbed at her mouth. "And I don't know what Mom is going to offer other than, *'At least you didn't marry an asshole like I did'*—"

"Okay, she's too close!" Avery slapped Brinkley's thigh and then smiled at their approaching mother.

"Hi, Mom," all three sisters sang.

"Hi, Elizabeth," their mother sang, squeezing her daughter in a hug. "So nice of *Elizabeth* to invite her mother to brunch. I didn't get a text from the rest of you."

"Why are you dressed like a spy?" Avery wondered.

"Excuse me, Avery," Mama Donna said, using her butt cheeks to nudge Avery further into the booth so she could sit. She took off her sunglasses and unraveled her red scarf, placing it on the table. "This is the style. Nana always wore headscarves, so I'm carrying on the tradition."

"Nana always looked stylish." Elizabeth nodded. "And you always do, too."

"You're just kissing up to Mom because you disinvited her to your wedding," Brinkley said.

"Anyway ..." Mama Donna picked up a menu only to put it back down. "What did I miss? Sorry I'm late. I was getting my nails done." She flashed her bright red sparkly nails at the table. They matched her scarf.

"Nothing! Let me see your nails," Brinkley chirped and grabbed Mama Donna's hand for closer inspection.

But Avery could hear a tremble in Brinkley's voice.

"Brinkley feels like something's missing in her marriage," Elizabeth blurted out.

Mama Donna leaned across the table, towards Brinkley. "How are you unhappy with your marriage? Chase is such an amazing guy."

"I am aware," Brinkley said flatly.

"Oh, and apparently Dad never wanted Avery? Is this true?" Elizabeth asked.

"What?" Mama Donna gasped, now looking at Avery.

"Yeah, apparently Dad told Avery he never wanted her. Only you did," Elizabeth said. "It actually makes a lot of sense. At first, I thought Dad paid for Brinkley and my college tuition but not Avery's because Avery was being stubborn about her major and you two lost a lot of money in the divorce, but ... now he lives in a big house and bought his fiancée a huge ring, so ..." Elizabeth appeared to think for a moment as she sipped on her orange juice. "It makes a lot more sense that he didn't want her, so he's always left you to take care of her," she concluded.

"Elizabeth, that's a terrible thing to say!" Mama Donna cried.

"Dad's the one who said it," Elizabeth argued.

YOU DON'T KNOW NANA

"What is wrong with him?" Mama Donna looked back at Avery. "Why would he tell you that? Was he mad?"

"Um ..." Avery looked at her mother's eyes searching hers. "He wasn't mad. I think he was just being honest?"

"That's horrible!" Mama Donna said, twirling a strand of hair around her finger with her mouth still dangling open in disgust.

"Agreed," Elizabeth said. "But is it true? Did Dad really not want another kid?" Before Mama Donna could answer, Elizabeth added, "I told Brinkley maybe another baby is what's missing from the marriage."

Mama Donna slapped her hand on the table, making the silverware clink. "Okay, Elizabeth, I think you're starting to sound cuckoo. Another kid? You don't just get pregnant to fill a void in your life."

Avery tilted her head. "Are you speaking from experience, or ..."

"Mom, why don't you stop acting surprised about everything that pops out of my mouth and shed some light on this situation?"

Mama Donna studied Brinkley for a moment. "Why do you feel like something's missing from your marriage?"

"I don't know, Mom. Chase is always busy with work and—"

"You feel like he's out there fulfilling his dreams while you've decided to devote your life to children?"

The table was silent. For once, Avery thought, her mother was actually making sense.

Brinkley leaned into the booth. "Well, yeah, kind of ... but ... I'm happy for him. I really am. And I love being a mom, so ..."

A smirk spread across their mother's face. "I'm sixty years old. You all treat me like I'm cuckoo, but I've learned a few things."

"But it's not like I resent becoming a mother," Brinkley said. "My kids are my life. I feel lucky I get to devote all my time to raising them—"

"Maybe they shouldn't be." Mama Donna shrugged, and reached

for a home fry on Avery's plate.

"What?" Brinkley said, her voice quiet.

"Maybe they shouldn't be your whole life. One day they're going to grow up and get their own, you know," Mama Donna said, and then glared at each of her daughters. "And then they'll become best friends who go to brunch without you."

"Mom—" Brinkley started, but their mother held up her hand in a "stop" sign.

Wonder where she learned that from, Avery thought.

"It's part of being a mother," Mama Donna said. "It's not an easy job. Your kids need and take so much from you. You can't let them take everything or else you'll grow up bitter with nothing left."

"Is that what happened to you?" Avery wondered aloud.

Ignoring her, Mama Donna leaned back in the booth and narrowed her eyes at Brinkley. "It sounds like you're entering a new season of life, my dear. When I was done having kids, I went through one, too."

"And what did you do about it?" said Brinkley.

"Took a lot of Ambien," Mama Donna announced, and popped another potato into her mouth.

"What?" Brinkley said, looking ready to burst into a puddle of tears. "Why is everyone around me doing drugs?"

"Oh, honey, it has nothing to do with you." Mama Donna shook her head. "The world is hurting. Anyway, when I realized that wasn't a cure, or healthy for that matter, I tried a bunch of different things. I made new friends. I traveled. I filed for divorce and fell in love with Jesus—" Mama Donna gasped, a light growing in her eyes. "You know what, Brinkley, you probably need religion in your life. I don't care which one you connect with – well, so long as it's a religion, and not a cult, but then again almost every religion began as a cult—"

"Religion ..." Brinkley repeated, and Avery couldn't tell if she believed it.

"Or some kind of spiritual practice," Mama Donna continued. "Your generation is so deprived of meaningful ritual, and a spiritual way to make sense of this world."

"Okay," Brinkley mumbled, and nearly buried her head into her omelet.

Mama Donna reached across Avery to take Brinkley's hand. "Look, my point is – kids are a beautiful gift. But ..." She tilted her head and shrugged. "They can be real a pain in the ass. Trust me, I had three of you. And even though I love each of you, and you gave me the happiest years of my life, it was a lot of *work*."

"We *all* gave you the happiest years?" Avery said. Nausea was starting to settle in, and she wanted to confirm this while she had the courage and the chance.

Mama Donna looked right into Avery's eyes and Avery could see flecks of a honey color illuminated in the sunlight. "Yes, Avery. *All* of you. You don't know how many nights I prayed to have a baby like you."

Avery felt her muscles grow tense, as if her body were transforming into a wall to safeguard her emotions. *Really?* she wanted to ask, but she didn't want to show that she needed confirmation. So, Avery allowed her mother to move on, never revealing how much hearing those words meant to her.

Looking back at Brinkley, Mama Donna gave her daughter's hand a squeeze. "You and Chase have a beautiful, healthy family, and you both love each other. What you're going through is normal. You will get through it." Mama Donna let go of Brinkley's hand. "And you will be a better person, and have a better partnership, for it."

Avery watched as their mother's words seemed to sink through Brinkley's body, grounding her to the seat.

"Well look at Mama Donna, coming through with all her wisdom," Elizabeth said, clapping before raising her glass for a cheer.

Brinkley kept her eyes focused on their mother. "So, what am I supposed to do?" she said.

"No one knows," Mama Donna said, and popped another potato into her mouth. "At least you didn't marry an asshole like I did."

Chapter 61

Avery was trapped behind the mahogany counter of the bar, staring through the window at the cumulus clouds that had appeared as splattered dots floating across the blue sky.

When it wasn't Wednesday, Raymond's visiting day, Avery resented working the late afternoon shift. Except for the occasional bar crawl or sports game, business was usually slow, which meant tips were low. The combination of free time and worry was an anxiety-inducing duo.

Today, however, she was at least grateful for this time for her mind to wander. As she stared at all the people passing across the bar window, she imagined herself among them, going somewhere. She just had no idea where.

Well, she loved to imagine hopping in her car, driving through America's Midwest, stopping in plains and deserts before arriving at lush forests and beaches. But midway through this fantasy she imagined her car breaking down, with no money for food or shelter or an auto repair, and she'd end up getting killed by a bear, per her mother's prediction.

As the excitement of the unknown lingered too long and transformed into fear, a man with a familiar, burly build, a shiny bald head contrasted against a dark, thick beard, pushed through the crowded city streets and caught Avery's eye. She watched as he paused in front of the entrance to her bar, looking up in the direction of the bar's sign before letting himself in.

The chime above the front door rang.

"Dad?" In all her years of working at this place, her father had never bothered to visit before.

"Avery! Hey. I called Brinkley. She said you'd be working today."

She lingered behind the bar, but as her father neared her, Avery walked around to greet him with a hug.

"I was in the city meeting a client," he said, pulling away from the hug. "Figured I'd stop by."

"Cool ..." Avery nodded. "What can I make for you?"

"This is where you work, huh?" His eyes were scanning the place. "Feels a bit ... dingy, no?"

"Not as dingy as the dungeon of the mind," Avery said under her breath, transfixed once again by the window.

"What?"

"Nothing. Do you like bourbon?"

"Yeah, sure."

Avery placed a rocks glass on the counter. "I've been told I make the best old-fashioned."

"Oh, I'm so proud," her dad said, the sarcasm clear.

Avery bit her tongue as she added a dash of bitters to the glass.

"How have you been?" she said. "Haven't seen you since Lily's birthday party."

"Yeah ... You never came to the barbeque I hosted. Brinkley and Elizabeth showed up. It was beautiful weather, delicious food. They got to meet Sin and my new pet. You should have come."

"Wait, you and Sin have a pet? Aren't you allergic to pets?" *And how did my sisters fail to mention this?* Avery thought, annoyed. She had listened at length about how something was missing from Brinkley's life, and how Elizabeth was removing basically everything from her life, yet no one could mention how their very allergic father had bought a pet?

"Yeah, Sin wanted a ferret," he said, his lips pressing together in a mixture of a scowl and a smile. "I have medication."

"Wow," was all Avery could bring herself to say as she processed this news. "Then you must be, like, *really* happy with Sin."

As he rubbed his thick, graying beard, Avery noticed her father's eyebrow twitch at her words.

"Yeah, I am," he said, his fingers becoming tangled in the beard.

"Yeah, like you're willing to give up *breathing* for Sin," Avery said, widening her eyes at her father. Sometimes communicating with her eyes was safer than using words around him.

Richard continued to rub his beard as he eyed his daughter. He cleared his throat. "I've never met anyone who treats me better than her, so..."

"You are either the happiest with your life, or the most indifferent to it, but," said Avery with a shrug, "you're a grown man, Sin's a grown woman, so I'm sure you both know what you're doing."

Richard stopped rubbing his beard and blinked. Before he could think too long about her words, Avery switched the conversation.

"So yeah, I'm sorry I missed the barbeque. I heard it was fun," Avery lied. What she had heard was that Elizabeth had lost her damn mind and shattered a casserole dish. And that was before their father had announced he was getting married two days before her.

As Avery eyed her father now, she wondered if Elizabeth had told him about her new wedding plans yet.

"It was a lot of fun," he said. "You'll need to come to the next one."

"Yeah ..." Avery glanced out the window before looking back at her father. Each time she saw him, there seemed to be a new wrinkle that marked his face, a new patch of gray taking over his thick beard.

"You popped into my mind a lot during the trip," Avery admitted, stirring the drink a little too quickly.

Richard remained silent, either not caring about her thoughts of him, or too scared to inquire further. But it was rare that Avery spent one-on-one time with her father these days, and his random visit to the bar seemed to be a sign from somewhere bigger than herself, so before she could convince herself otherwise, she blurted:

"Do you remember that weekend we spent camping together – the weekend we came home and saw Nana and Mom loading all those boxes of stuff into the car?" Avery used the edge of her bar knife to peel a piece of an orange's skin, trying her best to be careful with trembling hands. Placing the peel onto the edge of the glass, she set a coaster down and placed the drink in front of her father. "Do you remember that?"

Still eyeing her, he raised the glass to his mouth. "Yeah. Your mother was trying to take everything from me." He took a gulp and placed it down. The glass clinked on the finished wood, and his gaze dropped towards the sound. "Including you."

"I remember Nana pulling me away from you that day ..." Avery said, feeling her mouth grow dry. She readjusted his glass back onto the coaster.

"And you obeyed her," Richard added, his eyes glaring at her.

Avery kept her gaze steady on her father.

"Yeah," she accepted, feeling her palms grow sweaty. She wiped them on her pants and, instead of crossing her arms, leaned into the counter, towards her father. "For a while I felt guilty about that."

Her father remained silent, but he looked away.

"Sometimes I still do," she confessed. "I cut Nana out of my life because I was so angry at her for that. For the whole way she handled the divorce. I was angry at myself, too."

Without a word, her father raised his sweaty glass and took another swig of his drink. For a moment, his face was magnified into a blur behind the glass. Then all his wrinkles and untamed eyes became clear.

"I want you to know I'm sorry," she said once he set down his drink. She expected to feel lighter after apologizing, but her body remained heavy and barely breathing. Because in this relationship, Avery found herself apologizing not for her own healing, but for her father's. It was becoming clear to Avery she would not be able to have the relationship she so desperately craved with her father if he himself did not heal.

Richard's eyes remained cast downwards.

There was a feeling tugging Avery in a new direction, but she continued talking.

"Like I said, I thought of you a lot during camping," Avery said again. "You've been through a lot in life, with your own dad, and by the time I was born, you and Mom were already going through so much, so ... I don't think we had the proper chance to have the bond we could have had ..."

Holding her breath, Avery watched as her father shifted in his seat before reaching for his drink again. He didn't say anything when he brought it to his lips. Another gulp traveled down his throat. He set the glass down.

"You were so mean to me when you were younger," was all he said in a quiet voice. "I still think of the time you told me you didn't want me to have custody. Said you didn't care if you ever saw me again."

Avery blinked and felt her body begin to recoil.

"Why?" she said, crossing her arms. "I ... I was a child, Dad." *And I was scared.*

Avery felt her head pound with every exhale that passed without an explanation. Perhaps it was the way he was sitting, his back hunched in self-pity, even though his forehead creases and graying beard showed he had experienced time. Much more time than her.

Or maybe it was the fact that she had shown more grace than was required of her, and it still wasn't enough. Here he was, a middle-aged man who had devoted himself to things other than his wife and children, and yet found himself alone in a bar because he had devoted himself to nothing at all.

After minutes had passed, still without an explanation, Avery took the empty glass in her hands. "Would you like another drink?" she said.

"Yeah, sure," he said, still not looking at her. "That was okay."

Chapter 62

The sound of Daisy's snores could be heard from the top bunk as Brinkley finished reading their bedtime book of fairytales.

"Mommy?" Lily looked at Brinkley with her big, amber-colored eyes.

Brinkley shut the book and snuggled closer to Lily. "Yes, baby?"

"I saw a dead butterfly at summer camp."

Brinkley wrinkled her eyebrows, as much as they would wrinkle, anyway. "You did?" The wheels in Brinkley's head began turning, trying to figure out where her daughter was going with this. "I'm sorry, baby, sometimes—"

"When a butterfly dies," Lily interrupted, staring intently at her mother, "where does Nana go?"

Great, was the first word that came to Brinkley's mind, but she didn't have time to respond, because Lily, apparently, had already formed a case.

"If she can become another butterfly," Lily continued, "why can't she become another Nana?"

"You are ... so thoughtful," Brinkley said with a smile that felt too wide for her face.

Lily blinked, self-assured enough in her intelligence and wanting answers more than praise.

Brinkley should've known this butterfly tale would come back to haunt her. After all, what was Brinkley expecting to tell her daughter in the winter, when butterflies were no longer fluttering by? That Nana was now on a great migration and would come back in the spring?

Actually, that wouldn't have been half bad ...

"Mommy?" Lily said, still staring at Brinkley, waiting for answers.

The truth was, Brinkley had been hoping, with Lily's transition to kindergarten and everything else life brought a five-year-old, that the topic of Nana's death would fade from her daughter's mind. It's not as though Brinkley was expecting Lily to forget Nana, but perhaps forget about her death for a few months. Or a few years. Then, when Lily was a bit older, and more time and distance had formed between her life and Nana's passing, *then* they could have a more honest conversation about ... well, death.

Brinkley shuddered, focusing her attention back on Lily, who was still looking at her with those innocent-yet-intelligent eyes.

No, Brinkley could not have this conversation with her daughter now.

Placing the book on Lily's nightstand, Brinkley rose from the bed and began to pull the pink ballerina covers to her daughter's chin.

"Nana ..." Brinkley began, but already lost her words. Where the hell was Chase, their father, during these talks? Why did it always fall on her to wrap the complexities of life into a non-threatening, age-appropriate bow for their children?

"Yeah, Mommy, why can't Nana become another Nana?"

This girl is persistent, Brinkley muttered in her mind, feeling her daughter's eyes tracking her every move like a detective investigating a crime scene. Realizing her daughter was not going to let her run away from this question, Brinkley sat on the edge of Lily's bed with a sigh.

"I'm not sure, Lily," Brinkley admitted. Her truth sounded harsh in the pastel-colored room.

Lily remained staring at her mother, but with raised eyebrows.

"Some people believe in this thing called reincarnation; other people believe in this thing called heaven—"

"Ronald told me about heaven," Lily interjected with a roll of her eyes.

Did my five-year-old just roll her eyes?

"Ronald from summer camp?"

"Yeah. The one who picks his nose and eats his boogers."

"Lily, I don't think that's very nice—"

"Why? That's what he does."

"Well ..." Brinkley said, while her daughter remained still. "I'm sure he does other things. Nice things you could use to describe him."

"No, he's not very nice. When I wanted to be line leader, he told me I can't because boys rule the world and girls are the assistants."

That little booger-eating piece of shit, Brinkley thought as she plastered a smile on her face.

"Well, I'm going to talk to Ronald's mother and father because anyone can rule the world. In fact, the world would be a better place if there were more diversity in the leadership, Lily. It sounds like Ronald might need some help." Brinkley could feel an edge enter her voice as her heart thudded in her chest. "And next time he tries intimidating you out of being line leader, you tell him that you are a leader, and he better watch out. Okay?"

Lily just crinkled her nose. "Okay."

As if in agreement, Daisy released a groan from the top bunk.

"I think you're getting too loud, Mommy," Lily whispered as Brinkley checked on her younger daughter, who was still sleeping, lost in her dreams.

Brinkley sat on the edge of Lily's bed with another sigh. "I know,

I'm sorry," she whispered. "What did this Ronald tell you about heaven?"

"He said it's where dead people go. But only good dead people," Lily said, her usually squeaky voice quiet. "It's where all the good dead people meet and there's a lot of cake and stuff."

"Well ..." Brinkley sucked in her breath. Did she want her daughter to believe in heaven? Did Brinkley even believe in heaven? Better yet, was Ronald's probably sexist version of heaven the one she wanted to take root in her young daughter's developing mind?

And once again, where the hell was Chase to help her with this? Did he even care what their daughters believed about the afterlife? Last Brinkley checked, Chase was agnostic – but how many years ago was that?

Brinkley could feel her heart beating faster.

"You know what, Lily, it's past your bedtime. Let's talk about this tomorrow?"

"But, Mommy!"

"Shh! Daisy's sleeping."

"But I wanna know where Nana is!"

"She's in heaven!" Brinkley snapped with a whisper. "She's in heaven with your grandpa, and ... God, and ... Jesus ..."

"I love God," Lily declared.

"That's amazing," Brinkley whispered, nodding as she pulled the covers up to Lily's chin. "You should love God. He's great."

"God's a boy?

Oh great, now I'm feeding into this patriarchal nonsense. Sucking in a breath, Brinkley tried again.

"Look. God is not a boy—"

"God's a girl?"

"He's neither. He's both," Brinkley tried, the words rushing together as her head shook back and forth as if to signal, *Don't listen to this mother; she has no idea what she's talking about when it comes to death and religion.* Brinkley tried again: "He's— I mean ... not he, because He's not a boy ..."

A small chuckle escape Brinkley's lips, but Lily just blinked.

"So, God's non-binary?" Lily suggested.

Brinkley tilted her head. "What?"

"Non-binary," Lily repeated. "Someone who isn't a boy or girl."

"Yes, I've heard of non-binary ..." Brinkley said, eyeing her five-year-old. "How did you learn that word?"

"At camp," Lily said. "It's not a hard word, Mommy."

Brinkley felt the corners of her mouth curl, but before she could respond, Lily said,

"So, who is God, Mommy?"

"I don't know if it's a who ..." Brinkley took one look at her daughter's scrunched face and decided to stop the wheel of questions. "Look, God is ... great. And God is good," Brinkley tried. "And we thank God for our food, and for everything else that's good in the world."

"Hey, that's what we say before we eat sometimes."

"Uh huh ..." Brinkley nodded.

"If God's so great then, why did He let the butterfly at summer camp die? And Nana die?" Lily's eyes widened as she talked. "Am *I* going to die?"

Brinkley leaned towards her daughter's forehead and planted a kiss on it as she spun the parental lie as old as time. "You have nothing to worry about, Lily," she promised, looking into her daughter's eyes. "Your daddy and I love you and Daisy so much and we will protect you forever, okay?"

"Okay ..."

"Now it's bedtime, okay? We can talk more in the morning, but you need sleep."

Lily looked at her mother as if to challenge her, but Brinkley's face wasn't playing games.

"Okay," Lily squeaked. "Goodnight, Mommy, love you."

"Goodnight, sweetie."

The moon was almost full when Brinkley stepped onto her backyard patio. She could see its edge curve into itself, into its seemingly random craters and shadows, reflecting the sun as a night light in the dark sky.

Brinkley saw her husband lying on their patio couch, staring at the same thing. There was no screen blocking his face, no rectangular glasses guarding his eyes. Only him, sitting in their outdoor couch, surveying a sky, but sharing no words.

"Hey," she breathed, surprised at her own voice. "I didn't know you were out here. Figured you were working."

She remained standing by the door. Even though this was Chase, her husband, the father of her children, they had barely talked since their argument at the restaurant. She didn't realize how distant his presence had become, but without work, errands, or the kids running around to distract them, Brinkley almost felt as if she were in the company of a stranger.

"No," he said, still staring at the moon. "There will always be more work to do. I needed a night."

It's about time, she thought, but remained by the door.

With a tightened jaw, he turned his head to look at her. "Will you come sit?"

Brinkley made her way over and took a seat on the couch across from him.

"Are the girls asleep?"

"Yeah ..." Brinkley said, studying him for a moment. "Lily had some questions about God tonight."

"Really?"

"Yeah. You know I told her butterflies are like a visit from Nana, right?"

"Yeah?"

"Well, she saw a dead butterfly at camp, so ..."

Chase's laughter sounded like a familiar song dancing in the night. Brinkley hadn't realized how much she missed the sound until it filled her ears now.

"Yeah, you can bet how that went," Brinkley couldn't help but chuckle. She glanced at him again, but his focus was still on the moon.

"Do you ... believe in God? Or the afterlife or anything? I know years ago you said you were agnostic ..."

"Oh man," Chase said, raising his eyebrows as he looked at her. "Sometimes I do. Other times I have no idea. But I guess that's how a lot of people are."

"But a lot of people really do believe," Brinkley countered. "My mother one hundred percent believes there is a God."

"True," he said, his gaze dropping to the stone beneath them. "Sometimes I envy people like that."

"Really?" Brinkley tilted her head, observing her husband as the corners of his eyes creased into a soft smile. "Sometimes I do, too," she admitted before the sound of crickets filled the silence between them.

Finally, Chase sucked in a breath. "Brinkley ..."

Brinkley felt her chin lift, ready to hear what he had to say.

"We haven't really ..." he began, his voice quiet, "talked about anything."

Brinkley remained silent for a moment; the sound of the crickets' song was enough noise.

"What is there to say?" she finally wondered out loud, when Chase did not remove his focus from her.

In Brinkley's mind, she had already shared her feelings about Chase's work schedule and her growing unhappiness, and she hadn't been met with much of a response. The imagined circles under her eyes grew darker at the thought of trying to explain herself even further.

"I would hope something," Chase said, and his tone felt new to her. His words were shorter, more forceful than usual. She watched as he clenched and then released his jaw. "Do you think ... Do you think you'd want to try counseling?"

"You think I need counseling because I'm unfulfilled in our marriage?"

"No—"

But Brinkley didn't want to hear Chase try to explain himself. "I'm sorry my emotions are not the convenient way to feel," she said, too angry to care how sarcastic her tone sounded. "When all your dreams are coming true." Even though she saw a pained expression cross his face, she couldn't stop defending herself. "But it's how I feel, Chase," she said. "And I'm sick of feeling bad about it."

"Brinkley, can you get out of your own way for one damn minute and listen to what I'm actually saying? I'm not asking you to feel bad," he said, his tone softening but his jaw still tight. "You're allowed to feel whatever you feel, I'm just ..."

"You're what?" she demanded.

He glared at Brinkley, and Brinkley glared back. Their lips were pressed together, their nostrils flared. Only their eyes seemed to be searching each other for hints of vulnerability.

"I'm trying to understand, Brinkley," he said, and the creases that marked his forehead deepened. "Our last anniversary you were saying how happy you were, raving about how our family felt complete. I'm confused about what the hell happened."

"I don't know, Chase!"

"Well, I've been picking apart the past year in my mind, going over and over our interactions, our moments, trying to find out what went wrong, what I did wrong – and I know we haven't been perfect, but—" Chase stopped speaking, as if the words had gotten stuck somewhere between his mind and his mouth. His eyes seemed to plead with her, but she didn't know what they were asking. "I thought it was normal," he finally said, his voice strained as he clenched his jaw tighter. "I thought ... With all the changes we've been going through, having kids, moving, starting the business ..." He shook his head, letting his eyes get lost in the night before meeting hers again. "I thought it was normal. I didn't know how deep it was cutting."

"And what – you thought it would magically go away?" Brinkley said. Tears began to form in Brinkley's eyes, blurring her vision so that her husband was an indistinct, faceless shape coming towards her. "I've been so lonely, Chase. I've been so lonely, and you've slept next to me every single night. You think that's normal?"

Brinkley wiped her tears and Chase came back into view, but only for a moment until the next ones dripped from her eyes. Now she felt her husband's arms engulf her. She leaned her cheek on his shoulder. The more she cried, the blurrier the world around her became.

Brinkley watched as her tears spilled over the empty space where she had once worn Nana's rose quartz ring, and onto her platinum wedding band. Chase remained holding her, rubbing his hands over the fabric of her T-shirt until her sobs slowed to a stop.

"I would get bouts of feeling it before – feeling like there was this void, this emptiness," she tried to explain with a strained voice. "But ever since my nana died ..." She trailed off as she pictured Nana handing her the ring with her shaking hands. "The feeling hasn't gone away. It feels like it's taken over my mind." Sniffling, Brinkley buried her head deeper into her husband's chest. "Maybe I do need counseling."

She heard her husband suck in a long breath.

"When I mentioned counseling," he said, each word cautious, "I meant couple's counseling." Chase continued rubbing his wife's back until her sobs slowed to a stop. "You don't need to go through this alone," he promised, keeping his arms around her but pulling back so he could meet her gaze. She noticed his eyes were reddened. He used his thumb to wipe the remaining tears from her cheeks. "And I'm sorry for ever making you feel like you had to—"

"Chase—"

"No, let me speak," he said, still searching her eyes. "I've been so consumed by work and thinking that I'm this great father and husband for building this company and pretending like everything was okay ..." He shook his head. "When really, I'm the only one who wanted this company.

"I'm sorry. I saw the signs you were unhappy. *I heard them,* and instead of addressing it, I acted like they were normal and could be fixed with a vacation, or a renovation ..." Chase continued shaking his head as he spoke. "But—"

Brinkley felt her muscles tense once he said the word "but". Of course he had to add a "but".

"You've also pushed me away—"

"What! What are you talking about? You work nonstop, Chase. There's no chance for me to push you away when you're not even here!"

"But I *am* here," he said, and because his tone had changed so quickly, Brinkley closed her mouth, realizing it was his turn to speak. "I'm not here all the time but I *have been right here,*" he said, enunciating each word clearly. "Yet every time I try being intimate with you, you push me away. Every time I try stepping it up and helping with the girls, you push me away. This whole year, Brinkley, you have pushed me away. And I know I've been working insane hours and I need to fix that ..." he paused, his eyes looking intently into hers.

Shifting her weight, Brinkley broke their gaze, looking up at the night sky instead.

"But I have tried, Brinkley," Chase promised, grounding her back to earth. "Sometimes I feel like no matter what effort I make ..." Chase's voice trailed off.

Brinkley snapped her attention back to him. "What?"

"Sometimes I feel like ... you're just not attracted to me any more. And ... it's not easy, always getting rejected—"

"Come on Chase, I don't constantly reject you. And you're how old? You can't handle rejection?"

"I'm being honest with you right now, Brinkley."

The vulnerability hung in the air, ready to snap them apart or bring them together as Brinkley closed her mouth.

"You're my wife, and ... it doesn't feel good. I mean, how would you feel if you felt like you were always trying—"

"But what real effort are you making, Chase?" Brinkley couldn't help but interrupt as she felt the flood of words rushing from her mind. "By trying to sneak in sex when we both have somewhere to be? By turning our nursery into an office, of all things, without even asking me about it? By helping with the girls after you've already seen me struggling and I literally have to ask you to help, or spell out what to do?"

Chase stared as Brinkley's truth continued spilling out.

"Are you really trying, Chase? Because your efforts seem like they're convenient for you. Meanwhile everyone important in my life has shoved down my throat how lucky I am, how great you are, and I don't get any credit." Brinkley's voice cracked as she could feel the tears welling in her eyes. "Not from my friends, not from my family ..." She was sobbing now, collapsing her head into her hands.

"Brinkley ..." He tried taking her back into his arms, but she pulled away from him.

"And I want to have sex with you, I really do, but I can't do that when I don't even feel like we're connected any more. Like, what's connecting us besides the kids?" She looked up from her hands to see him through her teary eyes. "Not to mention my body—"

"Your body is hot, Brinkley. What are you talking about?"

"No, it's not. You're lying!"

"Brinkley," he said, snatching her hands away from her face. "I love your body—"

"Well, I don't! It doesn't even feel like mine, and I feel *awful* for feeling that. And I know I'll never get my body back because I'm too lazy and like wine and cheese too much, and don't want to start an amphetamine addiction." Brinkley was full on sobbing as she spoke, using the neckline of her shirt to wipe the snot dripping from her nose.

"Brinkley ..." Chase's voice was soft, but she could tell he was grimacing as he watched her using her shirt to wipe her nose. She had hit a new low. "Brinkley," he said her name again, leaning his face towards her. "I love you. And I love the way you look. You are not lazy; you're too hard on yourself."

Brinkley sniffled up some snot.

"This year has been a hard one," he confessed. "I've missed out on a lot. I know I have. The girls don't run up to me after work any more. Any time I'm alone with them, they cry for you. You and I have been so ... different. Distant, even when we're together ..."

Brinkley wanted to reach out and hug her husband, but she was scared any movement would snap them both out of the moment.

"And it's my fault for not doing something about it. I've been so distracted and focused on work, and building my business, making money ..."

A pang of guilt ran through Brinkley as she thought of the distance she'd been feeling between her and Chase. Brinkley had left him out of her feelings, thinking he was the lucky one, building his business while coming home to his wife and kids. That was the dream men were too often sold – make the money, advance your career, and get a wife who can raise the family and take care of the house. She had never considered what could be occurring in her husband's inner life as he lived the reality of that fantasy. The stress of being the financial provider, and the sadness that could come from missing family moments for work that would never love you back.

"No matter what we go through," he finally broke the silence, raising his eyes to meet hers, "let's go through it together, okay?"

When she didn't respond, he pulled her into a hug.

"This year has been a hard one," he repeated. "But I want to have the chance to make it up in the ones to come. I'm sorry, Brinkley."

With her cheek resting on his shoulder, she closed her eyes.

"I'm sorry too, Chase," she breathed, clutching him closer. "I'm sorry, too."

Chapter 63

"I do not want to go to work," Avery groaned, noticing the time on her microwave.

She hated analog clocks. With no *tick* or movement of the minute hand to mark the passage of time, the alien green numbers haunted her with every unannounced transformation they made.

"I thought you loved working Wednesdays," Izzy said, shifting in her seat cushion on the floor of their kitchen, which doubled as their living room.

"I did," Avery said, then quickly corrected, "I do. But Raymond comes on Wednesdays, and the last time I saw him, he basically said his dying wish was that I wouldn't be working at the bar any more." Avery flung her hair into a messy bun as she spoke. "And I've thought and I've written about it, but I have nothing for him. I have no idea what else I could be doing with my life. I mean, if we're talking fantasy, sure, I'd be on a road trip across America right now. But when we're talking reality?" Avery raised an eyebrow in the air, as if Izzy had asked an offensive question. "I need money."

"Jeez."

"What?"

Izzy clicked her tongue. "It's a lot of pressure for him to put on a stranger."

YOU DON'T KNOW NANA

"He's not a stranger, though. He's Raymond. Ray. A ray of sunshine in an otherwise dingy bar."

"I don't know, Avery," Izzy said as she chewed on a chip, "I get that you two are trying to recreate a whole *Tuesdays with Morrie* vibe, but I'm starting to agree with Mama Donna on this one."

"What do you mean?"

"This guy could be a total creep."

"What? Izzy, he's not telling me to quit my job and go live with him, for crying out loud – which, if he did, I wouldn't not consider it, because that's how non-creepy he is, and how high rent is becoming in this city."

Izzy grunted as she eyed her.

"Okay, maybe he's not what's creepy," Izzy conceded. "But the amount of influence you're giving him over your life is."

"Wait, what?" Avery said, her voice quiet.

Izzy rolled her eyes. "This dude told you a week ago that his dying wish is for you to quit the bar – now you feel pressured to have some sort of update on your life. For who? Him?"

Avery blinked.

"Does he pay your bills?"

"No ..."

"Then how you choose to survive isn't this dude's problem," she said. "Just because you didn't live up to your nana's expectations doesn't mean you need to start fulfilling everyone else's."

"This has nothing to do with my nana," Avery said, crossing her arms. "I'm telling you, when I went hiking, something happened. I made peace with all that."

"Mm-hm," Izzy said, side-eyeing Avery before blurting out, "Avery, this has everything to do with your nana, and Mama Donna, and your dad." Izzy paused, chip in hand, before adding, "And your whole childhood, while we're at it. And your life will continue having

400

everything to do with them until you make a change."

The words felt as if her friend were smacking her.

"I'm trying! I'm trying to make a change! I just don't know what that change needs to be. That's. My whole. Problem!"

Izzy chomped on another chip, never breaking eye contact even as she began to pick remnants out of her teeth. Avery watched with disgust as she worked her way from the front to the back.

"You look like a serial killer."

Rolling her eyes, Izzy tipped her head back to pour the remaining crumbs of the chip bag into her mouth.

"I feel like you've been on a ... witch hunt for answers or something." Izzy dusted all the crumbs from her denim shorts. "This Ray guy is not some wise wizard. He's not even your grandfather. He's not going to know what's good for you better than you do."

Avery scanned her mind for words, for a response, but Izzy continued speaking before Avery could say anything.

"I mean, some old man, who quite honestly might have dementia or a drinking problem – or could have been a real fraud for all we know – tells you he wants you to find a new job and all of a sudden you believe him?" Izzy narrowed her eyes at Avery. "If you're not happy in your job, by all means, find a new one. But don't go searching for something else just because other people want it for you."

Avery lingered in their stare, but Izzy seemed content with all she had said and wasn't going to offer more.

"It just ..." Avery considered her words and pulled in a breath before continuing: "It can be an unsettling feeling, to feel like I haven't lived up to anyone's expectations. To feel like I've even failed at my own," she said to no one in particular, and it was as if speaking the words helped her notice their weight.

When she had first moved to the city, getting out of her home environment and into an apartment of her own had done her well, instilling a newfound happiness and hope within her. She felt like she could be in control of her life for the first time, and the city skyline was much more mesmerizing compared to the suburb she had grown up in. Her attention was easily pulled into the hum that kept a city alive: the tidbits of conversation she'd hear while going for a walk; the murals that seemed to grasp her gaze, beckoning her to linger, if only for a moment, and consider their contents; the lights that would keep the streets aglow, never allowing her to feel ashamed for not being able to fall asleep.

But everything seemed to lose its luster eventually. It didn't take long for Avery to realize she was never going to be in control of her life, only parts of it. The tidbits of conversation were so frequent, that the endless noise was starting to give her headaches, and she had been searching the murals for meaning but could never find any. Even the lights that had once kept her company were now overstaying their welcome, blocking what she now craved most, which was to sit beneath a starry sky and feel its hope.

With lips pressed together and eyes lost in a daze, Avery allowed her focus to land on their kitchen sink. Dirty dishes were piled high. The longer she stared, the more those dishes felt like a symptom.

Izzy, on the other hand, was busy licking her fingers. So loudly, in fact, Avery couldn't get lost in her own self-pity.

"Did you really just lick chip sauce from your finger?" Avery said.

"Yes, yes, I did."

"You know that kills me."

"It's delicious, Avery. Live a little," Izzy said. "Now don't try to change the subject because you feel all vulnerable."

The cons of knowing someone too long, and too intimately – they begin to know you too well, Avery thought.

"Now look, you're not a con artist, you're not a murderer—"

"You set such high standards for me."

"I'm just saying," Izzy said, leaning on her hands. "So what if you lost touch with what you want out of life? That's okay. Of course it's unsettling, but just because you feel like you've failed at your expectations doesn't mean you need to go crazy purging your whole life. In fact, it probably just means you need some new ones." Before Avery could even process her friend's advice, Izzy tossed the chip bag aside. She was on a roll and wasn't going to let a snack slow her down. "Does this Ray guy even know what the job economy is like right now? Or that a new part of the world is on fire like every other week, and we can't even spend time in mourning because any moment humanity could be wiped out by aliens, war, a plague? I mean, we're not growing up in the age of making dreams come true any more, are we?"

"But you're making *your* dreams come true. You've always wanted to be a teacher."

"Avery," Izzy widened her eyes at her friend. "Teaching is my job. It's fulfilling, but it's not my *dream*."

Avery glanced at the floor, considering this.

"If you don't know what to do with your life, just sit with yourself and admire how far you've come," Izzy said, pulling Avery's focus back to her.

Sunlight spilled through the room, turning Izzy's eyes into a deep shade of gold. Their gaze remained locked in understanding.

Avery expected to feel resentment at the stinging constriction in her throat, but before she could think, Izzy wrapped her in a hug. She thought back to those adolescent years when each step had felt heavy, had required all her energy to take. When it had felt as if there were no place for her in the world she had been born into. It all seemed like a blurry, dark dream.

Even though she often worried the emotional shadow of that time was lurking somewhere, watching, waiting for a moment she'd be vulnerable enough for it to pounce once again, she *had* come a long way, and had a long way to go.

Chapter 64

Brinkley raced through the side door of her house, trying not to let the heavy bags of groceries slip from her fingers and splatter all over the floor. As she set the bags on the marble island of her kitchen and was ready to return to her car to retrieve more, she heard voices echoing from upstairs. Before she called for her husband, she realized the voice was feminine.

A female voice.

Her world froze.

She could feel beads of sweat growing on her face as she tried to eavesdrop on what was going on, but her thoughts were jumbled. All she wanted to do was run to the bathroom and throw up the vegetable panini she had eaten for lunch.

Tiptoeing closer to the spiral staircase, she now heard her husband's voice echoing off their high-rise ceilings.

So, he was having an affair.

All this time she had been consumed by what was wrong with *her*, what was missing from her life, thinking this bastard was constantly working. Never had it occurred to her that her husband could be cheating on her.

And the girls – was he really having an affair while the girls were in the house? He said he could pick them up from summer camp today. Said he had time in between showings. Was he bringing strange women around her daughters?

The thought was enough for her to snap out of the frozen panic she was in and storm up the spiral staircase.

"Where are my babies?" she shrieked as she hit the top of their spiral staircase and sprinted towards the echoing voices. "Where—"

She froze in the doorway of the nursery room. A short woman with a brown bob, peach-colored lips, and thick, square glasses looked at her with a smile. The woman was beautiful, but fully clothed and standing yards away from her husband, who was also fully clothed in a work suit, with his hair combed to the side and his rectangular reading glasses perched atop the bridge of his nose.

Brinkley felt her heart beating, but it was harder than normal, and for a moment she worried she was having a heart attack as Chase tried greeting her with a kiss.

"What's ..." She tried to speak but her mouth betrayed her as she looked around the nursery, which she realized was filled with racks of clothes and a full-length mirror.

"I have a surprise for you," Chase said, smiling with his dimples. "And it's not an office, don't worry. This is Tiffany." He extended his arm towards the woman. "She's a stylist."

How cool of her. Brinkley glared at her husband, then at the woman.

"I know shopping has been hard for you lately, so I thought a stylist might be able to help."

"Wait what's going on?" Brinkley breathed, placing her hand on her hip. "Start from the top. Where are the girls?"

"The basement," Chase said. "My mom's watching them—"

"Wait, Betty's here?" Brinkley said, feeling the brightness glow in her eyes. "She's been here the whole time?"

"Yeah, I told her I had a surprise for you, and wanted you to be able to enjoy it without the girls, so—"

"That's so nice of her!"

"Yeah, so I was doing some research ..." Chase continued, appearing completely oblivious to the fact that Brinkley had almost murdered him for an affair he hadn't committed just five minutes prior. "And one of the things that can help with body changes is getting new clothes ..."

"Wait, so ..." Brinkley trailed off, looking at the racks and racks of clothing with a gleam in her eye.

"And you've been holding on to all your old clothes for years, beating yourself up about not fitting into them," Chase paused, his eyes smiling as their gaze met. "And it's not fair that you're comparing your body now, to the one you had when you were younger—"

"Lily and Daisy wrecked my body."

"But they didn't," Chase said, his voice firm. "They changed your body. I thought," he said, and scratched the back of his combed hair, "I thought maybe a new wardrobe, one that's not based on an old version of you, would help?"

"Chase ..." She felt her heart beating faster at this admission, but was unsure if it was from excitement or fear.

"I didn't get rid of any of your old clothes, or anything," he said quickly. "I wanted you to decide what to do with them, but ..."

Brinkley felt a pang of guilt run through her, as she imagined throwing out her old skinny jeans. She had been holding on to them since before giving birth, determined to one day fit in to them again. Throwing them away felt like throwing an old goal away. A goal she had desperately wanted to achieve the past three years.

"I think a fresh start could be healthy," Chase finished.

As he looked at her, with his earnest eyes and the racks of clothes behind him – the proof of his effort, his care – Brinkley visualized this fresh start. Tried to imagine what it would feel like to walk into a closet full of clothes that fit her, no longer subjecting herself to her own body shaming.

To get rid of her old clothes would require Brinkley to accept new ones. Ones that were larger but would fit her.

She continued visualizing this fresh start, where she could be confident in her own skin, for her husband, for her daughters, mostly for herself. Oh, no. She was crying even more than her mother these days.

"This is ... so nice, Chase," was all she could muster without breaking into full-blown tears.

"I love you."

"I love you, too," she said, her voice cracking as she hid her face in his chest and tried to calm down. She hadn't even introduced herself to the stylist and was already having a breakdown.

"Tiffany will show you what she picked, and then just ... I don't know. Pick what you like."

"*Anything* I like?"

"Anything you like."

"This is probably costing a fortune, Chase," Brinkley whispered to her husband. "I can't just pick anything. What's the budget?"

"Hun," Chase said, putting his hands on her shoulders and looking into her eyes, "you have raised our family and supported me behind the scenes for years. Accept this from me, please." Before Brinkley could cry even more, Chase added, "And Tiffany knows the budget. She'll cut you off. Now, I do have to return to work ..." Chase offered the admission slowly, scratching the back of his head.

"It's okay!" Brinkley sang, giving her husband one last hug. "Go, enjoy! Work hard. I'll see you tonight."

"Okay," Chase breathed, looking as if he had just dodged a bullet. With one last kiss, he disappeared down the hall.

Brinkley turned to the stylist with a smile from ear to ear. "I'm so sorry I didn't introduce myself. I'm Brinkley."

"Oh, no worries," Tiffany shook her hand. "So, when your husband called me, I asked him to describe you a bit to help me select your pieces—"

"You did?"

Everything this woman was saying made Brinkley feel like she was going to cry happy tears.

"Yeah, so he described you as very caring, and fun – sometimes a little over the top – sexy and elegant—"

"He did?" she choked, her voice ten pitches higher than normal.

"Yes!" Tiffany said, tipping her head, her hands on her hips as if insulted that Brinkley would second-guess that. "He said you absolutely love delicate things, like flowers, and candles, and butterflies—"

"Oh, gosh," Brinkley chuckled.

"But he also said you're one of the strongest people he knows."

Brinkley felt the world around her become still, before she heard herself break into full blown sobs.

Tiffany wrinkled her eyebrows, watching Brinkley's shoulders heave.

"Um ..." Tiffany said, looking around the room before pulling a packet of tissues from her briefcase. "Here you go."

"Thank you so much," Brinkley said in between sobs. "I'm sorry, I don't know why I'm crying, I just—"

"Brinkley," Tiffany said, wiping her square eyeglasses as if to get a better look, "you are a beautiful woman. This might be an emotional experience, but it's time for you to let it out and let it go. Whatever that means for you."

Blowing her nose, Brinkley felt her head nod. "I just ... I haven't really been shopping, or trying on clothes in years—"

"And how has that been working for you?"

Brinkley looked around her, at the racks of an elegant, sexy, delicate yet strong wardrobe. Her heart was still thudding, but her head nodded anyway.

"You're right," she admitted. "It's about time I try something new."

Chapter 65

"So, Raymond," Avery said as she set down his old-fashioned, "I think you should know that, even though I value our friendship, I have no plans to quit my job here at the bar."

The wrinkles around his eyes draped his face as he squinted at a place far away. "I never told you to quit your job ... Did I?"

Oh, no. He is senile.

"Ray, last Wednesday you said you don't want to die while I'm still working here," she said. "You told me I had, like, depth. And experience. And it seemed very important to you that I do something with that. Even though you didn't offer any suggestions of what I could do, which I found kind of annoying—"

His deep-hearted chuckle broke her off.

"Oh dear, Avery, you don't think I have very long to live, do you?"

She studied him, but his chuckle turned into a laugh.

Okay, it's not that funny, Ray.

"I forgot," he said, and wiped his eyes, "your generation is so quick with things. I'm glad you kept your job! You would've left without saying goodbye."

"I'd say goodbye," she said, crossing her arms.

"Now, no one knows when their time is up," he said, regaining his composure. "But I think I still have a few years in me. I just want you to think about it, Avery. What else you'd rather be doing with your life."

Avery raised an eyebrow.

"Bartending is a passion for some," he said with a shrug. "But it's not that way for you, is it?"

She sighed, leaning her elbow on the counter across from him. "At one point it felt like it was. Now, I don't know. But it pays my bills and I get to meet a bunch of different people, so ..." She glanced through the window before looking back at him. "What more could I ask for in this day and age, Ray? Every day humanity doesn't destroy itself is a success to me, so ..."

With his deep-set eyes that had witnessed so many years of life, Raymond stared right through her.

"Purpose," he answered. "You could ask for a purpose. And even if you spent your whole life searching for one, at least you lived in that pursuit."

He raised his old-fashioned to his lips and took a drink.

Avery watched him for a moment, but he remained still. His hand still cupped the drink even as he set it on the counter.

"And what was your life's purpose?" she challenged.

He kept his eyes on the glass. "I don't know if I had one."

"What?" She nearly jumped at this admission.

"I poured all my efforts into my job, and my wife ... staying healthy and keeping friends. But aging takes all that away from you. And aging wasn't easy for me. Where's the life I had spent all my time building now?"

"Ray ..." was all she could say as she looked at him. In all her years of knowing him, in all the conversations they had shared about love and loss, she had never seen him look so sad.

He seemed to bite his own tongue as he took another drink and tried to regain composure. "Look," he said, and his eyes were pleading, "I lived a good life. But I don't want you making the same mistakes I did."

"I'm ... I'm sorry to hear that," Avery said, but felt more words crawling up her throat. "But what about now? What's your purpose now?"

"Oh, Avery," he said, his voice raspy, "I'm too old now. I watch my children and my grandchildren grow every holiday and I pass the time."

Avery watched as her mind let this man, this man who had once sat so high, fall from his metaphorical pedestal.

"Ray," she broke the silence just as the chime above the front door rang and unfamiliar customers strolled in, "you just told me you think you have a few more years. I don't want you to die while you're still coming here every Wednesday for your weekly source of human interaction." She greeted the new customers and left a couple of drink menus at the other end of the bar before looking back at Raymond. "I'd much rather be visiting you in, like, an independent living community where there's probably dance parties and maybe a pool."

Avery brought her face closer to his, to make sure he could look into her eyes when she made her promise. "I would visit you, okay? And you could still visit me every Wednesday."

He didn't say anything, but he scrutinized her eyes.

"And I know those places can be scary, or, like, way too expensive, but let's talk about it. Maybe there's a cool bingo night we could attend—"

"Just because I'm old, doesn't mean I like bingo."

"Come on, Raymond, who doesn't like bingo?"

Raymond rocked his head back to finish the last of his drink.

"If I'm being honest," she said, keeping her voice low so the other customers couldn't hear, "I don't plan on working at this bar much longer. But I've been taking life one step at a time. For a while, it's all I've felt capable of doing, and I'm just now starting to reconsider my potential. But for now, my purpose is to simply experience life, whatever it throws my way, and to hopefully make it feel a bit more joyful for anyone who walks through that door."

Raymond's gaze remained on his nearly empty glass, before the words seemed to settle into the corners of his eyes, and he offered a long, slow nod.

"You should be proud of yourself, Avery."

"I'm learning," Avery chuckled, but kept her eyes trained on him. "And look, I know it feels good to finally feel comfortable with life, Raymond, but you still have life to live. Let me help you."

Raymond remained quiet. She walked to the other end of the bar to take orders from the new customers, but his soft, strained voice called her: "Avery ..."

She turned her head to look at him. His eyes were bathed in light as he looked at her, the wrinkles around his mouth deepening at the corners.

"Thank you," he said, and when his lips pressed together, Avery could see his mouth was curved into a barely perceptible smile. "That means a lot."

"You're welcome."

Chapter 66

I t was the day of Elizabeth and John's casual wedding celebration. After Brinkley's wardrobe overhaul, she was especially in the mood to throw a party, so she had called Elizabeth and demanded to throw a wedding celebration for her and John.

Brinkley had been elated when Elizabeth had called back and given her the green light, even though the Astors would not be in attendance. Apparently, John was unwilling to extend the invite, but it wasn't Brinkley's place to get involved, and she was overjoyed that she, at least, would have a chance to celebrate her sister and future brother-in-law. Elizabeth had been her best friend while growing up. They'd played with dolls together until they were way too old, hid in the closet when their parents' arguments were especially bad, covered each other's lies during those teenaged years of parties and sneaking out, and shared countless nights of laughter that had turned into cries. It didn't feel right to let her little sis' run off and get married without *any* party to celebrate.

This morning, Chase had to meet potential new clients and conduct interviews for new real estate agents to add to his team, but Brinkley managed to kiss him goodbye without the usual bitterness over his work schedule. He promised he would be back in time for the celebration, and Brinkley was trying to practice trusting him and

YOU DON'T KNOW NANA

herself more. So, she had set her alarm for six am sharp to fill the balloons, finish setting up decorations, get the girls ready, and get herself ready.

She had chosen to wear a flowy, dusty-pink wrap dress that had a silk bow around the waist to accentuate her curves. Tiffany, Brinkley's new BFF – not really, but Brinkley liked to dream – had helped her pick it out. Brinkley was still getting used to feeling comfortable, even proud of her curves. Even thinking of her body as curvy was a new practice for her.

Retraining her mind would take time, but Brinkley was determined. She was not going to raise her daughters to feel uncomfortable in their own changing, sacred female bodies. Which meant it was necessary to learn to feel comfortable in her own.

And when she had looked at her reflection in the mirror this morning, with her hair dipping just below her shoulders, in soft waves around her face, a light dusting of makeup framing her eyes, Lily, standing behind her, had gasped and said, "Mommy, you look so beautiful!"

Even though Brinkley had insecurities, she was only just learning about herself, and she made the conscious decision to believe her daughter. The past few years, it had become hard for Brinkley to see herself through the eyes of the people who loved her. But she was going to try anyway.

Now, with the party all set up to celebrate, Brinkley found herself tiptoeing to the drawer of her vanity and staring at the rose quartz ring Nana had gifted her only a couple of months ago. It was stunning as ever, sitting there in the drawer, not caring whether it was on display or hidden as it had been the past few weeks. Brinkley picked it up and slid it on her right ring finger.

The pink rose quartz matched her new dress, but that's not why she was putting it on.

416

Brinkley was ready to face her nana's secrets because Brinkley was no longer carrying the burden of her own. Her life and her marriage were not perfect. Her husband was not perfect, and she was not perfect. They had nearly crumbled under the weight of perfection, and so it was okay that Nana's ring was no longer a symbol of perfect love. It was a symbol of real love, of the real work needed to raise a family and maintain a healthy relationship.

Around two pm, after Brinkley had finished setting up the catered food outside, hanging balloons, framing pictures of Elizabeth and John over the years, and giving Lily and Daisy white and pink flower petals to toss around the house, Elizabeth arrived.

All of Brinkley's efforts to throw her sister a wedding celebration felt worth it when Elizabeth walked through the front archway of white balloons with bright eyes and a dropped jaw. By the time she entered the house, with fresh white flower petals dispersed over every tabletop and pictures of her and John in gold frames lining the walls, Elizabeth was in tears.

She was dressed in a white tailored jumpsuit with a high neckline and thin spaghetti straps. For a moment, Brinkley felt a tug in her heart as she saw her sister with her long hair let loose around her face, cascading down the back of her elegant white outfit.

Brinkley imagined Elizabeth looking even more magical in her lace wedding dress, walking down the aisle to meet the love of her life. But as Elizabeth came in for a hug, a smile on her face and romance in her eyes, Brinkley could see her sister was happy. And Brinkley knew that no fantasy could compete with something as mystical as experiencing authentic happiness.

Shortly after the bride-to-be's arrival, Avery and Mama Donna arrived, their hair windblown from riding in Mama Donna's white convertible. After brushing and spraying their hair, all four women were now seated at the white marble island of Brinkley's kitchen, helping themselves to scoops of fresh cut fruit and a bottle of champagne. Lily and Daisy were busy playing in their playroom.

"Where's Chase?" Mama Donna inquired.

"He had an early meeting with a designer." Brinkley bit a strawberry. "I told him to come the same time as John and Dad."

"What?" Elizabeth and Mama Donna gasped.

"What?" Brinkley asked, looking between them. "I wanted us to have a couple hours for girl time."

"No, Brinkley," Mama Donna said, emphasizing her name, "you invited your father? Now he's going to bring his girlfriend—"

"Fiancée," Elizabeth corrected, but was nodding along.

"Oh my gosh," Brinkley groaned. "What did you think would happen when you filed for divorce, Mom? You thought our dad would just disappear?"

"He disappeared enough when you guys were little," Mama Donna retorted. "So yeah, maybe I did."

Before Brinkley could release another groan, Elizabeth broke into giggles.

"Well," Elizabeth said, "I guess he's going to find out today."

Brinkley froze while reaching for more champagne, and eyed her giggling sister. "What are you talking about?"

"John and I haven't told Dad we changed wedding plans yet. Did you at least tell him when you invited him today?"

Brinkley blinked. "I mean, I told him to come over for a wedding celebration. I figured he'd assume it was for you and John, but then Daisy ripped another head off Lily's doll, and I had to go deal with that ... I don't remember telling him anything!"

Avery laughed.

"Mom!" Daisy's voice yelled from her playroom. "Mom, come here!"

"One second, honey!" Brinkley called, then looked at Elizabeth. "Why didn't you tell Dad yet?"

Elizabeth tilted her head to stare at the ripe strawberry between her fingers. "I don't know ... I guess his total lack of regard for John and me liberated us from having any regard for him."

"It's been a second, Mom!" Now the voice sounded like Lily's.

Elizabeth continued speaking against the screams. "John and I wanted to enjoy these last few weeks of our engagement—"

"Why aren't you answering, Mom?" Daisy's voice called again.

"I'm just gonna ... go get your kids," Avery muttered and then disappeared into the other room.

Brinkley brought her fingertips to the bridge of her nose and tried to massage the tension between her eyes. "I am so sick of hearing my name today," she said, closing her eyes.

"Well, to be fair, your name isn't 'Mom'," Elizabeth said.

"Huh," Mama Donna grunted. "Once you have kids, it is."

"If I had kids, I'd have them call me something a lot more fabulous like ... Queen, or ... Empress," Elizabeth mused.

"I'm glad you don't want any, then," Brinkley quipped. "What were we even talking about?"

"We were talking about your asshole father," Mama Donna said.

"Mom, do you really need to call him an asshole every time you refer to him?" Brinkley asked.

"In all fairness," Elizabeth said, "he calls her an asshole, too. To be honest, I always found it endearing that they picked the same curse word for each other." Before Brinkley could roll her eyes, Elizabeth continued: "Anyway, Mom's right. We were talking about Dad and how he's about to find out my change of wedding plans."

"Oh my gosh, I'm getting nervous about it," Mama Donna said, but with a smile and a dazzle in her eyes.

Elizabeth sat up straighter. "Maybe when he walks through that door and sees all the decorations, I'll just look at him," she imagined out loud, looking at somewhere above her. "I'll look at him and I'll say, *'You're welcome. My sacrifice has preserved peace among this family and John and my future.'*"

Before Brinkley could call her sister insane, Avery appeared in the kitchen without the girls.

"Where're my babies?"

"Your girls are tough negotiators," Avery said.

"Yeah, Chase has been teaching them that," Brinkley said. "Where are they?"

"They were calling you to put on a movie, so I set them up in their room. They said they're not hungry now and they'll be down later."

Elizabeth narrowed her eyes. "What did you negotiate, then?"

"What?" Avery asked innocently.

"Sounds like Lily and Daisy set the terms for the whole deal," Elizabeth said. "What did you get?"

Avery blinked, and then a blood-curdling shriek echoed down the stairs.

"Nana!" Lily's voice, the sound of her little feet thudding down the stairs. "Mom, Mom, a butterfly flew past our window! Nana's here!"

Apparently, the dead butterfly at summer camp hadn't been enough to crush Lily's beliefs.

"What kind of sixth-sense shit—" Elizabeth started.

"Mom, you love God—" Brinkley started.

"Oh, I do ..." Mama Donna nodded at her daughters. "I really do. You all should, too."

"Would you ... want to teach Lily about God?" Brinkley asked. "She's been asking about heaven and stuff lately, and—"

"Say no more, Brinkley!" Mama Donna said, hopping out of her seat.

"I mean, you don't have to teach her right now."

"Yeah, Mom, where are you going?" Elizabeth said. "This isn't Bible Study. This is my wedding celebration. Stay with me!"

"Okay, okay," Mama Donna said, throwing her hands in the air as she resumed her seat. "Sorry, I got a little excited. I like when you girls ask for my help."

The older Brinkley got, the more similarities she noticed between her and her mother. And perhaps it wasn't such a bad thing. In fact, she considered as she eyed the rose quartz ring on her finger, it seemed to be a natural progression of passing on your life.

Chapter 67

The sound of Lily's feet racing down Brinkley's hallway could be heard from Elizabeth's seat at the head of the kitchen table.

"Mom! Daddy and Uncle John are here!" Lily announced.

"Oh, I can't wait to see them," Mama Donna said, already rising from her seat and disappearing from the kitchen with Lily racing close behind.

Brinkley looked at her sisters as the usual greetings echoed through the foyer. "If only she loved us as much as she loves them."

"My self-esteem would've been a lot higher growing up," Avery said.

"I wouldn't have been so deceived by John's family," Elizabeth added.

"I would know how to be satisfied with myself, my life," Brinkley chimed in, looking at something in the distance of the kitchen.

"Hey, what age do you think we'll stop blaming our parents for everything?" Elizabeth said.

"At whatever age we can stop parenting them," Brinkley said with a snort.

"I don't know," said Avery, crossing her arms. "I think whatever age we decide to take responsibility for the lives we're choosing now.

I think that's when we'll truly be free."

Elizabeth and Brinkley blinked, turning their heads towards her.

"I don't know," she said again, tucking an invisible piece of her hair behind her ears and looking at the ground.

"It sounds like you do know," said Elizabeth.

"Well," Avery said, raising her eyes to meet her sisters', "I'm still figuring out what it specifically means, for me, I guess."

Brinkley opened her mouth, but just then Lily's voice squeaked through the kitchen.

"And here," she said as she led the group past Brinkley's marble island with an outstretched hand, "is the kitchen."

"She took us on a tour," John explained.

"Yep," Chase said as he hugged his wife, "she showed us the guest room, her playroom, the laundry room ..."

"No ..."

"Opened the door before I could stop her," Chase said.

"It's okay, Brinkley," John said as he greeted Brinkley with a hug. "Every family uses a room as storage, to hide what they want from guests. It proves you're alive."

John released himself from his hug and grabbed Elizabeth's face in his hands with a soft smile. He gave Elizabeth a kiss and then brought her hand to his heart. "Darling, may I talk to you in private?"

"What? Why?" Elizabeth asked.

"Ah, I forgot, privacy is dead," he said, but was already leading her away from her family and into Brinkley and Chase's empty stone hallway.

With both hands on her shoulders, he let out a breath through his flared nostrils.

"John, what is it?"

"My mother will be attending."

"What!"

"So will my father," John continued. "And my sister. And Jared."

"John, what the hell?"

"Elizabeth—"

"John, we talked about inviting your family. I encouraged it! But you're the one who said no, insisted you didn't want them. Why are you springing this on me last minute?"

"Elizabeth," he said, his hands still on her shoulders and bending his knees, so his eyes were level with hers, "Elizabeth, I'm sorry. The closer the date got, the more I panicked. Before we get married, I think we need to face them and release all our demons—"

"John. The fact that you're referring to your family as demons—"

"Because they haunt me, Liz!" John said, his voice echoing down the empty hallway. "They haunt you, too. I thought more about what you were saying, and you were right."

Elizabeth felt her face soften.

As if he noticed, he repeated, "You were right, Liz. I think we should give my family one last chance to try to be there for us." John's eyes darted between her own. "Whether they're happy or angry or sad for us, they deserve a chance to just be with us before their only son gets married."

Elizabeth parted her lips for a moment. His eyes were still searching hers.

"I mean, I agree, but why didn't you tell me this earlier? I would've, like, taken a Xanax or something!"

"You want the truth?"

"Yes, John, obviously I want the truth."

"I was so happy we were happy ..." John swallowed. "I didn't want to ruin it. But when I woke up this morning, I realized I needed to at least invite them."

Elizabeth continued glaring at John before letting out a sigh. "Okay ... I get it."

"Thank you." He pulled her into a hug just as the doorbell rang.

"Sorry, sorry ..." Brinkley said as she passed Elizabeth and John in the hallway and sashayed to the front door.

"Hi!" Elizabeth could hear Brinkley's voice sing.

Elizabeth heard her father's voice first. Then she heard the baby-like pitch that could only belong to Cynthia. She looked up at John, who already had a nervous, perhaps even excited, look on his face.

And so it begins...

Chapter 68

Brinkley, Avery, and Donna had tiptoed to the edge of the kitchen to eavesdrop on John and Elizabeth's argument. Chase had acted appalled by this invasion of privacy, following Lily and Daisy into their playroom instead.

It took only a few seconds until the opinions were unleashed.

"She needs to be nicer to him," Mama Donna weighed in with a whisper. "That's his family."

"If Chase sprang that on me, I'd be mad," Brinkley said. "And I love Chase's family."

"Aw, I think they're making up!" Mama Donna said with a smile.

When the doorbell rang, Avery and Mama Donna remained in their hiding spots as Brinkley headed to the front door.

Richard's raspy voice soon filled the air.

"That balloon archway out front. It's beautiful! Brinkley, this is so nice," Avery heard her father say. "Is this all for me and Sin?"

"Hah!" Avery laughed, and then snapped her hand over her mouth.

"Haha, Dad," Avery heard Brinkley say, either playing along or not playing at all.

Mama Donna yanked Avery's arm so they could hustle back to the table as footsteps clicked closer.

"What?" Richard's voice asked.

"Oh, crap, that's right ..." Brinkley breathed as she came into view of the kitchen. Her hand was smacked against her forehead. "They didn't tell you."

"What?" Richard asked.

"Hello," Avery sang, rising from the seat she had just taken, but Richard and Sin's focus remained on Brinkley.

"This is for John and Elizabeth," Brinkley began.

As if on cue, John and Elizabeth appeared into the kitchen.

"We're getting married in one week!" Elizabeth said, flashing a smile. "No one's invited, so we're celebrating today!"

"What?" Richard asked again, visibly dumbfounded now.

"You're welcome," she said, hugging her father and then releasing the embrace to hug Sin. "You're welcome," she repeated.

John, smiling, also squeezed them both.

"What is going on?" Richard demanded, recoiling from John's hug.

"So," Elizabeth said, clasping her hands together and widening her eyes just a bit, "John and I realized a traditional wedding is not our thing."

John wrapped his arm around Elizabeth's shoulders with a grin. "Yeah, we were not happy with it – the idea of it, planning it, all of it. So, we shook our tree of life and realized the rotting relationships will fall from our branches and the healthy, growing ones will prosper."

Avery watched as her father's eyes narrowed at John, then Elizabeth.

"Do you even know what he's talking about?" Richard said to Elizabeth. "Is this some kind of joke?"

"Richard ..." John cleared his throat, tapping his hand against Richard's back. "This isn't a joke. This is our life. And we're taking it back."

"Brinkley, what the hell is going on?" Richard said, leaning towards Brinkley but speaking so everyone could hear.

"Um, so, Elizabeth and John are eloping," Brinkley said softly, and cleared her throat. "But they're telling everyone, so I guess it's not an elopement, but anyway, this is their wedding celebration. I, um, I forgot to mention that detail. And I guess they did, too."

With a cocked eyebrow and his mouth hanging open, Richard stared at the happy couple, turned his back to face the food, then glanced at Elizabeth and John once more.

"And this isn't a joke?" he asked once more.

Avery was still standing from her seat. She had originally intended to greet her father and Sin, but with one look at Sin's pout and Richard's scowl, she decided to sit back down.

"I'm sorry, Dad," Elizabeth offered, her tone still bright. "It's kind of been a whirlwind, canceling one wedding and then planning another within, like, a month. But you two know how wedding planning is."

Richard shut his mouth, eyeing the quiet room. "And you all knew about this?"

"I did," Mama Donna said quickly with a nod. "I wasn't happy about it, but I don't blame them given the circumstances of, you know, your conflicting dates."

"Give me a break, Donna ..." Richard rolled his eyes. "My date didn't have to be this much of a problem. If John and Elizabeth ..." He paused to scrutinize his daughter and future son-in-law, as if still waiting for the moment they would admit this was all a joke, but that moment never came. "If they want to run off and get married because they don't want to do a traditional wedding, that's on them."

Sin looked like an emotionless mannequin as she stared at everyone with wide eyes, perhaps wondering for the first time what kind of family she was marrying into.

"Okay," John's deep voice broke in. He clapped twice, then rubbed his hands together. "I think we could all use a drink, right? My family is on their way."

Chapter 69

Mrs. Astor tiptoed her way into Brinkley's house with her nose quite literally in the air as she surveyed her surroundings.

Elizabeth felt she might throw up the glass of champagne John had insisted they chug before his family's arrival. Cementing a smile on her face, Elizabeth tried to make her voice sound bright and bubbly as she leaned in for a hug.

"Mrs. Astor!" Elizabeth greeted with a voice two octaves higher than usual. "You look beautiful. Thank you for coming."

How generous of you to spend time with my improper family, she thought through a tight smile, but opened her arms wide for a hug. Mrs. Astor offered a one-armed hug.

"Oh," she said, already releasing herself from Elizabeth's embrace, "hi. How are you?"

"Great," Elizabeth said, still trying to keep her voice bright and bubbly, but the ice in Mrs. Astor's current tone was making her heart beat faster. *I mean, this is my wedding celebration, after all ...* "I'm happy we were able to get our families together to celebrate," Elizabeth added, her cheeks starting to hurt from the forced smile.

"What is there to celebrate, darling?" Mrs. Astor said and looked Elizabeth up and down before turning to give one-armed hugs to the rest of Elizabeth's family.

Elizabeth snapped her head towards John. "I need another drink."

Once the two families began to intermingle, remembering one another from John and Elizabeth's engagement party six months prior, Elizabeth pulled her fiancé into the playroom just as everyone was heading to Brinkley and Chase's outdoor patio, and shut the door behind them.

"John, your mother hates me. It's official," she said. "I tried being all warm and welcoming, and she was so cold to me. I thought I was going to turn to stone."

"She was cold to me, too. She only offered one air kiss," John said, looking towards the closed playroom door. "At least my father offered two."

"I feel so uncomfortable," Elizabeth groaned, smoothing over her white jumpsuit.

John snapped his head towards her. "Why? This is our party."

"Because, John," Elizabeth said, now smoothing her fingers through her hair, "she's going to be my mother-in-law. As cold as your mother can be, her self-assuredness is also quite fabulous, and I thought we were going to, like, drink Champagne together and sit around the fire pit, gossiping about her rich neighbors—"

"And when in your life did you think that?" John said.

Elizabeth paused, looking at John's loose waves freed from their gel, strands of them nearly dropping to his eyes and framing his face.

"You're right," she said with a nod. "I was a puppet back then. A smiling and nodding puppet, giving everyone else control of my strings."

"Now listen to me." John's hands gripped her shoulders as if their life depended on what he was about to say next. "We are going to enjoy this day with one goal in mind. That's it. One goal."

"Right." She nodded again. "What's our goal?"

"To celebrate us," he said firmly. "Our love. The ten years we've shared together, and the many more to come."

"Many more?" Elizabeth asked and could feel a smile spreading across her face.

"Many more. There is no one in the world, Elizabeth, who I would rather explore this life with than you. Wherever it may lead. All this ..." He waved his hand around.

"All ... what?" Elizabeth looked around the playroom, trying to see what he was waving his hand at. "All the toys?"

"Well, sort of, but think of the toys as symbolic of the distractions—"

"Okay, John, I love you, but your mother is one scowl away from making me flip a table, so can you please speak in literal terms for five minutes?"

Closing his mouth, John took Elizabeth's hand in his and looked her in the eyes. "This party is not our wedding. People can come, and they can choose to celebrate or act like fools, but our wedding day is already protected, Liz," he said. "No matter what these people do today, it doesn't matter. Because in one week, we are going to get married, by the Atlantic, and start new lives together. On our terms. And no one will be able to ruin or take that day away from us."

They lingered in this moment for a minute until John squeezed her hand. Elizabeth nodded. It was time to face the music.

John led his fiancée onto Brinkley's backyard patio, where everyone had congregated, and the music was blaring through the speakers.

"Oh good, people are already past small talk," John said. "I'm going to grab a drink, darling. Would you like anything?"

"Yes," Elizabeth said. "But I can get it. You go enjoy." Her eyes narrowed onto Mrs. Astor, who was seated at the patio table, frowning at something on the lawn. Following Mrs. Astor's frown, Elizabeth saw Avery swaying her uncoordinated body back and forth, drink raised in the air, singing – or at least trying to sing along – to an explicit song.

"This one's for you, Elizabeth!" she cheered when seeing her sister and raised her beer even higher before taking a gulp. "I came to celebrate!"

Elizabeth tried to offer a smile before making her way to Brinkley, who was also watching Avery sway, but with much more admiration than Mrs. Astor.

"Avery requested this song," Brinkley explained once Elizabeth approached. "Do you think the lyrics are okay for Lily and Daisy?"

Elizabeth looked towards the lawn, and noticed Lily and Daisy also swinging their hips back and forth, though with much more rhythm, if she was being honest.

"It's fine, they'll grow up empowered," Elizabeth said. "But why did Avery request this, of all songs? My mother-in-law is sitting right there and already hates me. The last thing I need is for her to hear these lyrics and think I'm—"

"Naughty?" Brinkley finished with a smirk.

"Well, yeah."

"Oh, please," Brinkley groaned. "If Betty were here, she'd find it hilarious. I mean, you did cancel your entire wedding to run off and marry her son. It is a little ... naughty, no?"

Elizabeth wanted to smack the smirk right off her sister's face.

"Look, Avery thought Mrs. Astor came in a little ... pouty, and after all the BS you've been through with his family and our family, she just wanted to liven things up a bit. Make sure you had a fun time," Brinkley said, before quickly adding, "She's sacrificing herself so you can smile."

Elizabeth watched as Avery continued gyrating her hips on the lawn.

"Maybe she started dancing for me, but I think she's doing it all for herself now, Brinkley."

Before Brinkley could respond, their father's voice broke through:

"Do you think your neighbors would spare a hungry man a steak?" Richard bellowed from across the patio, clutching his belly with a laugh.

Mrs. Astor's face finally cracked into a smile. "Please see if he'll spare two," she cooed from her seat.

"Make that three!" Mr. Astor joined in from the cooler.

"Why don't you all go to the neighbors and check?" John shouted from his spot at the grill with Chase, maintaining his gaze on his parents and future father-in-law as he stuffed a tofu kebab in his mouth. He didn't bother to close his mouth as he chewed.

Elizabeth was waiting for Brinkley, the queen of entertaining, to give a nervous laugh or attempt to diffuse the situation, but Brinkley's eyes were glued to her daughters, who looked like they were having the best time forming a dance circle with their aunt Avery.

"They are just too cute," said Brinkley. "Those dance lessons are really paying off." Maybe Brinkley hadn't heard.

"People are already complaining about the food," Elizabeth groaned.

"So what?" Brinkley took a sip from the glass of champagne in her hand. "If they want to starve, let them starve, you know?"

Elizabeth blinked. Was this Brinkley talking?

"This party is for you, Elizabeth. Well, you and John. But I did it mostly for you," Brinkley said. "So maybe this is a good time to realize who's here for you, and who's always just been here for themselves, you know?"

The advice planted itself in Elizabeth's mind as she looked back at Avery and her two nieces, all smiling and swinging their hips to the music.

"Should we join the dance?" Elizabeth said.

"If you want to dance, I'll dance," Brinkley said.

After a few more songs and drinks, the sun dipped in the sky and cast the world in a rich copper hue before nighttime took over. Whether it was the alcohol, or the freedom that people feel with more time and less light, the dance circle doubled in size to include John, Chase, and Mama Donna. Even Jordan and Jared, and Richard and Sin, made an appearance. At one point, Jordan moved to the middle of the circle to showcase her pregnant belly.

As Jordan began dropping it low, Brinkley whispered, "So, do you still hate Jordan, or do you think ... maybe ... you and Jordan could become friends?"

Elizabeth couldn't help but laugh as she watched her future sister-in-law only gain more momentum with each cheer from the crowd.

"Jordan! Jordan!" Avery chanted.

"Honestly," Elizabeth said, her cheeks hurting from all the laughing, "I never hated her. Or any of the Astors."

Brinkley cocked her head to the side, eyeing Elizabeth.

"I didn't! I just hated who I let myself become around them."

A hint of a smile flashed across Brinkley's face, but Elizabeth wasn't sure if she had imagined it as Brinkley looked back at the dancing crowd.

"Besides, I don't want to carry any baggage into my rebirth as an Astor, you know?"

Before Brinkley could respond, Avery had joined Jordan in the middle of the circle, a bottle of champagne in her hand as the two women giggled and danced together.

"Cheers to love!" said Avery, her eyes shut as she waved the bottle of champagne in the air.

"Oh, wait, wait, you're spilling!" Jordan said before hopping out of the circle, her baby bump bouncing with her.

Avery opened her eyes, looking at no one in particular. "Love is the answer, you guys!"

"Oh, Lord," Brinkley breathed to Elizabeth. "Is Avery okay?"

"I mean, she seems okay to me," said Elizabeth, then released a cheer for their littlest sis.

"Elizabeth, she has a whole bottle of champagne in her hand!"

Elizabeth waved her hand to shoo away her sister's judgment. "Let her live. We're all here to celebrate." Elizabeth's eyes traveled to Mrs. Astor, who was still seated at the table. "At least, most of us are."

When the music switched to a slow song, Jordan yelled from the perimeter of the circle: "Speech! Speech!"

Even Daisy stopped twirling. "Yeah!"

"I'll make a speech," Richard offered.

"Richard, no," Sin laughed, slapping his shoulder.

She slapped it a bit hard, Elizabeth noticed.

"Why not?" Brinkley asked Sin and then looked at their father. "You're the father of the bride – make a speech!"

"Okay, okay," said Richard. "Everyone gather round!"

"I'm scared ..." said Elizabeth.

Everyone was already gathered in a circle, with Richard at the center.

"Oh, here we go," Elizabeth heard her mother groan next to her.

Richard cleared his throat and looked at his audience. "Elizabeth and John, you have known each other for a long time. I didn't know what you were thinking at first, when you brought John around, but cheers to the happy couple!" he declared, raising his glass before receding into the circle. Within seconds, he popped his head back out. "And good luck."

"That's it?" Brinkley scrunched her face.

"It could have been worse ..." Avery shrugged.

Elizabeth felt her mouth open as she looked around, but everyone, sobered by the speech, was regrouping towards the people they knew best.

As Chase switched the slow song to something faster, Elizabeth felt her mouth close as John pulled her in tighter. And before she knew it, beneath the sky, surrounded by family, her fake smile transformed into something real.

Elizabeth looked around, at her sisters dancing by her side and her mother swaying her body to the music, so free in her movement. It reminded Elizabeth of the way her mother used to dance when they were all younger, and Elizabeth's father would be gone for the weekend, leaving Mama Donna with her daughters. The four of them would dance in their mother's bedroom to Fleetwood Mac and talk for hours by the foot of her bed.

Then she watched as the champagne bottle slipped from Avery's grasp, spilling its bubbles across the lawn. Avery eyed her surroundings before kicking it aside and continuing to rock her body to the beat.

Elizabeth switched her gaze to her nieces, who had been twirling across the grass but were now rubbing Jordan's belly, fascinated by the baby growing inside. Jared was still silent, and Elizabeth realized she could count the number of words they had ever exchanged on one hand. But still, he was standing there, close behind his wife.

She glanced at Mrs. Astor, who appeared more like an ice sculpture than a guest, as she was still glued to her seat with her posture straighter than ever. Her red lips were pressed into a thin line, her chin cocked in the air, hands clutching a delicate wine glass. The only thing noticeably moving was the red liquid, swirling around and around in the glass, and some of it slipped over the rim, spilling onto her silk blouse. Mr. Astor reached for napkins, but his hand was swatted away.

Oh, dear, Elizabeth thought, biting her tongue.

Finally, she tilted her head to look at John, who had his arms wrapped around her, squeezing her close to him. He still had barbeque sauce on the corners of his lips from shoving tofu kebabs into his mouth, but she squeezed his face to hers and planted a kiss on his lips before wiping the sauce away.

She began to visualize her wedding day, her actual wedding day, when there would be no one to please, or entertain. Only the sun, moon, and stars, the sound of rolling ocean waves, and the love of her life would be there, ushering her into the next season.

For a moment, Elizabeth felt cradled by love, as if a deep bliss was awakening within her. The kind of bliss that can only come from following one's heart.

"To Elizabeth and John!" Richard raised his glass, walking back from the cooler to rejoin the dance circle.

Elizabeth smiled and hugged her father. "I love you," she said into his ear.

And she meant it. Because this was not her wedding day. She hadn't given him, or anyone else, the power to ruin or control that, so she could still hold love for all of them.

Chapter 70

Avery blinked her eyes open to soft early morning light streaming through her frayed, sheer curtains. She kept her head on her pillow for a moment, resting in the silence with herself.

Today was the day of Elizabeth and John's bonfire.

She untangled herself from her covers and wiped the crusts from the corner of her eyes. Blinking her blurry world into clarity, she looked at the sliding door to her small closet that lay by the foot of her bed. It was a door that guarded many secrets.

Tucking her hair behind her ears, Avery took a moment to stare at the door. To feel her heartbeat as she confirmed in her mind, once and for all, what she was going to do.

Without resting any longer, Avery climbed towards the closet door and slid it open. There was a big box on the top shelf that contained all her journals. Every single one she had kept since she had learned how to write. Their pages contained half her life. Her achievements, and fears, her thoughts, and emotions. They contained her perspective of her own history, the inner workings of her mind, and details of the different phases she had grown through.

And she was going to burn them all. Tonight, at the bonfire. Every page.

The only journal she wasn't going to burn was the one Nana had gifted her. She had other plans for that one.

Avery parked her car at the entrance of the cemetery, and walked along the well-maintained road that intercepted through the lawn.

The tan leather journal was clutched in her hand as her footsteps clicked along the road. She crossed through the patch of grass, still wet with dew, to Nana's gray headstone.

Standing tall, she observed the rolling green hills around her, dotted with marble and granite headstones. Surrounded by so much death, Avery felt neither scared nor sad. None of these headstones were hiding. There were barely any trees left to hide behind, as all of them must have been cleared years before to make room for the human skeletons that had nowhere left to go on this earth.

Death, and the mix of emotions that come with it, was in plain sight here, unashamed of its role on this earth.

Avery knelt, the wet grass padding her knees.

In loving memory of Elena Wilson.

A beloved grandmother, mother, wife, daughter, and friend, the stone read.

Her nana had experienced eighty-six years of life, but the details of that life would get lost in time, leaving nothing but this stone behind even as her impact lingered.

Avery unraveled the leather string that kept the journal bound. She peeled open the cover, freeing the yellow pages to breathe, and flipped past Nana's sprawling two-word scribble, past her own reflections and revelations, and stared at the newest entry she had penned this morning.

She inhaled, breathing in the sickly sweet, humid air, and stared at her messy handwriting, with all its loops and curls, and lines drawn through words, replaced with more honest ones.

"Dear Nana," she whispered out loud and then scanned the cemetery for any visitors.

Of course she felt self-conscious, dramatic even. Yet there was something within her demanding she did this, that she owed it to herself to be vulnerable. And it was stronger than any insecurity.

"Dear Nana," she tried again. "I'm sorry."

The world remained still. No one, not even a bird, was watching her. Just her and her words, in the presence of death.

"I didn't want to take sides. When I was younger, I thought you had superpowers. My parents were always fighting. Sometimes it got too bad, and you would take me inside your home, and it always felt safe ..." Her voice was becoming strained. She felt tears that had formed travel through her eyes, trying to escape. "But when the divorce happened, nothing felt safe. Not even you. And I didn't think I could ever admit I was mad at you. So, I never gave myself a chance to forgive you, and our distance became the centerpiece of our relationship.

"Before you died, you offered a few words to everyone for closure. But the words you told me felt like a continuation of a past I wanted to let go of. I was hurt. Not because the words you told me were inherently bad." Avery tightened her jaw and blinked, letting a pair of tears fall from her eyes and slip onto the paper. "But because they were partly true."

The ink of one of her words smeared from the tear that was now settling and expanding through the page.

"You don't know where I've been, Nana. But I know. I have thousands of pages and years' worth of words documenting those mental and physical experiences. And I didn't let anyone in during those years, not because I was trying to hurt you, or anyone, but because I was trying to protect myself – sometimes even from myself."

Avery offered herself a pause, to reread those words once more.

I was trying to protect myself.

She couldn't help but shut her eyelids tightly, only allowing her body to release its tension when she opened them once again. The headstone stared back at her.

"I'm sorry," she said. "I've carried a lot of guilt, but I've never apologized to you. Or myself. And I'm so, so sorry."

Avery looked at the grass growing around Nana's grave. "And I forgive you. Even if you were never sorry." She sucked in another breath before releasing it all into the empty air. "I forgive you," she repeated, this time to herself. The world around her responded with silence.

"I regret we can't have this conversation in person. But I'm learning that sometimes tragedies are what're needed to push you to grow. And your death, Nana, has had a great effect on my life."

Avery paused in the soothing yet intimidating silence of the cemetery. Her fallen teardrop had already begun drying on the page. The blurred word was becoming a smudge.

"I don't know why you gifted me this journal. Maybe you had your own grudges against me. The years I would let pass without a call or visit," she said. "Or maybe you gave it to me in earnest, wanting to give the gift of writing back to me, since you couldn't give it back to yourself."

Avery felt the corners of her mouth curl as she glanced at the tattoo of a pen on her forearm. Only a few months ago, she had regretted this tattoo. Now when she looked at it, she felt something smile within her, at the wisdom of her younger self.

Then she ripped the page out with one clean tear. "All I know," she said, ripping out the rest of the entries, "is that this journal helped me. Thank you. No matter your intention, you have been a teacher to me. And for that, we will always be connected."

Avery ripped out the last page, the only page Nana had written those two words on: *Dear Self.* She placed all the ripped entries into a neat stack and folded them into her pocket. The journal was now empty, freed from any words. She circled the leather strap around, and placed the journal on an adolescent, leafy green tree a few feet from the headstone. Avery knew she would continue writing, but she was ready to write in her own book. Perhaps her nana's would help someone else.

With one last look towards Nana's headstone, the words floated off Avery's lips: "Goodbye, Nana. I love you."

Chapter 71

A suitcase lay open on Elizabeth's king-sized bed, full of neatly folded dresses and lingerie, but Elizabeth was on the other side of the room, lingering near her and John's antique wooden wardrobe. The crimson-red pouch Nana had gifted her was in the palm of her hand. Her fingers were smoothing over the gold fleur-de-lis embroidery, as if they were handling something delicate rather than something sewn.

"Darling?" she heard John call, but before she could answer, he had already poked his head through the doorway. "Darling, I'm going to pick up beer for the bonfire tonight. Is everyone still coming?"

With her eyes still studying the pouch, Elizabeth nodded. "Called them all to confirm this morning. Only my mom can't make it."

Looking up from the gift in her hands, she saw John standing with a crooked, slight smile on his face, his dark hair falling in waves. He eyed the open suitcase on their bed before glancing back at her.

"I thought you were done packing?"

Clasping her palm around the pouch, Elizabeth offered a small shrug. "Adding a few last things."

John inspected the object in her hands before raising his eyes to meet hers. The late morning sunlight was spilling through their window, washing their bedroom in its brilliant, earthy hues. His eyes were studying her, appearing as two stormy seas full of made-up ideas and murmuring words, always ready to take what it saw and create something new.

She opened her palm around the pouch. "What do you think of me bringing this?"

"What do you think about it?"

Analyzing the pouch once more, Elizabeth offered a slight tilt of her shoulder. "The last time I saw Nana, she said something to me right before she gifted me this."

"She did?" John took another step through the door so his whole body now took space in the room. "You didn't tell me that."

"I didn't?"

"No," John said, "you just told me what she gave you."

A small smirk and an exhale through her nose passed Elizabeth's face when she stared at the object in her hands. "I think I was focused on the wrong things a few months ago."

"I think we both were," John agreed, then tilted his head. "What did she tell you?"

"She said she loved hearing stories of our travels," Elizabeth said, feeling a soft smile at the memory. "Said we made her feel alive again, and that even when she's in heaven, she'll still come to me to brighten her heart."

"Are you serious?" John said, his face suddenly twisting.

"What?" Elizabeth asked, feeling her body freeze as she tried to understand his expression.

"How did you keep that from me?" he said. "Elizabeth, to make someone feel alive – that's incredible."

Elizabeth couldn't help but laugh at John's elation over Nana's last words, and at her own ignorance over just how remarkable those sentiments were.

"You are incredible," John said, stepping towards her now. "You make life more vibrant, Elizabeth. You always have. It can get quite dull, getting older, but, knowing I'll have you to grow old with, to know I'll always have your love and support to continue creating a life with ... it makes the years to come all the more exciting."

"John ..."

He hushed her words with a kiss on her lips.

"*We* are incredible," she corrected once he pulled away.

John tucked a strand of her hair behind her ears. "What do you think you'll do with the pouch?"

"I'd like to pack it," Elizabeth said. "Take a piece of her with us." When she looked back at her future husband, he was smiling, but she felt a heaviness wash over her. "I want to give Nana the benefit of the doubt," Elizabeth explained. "In her life, and in what she was maybe trying to say about ours, when she gifted me this pouch."

"I think that will serve you well," John said with a nod.

"I miss her ..." On a deeper level, she'd always been aware of the space her nana had left behind. But now that she was packing for her wedding trip and would be flying above the clouds, leaving her family behind to start a new chapter in her life in less than twenty-four hours, the truth of that sentiment was no longer the background music of her mind.

"I know you do, Liz," John said, stepping towards her grief. Within seconds, she was engulfed in his arms, his love, and as he held her, she snuggled closer, the crimson-red pouch still in her hands.

"I wish she could see us this week, to witness us get married," Elizabeth admitted, and then realized her words and added with a chuckle, "Of course, we chose to disinvite everyone and now the one person I want to invite is gone. Maybe my mind is just playing tricks on me."

"Well, maybe she will be there with us," John said, squeezing Elizabeth tighter. "Maybe all our loved ones will be. We have no idea how life or death really works. But she said when she went to heaven, she'd still come to you to brighten her heart. So maybe you should trust her."

Elizabeth closed her eyes and tried to allow Nana's last words to finally take root in her mind.

Chapter 72

"Hey, I've got a great idea!"

Brinkley's ears perked up at the sound of Lily's voice. The tone was already making her suspicious, and she felt her body lunge from her lawn chair, ready for action.

"I'll pretend to be the Jell-O monster, and I'm going to eat you!"

"Lily," Brinkley called from her lawn chair, about to scold her oldest daughter for teasing her youngest. Just as Brinkley set her iced coffee onto the table and was ready to diffuse the situation before anyone got smacked, Daisy, who must have forgotten Brinkley was sitting right there, started giggling and running from Lily, who was growling and chasing her as "the Jell-O monster".

Brinkley squinted her eyes at her daughters, watching as they moved their bodies with abandon and expressed the laughter of their young souls. It was all very picturesque, except for the fact that Brinkley had been woken up countless times in the middle of the night by Daisy's fear of this so-called monster. For months, Daisy had been tucking herself between Brinkley and Chase, her growing limbs sprawling across Brinkley's side of the bed and whacking Brinkley in the face. Brinkley had put up with it because she had thought her daughter was terrified.

Now Brinkley realized she had put up with it for too long. She vowed to herself then and there, as Daisy nearly tripped over herself because she was laughing and running so hard, that her youngest daughter was officially kicked out of Mommy and Daddy's bed. Daisy would have to learn how to laugh at her fears in the darkness the same way she had apparently learned how to in the daylight.

Leaning into her lawn chair, her iced coffee back in hand, Brinkley found her gaze lingering on the empty baby swing of the playset. Her daughters were growing up so fast. Sometimes it felt as if their futures were right around the corner, ready to steal these moments, no matter how exhausting, because that's how much these moments were worth.

The sunlight dazzled against her rose quartz ring as she brought her glass of coffee to her lips. She paused, surveying it.

You are a wonderful mother and wife.

Nana's voice was in her head, but it was much grainier than when she had said the words. Her nana was becoming closer to a memory than a reality now, and the thought lifted and burdened Brinkley's heart.

Without taking a sip, she lowered the iced coffee from her lips and examined the beautiful ring.

How odd, that people could be filled with so much self-doubt, that even a compliment could seem like mockery.

The rose quartz stunned in the sunlight as Brinkley repeated those last words in her head.

You are a wonderful mother and wife.

Her daughters' laughing melody dispersed through the late summer air. Brinkley pictured herself pregnant, sacrificing her body to bring in new life, not just for herself, but for her husband, and life itself, too. In the delivery room, Chase had never left her side. She remembered the way he had looked at her after each birth, his face flushed red with inexplicable emotion, the corners of his eyes slightly wrinkled. It was

448

a look she never wanted to forget.

You are a wonderful mother and wife.

She watched as Lily and Daisy continued running in no particular pattern, past the empty baby swing and towards the shelter of the sycamore trees, where they joined hands and decided to run together. Memories of pushing Daisy in that little swing filled her mind, back when this house was new and Chase still had hungry ambitions for more. While he would work, Brinkley remembered balancing Daisy on one hip while trying to keep Lily feeling just as loved as ever before, even though her parents' time and attention had now been split into a million different directions. So many sleepless nights during those years, yet she would relive them all in a heartbeat.

You are a wonderful mother and wife.

She closed her eyes and imagined her life now. Lily turning five, Daisy developing fears. Chase's never-ending hunger, her own growing void. For a moment Brinkley tried to envision Nana, holding her hand for one last time, acting as her guiding light.

And then Brinkley remembered what Nana had said.

You have always been a light in my life.

The words filled her mind. As Brinkley allowed herself to get lost in the inky blackness behind her eyelids, she felt her throat constrict. But she didn't keep it constricted. She allowed herself to grow lost in this emotion.

When she opened her eyes to the world once again, her daughters emerged from the sycamore trees and were now helping each other climb the ladder to their slide.

Brinkley didn't hesitate a second longer. She pulled her phone from the pocket of her new linen shorts, and opened the search engine.

Letting go of her old clothes and filling her closet with new ones was a good start, but Brinkley knew it was only going to help the reflection she saw in the mirror. And Brinkley needed something deeper than that. She began to type her request into the search engine, no longer asking the blank page what was missing from her life, but searching for a therapist who could help her recover it.

There *was* something missing from her life, and she had a sneaking suspicion it was her. She wanted to reclaim those lost parts in all their beauty and ugliness, but she was exhausted from trying to do it alone. Therapy seemed like a safe place to learn.

You are a wonderful mother and wife.

"And I am so much more than that," Brinkley whispered to herself, her voice so quiet, it was only audible because it had been screaming in her mind. She wanted to shout those words to the skies, even if no one would hear her echoes but herself.

Brinkley almost laughed out loud thinking of how offended she had acted when Chase had suggested counseling. The tricks her mind could play, to preserve its own ego. But Chase had offered his help, her family had offered theirs, and while she appreciated all their attempts and advice, Brinkley was aware that no one was walking in her shoes, lying in her bed awake in the middle of the night. So, with a sigh, she scrolled through the list of therapists, reading their short bios as she could hear her daughters playing in the background. Brinkley found a handful of people and decided to contact them.

Once she sent the messages, she felt her body lean further into the lawn chair. The sun was beating on her face, but there was no tension between her eyebrows. She remained sitting, watching her daughters run, even though they were no longer running to or from anything or anyone.

"I was wondering where everyone was."

Brinkley turned to see Chase, changed out of his business suit he had put on this morning and into workout shorts and a T-shirt.

"Chase?" she had to confirm. It was still work hours, after all.

"Hey," he said, and seemed to hesitate, but leaned in for a kiss anyway.

She wrapped her arms around him with a lingering kiss. It wasn't too long before their daughters noticed and ran towards them.

"Daddy!" they both shrieked, as if Chase were a celebrity.

Brinkley didn't mind. He might be their celebrity, but she was their mother.

Chase didn't hesitate to drop to his knees and turn into a tickle monster.

"What are you doing here?" Brinkley said. "What time is it?"

"Around three," said Chase. "I left work a little early. Figured we could have some family time before Elizabeth and John's bonfire tonight."

"Really?" Brinkley heard herself ask.

"Daddy, Daddy, Daddy!" Lily and Daisy kept shouting in unison. "Take us to the tree house!"

"One second, girls," he said, then resumed his focus on Brinkley. "Really, Brinkley. I love you."

She reached for his hand when he said the words, their daughters still clinging onto him. "I love you, too."

"For better or worse?" he said, getting tugged across the lawn by Lily and Daisy.

"For better or worse," she said, then couldn't help but smirk. "Although I really prefer the better part."

You live such a lucky life, Nana's voice concluded, and Brinkley smiled at her husband as he followed their daughters to the trees.

I know I do, Brinkley agreed. *I work hard for it. Thank you, Nana.*

Chapter 73

A crescent moon glowed in the dusty night sky, the kind that couldn't get any slimmer without disappearing completely. "We couldn't have asked for a better night," John marveled, as if reading Avery's mind.

But the statement brought Avery back to earth, where everyone was seated on wooden stumps surrounding Elizabeth and John's fire pit. The flames were alight, every now and then sending a burst of glowing embers into the air. The longer Avery stared, the more she began to resent the small flames.

"You know, I'm not going to lie," she said, tilting her head, "I pictured the fire to be much bigger."

"Same," Brinkley said, her own eyes clearly mesmerized and disappointed by the ever-changing flames.

"The fire of the mind is always bigger," John said.

"And we don't want to start a forest fire," Elizabeth added, studying her marshmallow as it hovered near the flames.

"So, um ..." Chase's words trailed off as he readjusted himself on his wooden stump. "What now?"

"Yeah, when do we start burning stuff?" Avery asked.

"Now," said John, removing his flaming marshmallow from the pit and blowing it out as if it were a candle.

Avery held her breath, but she couldn't hold it for long. John set the burnt marshmallow on top of a graham cracker and then eyed his accomplishment before setting a square of dark chocolate directly in the middle and placing another graham cracker on top, careful not to press the two crackers too hard together. With a smile to himself, he popped the s'more into his mouth while everyone around him continued to scrutinize his every move, waiting for the moment he would reveal what this bonfire was all about.

While finishing his chews, he reached into the pocket of his jeans and pulled out a packet of papers. John tore the papers into fours and tossed them into the fire with no more than a shrug. Avery watched as the pieces fell as soft as snowflakes.

Everyone waited a few minutes in silence, watching the papers curl onto themselves before disintegrating into black nothingness.

"Is that it?" Brinkley was the first to ask.

"What? You wanted more?" John said.

"I mean, yeah," said Avery. "Elizabeth, you made it seem like this was going to be some life-changing experience."

"Avery, is that what I actually said or is that what you wanted to hear?" Elizabeth said, sitting straighter as she removed her goldened marshmallow from its spot hovering over the flames. She waited a moment before popping it in her mouth, staring at Avery for a response while she chewed with raised eyebrows.

Avery's mouth hung open. She looked at Brinkley.

"Brinkley," Avery said, "did she not make it seem life-changing?"

Brinkley's nose scrunched. "It might be a misunderstanding?"

Avery's face twisted into disgust at Brinkley's justification. She turned back to John and Elizabeth, her arms crossed. "You don't even say a prayer? Do a ritual?"

"I mean hey, if you want to say a prayer, go for it," said John, and looked around the group. "Who's next?"

"Wait, that's all you have to burn?" said Avery, tilting her body from her wooden stump to try to see if there was anything else behind John's back.

"For this month, yeah."

"But ... what happened to burning all your old work, memories – Elizabeth even said we could burn receipts for crying out loud—"

"Look, we burn all sorts of things," John said, "but this happened to be a productive month for me. I ended up writing some of my best content. Go figure."

Before Avery could respond, Elizabeth rolled her shoulders back with a bright smile.

"I'll go next!" she said, reaching into the cream-colored canvas bag she had brought to the fire and removing ... a piece of paper. One lonely, single piece.

She tossed it into the flames as if throwing a Frisbee.

"You've got to be kidding me," Avery muttered, before hearing the panic rise in her own voice: "That's all you have?"

"Yeah," Elizabeth said, staring at her. "It was a copy of our old wedding deposit."

"Avery, why are you freaking out right now?" said Brinkley.

"What else is in your bag?" Avery said to Elizabeth. "You brought a whole bag outside for one piece of paper?"

Elizabeth wrinkled her eyebrows. "No," she began, shuffling through the canvas bag, "I have bug spray, water, tampons, sunscreen I forgot to throw away, because it makes me break out—"

"Whatever ..." Avery looked away and took a swig of her beer.

"Avery, what's wrong? Why are you upset John and I don't have more stuff to burn?"

"Yeah, more isn't always better," John added, shaking his head.

"Nothing, it's fine," Avery tried, but she could hear the dejection in her own voice. "You just made it seem like this was going to be some big ritual, with papers burning as far as the eye could see ... I'm not mad," Avery clarified when no one responded. "I'm just ... embarrassed."

"Hey, hey," John said, shaking his head, "no need to be embarrassed here."

"Yeah, why are you embarrassed?" Elizabeth said, but soon added, "What'd you bring?" She leaned forwards with an arched eyebrow, surveying Avery's surroundings.

"Brinkley and Chase, what did you two bring?" Avery snapped her gaze towards them.

"Well ..." Chase glanced at Brinkley before reaching into his sweatshirt pocket and pulling out a packet of papers. "I brought old plans for our nursery renovation," he said, and threw the folded packet into the fire.

"What renovation were you two planning?" Elizabeth said. "And when?"

With a roll of her eyes, Brinkley said, "Chase was trying to be sweet and surprised me with plans to turn the nursery into an office, but ..."

"You realized it should become a spa?" Elizabeth tried to finish.

"Um, no," Brinkley said with a small shake of her head before stealing a glance at Chase. With a sly smile, she said, "We've decided to scrap our plans and pick something together."

"And?" Avery said. Brinkley loved drawing out the suspense. "What did you two decide?"

"We're turning the nursery into a study," Brinkley beamed.

"Isn't 'study' a synonym for 'office'?" John proposed with squinted eyes.

Brinkley ignored him. "It'll be a place for Chase when he's working from home, and a place for me when I want to read books in peace and quiet," she said, still beaming. "I was even thinking of taking Mom's advice about, you know, needing a spiritual practice in my life, and turning my book club into a spiritual study, if any of you are interested."

"Aw, John loves to read," Elizabeth said.

"So, what does that mean, Elizabeth?" Brinkley said. "Are you interested, or are you speaking on behalf of John?"

"I just love that he loves to read ..." Elizabeth shrugged. "But I'm out. I plan to have nothing planned for the next year. I need to reclaim my free time, you know?"

Brinkley blinked.

"Can we move it along?" Avery said, snapping her head toward Brinkley. "I am so excited for your renovation and all, but what did you bring?"

Please tell me it's larger than a packet of papers.

Brinkley reached for her black, oversized bag, and pulled out ...

"Jeans?" Elizabeth squinted at the object.

"Yes," Brinkley said with a long sigh and a nod. "Ladies, it's time to accept my new, post-baby, early thirties body, and burn my old skinny jeans."

Avery felt her own eyes smile as she stared at the outdated object of clothing.

"Don't burn them," Elizabeth objected. "They're cute – I'll take them!"

Brinkley eyed the article of clothing in her hands before looking at Elizabeth.

"Okay," she said, and passed the jeans to John, who placed them in Elizabeth's arms. "It feels good to offer them new life," Brinkley added as she watched Elizabeth happily fold the jeans into her canvas bag. "Good-bye, mid-twenties. It's time for new hopes and dreams. Bigger ones, that don't involve fitting into smaller clothes."

"I'm proud of you, Brinkley," Avery said.

She watched her sister break her gaze from the canvas bag, and when Brinkley made eye contact with Avery, Avery could see the flame alight in her sister's eyes.

"Thank you," Brinkley said. Her voice was quiet, but it was clear.

"It's your turn, Avery," Elizabeth said, and Avery realized the only person left was herself. "What'd you bring?"

"Um ..." Avery stammered, keeping her eyes focused on the dancing flame. "I brought ..." She scratched the back of her head. "I brought all the journals I've kept since I was in second grade, so ..." She cleared her throat. "It's a bit more than a packet of papers ... or jeans ..."

"That's incredible," said John.

"Wait, what?" said Elizabeth, her eyes narrowed on Avery.

"You want to burn your journals?" said Brinkley. "You can't do that!"

Chase remained silent.

Avery kept her gaze on the flames feasting on the charred, disfigured papers.

"Where are they?" John asked.

"In my car," said Avery. "The box was too heavy for me to carry across the lawn, so ..." Before Avery could decide how she wanted to finish her statement, John lunged from his stump and disappeared into the night.

"Where is he going?" Avery asked Elizabeth, even though the nausea in her stomach was telling her the answer.

"Darling?" Elizabeth called into the dark night. "Darling?"

Just then, the light of a phone glowed in the darkness. Everyone watched as it weaved through the wooded backyard and disappeared towards Elizabeth and John's driveway.

"He's clearly retrieving Avery's journals," Brinkley groaned, glaring at Elizabeth. "He's your future husband, put a stop to this."

"Yes, he's my future husband, but that doesn't mean I control him."

With a roll of her eyes, Brinkley's gaze landed on Avery. "Avery, we can't let you burn your old journals."

Avery looked at her sister, but she felt her mind was somewhere else as she crossed her arms against her chest and tried to breathe.

"Yeah, this is not what I had in mind when I invited you over," said Elizabeth. "I told you to bring letters and receipts, and you're ready to burn the written history of your entire life?"

Sitting still, Avery let their words flow into the night, imagining herself throwing her journals into the fire, watching them become devoured by the small flames, wondering how it would feel.

"John!" Elizabeth's voice cut through.

When Avery raised her eyes from the fire pit, she saw John, but he was empty-handed.

"John, we thought you were getting Avery's journals," said Elizabeth. "Where the hell did you go?"

John just looked at Avery. "I, uh, I need the keys."

Chapter 74

When Avery and John lugged her box of journals to the small fire, everyone, of course, went into panic mode.

"Tell me you at least have these typed and backed up," Elizabeth said.

John winced. "Darling, who wants to back up their private life like that?"

"She's never kept a journal ..." Avery shook her head with John.

"Well, he's never had a real phone!" said Elizabeth. "You're going to listen to a guy who still uses a flip phone?"

"Yeah, Avery, you can't burn all these!" said Brinkley, as if the journals were alive. "These contain your whole life. Chase," she said, nudging her husband, "tell her she'll regret this."

"It's part of my life," said Avery, but the longer she looked at the box, the more the details inside came alive. Her first day of second grade was documented in there, for crying out loud. "Majority of it," Avery corrected again. She suddenly had the urge to throw her body in front of the box and protect it from the hungry flames.

Chase maintained a neutral face when Avery looked at him. "Any thoughts?" she asked him. "You're the only one who hasn't gone into hysterics."

"Chase, tell her she'll regret this," Brinkley scolded.

"I mean, they're her journals," said Chase, pushing his glasses up the bridge of his nose before looking at Brinkley. "If you're so concerned about it, why don't you try keeping one for yourself?"

"Avery," Elizabeth said, "why don't you take more time to think about this, and if you still want to burn them, you can bring them to next month's bonfire?"

Now Avery groaned.

"I did think about it!" she yelled across the whipping flames. "I thought we were all coming here to see some big, giant bonfire, and everyone would have stacks of ... of ... of their never-ending hopes and unfulfilled dreams, their questions and failures." Avery looked at each family member, with their faces frozen in panic amid the hot flames. "I thought we'd all have more to throw in. Now I feel like I'm the only one with all this ..." She looked at the nondescript brown box ... "baggage." She glanced up at her sisters, who stood across from her, their eyes glued to her but their mouths dangling open. "This baggage you're trying to convince me to keep, and yet none of you are the ones carrying it."

Brinkley and Elizabeth eyed each other before looking back at Avery.

"I don't want you to hold on to baggage, Avery," Brinkley defended. "I just don't want you regretting this later. Think of all the moments of your life you have in there. They're not all bad! What if you get older and want to pass them on to your children?"

"I don't think my future children need to read about how I lost my virginity," Avery retorted.

"Brinkley has a point," Elizabeth argued, but her voice had softened. "Even if you don't share your journals with anyone – what if you get Alzheimer's, or some other tragic thing wipes your memory? You'll regret not keeping them around."

"If I don't have a memory, I won't remember writing in them, anyway," Avery said.

Clearing her throat, she tried to mutter something, but it was unintelligible even to herself, so she decided to get back to her own task at hand.

"Avery, you don't have to do this!" Brinkley said as Avery opened the cardboard box containing her journals. "Let's just slow down."

"Yeah, Avery, knock it off," Elizabeth said.

Before Avery lifted the last two flaps of the cardboard box, she saw the first layer of the many journals that were packed. As she stared at the covers, she remembered the different stages of her life contained inside each one.

The journals that contained the thoughts of her depression, tales of self-loathing and dreaming she'd wake up as someone else. Or drift into an endless sleep. Then there was the one from middle school, when her parents had been in the beginning of their divorce, her black-and-white world becoming complex with shades of gray while she was still young enough to be unguardedly honest about it all. There was the journal when she'd detailed what it was like to fall into teenaged love, and then experience the ensuing heartbreak. At the time, she had believed she would never be able to love as hard, thinking her body could only sustain a hurt like that once. Now she could feel the knowing smile spread through her mind. Her understanding of love and loss, of herself and her power, had been innocent then.

Finally, her eyes lingered on a simple, nondescript black journal with a small, golden sun engraved in the middle. It was the last journal she had written in before she'd graduated high school. The world had seemed promising to her then. She had finally become an adult, free to grow where she wanted and do as she pleased, and she was moving to the city. She didn't know then what her adult world would contain. Underappreciated jobs and long hours, a cycle of depression only to feel healthy again, and go on living and partying, rinsing and repeating. Until the words stopped flowing, just as bored as she was.

But she also hadn't known, when she had written in that journal, excited to begin her life in a city, all the different people she would meet and moments she would experience. The conversations she would share, the heights she would walk beneath. Avery realized that everyone had a story, filled with joy and sadness and everything in between. And everyone had a way of retelling their story, trickling the information into a stranger's ear, or letting it roll off their tongue like a steady stream, casting themselves as the victim, the villain, the courageous protagonist, the unseen wallflower. A little bit of everything or nothing in between. And through her years of living and working in the city, meeting different people and hearing their stories, Avery realized everyone had their own way of coping with it, determining its ending.

And there was something sad and nostalgic and joyful about that, and about all these moments that had made it onto the page. It was all just a story she had written. Sure, she had gone through those experiences, but the words had been written from the perspective she had had at the time. And now that she had discovered a new one, she was ready to let these old stories burn, and return to the earth.

"Avery, what are you thinking about?" she heard one of her sisters ask. "Please tell me you're reconsidering this."

Avery squinted at her hidden memories, silently thanking them one last time.

As everyone protested what to do with a past that didn't belong to them, Avery's focus remained on the history of herself that stared back at her. The longer she looked, the more her journals seemed to be smiling with all their secrets, nudging her along. She picked up the nondescript journal with its black cover and golden sun, ripped the pages free, and threw them into the fire. The flames frolicked and hovered around the paper before they consumed it. Embers went flying through the dark air. In the distance, Avery could hear Brinkley and Elizabeth shriek.

The flames grew for a brief flicker in time, until they accepted her words.

Avery laughed at the sweet release, and caught John laughing, too.

"Avery," Brinkley tried once more, "are you sure?"

"Brinkley, I think she's sure," Chase said and then quickly covered his mouth with a swig of his beer.

"Brinkley, Nana said she had no idea where I've been," Avery said with a forceful voice into the night air, not because she was mad but because her emotions were stirring inside, needing to be heard. "Well, guess what, I do know where I've been. I have thousands of pages to remind me, to keep me stuck there."

Everyone remained silent, ready to listen to the words Avery had to say, now that she was ready to burn the words she had written.

"I love these journals – they served a great purpose," Avery admitted, and picked up another journal, this one crowded with bare trees on the cover. "I won't forget where I've been – trust me, it's burned in my memory – but..." She tossed the book into the glowing fire. This time everyone silently watched the pages burn. When no one spoke, Avery swallowed. "I want to let these old perspectives go. Make space for new ones," Avery said, keeping her chin lifted.

Before anyone could try to infiltrate her dreams with their own hopes and opinions, Avery dug through the box and picked up a thin journal. It had a picture of a pink rose against a piano on the cover. It was the first journal she had ever written in, its contents filled with big letters and misspelled words, from a time when a couple of sentences had been enough to document her day.

She placed it in Brinkley's hand. "You can help me if you want."

The flames were busy consuming the journal Avery had just thrown in, but Avery watched as Brinkley added the one she'd been handed into the mix.

Avery gathered three more journals from the box, handing one to each of her family members.

"Toss them in," she said.

"It did feel kind of good," said Brinkley.

Avery inhaled, her chest expanding. John laughed, still clutching Elizabeth's hand, standing by her side as they both dropped Avery's journals into the fire.

Avery's gaze became transfixed by the ever-blackening, ever-changing pages of her past as they crumpled and darkened into themselves in a strange dance with their own impermanence. She thought of herself as a young girl scribbling ferociously by the light of her old nightlight, trying to make sense of the world she had been born into while still unaware that's what she had been trying to do, and her adolescent years, when she would write her fears of feeling like this world was not meant for her.

She visualized herself as a young woman, camping solo, finally free of her family problems, only to realize that no matter how far she traveled, her problems would always follow, because the real problem was not external or something she could run away from.

The real problem was the way she had been treating her mind.

Now, Avery sucked in a breath, tilting her chin to look at the crescent moon offering a glimmer of light in the night. Various stars dazzled the sky, and Avery knew from her nights camping that there were many more twinkling, even when she couldn't see them.

The fire glowed against the darkened night, its crisp yellow flames striking the air around it, never lingering longer than a sliver of a moment. Avery exhaled.

Her emotions over the years had not been trying to hurt her. This whole time, they had been trying to help her.

To help her grow into the woman she was now and had yet to become.